NORTH CAROLINA
STATE BOARD OF COMMUNITY
LIBRARIES
WAKE TECHNICAL COMMUNITY

WITHDRAWN

D0999978

JOSEPH CONRAD: BETRAYAL AND IDENTITY

Also by Robert Hampson

Joseph Conrad, *Lord Jim (editor with introduction and notes by Cedric Watts)*

Rudyard Kipling, *Something of Myself (editor with introduction and notes by Richard Holmes)*

Joseph Conrad, *Victory (editor)*

Joseph Conrad: Betrayal and Identity

Robert Hampson
Lecturer in English
Royal Holloway and Bedford New College
University of London

St. Martin's Press

823.912
C754

© Robert Hampson 1992

All rights reserved. No reproduction, copy or transmission of
this publication may be made without written permission.

No paragraph of this publication may be reproduced, copied or
transmitted save with written permission or in accordance with
the provisions of the Copyright, Designs and Patents Act 1988,
or under the terms of any licence permitting limited copying
issued by the Copyright Licensing Agency, 90 Tottenham Court
Road, London W1P 9HE.

Any person who does any unauthorised act in relation to this
publication may be liable to criminal prosecution and civil
claims for damages.

First published in Great Britain 1992 by
THE MACMILLAN PRESS LTD
Houndmills, Basingstoke, Hampshire RG21 2XS
and London
Companies and representatives
throughout the world

A catalogue record for this book is available
from the British Library.

ISBN 0–333–45741–2

Printed in Great Britain by
Antony Rowe Ltd
Chippenham, Wiltshire

First published in the United States of America 1992 by
Scholarly and Reference Division,
ST. MARTIN'S PRESS, INC.,
175 Fifth Avenue,
New York, N.Y. 10010

ISBN 0–312–07273–2

Library of Congress Cataloging-in-Publication Data
Hampson, R. G.
    Joseph Conrad: betrayal and identity/ Robert Hampson.
        p.   cm.
    Includes index.
    ISBN 0–312–07273–2
    1. Conrad, Joseph, 1857–1924—Criticism and interpretation.
I. Title.
PR6005.04Z74187   1992
823'.912   dc20   91–37676
                                                              CIP

For Hans van Marle
with respect and affection

Contents

Acknowledgements

I would like to acknowledge my debt of gratitude to the late Patrick Yarker, who guided the early years of my research on Conrad, and to Leonee Ormond, who supervised the completion of my doctoral thesis. I would like to thank Lindsay Badenoch, Mary Nyquist and, in particular, Gerlinde Roder-Bolton, who commented on earlier stages of some of these chapters. I would also like to thank Chandra Ghosh, Hans van Marle, Sibani Raychaudhuri, John Stape, Jane Temperley and my colleagues at Royal Holloway and Bedford New College – Peter Caracciolo, John Creaser, Tony Davenport, Martin Dodsworth, Andrew Gibson, Warwick Gould and Katie Wales – for their encouragement, support and stimulation. I am grateful to the British Library and the University of London Library; to the University of London Computer Services unit for transferring my typescript to disk; and to Royal Holloway and Bedford New College for granting me sabbatical leave to complete the book. I am particularly indebted to the Manuscript Division of the British Library and to the Trustees of the Joseph Conrad estate for permission to quote from the manuscript of 'The Rescuer'.

Introduction

I

Thomas Moser, writing in the mid 1950s, referred to 'a new and serious interest in the novels of Joseph Conrad' since the end of the Second World War, that had grown out of the rediscovery of Conrad in the 1940s by M. C. Bradbrook, Morton Zabel and F. R. Leavis.[1] In Conrad's own life-time there were already two book-length studies of his work, and in the decade after his death there was a succession of memoirs and collections of letters.[2] In the 1930s, critical attention to Conrad's work was already under way with studies by Gustav Morf, R. L. Mégroz and Edward Crankshaw; but J. D. Gordan's *Joseph Conrad: The Making of a Novelist* (1940) marks the start of serious, scholarly study of Conrad.[3] Certain critical works of the 1950s, notably Douglas Hewitt's *Conrad: A Re-assessment*, Moser's own work, *Joseph Conrad: Achievement and Decline,* and A. J. Guerard's *Conrad the Novelist*, were to become very influential: indeed, they created the paradigm within which most subsequent Conrad criticism has been written.[4]

One of the most important parts of the paradigm was a construction of Conrad's writing career in terms of 'achievement and decline', and one of the aims of this book will be to challenge that model by paying particular attention to the early and late fiction. Hewitt, for example, omitted the 'books of the early "Malayan period"' from his 're-assessment' because they were 'not of much intrinsic interest' (p. 7). Moser, similarly, dismissed them as 'apprentice' work (p. 50). Although the early work is now receiving more critical attention, most criticism of Conrad still concentrates on the works produced in the period that begins with *The Nigger of the 'Narcissus'* and ends with *The Shadow Line*.[5] John Palmer produced an early attempt to challenge the paradigm in relation to the late novels. As he correctly observed:

> The result has been to impose a false symmetry on the Conrad canon: to undervalue some works and overvalue others, and to blur the distinctions whereby we might see how Conrad's later works do and do not represent a decline.[6]

1

Palmer, however, also sought to assert that psychological, philosophical and symbolic subtleties in Conrad's work were secondary
to moral interests: his challenge to the 'achievement and decline'
paradigm was a conscious attempt to return to an earlier view of
Conrad 'as a simple, rational man with a conservative ethic and love
of the sea'.[7]

Ironically, it was precisely Moser's privileging of 'Conrad the
moralist' that led him to undervalue Conrad's later work.[8] Moser's
particular case is worth dwelling on for a moment since it highlights
a methodological problem for Conrad criticism generally. Moser's
negative evaluation of the late fiction was a product of the limitations of his own approach, even though that approach had worked
well enough with the fiction of Conrad's middle period. The problem is that a single line of argument cannot readily come to terms
with a radical change in Conrad's interests or a radical change in
Conrad's techniques. Indeed, Moser complained of the Conrad of
the later novels that he 'was looking at things in a new way; he was
turning his back on moral judgement' (p. 130). In effect, many critics
of Conrad's late fiction have repeated this cry: having developed a
critical approach for the middle-period fiction, they are very reluctant to develop a different approach that would be appropriate to
the late fiction, and yet such a change is necessary because Conrad in
these novels is 'looking at things in a new way'.

II

In *Conrad the Novelist*, Guerard justified psychological explorations
of Conrad's work by the argument that the artist dramatises what
later theory conceptualises: 'A novelistic portrait may show psychological intuition through its accurate dramatization of mental
processes and significant notation of behaviour'.[9] Guerard's own
psychological interests were mainly focused on the idea of a
descent into the self, which he combined with the anthropological
concept of 'the night journey': 'an essentially solitary journey involving profound spiritual change in the voyager' (p. 15). This
approach produced stimulating and suggestive readings of 'Youth',
'Heart of Darkness', 'The Secret Sharer', *The Shadow Line*, *The Nigger
of the 'Narcissus'*, *Lord Jim* and *Under Western Eyes*, but it broke down
when it reached *Nostromo* and *The Secret Agent*, and it was unable to

cope with *Chance, Victory, The Rover, The Arrow of Gold* and *Suspense*. The approach proved to be restricted to the genre of 'spiritual auto-biography' and unable to do justice to other kinds of writing. Guerard also flirted with 'the psychology of composition' (p. xii), but this was largely manifested in a tendency to ascribe narrative-techniques to 'temperamental evasiveness' rather than to conscious artistic decisions, and as a way of underwriting the idea of Conrad's 'late novel decline'.[10]

Guerard's brief forays into the 'psychology of composition' suggest one of the drawbacks to psychological approaches to literature. The psychoanalytic method developed in relation to personality disorders and psychological malfunctioning, and the application of that method to literature can very easily replace the artist with the neurotic. This is epitomised in Bernard Meyer's *Joseph Conrad: A Psychoanalytic Biography*.[11] Meyer attempts to use Conrad's fiction as 'source data for a psychoanalytic biography' (p. 10). To do this, he assumes the existence of 'a few standard themes which may be interpreted with a fair degree of confidence' and 'a limited number of symbols which appear to possess universal application to basic biological themes' (p. 11). In other words, Meyer offers a Freudian reading of Conrad's plot situations and a decoding of certain objects or images in Conrad's narratives according to Freudian theories of dream symbolism; he then attempts a psychoanalytic account of Conrad by relating this reading of the texts to certain events in Conrad's life.[12] Meyer is at his best when he is closest to orthodox biography: he produces a suggestive account of Conrad's 1887 'injury' on board the *Highland Forest* and he makes a convincing case for the importance of Stanley's exploits as a context for Conrad's journey to the Congo. However, when he approaches literary commentary, the crudeness of his method becomes apparent. Although he does not present himself as writing literary criticism, his approach obliges him to make literary interpretations. His approach, like Guerard's, valorises the 'journey into the self' (even *The Secret Agent* is discussed in these terms). He praises Conrad's 'willingness to search his inner self', as if this were the single most important feature of the art-work. More damagingly, he penalises work in which Conrad displays an unwillingness to search 'his inner self'. Accordingly, he is critical of deviations from autobiographical truth in *The Arrow of Gold*. And, not surprisingly, he readily accepts the idea of Conrad's 'late novel decline':

> Psychologically, it would appear that he could no longer afford those introspective journeys into the self that constitute the greatness of the impressionistic art he created during the years of his close association with Hueffer.   (p. 243)

In this approach, there is no place for work that is the conscious exploration of ideas that are not of direct, personal, psychological relevance.

Meyer acknowledges some of the psychoanalytic objections to the psychoanalysis of an author through his work; but it is worth developing the main objections here. First of all, psychoanalysis is based on the utterances of the analysand produced in, and in response to, the analytic situation. Secondly, the relationship of the analyst and the analysand also plays an important part in the psychoanalytic process. Freud emphasises the importance of this relationship for the analysand (in terms of transference), but it is also important for the analyst.[13] It is clear from Freud's own accounts of case-histories that the analyst's interpretation was influenced by the analysand's responses to his suggestions.[14] The dialectical relationship between analyst and analysand is very different from the imposition of a psychoanalytic reading upon an author through his/her work. At the same time, there are also literary objections to Meyer's project. First, the literary text is not dream-material, nor the product of free association, but an artwork in which whatever is supplied by the subconscious is mediated through various conscious artistic decisions and through various quasi-autonomous literary forms and conventions. For example, Meyer talks about Conrad's 'fantasies of rescue' (p. 83) without taking into consideration the fact that rescue is also a traditional narrative motif. His account of 'The Duel' (pp. 198–201) in terms of a 'loving attachment' between two men who are ostensibly rivals (that is, as an Oedipal conflict which is resolved by minimising the importance of women) reveals more serious limitations. Meyer finds 'little to account for the perpetuation of their feud' (p. 198) because he ignores material that is not amenable to Freudian decoding: in this case, the historical context, with its significant political changes; the geographical, social and temperamental differences between D'Hubert and Feraud; and, above all, their different concepts of honour which trap them within this constantly renewed conflict. Fredric Jameson's account of the Deleuze/Guattari critique of Freudian interpretation is relevant here:

> What is denounced is . . . a system of allegorical interpretation in
> which the data of one narrative line are radically impoverished by
> their re-writing according to the paradigm of another narrative,
> which is taken as the former's master-code or Ur-narrative and
> proposed as the ultimate hidden or unconscious *meaning* of the
> first one.[15]

In his reading of 'The Duel', Meyer ignores non-psychological
material encoded in the narrative in order to offer the Freudian
narrative as the unconscious but ultimate meaning of the text.

Finally, Meyer's approach (like Guerard's) does not allow for the
possibility that Conrad himself might use psychological ideas consciously in his fiction. Richard Brown has written, of a similar issue
in Joyce studies, that 'it seems rather demeaning to assign Joyce to a
particular sexual personality or unconscious figuration . . . when
Joyce himself knows as much of the literature and theory of sexuality as the interpreting critic'.[16] As Frank Sulloway has shown,
many of the ideas we think of as Freud's were already in existence in
the work of earlier psychologists, criminologists and sexologists.[17]
And Paul Wiley pointed out long ago that many of Conrad's psychological perceptions – 'of the division of personality, of the conquest of mind and will by the irrational, of the maladies that inhibit
action' – are in close accord with 'the tendencies of mental science in
his time, whether manifested in literature or in the casebooks of men
like Charcot, Janet, Prince and James'.[18] I would argue that this
'accord' is not merely coincidence: Conrad was aware of both pre-
Freudian and Freudian psychology. Galsworthy records Conrad's
liking for 'the writings of William James'; Freud's work on hysteria,
for example, was available in English in 1912; and Conrad's interest
in psychology is also evidenced by the fact that he owned the 1916
English translation of Jung's *Psychology of the Unconscious*.[19] As I shall
show, Conrad's exploration of identity in his early fiction was shaped
by certain nineteenth-century ideas about sexuality, and his exploration of sexuality in his later fiction was informed by some
awareness of Freudian psychoanalysis. Jeffrey Berman has described
Chance as 'a kind of encyclopaedia in its detailed case studies of
mental illness, including traumas, repressive sexuality, oppressive
guilt, Oedipal strife, and hysteria'.[20] *The Arrow of Gold*, in particular,
has been misread (and consequently undervalued) by the failure
to recognise Conrad's conscious use of psychoanalytic theory and

practice in his late fiction. Conrad's late novels have to be placed in the context of the 'heated and sustained discussion' of sexual matters that Richard Brown describes.[21] In this context, the late-novel concern with the relations between men and women becomes less an old man's reversion to the themes of his earlier fiction and more the mature writer's engagement in the urgent debates of his time.

III

This book has its roots in the work of Paul Kirschner, Zdzislaw Najder, Eloise Knapp Hay and Avrom Fleishman.[22] Paul Kirschner, in particular, suggested a way of looking at Conrad that drew on psychological ideas without subjecting Conrad's work to the reductionism of earlier psychological approaches:

> Critics who interpret Conrad's fiction in the light of psychoanalytic theories often seem more inspired by Freud or Jung than by Conrad himself. . . . I have found it more rewarding to regard Conrad as a great psychologist who knew what he wished to say, and to approach his work as the deliberate expression, in art, of his ideas about human nature.[23]

Kirschner argued that Conrad presents 'his own particular vision of the self' through 'a multiplicity of characters and events'.[24] Kirschner also argued that there was a continuity between the different phases of Conrad's work:

> The political novels may then be seen as a prolongation into society of the principles of individual psychology established in the earlier works. . . . And the later novels may be studied as the application of the same principles to the sexual condition of mankind.[25]

For Kirschner, these three phases could be classified, in terms of Conrad's 'vision of the self' in each phase, as 'the self in the dream', 'the self in society' and 'the sexualised self'.

Kirschner's emphasis on the continuity of Conrad's fiction had a number of beneficial side-effects: besides bringing Conrad's early and late fiction back into critical consideration, it drew together the psychological and political dimensions of Conrad's work. Guerard, for example, tended to minimise or exclude the political aspects of Conrad's fiction. He noticed, for instance, the political complexities of the world of *Almayer's Folly*, but he saw this as a defect in the novel rather than as a sign of the 'psychopolitical' cast of Conrad's imagination.[26] Eloise Knapp Hay, in the first book-length study of Conrad's politics, noted that 'accidents of national origin and family background' compelled Conrad 'from earliest childhood to see in life a political dimension that strongly affected his perspective of all human affairs'.[27] Hay understood the significance of the merchant navy for Conrad ('the organisation of a ship presented Conrad with the model of a stable social order' [p. 53]) and the connection between this 'model' and Apollo Korzeniowski's political ideas, but she failed to make certain psychologically-significant distinctions. She failed to distinguish between the code of honour and the self-ideal in her account of *Lord Jim*, and she similarly failed to distinguish Kurtz from the other colonists in her analysis of 'Heart of Darkness'. Furthermore, she did not provide an adequate account of the changes and developments in Conrad's political ideas. Avrom Fleishman's *Conrad's Politics* showed how, in *Nostromo, The Secret Agent* and *Under Western Eyes*, Conrad was exploring, in turn, organicism in relation to neo-colonialism, organicism in relation to contemporary English society, and organicism in relation to both Russian absolutism (whether czarist or revolutionary) and Western 'social contract' democracy. (The further comparison, with American democracy, was dropped from the novel in the course of the final revisions.) However, while Fleishman was right to read *The Nigger of the 'Narcissus'* as an explicit expression of organicism as an ideal, *Nostromo* and *The Secret Agent* are less positive than Fleishman suggested: they register, instead, Conrad's sense of the gap between the organicist ideal and contemporary reality. Furthermore, while Fleishman presented a clear and often penetrating account of the novels as 'dramatic expressions of a complex political imagination' (p. ix), he also underestimated (like Hay) their psychological dimensions. To paraphrase Frederic Jameson, there is no gap between the public and the private, between the social and the psychological, between 'society' and the 'individual'.[28] Accordingly, changes in Conrad's political ideas interact with his psychological explorations, and the interaction between Conrad's ideas about identity and his ideas about society will be one of the themes of this book.

IV

The central concern of this book is Conrad's exploration of the nature of identity through his novels, and it is constructed according to the idea expressed by Royal Roussel that the sequence of the novels was not 'the result of a series of arbitrary choices' but rather 'the progressive working out of possibilities which are inherent in the perception from which all the fiction flows'.[29] It begins with an analysis of incidents of betrayal (both of one's self and of others) in Conrad's early novels to show how Conrad used these incidents to explore questions about being and identity. Chapter 1 considers *Almayer's Folly* in terms of (a) Almayer's attachment to his self-ideal and (b) Nina's conflict between the identity imposed upon her by her father and an instinctive self she apprehends through her relationship with Dain. Chapter 2 presents an account of *An Outcast of the Islands* in terms of Willems's unshared self-ideal and the subsequent disintegration of his false-self system. Bruce Johnson has analysed the similarities between Almayer and Willems:

> Their principle talent is for denying responsibility, for attributing their misfortune to anything rather than to their own failure of will, their own actions or inertia. Ultimately both men create from their enforced isolation a dream of identity requiring no power of will to sustain it.[30]

These two chapters explore that 'dream of identity' as a context for the later consideration of *Lord Jim*. In Chapter 3, Conrad's failure to complete *The Sisters* and 'The Rescuer' is examined as an important event in his early writing career. It is shown to have a particular significance in relation to Conrad's exploration of being and identity. As Bruce Johnson observed, 'all this early work uses roughly the same model', but, in the manuscript of 'The Rescuer', 'it apparently broke down entirely' to be replaced 'by something rather new in *The Nigger*'.[31] Chapter 4 then considers *The Nigger of the 'Narcissus'*, 'Heart of Darkness' and *Lord Jim* to show how Conrad uses the first of these works to articulate an ideal code of conduct (and the organicist concept of society on which that code is based) and then sets that ideal code of conduct against, first, the instinctive self (in 'Heart of Darkness') and, then, the ideal of self (in *Lord Jim*). Conrad re-examines, within this newly articulated ideological framework, some of the issues he had explored in his earlier works. Chapter 5 deals with *Nostromo* and *The Secret Agent*: in *Nostromo* the ideal code of conduct and the organicist model are brought up against a society dominated by 'material interests'; *The Secret Agent* expresses the disillusionment that follows from this collapse of Conrad's model in its picture of an atomised society characterised by conflicting self-interests. Chapter 6 discusses *Under Western Eyes* as the summation of the central concern of Conrad's earlier fiction: it presents a search for identity explored through acts of betrayal, but this search for identity now takes place within an explicitly corrupt society, whose corruption influences and limits the nature and direction of the search. Chapters 7 and 8 draw on the discussion of being and identity in the earlier chapters to argue for a revaluation of Conrad's later fiction. In his late novels, Conrad turns from the self in isolation and the self in society to a consideration of the sexual self. Chapter 7 examines *Chance* and *Victory* and suggests that they articulate a transition from radical scepticism to a positive attitude towards sexuality. It also argues that these novels represent a continuing willingness on Conrad's part to engage in technical experimentation, and that Conrad's willingness to experiment has to be met with a corresponding flexibility on the part of the critic or reader. Conrad's later novels challenge our preconceptions about his work and force us to change our method of reading. Finally, in Chapter 8, *The Arrow of Gold* and *The Rover* are explored as psychological novels. Their technical achievement is considered, and it is suggested that they represent Conrad's artistic maturity rather than a decline in his creative power.

In Chapter 1, *Almayer's Folly* is placed in the context of late-Victorian ideas about sexuality. Subsequently, to discuss betrayal and identity in Conrad's work, existential psychology is used to provide a conceptual framework and a vocabulary.[32] In the opening chapters of *The Divided Self*, R. D. Laing differentiates between existential phenomenology and clinical psychiatry: 'To look and to listen to a patient and to see "signs" of schizophrenia (as a "disease") and to look and to listen to him simply as a human being are to see and hear in . . . radically different ways'.[33]

Laing's criticism of clinical psychiatry and its perception of the schizophrenic is analogous to my earlier criticism of Freudian interpretations of literature. In both cases, interpretation is limited to the recognition of 'signs' and the de-coding of those signs according to an *a priori* system. To explain the distortions created by 'objective' clinical psychiatry, Laing uses the analogy of textual interpretation;

the terms of Laing's analogy could, however, be reversed to justify the use of existential psychology to avoid the distortions associated with the Freudian interpretation of literature.[34] Furthermore, as Laing states, only existential thought 'has attempted to match the original experience of oneself in relationship to others in one's world by a term that adequately reflects this totality'.[35] In general, existential psychology provides a language for the precise analysis of relations within the self and relations between the self and others, which is invaluable for discussing identity and betrayal. The following passage from *The Leaves of Spring* includes and defines many of the terms used in this book:

> Identity should be distinguished from being. By *being*, I mean all a person is. By *identity* I mean the pattern of experience and being by which a person is recognised by himself and/or others in his relations with others, i.e. who he is recognised or defined to be.
>
> Persons experience themselves directly and immediately. They also experience themselves through the eyes of others. A person's direct experience of himself is his being-for-himself, or his being-for-self. His experience of himself mediated by the other is his being-for-the-other. A person's definition of himself in relation to others is his identity-for-self. Whom he feels himself to be in the eyes of the other, or who he is in the eyes of the other, is his identity-for-the-other, or what I term his 'alterated identity'.
>
> A person may be confirmed or disconfirmed by the others in his experience-for-self: for instance, his identity-for-self may be confirmed by his identity-for-other. John, who sees himself as good, feels confirmed when he sees James seeing him as good.
>
> A person may interiorize or identify with the other's view of him. For instance, if John interiorizes the John he sees James seeing, when he sees James seeing him (John) as good, then John has identified with James's view of him. But this is not the same as confirmation, even if John saw himself as good initially. It is what I call *identification with his alterated identity*. And his identity-for-self now comprises an alterated component.[36]

As this passage suggests, the concerns of existential psychology make it particularly appropriate for a study of Conrad's novels.

1

Two Prototypes of Betrayal:
Almayer's Folly

In *A Personal Record* (1912), Conrad sets out to describe the beginnings of the two major phases of his life: his initiation to the sea and
his initiation to the life of a writer. The narrative begins in the winter
of 1893–4 with Conrad writing the tenth chapter of *Almayer's Folly*,
while land-locked in Rouen aboard the 'Adowa', which was to be his
last ship. But, as Guerard has noted, between this beginning which
was really an ending and the end, with his first contact with a British
ship, which was really a beginning, Conrad's memory flows freely in
time and space, and the resulting commingling of the two phases
suggests their essential continuity.[1] The question of continuity – in
its aspects of consistency, fidelity, identity – deeply concerned Conrad,
but it is through its obverse (through dislocation and betrayal) that
I intend to approach his work. Conrad's concern with betrayal is
evident right from the start of his writing career, and his first two
novels provide (in Nina Almayer and Willems) prototypes for two
distinct, though related, forms of betrayal, to which, with their accompanying configuration of motifs, Conrad was to return again
and again.

I

Conrad records, in *A Personal Record*, how he wrote that tenth chapter in sight of the Rouen cafe, 'the very one' visited by 'the worthy
Bovary and his wife' after their night at the opera.[2] He indulges in
the 'pleasant fancy' that 'the shade of old Flaubert' hovered 'with
amused interest' (p. 3) over him as he wrote, and this playful in-
vocation of a 'patron saint' is a clear acknowledgement of the connections between the two works.[3] Almayer, after the loss of his
daughter Nina, is reminiscent of the ageing Charles Bovary, after the
death of his wife. But more important are the similarities between

11

Almayer and Emma Bovary. They have the same ambitious impulse, the same infatuation with a dream. Emma's feeling that she is confined to a sphere too small for her endowments is clearly shared by Almayer – 'the only white man on the east coast' (p. 184) – who is confined to a far more obviously restricted area, the decaying, almost defunct Lingard trading post in Sambir. In their very different situations, each dreams of escape. Emma dreams of fame or, more often, of an intense romantic life, which she feels must exist somewhere. Almayer, in just the sort of exotic environment she longs for, feels he is in a prison, and has 'his dreams of wealth and power away from this coast' (p. 3) in Europe. He too has a dream of success – equally unrealistic – and equally doomed to failure. For, in their infatuation with their dreams, they lose sight of the reality in front of them. They include others in their dreams, without allowing for their otherness. And as Emma feels her dreams founder – first on Charles (on his inability to be other than he is, and on his lack of skill as a surgeon) and then on her lovers and the 'disillusionment of adultery' – so Almayer feels his dreams collapse because of his daughter, Nina, whose character is the unknown factor he egotistically takes for granted.[4] Because of his lack of love, in fact his disgust, for his 'savage' wife (p. 42), he has tried to forget (indeed, he has effectively forgotten) that Nina, his daughter, is as much part of her mother as of him, as much Malayan as Dutch, and must necessarily share some of her mother's nature. She always appears dressed 'all in white' (p. 17) (whereas the Malays are brightly dressed) and is always in 'European clothes' (p. 29) as part of his attempt to wipe out her mother's portion in her and to 'make her white' (p. 31). This piece of self-deception, so important for his dreams, is, by the same measure, central to their failure.

Nina's 'deception' becomes the focus of Almayer's bitterness. For, just as Emma feels that Bovary humiliated her by the failure of the operation on Hippolyte, and, later blames Léon for her disappointed hopes 'as if he had betrayed her' (p. 272) without ever questioning those hopes, in the same way, Almayer focuses his dreams on Nina, without admitting to himself her real identity, and then feels betrayed by her: 'his faith was gone, destroyed by her own hands; destroyed cruelly, treacherously, in the dark; in the very moment of success' (p. 192).[5] Flaubert, by his earlier analysis of Emma's behaviour, prepares the reader to understand the particular psychological mechanism behind this sense of betrayal and to question the validity of these dreams. He makes it clear that, in fact, it is Emma who is betraying Léon, as she did Bovary, with the 'subtle infidelity' of her dream of an ideal man, and an ideal love: 'a phantom fabricated from her most ardent memories, her most beautiful literary memories, her strongest desires' (p. 272). But Conrad, in *Almayer's Folly*, is not *primarily* concerned with this form of betrayal – the betrayals and self-betrayal of the romantic dreamer. Although Almayer, as Nina says, has betrayed his 'own countrymen' (p. 181) by selling gunpowder to Dain and would betray Dain, in turn, to the Dutch, these betrayals are not foregrounded – perhaps because they are only opportunist wrigglings in an unprincipled struggle for survival, and are not experienced by Almayer as conflicts in a moral world. Conrad's focus is neither on Almayer, nor on the other romantic dreamer, Tom Lingard, but on Nina. In fact, *Almayer's Folly* is not primarily concerned with the 'dreamer' (p. 35), with the inner relationship of his actual and ideal selves, nor with the betrayals he experiences and causes because of his dreams and his false ideal of himself. Instead, because Almayer's dreams are so much projected on to Nina, the focus shifts from him to her. The narrative follows her quite different problems of loyalty and betrayal.

The opening paragraphs of the novel announce two subjects: Almayer and 'his dream of splendid future' (p. 3) and Almayer's relationship with his daughter.[6] At this stage, however, this second subject seems to be subsidiary to (or part of) the first. The narrative emphasises the important place of Nina in Almayer's dream, but also the complicating factor of her 'mixed blood' (p. 3) which Almayer hopes to compensate for with his gold. A second complication is introduced in the person of Dain Waris. Dain is initially presented as part of the first subject, but, as the narrative proceeds, Dain is revealed to have a central role in relation to the second subject also. To begin with, however, Almayer's is the dominant consciousness. Almayer's memories of his youth in Macassar, which motivate the first analepsis, emphasise his optimism and ambition: 'Almayer had left his home with a light heart and a lighter pocket . . . ready to conquer the world, never doubting that he would' (p. 5). This romantic vision produces an over-valuation of others as well as of himself:

Almayer . . . would hear the deep and monotonous growl of the Master, and the roared-out interruptions of Lingard – two mastiffs fighting over a marrowy bone. But to Almayer's ears it sounded like the quarrel of Titans – a battle of the gods. (p. 8)

The analeptic account of Almayer's relationship with Lingard and his marriage to Lingard's 'daughter' introduces three themes which are developed further on return to the first narrative. First, Lingard's view of his 'daughter' anticipates Almayer's attitude towards Nina: when he suggests the marriage, he adds 'Nobody will see the colour of your wife's skin. The dollars are too thick for that, I tell you!' (p. 10). Secondly, Lingard's relationship with his 'daughter' establishes the theme of father-child betrayal: Lingard is another 'father' with plans for a 'daughter' which clash with her own. This is not surprising since Lingard does not understand her nature at all. To begin with, he has the sentimental idea that he 'orphaned' her: he does not know that 'she had been fighting desperately like the rest of them on board the prau' (p. 21). Similarly, when he marries her to Almayer, he does not realise that she had hoped to be his wife, or else, as we learn later, at least the wife of a 'warrior' (p. 148) like himself. This betrayal of her expectations is not stressed, but the theme of parent/child betrayals is foregrounded through an immediate juxtaposition with the reverse case. Lingard occupies a pseudo-paternal position in relation to Almayer (he invites him to 'call me father' – p. 11), but Almayer's acceptance of the proposed marriage is accompanied by his plan to dispose of this wife: 'while swearing fidelity, he was concocting plans for getting rid of the pretty Malay girl in a more or less distant future' (p. 23). Finally, there is the factor common to these two instances: the polarity of Dutch and Malay, white and brown. This is one of the most important constituents of the novel's social world and of its thematics. When Lingard made the proposal to him, Almayer thought first of the gold, and of the realisation of his dreams of Europe. Then he considered 'the other side of the picture' ('the companionship for life of a Malay girl, that legacy of a boatful of pirates') and felt within him 'a confused consciousness of shame that he a white man . . . ' (p. 10). When, at the end of this first analepsis, Almayer turns from the gold of his dream and the gold light on the river to the 'stones, decaying planks, and half-sawn beams' (p. 12) of the reality about him, he turns also to this sense of racial polarities. They are signalled at once by Almayer's attitude to his partner, Dain: 'It is bad to have to trust a Malay' (p. 18). In making such a comment to Nina, Almayer also shows his blindness to her position. Another kind of blindness towards her is intimated, moments later, through the observation that 'he liked to recall the time when she was little and they were all in all to each other' (p. 18). As the narrative will reveal, Almayer has built his dreams on a time which has long since passed by, and on a vision of Nina which isn't Nina. This is implicit in the different significance of Dain's return for each of them, although the different meanings of this event are not available until Chapter 5.

Chapter 2 introduces an extended analepsis which continues until the end of Chapter 5. It records the early years and steady decline of the Lingard trading post. It gives the impression of a background of intrigue and struggle – human activities that are imaged, and find their counterpart, in the Darwinian struggle of the vegetation of the jungle. It suggests a world of isolated egoists, of people trying to realise their separate dreams of power.[7] It stresses, above all, the isolation of Almayer 'alone in the midst of those adverse circumstances, deriving only a little comfort from the companionship of his little daughter' (p. 25). The chapter reveals how Nina came to have a central part in his dreams of success in the subsequent solitary years, when he was completely isolated, deprived of both her company and Lingard's occasional visits, dropped by his 'adoption' into the prison of this island from which he longs to escape.

Chapter 2 also develops the racial polarities of the background. It shows their effect on Almayer's professional activities (Lakamba helps 'the white man's enemies' [p. 24]), and it foregrounds their role in his personal life both in his wife's 'outbursts of savage nature' (p. 26) and in his defensiveness before his own daughter, whom he has sent away to be educated in Singapore:

> He could not take her back into that savage life to which he was condemned himself. . . . What would she think of him? . . . A civilised woman, young and hopeful; while he felt old and hopeless, and very much like those savages round him. (p. 29)

And so, when she arrives unexpectedly, Almayer 'thought with dismay' of the meeting of his wife and daughter, 'of what this grave girl in European clothes would think of her betel-nut chewing mother' (p. 29). Almayer projects his own disgust of Malays – which is part of his 'white man's pride' (p. 28) – inappropriately on to Nina. His dreams are not so much the result of love for Nina, but are essentially egotistic in origin. The dream is not for Nina: Nina is for the dream. In his dreams 'They would live in Europe, he and his daughter.' 'They would be rich and respected. Nobody would think of her mixed blood in the presence of her great beauty and his immense wealth' (p. 3).

It is not that he wants her 'respected', so much as himself. It is not her rehabilitation in the white world that he desires, so much as his own. It is his sense of 'shame' (p. 10) at being married to what he considers a 'savage' wife that provides the energy behind his dreams, not love for Nina. He wants to be accepted back (and accepted back at his own evaluation) with his 'transgression' forgiven and forgotten. It is because this is what he wants – and because he has internalised this judging (and, he hopes, ultimately forgiving) white world – that his awareness of Nina is so distorted. He knows she has 'mixed blood' (p. 3), but he doesn't allow for the implications of that fact in her relations to either the white or the Malay world. And yet this fact of 'mixed blood' – of half-belonging to two worlds – is the basic conflict of Nina's reality and personality.

Almayer's vision of events, then, cannot be accepted uncritically. Indeed, scepticism is encouraged. While Almayer's dreams and assumptions continue unchanged, information is supplied that cannot be contained within Almayer's world-view, but does not obviously break out of it only because it is so equivocally or unobtrusively presented. Captain Ford's 'explanation' of Nina's return is a typical example: it is elliptical and elusive, yet it contains an important warning: 'She was never happy over there. Those two Vinck girls are no better than dressed-up monkeys. They slighted her. You can't make her white' (pp. 30–1). Almayer, however, is ever ready to turn a blind eye to reality and to find evidence to support his self-ideal and his dream of power. For example, when visitors arrive out of curiosity to catch a glimpse of Nina, Almayer offers a very different 'reading' of the incident:

> Those Arabs and Malays saw at least that he was a man of some ability, he thought. And he began, after his manner, to plan great things, to dream of great fortunes for himself and Nina. Especially for Nina. (p. 32)

By this means, the central place that Almayer's vision of Nina has in his plans for his own future is steadily revealed. At the same time, it is clear that this vision of Nina does not correspond to the true Nina, although, because the narrative is focalised through Almayer, it is not yet possible to measure the discrepancy between the phantom and the real Nina. For instance, because the focus is on Almayer's fears of the first meeting of mother and daughter, it is almost possible to miss the otherwise surprising and significant fact that Nina's first action on her return is to lock herself away in conversation with her mother. This action supplies the answer to questions which are implicit in the narrative but which Almayer never thinks to ask. He never wonders why 'Nina adapted herself wonderfully to the circumstances of a half-savage and miserable life' (p. 31), nor why Nina spends so much time with her mother and accepts 'that savage intrusion into their daily existence' (p. 33) with such equanimity. He has his own 'explanation': 'she had (as he called it) her bad days when she used to visit her mother and remain long hours in the riverside hut' (p. 31). In other words, when she is not what he wants her to be, she is 'not herself' – a family dynamic that R. D. Laing would have recognised as a paradigmatic schizogenic situation.[8] It denies the child's real identity and maintains the parent's illusions, so that the child is trapped between its own sense of identity and the identity its parents assign to it. This is most clearly signified in Almayer's refusal to give full value to his daughter's 'mixed blood', to recognise the two sides of his daughter's nature. As a result of this refusal, he is bound to feel that she has 'betrayed' him. The schizogenic potential of the father/daughter relationship is, however, further complicated since Nina combines within herself two strands which the surrounding society polarises. In that polarised society, a conflict of loyalties is unavoidable – and 'betrayal' is necessary – if she is to find an identity.

Chapter 3 brings Nina's search for identity to the fore. First there is a reminder of the Sambir inhabitants' view of her as 'a silent figure moving in their midst calm and white-robed' (p. 38). But then, unlike them, the reader is given access to the thoughts and decisions that that silence masks. Her mother very quickly cast off the influence of her convent education, until she was left with only a misunderstood, talismanic 'brass cross'. And Mrs Almayer had at least had 'something tangible to cling to', but Nina, 'brought up under the Protestant wing of the proper Mrs Vinck', had not even 'a piece of brass to remind her of past teaching' (p. 41). In her search for identity, Nina goes over her past, and over the different heritages of the two strands that compose her being. Her past falls into three distinct phases – and her memory, or, equally, her lack of memory, of these phases leads steadily to a single conclusion. The first phase was that of her early close relationship with Almayer, but 'she seemed to have forgotten in civilised surroundings her life before the time when Lingard had, so to speak, kidnapped her' (p. 42) from Sambir. Yet it is upon this relationship, and this early period, that Almayer has built all his dreams. But just as it is understandable why he should remember those early years, so it is equally understandable, given her age and her subsequent experiences, why Nina should have forgotten them. In the second phase, in Singapore, she had had 'Christian teaching, social education, and a good glimpse of civilised life' (p. 42). But she had been unimpressed by 'civilisation': she had seen 'only the same manifestations of love and hate and of sordid greed chasing the uncertain dollar' (p. 43) as she saw in Sambir; and the 'virtuous pretences' of the white people had contrasted unfavourably with the 'savage and uncompromising sincerity of purpose' of 'her Malay kinsmen' (p. 43). This impression and the choice of that significant word 'kinsmen' were influenced by her personal experiences in Singapore – in particular, her rejection by the white community: 'her teachers did not understand her nature, and the education ended in a scene of humiliation, in an outburst of contempt from white people for her mixed blood' (p. 42).

The movement begun in Singapore has continued and gathered momentum under the influence of new experiences after her return to Sambir. She has lived on the river for three years 'with a savage mother and a father walking about amongst pitfalls, with his head in the clouds, weak, irresolute and unhappy' (p. 42), and, during these three years, she seems to have had only one important activity – listening 'with avidity to the old woman's tales of the departed glories of the Rajahs, from whose race she had sprung' (p. 43). These tales, in which 'men of her mother's race shone far above the Orang Blanda' (p. 42), leave their mark on her, with the result that 'she became gradually more indifferent, more contemptuous of the white side of her descent, represented by a feeble and traditionless father' (p. 43). Besides this incipient (but, so far, unexpressed) choice of sides by Nina, this third chapter reveals a further element of importance in Nina's relationship with her father. Nina's reaction to the news of Reshid's proposal of marriage shows clearly her readiness for love.[9] For this reason, her response produces 'a nameless fear' (p. 47) in Almayer's heart: not only is the world breaking in on his dreams for himself and Nina, but Nina herself seems ready to welcome it. Almayer's later attitude to Dain reflects not – or, rather, not only – racist feelings, but also a jealous possessiveness. Not only does Almayer base his dreams on his early relationship with Nina and love to recall 'the time when she was little' (p. 18), but he is also prepared to sacrifice her to those dreams. His constant thoughts of those times stand revealed as manifestations of a desire to prevent her from growing up, since growing up means growing away from him. If the child's chosen life is a betrayal of the parent's dreams, equally the parental ambitions are a block on the child's freedom and free growth to adulthood.

In the subsequent chapters, there is a gradual build-up and externalisation of these implicit conflicts. Nina, by her actions, creates her social identity and becomes irrevocably committed to her choice of sides. She has to find her place in either the Dutch or Malay camp. She has to decide between her father's dreams and her own needs – between betraying him and betraying herself. And yet, all the same, she has to betray some part of herself, since she really belongs fully to neither side. The elements are fused within her that are polarised in the external world. She is forced to choose between Malay and Dutch – between father and lover – yet, in herself, these choices don't exist. She is half-Malay and half-Dutch, which means that she is both Malay and Dutch. This is evidenced in her relationship with Dain – in her variations between eastern and western behavioural modes. Even though Dain, from the first moment, is reported to have felt 'the subtle breath of mutual understanding passing between their two savage natures' (p. 63), yet, at that first moment, Nina appeared 'shamelessly' before him like a white woman, and Almayer had to excuse her appearance, by saying 'White women have their customs' (p. 56). It was only after a pause of surprise, when she felt 'confused' because of the new sensations that she experienced under his glance, that she 'instinctively drew the lower part of the curtain across her face' (p. 55). Nina felt him to be 'the embodiment of her fate, the creature of her dreams . . . the ideal Malay chief of her mother's tradition' (p. 64), but that reference to 'her mother's tradition', while explicitly affirming kinship, simultaneously and tacitly attests to a difference, by reminding us of her father's different heritage. The 'mystery' element of her 'mysterious consciousness of identity with that being' (p. 64) celebrates the same fascination of closeness and separation, affinity and strangeness. In their later meetings, Nina behaves towards Dain 'as became a Malay girl', listening to him 'with half-veiled face and in silence' (p. 64). But, on the eve of Dain's departure, to try and express the depth of her feelings for him, she turns to a western mode: 'in the great tumult of passion, like a flash of lightning came to her the reminiscence of that despised and almost forgotten civilisation she had only glanced at' (p. 72), and she kisses him.

II

This ambiguity about Nina is not only internal, but external – not only felt by her, but felt by others. If she alternates, in her behaviour, between eastern and western modes, and seems to have the best of both worlds, in fact, each world notes only the alien part and excludes her because of it. When the Dutch officers visit Almayer, the 'young sub' shows the white world's reaction to her:

> 'She was very beautiful and imposing,' he reflected, 'but after all a half-caste girl'. This thought caused him to pluck up heart. (p. 126)

Her beauty and personality lose their value from the fact that she is half-Malayan, and a feeling of respect for her, as a 'beautiful and imposing' woman, gives way in his mind to a sense of her availability as a 'half-caste girl'. The vehemence of Nina's reaction is, therefore, completely understandable:

> I hate the sight of your white faces. I hate the sound of your gentle voices. That is the way you speak to women, dropping sweet words before any pretty face.   (p. 140)

Conversely, Malays like Lakamba and Babalatchi have no respect for her either. They are shocked by her westernised behaviour. While the Dutch officers are at dinner with Almayer and Nina, Babalatchi reports on Dain and his hiding-place:

> The white-man's daughter took him there. She told me so herself, speaking to me openly, for she is half-white and has no decency. (pp. 127–8)

Her own mother criticises her for speaking 'like a fool of a white woman' (p. 149). Even Dain, we are told, felt proud to be 'at the feet of that woman that half belonged to his enemies' (p. 172). Only to Almayer – and to her humble rival Taminah – is she a 'white woman'. Even then, for Almayer, it is a way of claiming respect for himself, while for Taminah it is a way of showing her scorn. Apart from them, to the Dutch she is a 'half-caste' (p. 126), and to the Malays she is the 'white-man's daughter' (p. 127) – a formulation that precisely marks her off as belonging neither to the Malay nor the Dutch world.

The ambiguity of Nina's nature is brought fully to the surface through her triangular relationship with Almayer and Dain. The conflict of ties – between father and lover – first appears after Almayer has discovered what he takes to be Dain's dead body. He is emotionally affected by the discovery – though not for Dain's sake, but rather because, with the death of Dain, he sees the final collapse of all his dreams. To gain sympathy from Nina, he tells her what those lost dreams were, how they centred on her, and what he takes to be 'the inner meaning of his life' (p. 102). His subsequent appeal for 'one word of comfort' rouses 'conflicting impulses' in Nina:

> With her heart deeply moved by the sight of Almayer's misery; knowing it was in her power to end it with a word, longing to bring peace to that troubled heart, she heard with terror the voice of her overpowering love commanding her to be silent. And she submitted after a short and fierce struggle with her old self against the new principle of her life. (p. 103)

The narrative here is deliberately misleading. The 'word' with which she could end Almayer's misery is not the general 'word of comfort' for which he asked, but a specific piece of information – namely, that Dain is still alive. The message spoken clearly by her silence is that, if she has to choose between her father and her lover, she will choose Dain. Her 'old self' has submitted to a 'new principle of life'. Almayer's blindness, however, is equally significant. He notices none of the, admittedly small, signs of this internal struggle, 'for his sight was dimmed by self-pity, anger, and by despair' (p. 103), just as later he does not see that Nina loves him, even though she has opted out of his dream to follow her own dream with Dain.

This conflict of ties – and the struggle of 'old self' and 'new principle' – is visible again in Chapter 10. In the last moments before she takes to the river and irrevocably commits herself to her 'new principle', she suddenly feels fear in the face of the unknown towards which this 'new principle' is leading her: 'the sudden darkness seemed to be full of menacing voices calling upon her to rush headlong into the unknown; to be true to her own impulse to give herself up to the passion she had evoked and shared' (p. 147). Held between conflicting forces – her old self and her new principle, the 'fear of finality' (p. 151) and the impulse to passion – Nina undergoes a long moment of paralysis, which her mother tries to break. She appeals first to Nina's ambition: 'I was a slave and you shall be a queen' (p. 149). Then, when Nina expresses the desire to see her father once more, she appeals to her love for Dain: she threatens to cry out and bring the Dutch soldiers down on him, if Nina takes another step towards Almayer. By bringing up this 'new principle of life', she gets Nina into the boat.[10] The narrative takes pains to prevent us from reading her hesitation as evidence of love for Almayer: 'At the bottom of that passing desire to look again at her father's face there was no strong affection' (p. 151). This is followed by another assertion, which, in this context, acts as corroboration: 'She felt no scruples and no remorse at leaving suddenly that man whose sentiments towards herself she could not understand, she could not even see' (p. 151). Nina's inability to understand the emotions and fantasies that Almayer has woven around her figure would not necessarily signify a lack of affection for him; and there is a discrepancy between what is shown of their relationship in earlier scenes and what is narrated here, which can be explained as a misogynistic voice that enters the narrative and colours the last part of the novel.[11]

In Chapter 10, Nina has to relive the conflict of ties between father and lover, and the conflict between old self and new principle, before she makes her decision and is pushed off into the stream. The chapter includes a lengthy summary of the process that Nina has undergone:

> She had little belief and no sympathy for her father's dreams; but the savage ravings of her mother chanced to strike a responsive chord . . . and she dreamed dreams of her own with the persistent absorption of a captive thinking of liberty within the walls of his prison cell. With the coming of Dain she found the road to freedom by obeying the voice of the new-born impulses. . . . She understood now the reason and the aim of life; and in the triumphant unveiling of that mystery she threw away disdainfully her past. (pp. 151–2)

This both parallels and contrasts with the earlier lengthy speech from Almayer in which he outlined the 'inner meaning of his life' (p. 102). These contrasting set-pieces bring together their different programmes for living: Nina's truth to impulse, and Almayer following the dream based on his self-ideal. Almayer tries to live in the future, and forget the present. Nina tries to live in the present, and to forget and escape from her past.

In the last two chapters the conflict of ties reaches its climax in the confrontations between the three members of the triangle. When Nina rejoins Dain, she has thrown away her past and her old self. The irreversibility, the final and suicidal nature, of this decision is conveyed by the imagery: 'she walked up to him with quick, resolute steps, and, with the appearance of one about to leap from a dangerous height, threw both her arms round his neck' (p. 171). But it is now, too, that the real nature of the ambiguity of Nina's character and the real complexity of the questions of loyalty and betrayal that face her are revealed. Though she is forced to choose between alternative commitments, the elements are not in conflict within her, and her problems do not end with making a choice of sides. This is seen particularly clearly in the case of the novel's brown/white polarity. There is a hint of what is to come, when Dain (in Chapter 11) describes his love of the sea to Nina:

> Her hair was over his eyes, her breath was on his forehead, her arms were about his body. No two beings could be closer to each other, yet she guessed rather than understood the meaning of his last words.   (p. 174)

Accordingly, when Almayer tells Nina 'Between him and you there is a barrier that nothing can remove' (p. 178), Nina's reply, though true, does not deny Almayer's assertion: 'Between your people and me there is also a barrier that nothing can remove' (p. 179). Indeed, Nina's claim 'now I am a Malay' (p. 180) is invalidated by the events on the islet in Chapter 12. As Dain watches Nina crying, he feels 'something invisible that stood between them, something that would let him approach her so far, but no further' (p. 187); and what that 'something' might be is suggested by his comment 'It is the white woman that is crying now' (p. 188). Though Nina can follow a 'new principle', and reject her 'old self', though she can apparently choose between white and brown, Almayer and Dain, there is still, even at the end, a 'white' part of her 'old self' that she can never, it seems, get away from. There is a 'new principle', but not a 'new self'. It is always potential, never actual in the novel.[12]

The events on the islet do, however, clarify the various questions of betrayal. Nina has been true to her impulses, and, if she has 'betrayed' Almayer's dreams, the betrayal has been forced upon her, as she says, by the unreality of the dreams (p. 190). Nina also draws a sympathetic picture of the struggles behind her other decision, her choice between white and brown:

> When I returned to Sambir I found the place which I thought would be a peaceful refuge for my heart, filled with weariness and hatred – and mutual contempt. Then I saw that you could not understand me; for was I not part of that woman? Of her who was the regret and shame of your life? I had to choose – I hesitated. Why were you so blind? Did you not see me struggling before your eyes? (p. 191)

Almayer's racism precluded understanding earlier, just as now his possessive jealousy precludes 'forgiveness'. There is a further complication: Almayer believes that his faith in Nina is the 'foundation of his hopes' (p. 192), but the real foundation is his attachment to an unrealistic self-ideal: 'She was a remarkable woman . . . all the latent greatness of his nature – in which he honestly believed – had been transfused into that slight, girlish figure' (p. 192).

It is not his 'latent greatness' that has been 'transfused' into her, but rather his self-ideal that has been transferred to her. He has made her into the custodian of 'all the latent greatness of his nature': she acts as a kind of 'external soul'. This is the clearest expression of Almayer's attempt to take over Nina for the sake of his self-ideal. By extension, to accept her autonomy would involve the surrender of that self-ideal. Accordingly, in Chapter 12, Almayer forces the choice between himself and Dain. For a moment, he considers that he might change 'his heart if not his skin' and make 'her life easier between the two loves' (p. 192); but he chooses to be 'betrayed', and he has the burden passed on to him of forgetting, and escaping from, the past.

III

The reader's response to this situation (and his evaluation of Nina and Almayer respectively) is, however, influenced by a misogynistic voice that steadily emerges in the narrative. Two of Moser's criticisms of the novel provide a useful starting-point for consideration of this topic: he complains of 'the inappropriate imagery used in connection with the lovers' and the 'inconsistency of the lovers' attitudes towards each other'.[13] As an example of this 'inappropriate imagery', he cites the descriptive passage that concludes the first account of a love-scene between Dain and Nina:

> The intense work of tropical nature went on: plants shooting upward, entwined, interlaced in inextricable confusion, climbing madly and brutally over each other in the terrible silence of a desperate struggle towards the life-giving sunshine above – as if struck with sudden horror at the seething mass of corruption below, at the death and decay from which they sprang. (p. 71)

The word 'inappropriate' supplies the key to the assumptions underlying Moser's criticism. Ian Watt suggests an alternative way of reading this unexpected conclusion to the scene: he notes how the representation of nature in this passage 'violently subverts the conventional assumptions of popular romance'.[14] Instead of 'a static landscape' there is 'nature in motion'; instead of 'exotic travelogue', the Darwinian 'struggle for survival'. Watt offers a similar answer to Moser's second criticism. It is not that the lovers' attitudes are 'inconsistent' but that 'the particular view of sexual relations' inscribed in the novel conflicts with the 'essential presuppositions of romance'.[15] Romance elements are again subverted by the insertion of another discourse. Watt, however, does not attempt to explore, contextualise or even define more clearly that 'particular view of sexual relations'.

On 24 September 1895, Conrad wrote to Garnett, arguing that 'every individual wishes to assert his power, women by sentiment, men by achievement of some sort – mostly base'.[16] Although Conrad was writing with reference to *An Outcast of the Islands*, this view of human motivation is already very much in evidence in *Almayer's Folly*. It lies behind Almayer's 'dream of wealth and power' (p. 3), his wife's 'dreams of the future' (p. 23), and all the scheming and intrigue that drives the overt and covert plots.[17] Ultimately, the 'power' men wish to assert by achievement in these novels is not so much actual power over others as the abstract idea of their own power: achievement is the way of realizing the self-ideal. For women, 'power' is both more and less direct. They have direct and actual power over one man, and, through that, have indirect and abstract 'power' by drawing on and working through his achievement. Mrs Almayer holds before Nina, on the eve of her departure, the temptation of power, and she reveals, simultaneously, her own thwarted ambition (pp. 149–50). She, like Almayer, seeks to find vicarious satisfaction in Nina's success: if she cannot be a great Ranee herself, she will be the mother of a great Ranee. All this depends, in turn, on Dain's success, and Mrs Almayer, accordingly, advises Nina how to gain 'power' over Dain. In the following chapter, on her re-union with Dain, Nina shows how well she has learnt the lesson. It is here that that lengthy description of the 'look of women's surrender' (p. 172), which was one of Moser's examples of the 'inconsistency of the lovers' attitudes', is to be found:

> She drew back her head and fastened her eyes on his in one of those long looks that are a woman's most terrible weapon; a look that is more stirring than the closest touch, and more dangerous than the thrust of a dagger, because it also whips the soul out of the body, but leaves the body alive and helpless, to be swayed here and there by the capricious tempests of passion and desire . . . bringing terrible defeat in the delirious uplifting of accomplished conquest.   (p. 171)

Nina's behaviour here is perfectly consistent with the idea of a will-to-power that has been released by her mother's teaching; and the sense of male powerlessness, far from being inconsistent with earlier representations, picks up a detail from that first love-scene between Nina and Dain, when Dain, 'at the feet of Nina, forgot the world, felt himself carried away helpless by a great wave of supreme emotion' (p. 68). It is possible, then, to read the passage as part of an extended consideration of the ambiguities of power and powerlessness.[18] Dain's 'conquest' is also his 'defeat'; his greatest feeling of pride comes from this self-abasement. Nina, too, is very much aware of the ambiguities of sexual power-relations: 'she would be his greatness and his strength; yet hidden from the eyes of all men she would be, above all, his only and lasting weakness' (p. 139). Also, as the passage proceeds, it produces more than just a sense of women's power over men. Specifically, what emerges is a male fear of 'passion and desire': sexual feelings are feared as loss of control, and, as in *An Outcast of the Islands,* the representation of sexual passion as enslavement elides into sexual passion as diabolic possession.[19] We arrive at a discourse of sexuality that is marked by the woman's will-to-power, intimations of male sexual anxiety, and the association of love with death and decay.

Conrad's formulation of his view of human motivation (in his letter to Garnett) finds an interesting parallel in Schopenhauer's *Parerga*:

Man strives in everything for a *direct* domination over things, either by comprehending or by subduing them. But woman is everywhere and always relegated to a merely *indirect* domination, which is achieved by means of man, who is consequently the only thing she has to dominate directly.[20]

It is, arguably, Schopenhauer rather than Darwin who lies behind Conrad's representation of nature in terms of 'the struggle for life'. For Schopenhauer, the 'Will' was the source of all phenomena. The 'Will', present and active in each of them, greedily demanding life, thus produced 'the horror of the struggle of all against all', a 'manifold restless motion' driven by 'hunger and sexual instinct'.[21] Woman's role, according to Schopenhauer, was as the agent of the Will: 'women exist in the main solely for the propagation of the species', and the Will works through them to phylogenetic not ontogenetic ends.[22] For Schopenhauer, satisfaction of the sexual impulse affirms life 'beyond the death of the individual', but, at the same time, it also involves an affirmation of 'suffering and death', since these too belong to 'the phenomenon of life'.[23] As Conrad intimates imagistically in *Almayer's Folly*, involvement in the processes of life is, simultaneously, involvement in the processes of death and decay.

There is another context which also needs to be taken into consideration. J. S. Mill commented on women's indirect control over men in a way that superficially resembles the statements of Conrad and Schopenhauer:

By entirely sinking her own existence in her husband; by having no will (or persuading him that she has no will) but his ... and by making it the business of her life to work upon his sentiments, a wife may gratify herself by influencing, and very probably perverting, his conduct.[24]

However, where Schopenhauer believed he was distilling the essence of female nature, Mill is describing the way in which woman's nature is distorted by the conditions of patriarchal society. Conrad's view of human motivation and of sexual difference has to be placed in the context of the Victorian debates about women and sexuality.

In particular, as J. D. Patterson has argued, Conrad's representation of women in his early fiction has to be seen in relation to the erotophobic nature of Victorian patriarchy.[25]

Since Steven Marcus's *The Other Victorians*, it has almost become customary to take William Acton's *The Functions and Disorders of the Reproductive System* as representative of official Victorian attitudes towards sexuality.[26] Despite its title, Acton's volume addresses itself almost exclusively to the male reproductive system. It is, indeed, constructed, both implicitly and explicitly, upon a denial of female sexuality: 'I should say that the majority of women (luckily for them) are not very much troubled with sexual feeling of any kind'.[27] However, as Otto Rank observed, man depreciates woman 'only consciously; in the Unconscious he fears her'.[28] In his account of male sexuality, Acton creates 'a world part fantasy, part nightmare, part hallucination, and part mad house', but behind this (and expressed through it) is a single, overwhelming emotion: 'fear – fear of sex in general and particular; of impotence and of potency; of impulse and of its loss; of indulgence and even of the remedies prescribed to curb it'.[29] Acton's work suggests that, for the Victorian male, sexuality was an area of deep anxiety, which expressed itself through this labyrinth of double binds. This is borne out not only by the explicit warnings against sexual indulgence, but also by some of Acton's curious digressions.[30] *Almayer's Folly* produces a discourse about sexuality that is marked by similar fears, and those fears are to be glimpsed, in particular, in the representation of Nina.

IV

Almayer's story is, like Jim's, the account of what becomes of a man 'gifted with a strong and active imagination' (p. 10) who dreams of triumphs which reality deprives him of all rational hope of fulfilling. It records, as Kirschner suggests, the annihilation of the unshared ideal of self.[31] At first, Almayer maintains his self-ideal by escaping from the 'unpleasant realities' (p. 3) of the present into dreams of the future – just as Razumov will do later. With the 'death' of Dain, all Almayer's dreams are shattered, and, for a moment, he sees clearly:

> It seemed to him that for many years he had been falling into a deep precipice. Day after day, month after month, year after year,

he had been falling, falling, falling; it was a smooth, round, black
thing . . . and now, with an awful shock, he had reached the
bottom, and behold! he was alive and whole . . .   (p. 99)

For a moment, he sees his wasted life free from any protective
illusions. The result, however, is a split of consciousness: he has the
experience of standing outside himself, and of seeing himself objectively, like a double or second self. This double vision enacts the gap
between his real and ideal selves:

He felt inclined to weep, but it was over the fate of a white man he
knew; a man that fell over a deep precipice and did not die. He
seemed somehow to himself to be standing on one side, a little
way off, looking at a certain Almayer who was in great trouble.
Poor, poor fellow! Why doesn't he cut his throat.   (pp. 99–100)

The problem he faces is how to survive the loss of his illusions of
success and the loss of his self-ideal. Suicide would be one way of
escaping this knowledge. Instead, Almayer turns to illusions of a
different sort, and tries to make an emotional claim upon Nina. He
reveals to her 'the inner meaning of his life':

I wanted to see white men bowing low before the power of your
beauty and your wealth. . . . I wished to seek a strange land . . . so
as to find a new life in the contemplation of your high fortunes, of
your triumphs, of your happiness.   (p. 101)

But he is 'deceived by the emotional estimate of his motives' (p. 102),
and his speech betrays the real motives that he conceals from himself: the way in which Nina figures in his dreams as a substitute for
himself, as the embodiment of 'all the latent greatness of his nature'
(p. 192). Ultimately, he has the same need as Jim for recognition of
his achievement by his own world and by his own 'race'.

The scene where Taminah wakes Almayer from sleep prefigures
his reaction to Nina's departure. First, Almayer's dream, in which he
is an Atlas with 'the crushing weight of worlds' (p. 158) on his
shoulders, serves as a reminder of both his egocentricity and his
dream of greatness. Then, the way in which Taminah's efforts to
wake him are incorporated into his dream, while demonstrating the
mechanism of dreams, at the same time provides insight into
Almayer's general situation:

Get away! But how? If he attempted to move he would step off into nothing, and perish in the crashing fall of that universe of which he was the only support.   (p. 158)

The 'anguish of perishing creation' (p. 159) when he awakes derives not just from the loss of his dream of worlds, but also from the anticipated loss of his world of 'dreams'. He has created a world, which he shares with no one, to correspond to his self-ideal. The 'death' of Dain threatens the 'dream of wealth and power' his self-ideal feeds upon. The departure of Nina, which he has not yet taken in, threatens his world and his self-ideal in another way. Later, when he learns that Nina is leaving, he feels again 'the whole universe unsettled and shaken by this frightful catastrophe of his life' (p. 192). He can no longer hope to redeem himself, and realise his self-ideal through Nina's success. The only way he can do 'his duty to himself – to his race – to his respectable connections' (p. 192) (i.e. to his self-ideal) is by trying to forget the 'disgrace' of this marriage, trying to forget the past on which his hopes were based and the future in which his self-ideal was to be realised.[32]

In the last chapter and a half, Almayer is shown trying to forget, but he is haunted by a phantom child, which torments him like a devil: 'wherever he went, whichever way he turned, he saw the small figure of a little maiden with pretty olive face, with long black hair' (pp. 201–2). This phantom child, not Nina, was the real basis of his hopes. In his despair, this phantom haunts him to remind him of his dreams and his self-ideal. Finally, he succeeds in forgetting, but it is only by wiping out consciousness with opium – a refuge which his self-ideal had earlier denied him.

Kaspar Almayer is Conrad's version of Emma Bovary. Her elevated self-ideal distorted her sense of reality and her expectations from others so that she felt betrayed by others when they didn't live up to those expectations. But the real betrayal was the self-betrayal produced by this false self-ideal. Further, this self-betrayal of hers meant that, rather than being betrayed by others, Emma Bovary was betraying them in her behaviour by her own inauthenticity and betraying them in her consciousness because of the phantom 'other' her own expectations created. But something like this could not stand as an adequate summary of *Almayer's Folly*. Almayer is not the dramatic centre of the novel. This, instead, is Nina, who is the prototype of a different sort of betrayal. Nina's problems are not those of an elevated self-ideal. Her problems are more obviously social problems: the problem of having to align herself with one of two opposed groups, when she belongs equally to each. Nina is in the situation where she is forced to betray a group to which she partly belongs for another to which she also partly belongs – and hence to betray part of herself. Through this situation, Conrad begins his exploration of the problematics of identity-for-self and identity-for-others. It is Conrad's second novel, *An Outcast of the Islands,* that has, as its dramatic centre and as the focus of its analysis, the sort of betrayal represented by Emma Bovary and by Kaspar Almayer.

2
The Unshared Ideal of Self:
An Outcast of the Islands

An Outcast of the Islands is concerned, like *The Secret Sharer*, with 'that ideal conception of one's own personality every man sets up for himself secretly', but it begins when the ideal has already been once betrayed:

> When he stepped off the straight and narrow path of his peculiar honesty, it was with an inward assertion of unflinching resolve to fall back again into the monotonous but safe stride of virtue as soon as his little excursion into the wayside quagmire had produced the desired effect. It was going to be a short episode – a sentence in brackets so to speak – in the flowing tale of his life: a thing of no moment, to be done unwillingly, yet neatly, and to be quickly forgotten.[1]

The narrative then traces the gradual discovery that the ideal has been betrayed, exploring the reactions to, and consequences of, that discovery. Whereas Nina's 'betrayals' sprang from having to commit herself to one of two opposed sides, to each of which she equally belonged, and from the problematic relation between identity-for-self and identity-for-the-other, Willems's betrayal is essentially self-betrayal, and only secondarily the betrayal of other loyalties, although it is through the betrayal of others that his self-betrayal is explored. Willems is the prototype of those Conrad heroes who betray an ideal conception of self and 'spoil' their lives. Just as Lingard provides the first glimpse of that other Conrad hero, subtly related to the first: the man who tries to follow an ideal code of conduct.

I

Chapter 1 of *An Outcast of the Islands* displays both the falseness of Willems's self-image and the concatenation of circumstances that

32

will render that self-image untenable in the society that Willems inhabits. Willems's self-image is one of 'unquestionable superiority' (p. 4), based on his sense of his own cleverness, virtue, and, above all, success. He is 'the successful white man', 'the rising man sure to climb very high'; and the material basis for all this is his role as 'the confidential clerk of Hudig and Co.' (p. 4). As a result of this 'superiority', Willems has adopted certain habits in Macassar. At home, he has become accustomed 'to tyrannise good-humouredly over his half-caste wife, to notice with tender contempt his pale yellow child, to patronise loftily his dark-skinned brother-in-law' (p. 3). He thinks of himself as 'their providence', and they apparently accept him in this role (p. 4). In his social life, too, there is the same boastfulness, the same patronising, and the same enjoyment (and over-evaluation) of his power: 'A man of his stamp could carry off anything, do anything, aspire to anything' (p. 9). He has apparently forced others to accept this self-image as their image of him. Yet the ironic overtones of such label-like phrases as 'the successful white man', at the same time, subtly problematise that self-image.

As the narrative proceeds, Willems's entire life in Macassar is shown to be based on a series of self-deceptions. The first of these is his belief that he knew 'all about himself': he 'believed in his genius and his knowledge of the world' (p. 6). In fact, he has 'an exalted sense of his duty to himself and the world at large' (p. 5). He is 'clever', but he is also ignorant, and, in his ignorance, he thinks his small world is the whole world. As regards his 'virtue', the 'straight and narrow path' of his existence as Hudig's 'confidential clerk' turns out to have had considerable latitude, while the 'confidential' part of his title fitly acknowledges the shadiness of some of the ways. As for 'honesty', he 'disapproved of the elementary dishonesty that dips the hand in the cash-box', but 'one could evade the laws and push the principles of trade to their furthest consequences' (p. 8). He has fallen into the same trap as Raskolnikov in *Crime and Punishment*: the trap of 'enlightened self-interest'. Like Raskolnikov he believes in taking 'the principles of trade' to their limit and in 'the special dispensation for the strong':

> Some call that cheating. Those are the fools, the weak, the contemptible. The wise, the strong, the respected have no scruples. Where there are scruples there can be no power.   (p. 8)

To cap it all, much of Willems's 'success', that will excuse such dishonesty, is actually based on the future. Like Razumov's, his identity is projected forwards on to the future, but, unlike Razumov, he is enjoying already that phantom future identity. Chapter 1 ends with what is, literally, a projected, exalted image of him, when he sees 'his shadow dart forward and wave a hat, as big as a rum barrel, at the end of an arm several yards long' (p. 10). He goes home 'dizzy with the cocktails and with the intoxication of his own glory', weaving 'the splendid web of his future':

> The road to greatness lay plainly before his eyes, straight and shining, without any obstacle he could see. He had stepped off the path of honesty as he understood it, but he would soon regain it, never to leave it any more . . . he would go on unchecked towards the brilliant goal of his ambition, Hudig's partner.   (p. 11)

The chapter ends where it started, but the reader is now equipped with greater knowledge. Besides the real insignificance of Willems's 'success' and the dullness of his 'brilliant goal', there is also the over-confidence with which he already identifies with his 'future'. The return to the imagery of the opening paragraph brings with it the reminder that he is 'off the path' already. The sinister appearance of Vinck towards the close adds to the sense of precariousness, since it is suggested that Vinck not only resents Willems, but also knows of his dishonesty. (He is, after all, 'Hudig's cashier'.) Willems's 'shadow', 'the shadow of a successful man', now takes on a further connotation: it is not only the exalted self-image that Willems pursues, but also a ghost. Willems's future identity, which is so much a part of his self-image, is as good as dead. The chapter ends with Willems standing 'contemplating mentally Hudig's future partner': 'He saw him quite safe; solid as the hills; deep – deep as any abyss; discreet as the grave' (p. 11).

The rest of the first section deals with Willems's discovery that his self-image is no longer a viable identity in Macassar. It explores the gap between his self-image and the way others regard him, between identity-for-self and identity-for-the-other, and establishes a pattern of betrayal, flight and rescue. Chapter 2 focuses on the prototypical instance that epitomises Willems's character, his flight from *Kosmopoliet IV*, but it also introduces Lingard's character as an illuminating parallel within this exploration of the self-image. The chapter opens with a description of the sea, likening it to 'a beautiful and unscrupulous woman' (p. 12).[2] But this mistress, instead of destroying Lingard, has endowed him with qualities that seem morally positive: 'his fierce aspect, his loud voice, his fearless eyes, his stupidly guileless heart'; 'his universal love of creation'; 'his straightforward simplicity of motive and honesty of aim' (p. 13). Above all, it has given him 'his absurd faith in himself' (p. 13). This echoes Willems's 'exalted sense of his duty to himself and the world at large' (p. 5). Each of them has an exalted self-image, but the juxtaposition brings out the differences, and the differences are related to their different working environments, the different worlds of sea and trade. Willems was 'found wanting' by the standards of the sea. He was 'hopelessly at variance with the spirit of the sea': he had 'an instinctive contempt for the honest simplicity of that work which led to nothing he cared for' (p. 17). In Chapter 3, this 'honest simplicity' of the sea is contrasted with the 'peculiar honesty' of trade, and Willems is shown as operating through perverted forms of sea-virtues. 'Work' and 'duty' appear as 'the tasks of restitution' and 'the duty of not being found out' (p. 21). Courage appears as 'that courage that will not scale heights, yet will wade bravely through the mud – if there be no other road' (p. 21). When Lingard rescues Willems for the second time (in Chapter 4), the key to this difference is given: the selfish individualism of trade is implicitly contrasted with the sense of responsibility of the sea. Where Willems is keen to evade the 'burden' of his wife, Lingard feels obliged to help:

> We are responsible for one another – worse luck. I am almost ashamed of myself, but I can understand your dirty pride. . . . I will see this thing through. . . . And I will have it all square and ship-shape. (p. 40)

Chapter 3 also recounts the discovery of Willems's crime and his reaction when it becomes public knowledge. The chapter starts from his sense that 'he was off the path of his peculiar honesty' (p. 21). The return to 'path' imagery serves as a reminder that his identity is projected on to the future, and that he has to remain on the same public course to maintain his self-image in the present. However, since this identity is not only projected on the future, but also based largely on identity-for-the-other (in fact, it incorporates identity-for-the-other), his problem is not a moral one of 'steadfastness of heart', but rather a practical one of concealing his crimes and transgressions. His real crisis comes not when he is tempted to betray Hudig, but when his betrayal of Hudig's trust is discovered and made public. It is not that his 'self-respect' is 'undermined' as Baines states, but that the 'humiliation' destroys his identity-for-the-other at the same time as being sacked removes the material basis of his identity-for-self.[3]

Accordingly, when he arrives home, he is surprised to find the house still there: his past 'was so utterly gone from him that the dwelling which belonged to it appeared to him incongruous standing there intact, neat and cheerful' (p. 23). The discovery of his crime has produced the same sense of 'dislocation' as Raskolnikov felt after committing the murder: his past 'seemed to be lying at the bottom of some fathomless chasm, deep, deep down, where he could only just discern it dimly'.[4] Willems, however, feels the dislocation only when his crime becomes known – not, like Raskolnikov, when the crime is committed: where Raskolnikov is trying to discover more about himself, Willems is more concerned with maintaining his self-image. Like 'Lord Jim' he refuses to accept his action as a sign of himself. His initial feeling is one of shame (not guilt), and that sense of shame 'was replaced slowly by a passion of anger against himself and still more against the stupid concourse of circumstances that had driven him into his idiotic indiscretion'. The narrator then briefly intrudes before returning to Willems's thought processes:

> Idiotic indiscretion; that is how he defined his guilt to himself. Could there be anything worse from the point of view of his undeniable cleverness? What a fatal aberration of an acute mind! He did not recognise himself there. He must have been mad. (pp. 22–3)

The narrative delineates a gradual process by which Willems moves from a suffocating sense of guilt to a disowning of that guilt. He first shifts the blame from himself to 'circumstances' – to the concatenation of events that tempted him. Then he makes it an issue of cleverness or stupidity: by changing the terms, he moves the deed out of the moral world of innocence and guilt. Then he invokes his self-image of 'undeniable cleverness', and, by asserting it, pushes the crime away from 'himself' as an 'aberration'. Rather than confront his self-image with the action, Willems splits himself into two parts (a momentary 'mad' self and his usual self) to rescue his self-image.

Nevertheless, he still experiences a sense of dislocation. Indeed, by splitting himself into two to deny responsibility for his own actions, he is insuring a sense of dislocation. On his return home, Willems realises that, even though he has rescued his self-image for himself (identity-for-self), he has irrevocably lost the social identity (identity-for-the-other) that his self-image was built upon. He immediately faces the problem of dealing with his family without the support of that identity. It is going to be more difficult to persuade them of his unstained 'superiority' than it was to persuade himself. In fact, the fear that he feels at the thought of meeting his wife cuts through the earlier process of evasion and makes him aware of the change that has taken place: 'Another man – and another life with the faith in himself gone. He could not be worth much if he was afraid to face that woman' (p. 23).

Here, for the first time, appears a characteristic aspect of Willems's psychology: his idealised self-image is counter-balanced by profound doubts of his own worth, and these two psychic positions act as the positive and negative poles of self-evaluation between which he alternates. While he waits for his wife, he slowly moves away from this negative pole of self-evaluation. He considers his wife's fear and passivity towards him, and he plays with various labels ('Willems the successful' [p. 24]) trying to reassure himself of his identity not from a subject-position but by acting as the 'other' for himself. Then he realises that the people who earlier recognised his superiority with such labels will now be recognising his shame with a different one: 'Willems the . . . He strangled the half-born thought' (p. 24). Rather than face the label 'thief', he rejects his 'friends' with scorn. This strategy has the further advantage that it simultaneously allows him, with that scorn, to reclaim his sense of superiority over them. He has regained some of the essential elements of his identity-for-self, but that identity is no longer publicly viable and no longer has a material base. Nevertheless, he clings to the hope of its continuing domestic viability. His speech to his wife is full of his regained sense of his own greatness and, correspondingly, of Hudig's unjustness to him. He ends his speech feeling he was 'a fine fellow': 'Nothing new that. Still, he surpassed there his own expectations' (p. 26). He has talked himself back into his old exalted self-image, but a measure of his distance from reality is supplied by his misreading of Joanna. Her response throws him back to the alternative negative pole of self-evaluation, as, in Kirschner's words, 'the

accumulated resentment of her submerged will' breaks out in revolt:
'You are nobody now. . . . You are less than dirt, you that have wiped
your feet on me . . . man from nowhere; a vagabond!' (pp. 27–8).[5]

By the end of Chapter 3, Willems feels 'as if he was the outcast of
all mankind' (p. 30), and, for a moment, he faces up to what he has
done:

> Nothing ever comes back. He saw it clearly. The respect and
> admiration of them all, the old habits and old affections finished
> abruptly in the clear perception of the cause of his disgrace . . . for
> a time he came out of himself, out of his selfishness – out of the
> constant preoccupation of his interests and his desires – out of the
> temple of self and the concentration of personal thought.
>
> (pp. 30–1)

Then, as with Jim later, the perception of disgrace at once gives way
to thoughts of home, of the home from which he now feels permanently excluded. Because of his ambition, he 'cut himself adrift'
(p. 31) from home earlier. Now, because of his disgrace, he feels cut
off permanently. He feels separated from his past, isolated in the
present, fearful of the future: 'For the first time in his life he felt
afraid of the future, because he had lost his faith, the faith in his own
success. And he had destroyed it foolishly with his own hands'
(p. 31). He had aimed at being a 'success', and that projected self-
image had provided his life with its meaning. But now he has
betrayed that self-image. In this situation, the negative side of his
self-evaluation asserts itself once more, and it is obvious why he
needs to talk himself away from it: the threat of insignificance is only
a step away from thoughts of non-existence.

His meditation, which 'resembled slow drifting into suicide'
(p. 32), is terminated by the arrival of Lingard. This second rescue,
which explicitly re-plays the start of his career in Macassar, suggests
the chance of a 'new start' – of being a 'new man' (p. 32). But first,
Lingard delivers a number of shattering blows to Willems's former
identity: he reveals various errors and illusions until 'the facts of the
last five years of his life stood clearly revealed in their full meaning'
(p. 34). However, while shattering Willems's old world-view, these
facts incidentally give Willems an opportunity to project his guilt
onto Hudig: 'While he worked for the master, the master had cheated
him; had stolen his very self from him. . . . And that man dared this

very morning call him a thief' (p. 36). He uses the fact of Hudig's deception to reverse the situation.

A similar mechanism operates with his wife, Joanna: 'He did not break his oath, but he would not go back to her. Let hers be the sin of that separation' (p. 38). Willems disowns the guilt of his own actions. He dissociates action from its significance, and revels 'in the extreme purity of his heart' (p. 38). He goes over his Macassar life, and manages to forget his downfall 'in the recollection of his brilliant triumphs' (p. 39). When Lingard tries to bring him back by demanding 'Whose the fault?', Willems ignores the question. He reverts at once to the other pole of self-evaluation, and uses the accompanying suicidal impulse as emotional blackmail to coerce Lingard into rescuing him. He refuses to face the consequences of his actions among the people he knows: 'I would rather hide from them at the bottom of the sea' (p. 39). He seeks to avoid the disconfirmation of his idealised self-image, the experience of the gap between identity-for-self and identity-for-the-other, because, if he loses that idealised self-image, he is left with the opposite pole of self-evaluation, the underlying sense of his own worthlessness. Even before he has reached the island, then, Willems has suicidal impulses and a tenuous sense of self (p. 36). On the other hand, the attempt to rescue the self-ideal is itself a self-destructive process. In the end, there will be only one place for Willems to 'hide' from his actions and only one way for him to escape from himself.

II

At this point, Conrad introduces Babalatchi: Babalatchi, like Lingard, offers an alternative model of being-in-the-world. Babalatchi has the same ambition, the same will-to-power, the same sense of greatness and cleverness as Willems. He too has run away; he too has experienced 'the sudden ruin and destruction of all that he deemed indispensable to a happy and glorious existence' (p. 52); but where Willems's flight is suicidal, running away to escape reality, Babalatchi's flight is designed to rescue something from the past. He is faithful to his leader and his leader's daughter – precisely the relations Willems is betraying by cheating Hudig and leaving Joanna. Furthermore, where Willems is running away rather than face the title 'thief', Babalatchi, who is also a thief, handles that fact by idealising it and giving it an heroic status. He is the 'piratical and son-less Aeneas' (p. 54) to Omar's piratical Anchises. His *modus vivendi* involves, not the pursuit of a shadowy ideal self, but the acknowledgement and idealisation of his own actions. Where Willems is rigidly trying to preserve a self-ideal, Babalatchi idealises what he is and thereby gains 'a true vagabond's pliability to circumstances' (p. 56): Babalatchi's mode of being maintains the continuity of his life, whereas Willems's evasions ensure dislocation.

The return to Willems, in Chapter 6, picks up exactly this point of dislocation. Willems's three months in Sambir have demoralised him, but, instead of feeling guilty for the actions that have spoiled his life, he has merely created a disjunction between past and present:

> He missed the commercial activity of that existence which seemed to him far off, irreparably lost, buried out of sight under the ruins of his past success – now gone from him beyond the possibility of redemption.   (p. 64)

His initial feeling, that he is cut off from his past, gradually becomes the feeling that he is 'left outside the scheme of creation in a hopeless immobility filled with tormenting anger and with ever-stinging regret' (p. 65). Willems, like Nostromo later, feels that he has wandered out of life: 'The man who, during long years, became accustomed to think of himself as indispensable to others, felt a bitter and savage rage at the cruel consciousness of his superfluity' (p. 66). He has avoided conscious knowledge of his actions, but he is troubled by an unconscious knowledge that manifests itself in mental and emotional turbulence, and he takes to restless wanderings 'in search of a refuge from the unceasing reproach of his thoughts'. It is in this mood that he meets Aissa:

> And Willems stared at her, charmed with a charm that carries with it a sense of irreparable loss . . . sleeping sensations awakening suddenly to the rush of new hopes, new fears, new desires – and to the flight of one's old self.   (p. 69)

This is not, as with Nina, the replacement of an 'old self' by a viable 'new principle'. The sinister overtones of 'charm' are immediately activated, and Willems's sense of the flight of his 'old self' gives way to a sense of diabolic possession: 'the fear of something unknown that had taken possession of his heart, of something inarticulate and masterful which could not speak and would be obeyed' (p. 72).

As in *Almayer's Folly* surrender to passion (and to natural processes) elides into ideas of diabolic possession, although here it is clearly Willems's alienated instincts that return in this form.[6] Part I completes the first stage of this process of 'possession', as Willems's 'gradual taming' (p. 76) of Aissa ends with his own capture: 'his very individuality was snatched from within himself by the hand of a woman' (p. 77). During his last meal with Almayer: 'He was keeping a tight hand on himself. . . . He had a vivid illusion . . . of being in charge of a slippery prisoner and within him a growing terror of escape from his own self' (p. 78). Rather than face up to his actions, he sought refuge even from his own thoughts. The price of that strategy has been the denial of aspects of himself, and that denial now destroys the 'safety' and the 'refuge' that were desired: 'There was no safety outside of himself – and in himself there was no refuge, there was only the image of that woman' (p. 80). He asserts, for a moment, 'the unstained purity of his life, of his race, of his civilisation' (p. 80), but that self-ideal can find no confirmation from outside himself and it is undermined by more powerful forces within. This last defence of 'superiority' goes and the flood of emotions swamps his self:

> He struggled with the sense of certain defeat. With a faint cry and an upward throw of his arms he gave up as a tired swimmer gives up: because the swamped craft is gone from under his feet; because the night is dark and the shore is far – because death is better than strife.   (p. 81)[7]

III

By the end of the first section, Willems has betrayed Hudig, his patron and father-in-law, and, in doing so, has destroyed the material basis of his self-ideal. In addition, he has left his wife and there are indications of the imminent betrayal of another father-figure, Lingard.[8] However, the betrayals in Part II are of a different kind, and their changed nature is connected with Willems's relationship with Aissa. These betrayals are equivalent to the betrayals forced on Nina in her 'choice of sides'. Both Willems and Aissa want to separate the other from their own people, and Aissa consciously wants Willems to betray his people as a way of committing him irreversibly to her. But where Nina's 'betrayals' of one side were, simultaneously, acts of commitment to the other, these betrayals are parts only of a steady disintegration, a process of loss.[9]

In Chapter 1, Willems is 'a masquerading spectre of the once so very confidential clerk' (p. 87). His clothes are 'soiled and torn' and, significantly, 'below the waist he was clothed in a worn-out and faded sarong' (p. 87).[10] For a moment, when he asks Almayer for assistance ('I want to become a trader in this place'), he has a brief flash of 'his old belief in himself' (p. 92). He temporarily regains 'something of his old assurance' (p. 92), enjoying, as before, a precarious future identity in the present, until Almayer throws him out.[11]

The rest of Part II is concerned with the Malays, to whom Willems now has to turn. Chapter 2 shows more of the forces that are operative in Sambir. It moves from an opening scene of chess-players in Lakamba's household to Babalatchi, manipulating Omar, Willems and Aissa as pawns in his own ambitious political schemes. It also shows the lovers' position from the Malay viewpoint: white men are 'the sons of witches' (p. 103), and Aissa is seen as betraying her people and her religion.[12] Her father complains that she has forsaken him 'for an infidel dog' (p. 104). The shifting narrative perspective constructs a relativist representation of cultures, but it is Willems's betrayals that are foregrounded as narrative focalisation returns to him:

> Willems measured dismally the depth of his degradation. He – a white man, the admired of white men, was held by those miserable savages whose tool he was about to become. He felt for them all the hate of his race, of his morality, of his intelligence.   (p. 126)

Willems is caught up in a plan to betray Lingard's secret. He tells himself that he is doing this for Aissa, but 'degradation' also does justice to both aspects of his dual evaluation simultaneously. The same action acknowledges both the ideal he is falling from (his sense of 'superiority', individual and racial) and also what he has become. He feels, momentarily, a perverse pleasure in his 'debasement' with the thought that 'what he had done could not be undone': 'He had given himself up. He felt proud of it' (p. 127).[13] However, although he is betraying one side, he will not be accepted by the other: he remains 'the white man' (p. 102). Furthermore, though he may be doing it for Aissa, he remains a 'white man' for her too: the lack of communication and understanding between them is emphasised. Her image of him is false: like Jewel in relation to Jim, she 'could not understand all he told her of his life', but the fragments she understood 'she made up for herself into a story of a man great among his people, valorous and unfortunate' (p. 75). Abdulla's arrival serves to remind him how different they are:

> She had disguised herself so because a man of her race was near! . . . This manifestation of her sense of proprieties was another sign of their hopeless diversity: something like another step downward for him. (p. 128)

Willems is aware of the bind he is in: 'he could not make clear to her the simplest motive of any act of his' and yet 'he could not live without her' (p. 128). He expresses his divided feelings about her in terms of a conflict of 'passion' and 'will', in terms of slavery and manhood: he feels contempt for himself as 'the slave of a passion he had always derided, as the man unable to assert his will' (p. 128). These 'warring impulses' arise, not like Nina's, from a clash of love and duty, of identity-for-self and identity-for-the-other, but from self-hatred and from conflicting self-evaluations. Duties and ties are acknowledged only in being denied. He tells Abdulla, early in Chapter 5: 'I shall never return. . . . I have done with my people. I am a man without brothers. Injustice destroys fidelity' (p. 131). The self-deception and the self-flattering evasions that lie beneath this rhetoric are pointed up by Babalatchi's song that ends the chapter: 'a tale of shipwreck and of thirst, and of one brother killing another for the sake of a gourd of water' (p. 138). No matter what Willems would like to believe, there are bonds that he is betraying; and the betrayal of a bond is precisely what this action signifies.

In Chapter 6, Willems is vaguely troubled by guilt-feelings at his imminent betrayal of Lingard: 'Why that hesitation to think, to speak of what he intended doing?' (p. 142). But he argues himself out of his doubts: 'His clear duty was to make himself happy. Did he ever take an oath of fidelity to Lingard?' (p. 142). Once more, Willems's specious reasoning is juxtaposed to Babalatchi's song to emphasise the betrayal that he is trying to deny, as the subsequent talk between Aissa and Willems makes clear. Aissa is worried that he will return to 'his people', but he reassures her: 'I have no people of my own'

(p. 143). He rejects the idea of group commitment while her words emphasise that the betrayal of group commitment is precisely what his betrayal of Lingard involves for her: 'When you have helped Abdulla against the Rajah Laut, who is the first of the white men, I shall not be afraid any more' (p. 144). The rest of this chapter under-mines the sense of peace this decision has brought by revealing the implications that Willems is trying to conceal from himself. While Willems lies beside Aissa, he is troubled by 'an indistinct vision of a well-known figure'. He 'felt a desire to see him vanish', and then he realises it is himself:

> It was some time before he recovered from the shock of seeing himself go away so deliberately, so definitely, so unguardedly; and going away where? It was like an evasion, like a prisoner breaking his parole.   (p. 145)

This clearly recalls the tight grip he kept on himself during his last meal with Almayer (p. 78), but the positioning of the passage also suggests a connection between his loss of identity and his denial of group-commitment.

In addition, the parricidal implications of this betrayal are clearly brought out in the subsequent scene between Omar and Aissa. Willems's 'dreamy immobility', as he lies with Aissa, is suddenly broken in upon by an 'apparition' moving closer towards him 'like the shadow of some nightmare' (p. 147). Willems suffers a spasm of paranoia as, for one second, he loses faith in Aissa and believes she is holding him down so that her father can kill him. But father and daughter struggle over him, and now he is as much 'horrified' by Aissa as 'grateful' (p. 150) to her. The narrative teases at the idea that Aissa has killed her father: there is a reference to Omar's 'apparently lifeless body' (p. 150) and the final glimpse of his head 'swinging . . . like the head of a corpse' (p. 151). The nightmare quality of the scene comes partly from the suggestion that parricidal emotions are involved when a child goes against parental wishes, but it comes also from Willems's fearful sense of lost control: 'the unreasoning fear of this glimpse into the unknown things, into those motives, impulses, desires he had ignored', 'the horror of bewildered life where he could understand nothing and nobody round him; where he could guide, control, comprehend nothing and no-one – not even himself' (p. 149). This can be read as his realisation of what life would be like in an alien culture, as an outcast, 'a man without brothers' (p. 131). But it is also his sudden enforced awareness of the autonomy of others and his glimpse into the darkness of his own motives and desires.

The immediate consequence of this scene is Willems's renewed desire to take Aissa away:

> He did not stop to ask himself whether he could escape, and how, and *where*. He was carried away by the flood of hate, disgust, and contempt of a white man for that blood which is not his blood. (p. 152)

Razumov's situation – and Razumov's problem of knowing where to go, when you are aligned with neither side – is prefigured in these two lovers caught between these two 'races'. Aissa, however, sees not his desire for her, but only his need to escape, and this awakens her own fears. She misinterprets: 'instead of forgetting all the world in her embrace, he was thinking yet of "his people" ' (p. 153). She fears going among his people as much as he fears staying among hers. But he is not thinking of returning to his people: he wanted her for himself 'far from everybody, in some safe and dumb solitude' (p. 152).[14] This urgent need to escape is really closer to his earlier desire to die with her: the grave is the only real 'safe and dumb solitude' (p. 152). And, in fact, in this situation, with his contempt for her people, and with his feelings so divided as regards her, his love for her is like suicide.

IV

The third section of the novel is mainly taken up with Almayer's retrospective account to Lingard of Willems's betrayal of Lingard's secret. Like the account of the meeting with Abdulla, this narration serves to counteract the diminishing effect of the narrative focalised through Willems. In Part II, Abdulla was surprised when he found himself confronted not by 'some old officer of Lingard's' but by 'an individual whose reputation for sagacity in business was well-known to him' (p. 130). In the same way, in Part III, Almayer's account of Willems's role in Abdulla's coup justifies Lingard's comment, 'Smart fellow that' (p. 164), whereas few of the other scenes with Willems would. By stressing values in Willems that are being wasted, the narrative gives some weight to his self-betrayal.

At the same time, however, the main function of this section is to reintroduce Lingard in order to give Willems's betrayal of him greater depth and significance. Chapter 4 focusses on Lingard's river. Willems has betrayed not only the basis of Lingard's economic plans, but also the secret key to his identity, the river that, like Samson's hair, is both a source of power and a site of vulnerability. But what is remarkable is that, though the river seems so important to his identity, Lingard does not go to pieces in the way Willems did when the material basis of his identity vanished. Indeed, Lingard seems mainly troubled by the incomplete nature of Willems's rascality: Willems hasn't run away; he hasn't 'shown any consciousness of harm done'. Willems lives in an amoral world where actions are dissociated from their consequences, whereas Lingard inhabits a world of responsibility. Willems's behaviour is a challenge to Lingard's idea of the moral simplicity of the world. At the same time, he does not acknowledge, by displays of fear or guilt, any sense of Lingard's 'power' and paternal superiority, and the unusual 'identity-for-the-other' implied by this also bothers Lingard. He 'can't see himself' reflected in Willems's behaviour towards him. Willems should feel guilty or afraid, but obviously does not, and by 'not playing the game', he nonplusses Lingard.[15] This dual shock to Lingard's world-view befogs his mind, and he drifts in search of some action to take him out of his confusion.

Many critics see in this confusion of Lingard's a prefiguration of Jim's paralysing identification with Gentleman Brown.[16] There was a strong suggestion of identification in the earlier incident, when Lingard rescued Willems and brought him to Sambir (p. 40), and Lingard's thoughts in Babalatchi's hut convey a similar feeling:

> How he had liked the man: his assurance, his push, his desire to get on, his conceited good-humour and his selfish eloquence. He had liked his very faults – those faults that had so many, to him, sympathetic sides.   (p. 223)

This is, however, a different sort of identification from that of Jim and Brown – or that of Jim and Brierly. In both these instances, the 'double' provides a shocking revelation of an aspect of self that the individual was either trying to conceal from himself or had not considered before. The double corresponds to, and activates, a concealed doubt about oneself. That element is missing here: Lingard felt 'considerable uneasiness' (p. 40) in his first identification with

Willems, but, in Sambir, there is no sense of guilt or shame. Lingard
has no guilt feeling about the qualities he shares with Willems:
indeed, he had 'liked his very faults'.[17]

It is the challenge to Lingard's world-view that is of prime importance. This is suggested by the events of Parts III and IV. For most of
Parts III and IV, Willems is absent. He is glimpsed only through
reports, and his behaviour seems wild and incoherent. Lingard in-
terviews, in turn, Almayer, Babalatchi, and Aissa before he actually
meets Willems himself, and the reader is involved in his questioning
partly because it confirms things about Willems, partly because it
reveals things about Lingard, but also because Lingard's questioning is impelled by his need to make an order within which he can act.
Lingard's questioning enacts the reader's own hermeneutic role.

Part III begins with Almayer criticising the destructiveness of
Lingard's 'infernal charity' (p. 161) and suggesting the self-destructive nature of his sentimental idealism. This is the first 'explanation'
offered of Willems's betrayal. It reflects the self-centredness of
Almayer, but it also mirrors fairly his experience of Lingard's promises and reveals one aspect of Lingard's character. Instead of helping
Almayer to make his fortune as he intended, Lingard has, in fact,
buried him in Sambir. And he is still making promises. He looks at
Nina and tells Almayer 'we shall make her somebody': 'that baby
would be the richest woman in the world. Here was something to
live for yet!' (pp. 193–4). While he outlines his plans, he builds her a
house of cards, and it is no surprise when the 'structure collapsed
suddenly before the child's light breath' (p. 196). *Almayer's Folly* acts
as a constant ironic frame of reference. Lingard's dream of riches
parallels Almayer's illusion of Nina's 'whiteness': each is the unsound foundation for a house of cards.[18] Lingard stands revealed as
a romantic dreamer who needs charitable actions and 'unselfish'
plans to support his self-image of superiority. His plans for Nina are
essentially the same as Almayer's, and have the same actual disregard for Nina herself: his words 'make her somebody' carry the
same implication as Nina's statement that her father has told her her
identity. What Lingard really seeks in his charity is 'something to
live for' for himself. But his drive to create meaning contains a clue
to his strength. He has lost both his river and his ship, but, unlike
Captain Allen in 'Freya of the Seven Isles' (who is emasculated by
the loss of his ship), Lingard has lost neither his identity nor his
optimism.[19] He believes in, needs, and tries to create an orderly
reality; and that sense of an orderly 'reality' supports his ideal code

of conduct. However, when he tries to bring Willems and his wife
back together ('Proper thing, of course. Wife, husband . . . together
. . . as it should be' [p. 190]), he not only fails in his aim, but actually
helps bring about the catastrophe.

The long chapter that ends Part III brings out more clearly both his
strengths and weaknesses. The keynotes of his character are his
'honest simplicity' and his 'benevolent instincts' (p. 198) (part-
product of 'the Sunday-school teachings of his native village'). These
find expression in his code of responsibility, his ideal code of conduct. The crucial difference between Lingard and Willems, beneath
certain surface similarities, is the difference between an internalised
code and a projected self-ideal. The distinction between internalisation and projection, in effect, is the difference between self- and
other-directed identity. Lingard's code of conduct grants him an
independence denied to Willems: Willems's dependence on Aissa is
only a more extreme version of his self-ideal's dependence on the
'other'.

This chapter begins with a long set-piece on 'men of purpose',
who, 'proud of their firmness, steadfastness of purpose, directness
of aim', 'walk the road of life . . . proud of never losing their way'
(p. 197). This introduces a revaluation of the road imagery normally
associated with Willems. Lingard may still be 'on the road' (unlike
Willems), but the road is 'fenced in' by 'prejudices, disdains or
enthusiasms' (p. 197). Lingard has the certainty of his simplicity,
but at a price. Nevertheless, he has been 'successful', even if his
ignorance has caused him to overestimate his success: 'he was amazed
and awed by his fate, that seemed to his ill-informed mind the most
wondrous known in the annals of men' (pp. 198–9). In this false
estimation of 'success' and unjustified sense of superiority, he is like
Willems.[20] In his case, 'success' justifies his belief in 'the simplicity of
life' (p. 199) and of moral choice: 'In life – as in seamanship – there
were only two ways of doing a thing: the right way and the wrong
way' (p. 199). His 'success' also confirms his faith in his own knowledge of 'the right way', and licenses his 'meddlesome' beneficent
instincts, which, reciprocally and covertly, express and support the
'superiority' which justifies them.[21] Lingard gives help which he
feels himself 'bound in honour to give, so as to back up his opinion
like an honest man': Willems's actions, on the other hand, are ultimately intended to prove things to others.[22]

There are still, however, obvious similarities between Lingard and
Willems in the social operation of their sense of 'superiority'. Conrad

analyses this particularly with regard to Lingard's developing relationship with Sambir. Lingard's initial motive of personal gain gives way to a liking for, and desire to help, the Malays:

> His deep-seated . . . conviction that only he – he, Lingard – knew what was good for them was characteristic of him, and, after all, not so very far wrong. He would make them happy whether or no, he said . . . (p. 200)

The 'superior' disregard for their autonomy quite clearly links paternalistic, colonial government and the sort of paternal love Lingard and Almayer demonstrate. Lingard's growing love for 'the land, the people, the muddy river' is very much a narcissistic love. He loves and helps them because their success reflects back on him. This discloses the covert way in which his 'altruism' generally supports his sense of superiority. It also casts light on his relationship with Willems: in particular, on his motives for rescue and on the difficulties he now faces about punishing him. Ultimately, his 'love', like Almayer's, is very much a controlling and possessive love: 'the muddy river . . . would carry no other craft but the "Flash" on its unclean and friendly surface' (p. 200).[23] And it is similarly self-deceiving. He tells Babalatchi that his actions in Sambir were 'for the good of all' (p. 226), but Babalatchi's reply reveals the reality of power beneath the paternalistic colonial discourse:

> This is white man's talk. . . . That is how you all talk while you load your guns and sharpen your swords; and when you are ready, then to those who are weak you say: 'Obey me and be happy, or die!' You are strange, you white men. You think it is only your wisdom and your virtue and your happiness that are true. (p. 226)[24]

This dialogue with Babalatchi again emphasises the interconnectedness of the 'political' and 'personal'. The political content of Babalatchi's speech casts light on the personal situation, on how Lingard, at the moment of the conversation, is similarly cloaking his revenge against Willems under the name of 'justice'. This is another way in which Lingard looks forward to Charles Gould: they are both involved in an egocentric ordering of the universe in which personal motives are masked by self-deceiving ideals.

Kirschner has pointed out how this relationship between Lingard and the Malays of Sambir in Part III repeats 'on a larger scale' Willems's relation to Joanna in Part I: the scope is suddenly widened 'to show the blindness of one race to another's independent self-determining will'.[25] On the basis of their 'superiority', each of them uses others without allowing them their autonomy, and, in consequence, each is eventually confronted with the existence of forces beyond their control: Willems when Joanna revolts, and Lingard through the loss of Sambir. This loss represents a double betrayal of Lingard: by Willems and by the Malays. Both have worked against him and helped Abdulla into his river, and both, by that action, have challenged his idea of a universe of which he is the benevolent deity.

In a sense, Lingard is as much responsible for these betrayals as Almayer was for his betrayal by Nina, and for exactly the same reason. Almayer was right about Lingard's self-destructive idealism, and Lingard's difficulty in punishing is partly because he is aware of the extent of his own responsibility. Lingard recognises that he can do nothing to recover his position in Sambir, but he is constantly being pressured, from without and from within, to act against Willems. He is concerned to 'understand' Willems's action and to find his own 'just' response because he needs to reassert his own simple view of the world and of morality.[26] At the same time, he needs to find an action that will fit with his ideal of conduct and maintain his position 'on the road'. This is suggested by the interesting parallels between the closing stages of the relationship between Willems and Lingard and the penultimate stage of the relationship between Willems and Aissa. Each is keen to 'understand' events in such a way that he rescues his ideal of conduct or his self-ideal. To this end, each depersonalises the other, just as earlier each refused to recognise the autonomy of the other (in the Malays and in Joanna respectively). But the variations between the two reveal the deep-structural differences that underlie the apparent similarities of loyalty to a self-ideal and loyalty to an ideal code of conduct.

V

Part IV opens in the darkness of the East Coast night. The darkness is not just a correlative of Lingard's state of mind, but suggests human confusion in the face of an indifferent and disorderly universe. As the narrative begins, he sits listening to Babalatchi's monotone, hoping 'that from the talk a ray of light would shoot through the thick blackness of inexplicable treachery, to show him clearly – if only for a second – the man upon whom he would have to execute the verdict of justice' (p. 223). Certain differences between Lingard and Willems are immediately apparent. Despite the 'darkness', Lingard still asserts certain values and recognises various bonds. These are the *a priori* ground of his world. When Babalatchi tries to flatter him by suggesting that he is 'not like the rest of the white men', he replies (in contrast to Willems) 'I am like other whites', and then continues 'I came here to see the white man that helped Lakamba against Patalolo who is my friend' (p. 222). He stresses the bonds of 'race' and of friendship, but he also implies that the bonds of friendship can override the bonds of 'race'. Secondly, despite the confusion (in fact, because of the confusion), Lingard still has a compulsion to act, to give order to things, whereas Willems and Almayer both give in to lethargy and immobility. Babalatchi's mono- logue acts as 'a thread to guide him out of the sombre labyrinth of this thoughts . . . out of the tangled past into the pressing necessities of the present' (p. 225). That sort of temporal continuity is something that Willems (with his evasions and dislocations) and Almayer (with his future-projected identity) both lack. It arises directly from Lingard's need to make a simple, orderly structure out of his ex- periences, to see 'the clear effect of a simple cause' (p. 239). This is why Lingard is so shocked by the 'ghastly injustice' of the situation; why the main concern of Part IV is with 'justice'; and why the approaching dawn is compared to 'a new universe . . . being evolved out of sombre chaos' (p. 236).

When Lingard finally meets up with Willems, he is led rapidly to the question: 'Was there, under heaven, such a thing as justice?' (p. 265). Willems's betrayal has unbalanced him by challenging his sense of the fitness of things. His anger at the betrayal gives way suddenly to a feeling of nausea, of menacing darkness pressing in on him, of the insubstantiality of things; and Lingard is dropped into a long moment of meaninglessness:

> He felt a great emptiness in his heart. It seemed to him that there was within his breast a great space without any light, where his thoughts wandered unable to escape, unable to rest. . . . Speech, action, anger, forgiveness, all appeared to him alike useless and vain. . . . He could not see why he should not remain standing there, without ever doing anything, to the end of time. He felt something like a heavy chain, that held him there. (p. 272)

Lingard asserts his old identity and breaks 'the chain' that has held him: 'The strong consciousness of his own personality came back to him. He had a notion of surveying them from a great and inaccessible height' (pp. 272–3). Then he talks 'steadily', laying claim to a slowly-extending area of order: 'I regret nothing. I picked you up by the water-side, like a starving cat – by God. I regret nothing; nothing that I have done' (p. 273). This recalls the earlier portrait of Lingard as someone whose 'idea of the fitness of things' it was 'not worth anybody's while' to try and counter: 'There is not much use in arguing with a man who boasts of never having regretted a single action of his life' (p. 235).

The implication is that Lingard is regaining his former 'certainty', but the increasing fragmentation of his speech, the sort of detail that momentarily obtrudes, and the way in which he repeats 'I regret nothing', all convey the struggle that is involved in this recovery of his old identity. His expressed lack of regret, for example, runs up against the fact that, by rescuing Willems, he himself started the process that has ended in his own betrayal. He has found an excuse for that 'mistake' by alleging an unforeseeable change in Willems ('you have been possessed of a devil' [p. 273]), but the inexplicability of Willems's action threatens Lingard's belief in a simple, orderly world.

When Lingard reaches his decision, he has found a solution for all these problems. His disclaims the bonds of 'race': 'You are neither white nor brown. You have no colour as you have no heart' (p. 276). Willems's betrayal of Lingard has invalidated that claim, as it has also invalidated the claim of earlier friendship: 'To me you are not Willems, the man I befriended and helped through thick and thin, and thought much of' (p. 275). His act of betrayal assigns to Willems a new identity, but Lingard has gone far beyond denying Willems his old identity to denying him his separate human existence: 'You are not a human being that may be destroyed or forgiven. You are a bitter thought, a something without a body and that must be hidden. ... You are my shame' (p. 275). His decision to leave Willems on the island resolves the dilemma of not wanting to leave him in the larger world, because he can no longer trust him 'amongst people' (p. 275), and yet not wanting to kill him because of 'the peaceful certitude of death' (p. 258). But the mental processes behind the decision are less rational than this might suggest: Lingard depersonalises Willems to surmount the problem of his disorderly action. Lingard acknowledges that he made a mistake with Willems, but Willems immediately becomes the 'mistake', and then changes into Lingard's 'shame' at the mistake. Willems is not just being depersonalised, he is being taken over and reduced to an element of Lingard's own personality. In the process, Lingard repeats, in miniature, Willems's psychological narrative. Willems's first action in the novel was an attempt to hide a mistake. Lingard's mistake is of a different ethical order (he did not commit a crime in rescuing Willems), but each of them initiates a course of actions without realising that the consequences will destroy his world. In taking responsibility for the consequences, Lingard is attempting to reassert his former identity, since taking responsibility for the weakness of others is part of that old identity. But he then projects his 'shame' at that 'mistake' on to Willems, which is the sort of manoeuvre Willems himself attempted.[27] Then, having incorporated Willems, he splits him off and buries him in exactly the way that Willems earlier (in Part I) and at this very moment splits off parts of his personality rather then recognise them.[28] There is the apparent difference that Lingard makes himself responsible for the weakness of others rather than blaming others for his own defeats: he rescues his self-ideal by responsibility, whereas Willems rescues his self-ideal by evasion; but, despite these differences, each is now reacting in the same way, projecting and splitting off to hide a mistake. Whether in pursuit of a self-ideal or following an ideal code of conduct, the individualistic ordering of will seems inadequate and self-betrayal seems inevitable.

The chapter ends with the undermining of both Lingard and Willems: they are dwarfed by 'a single crash of thunder' which makes their voices sound 'thin and frail, like the voices of pigmies' (p. 279). Further, as Kirschner notes, an ironic parallel with Ali specifically subverts Lingard's asserted 'superiority': Ali struts towards the landing-place 'thinking proudly that he was not like the other ignorant boatmen', since he 'knew how to answer properly the very greatest of white captains' (p. 279).[29] But Lingard's self-deception and self-betrayal are above all emphasised by being set against the psychological contortions of Willems.

VI

After Willems's entry in Chapter 4, coming down the plankway with a rush, his first words choked off by a fit of coughing, there is a long period of suspenseful silence during which Lingard's troubled thoughts and impressions occupy the narrative, as he looks at Willems, and then finally hurls himself angrily on to him. When Willems finally speaks, the unexpected calmness of his words indicates that he has changed again. Willems has been absent from the narrative for a long time, and that first rush and strangled halt matches the 'wild' image of him conveyed by other people's reports. Willems, to begin with at least, sounds very calm and collected. He makes Lingard seem, equally surprisingly, splenetic and unstable:

> 'Steady, Captain Lingard, steady!'
>   His eyes flew back to Willems at the sound of that voice, and, in the quick awakening of sleeping memories, Lingard stood suddenly still, appeased by the clear ring of familiar words . . . that fellow, who could keep his temper so much better than he could himself, had spared him many a difficulty, had saved him from many an act of hasty violence by the timely and good-humoured warning, whispered or shouted, 'Steady, Captain Lingard, steady.'   (p. 262)

This memory discloses the 'emotional and unstable' Lingard that his quest for order has concealed. It also signals that Willems has regained his old identity, and this is corroborated by the self-righteous way in which Willems reacts to Lingard's attack on him: 'That was a fine thing to do!' (p. 264). The ironic understatement suggests an inner calm that should shame the other's lack of control. Willems seems somehow to have forgotten his own actions to which Lingard is responding. He attributes to Lingard all the guilt of the situation: 'You have struck me; you have insulted me' (p. 264).

When Willems begins his account of himself at the end of Chapter 4, he displays not just the fact of dissociation but also the processes involved. His speech covers the various betrayals of others in his life, but his ordering and interpretation of events glosses over or excuses his actions. He begins by asserting his old self-image: 'I have always led a virtuous life' (p. 266). His justification of this incredible statement (Lingard is 'astounded into perfect silence') reveals the chaos of his moral thought. He quotes Lingard's early (false) estimation of him back at him: 'You always praised me for my steadiness' (p. 266). He redefines his first crime (his betrayal of Hudig) as 'borrowing' not 'stealing'. Then he moves his act out of the moral world ('It was an error of judgement' [p. 266]), and excuses his 'error of judgement' by reference to his finances: 'I had been a little unlucky in my private affairs, and had debts' (p. 266). The words 'error of judgement' and 'unlucky' are the keys to this process of reclaiming his self-image. They recall Willems's earlier excuses for his betrayal of Hudig and his earlier redefinition of guilt as 'idiotic indiscretion' (p. 22). The thematic and structural parallel of the betrayals of two father-figures, however, undermines the excuse by revealing the recurring psychological pattern. He thinks in terms of gambling and commerce. He thinks, in his book-keeping mentality, that he can 'pay back' or 'pay for' bad actions, and that, by 'paying back', he can cancel them out.[30] As he goes on, his speech reveals how the self-ideal itself was used to justify the actions that made it no longer viable: 'Could I let myself go under before the eyes of those men who envied me?' (p. 266). For the sake of his self-ideal, he betrayed not only Hudig, but the self-ideal itself.

Willems, however, seems unaware of this – or of other contradictions in his position. He asserts again: 'I have always led a virtuous life' (p. 266). And he defines this 'virtuous life':

> I drank a little, I played cards a little. Who doesn't? But I had principles from a boy. Yes, principles. Business is business, and I never was an ass. I never respected fools. They had to suffer for their folly when they dealt with me. The evil was in them, not in me.   (p. 266)

The mechanisms of Willems's 'peculiar honesty' are here laid bare: the two bases of his old identity, his 'cleverness' and his 'principles', and this saving clause of the 'evil . . . in them' by which he protects his self-image from the implications of his own actions. His statement of 'principles' perfectly illustrates this dissociation of action from self-image, and the vacuum in which his self-image and his 'principles' correspondingly exist: 'But as to principles, it's another matter. I kept clear of women. It's forbidden – I had no time – and I despised them. Now I hate them!' (p. 266). The untruth of this self-presentation is further evidenced by the direction Willems's speech now takes, and by the revealing vehemence of his unexplained shift from despising women to hating them. 'The evil was in them, not in me' provides the explanation: to rescue his self-ideal, he projects on to others, particularly, for reasons which will become obvious, on to women.

VII

When he starts speaking again, he tries to justify his betrayal of his wife and of Lingard. As regards his wife, he blames his betrayal of her on her non-recognition of his superiority: 'She was nobody, and I made her Mrs. Willems . . . You ask her how she showed her gratitude to me' (p. 267). But he is on very shaky ground, and he does not go very far with this argument.[31] He switches to his betrayal of Lingard. He blames first Lingard: 'you came and dumped me here like a load of rubbish; dumped me here and left me with nothing to do – nothing good to remember – and damn little to hope for' (p. 267).[32] Then he blames 'that fool, Almayer' and, finally, Aissa (p. 268). To some extent, what Willems says is true. Lingard did dump him in Sambir 'with nothing to do'; Almayer did hate him and make life awkward for him; and Aissa did take control of him:

> I wanted to pass the time – to do something – to have something to think about – to forget my troubles till you came back . . . she took me as if I did not belong to myself . . . I did not know there was something in me she could get hold of. . . . She found it out, and I was lost. . . . I was ready to do anything. (p. 269)

But in each case he minimises his own responsibility. He was actively searching for a refuge from his thoughts. He had made the decision to avoid his guilt rather than to face it, and that was symptomatic of a more basic choice: to maintain his self-ideal rather than to re-value it. In pursuing his self-ideal, he had lost touch with his instinctual self, and that alienated self was the 'something' she had got 'hold of'. In relating to her, the denied instincts came into play. 'I did not belong to myself' is a true description of his situation, though not in the way he thinks.

As if to stress this, at this very moment, he is following the same self-evasive strategies. He tells Lingard:

> As far as you are concerned, the change here had to happen sooner or later; you couldn't be master here for ever. It isn't what I have done that torments me. It is the why. It's the madness that drove me to it. It's that thing that came over me. (p. 270)

Like Lingard, he is trying to find an explanation that will maintain his world-view and his old identity, and will not require any revaluation of either. First, he blames Aissa for controlling him. Secondly, as with the betrayal of Hudig (and as with the betrayal of Joanna through the relationship with Aissa), he minimises the deed itself: he makes the loss of Sambir inevitable and himself the mere instrument of necessity. He stresses that he was acting under com- pulsion – not just from Aissa, but also from his own 'madness'. This latter, the 'madness', 'the thing that came over me', is a way of disowning rather than of accepting and integrating aspects of self, as the expressions themselves make clear. Only once does he refer to 'my madness' (p. 274). The idea of 'madness' acts as a block to further inquiry. Willems disowned his guilt earlier in relation to Hudig by splitting off a piece of himself labelled 'madness' rather than accept the identity-for-the-other of 'thief'. And this is exactly the way Lingard will isolate, disown and 'bury' his prodigal son, his 'shame', Willems.

Willems's 'madness' is closely associated with Aissa. He tells Lingard: 'Every time I look at her I remember my madness' (p. 274). Later, he demands: 'Take that woman away – she is sin' (p. 278).[33] Just as Lingard depersonalises Willems, and projects his shame on to him, incorporating him and then splitting him off; so Willems depersonalises Aissa, projects his guilt on to her, and wants rid of her. But Aissa represents to him more than just his guilt from betray- ing Lingard. He has regained his 'old self', but, as the dialogue with Lingard proceeds, his initial calmness rapidly gives way to an excite- ment of tone: Willems moves from calmness to excitement as Lingard conversely moves from unstable anger to 'sombre deliberation'. An excitement is disclosed beneath the apparent calmness of Willems's regained 'identity', just as unstable anger underlies Lingard's 'delib- eration'. And it is significant that, in this excitement, it is the earlier 'parricidal' incident that rises to the surface of his mind: 'You don't know through what I have passed. Her father tried to kill me – and she very nearly killed him' (p. 270).

This incident epitomised for Willems the new world he was living in – an insane world of actions whose causes and background he did not understand. But the most disturbing part of the experience was the glimpse into the darkness of his own motives and desires, in- cluding the knowledge of his own parricidal action in the betrayal of Lingard. He is troubled not just by her lack of restraint, but also by his own: 'She goaded me to violence and to murder. Nobody knows why. . . . Fortunately Abdulla had sense. I don't know what I wouldn't have done' (p. 270). In fact, he would rather not know what he might or might not have done. After the shock of these experiences, he does not want to come to terms with these 'dark impulses'. He has re-pressed them and split them off inside himself as 'the madness' (p. 270), as 'something in me she could get hold of' (p. 269). The paranoid implications of this latter statement are obvious. His fear of his own impulses is a fear of loss of control. This fear of loss of control is manifested internally as a fear of madness and externally as a fear of sexual or emotional surrender.[34] His repressed and alien-ated instincts are projected on to Aissa, and then experienced as threats. She is experienced as something either evil or animal, which reveals his attitude towards his own instincts, and the nature of the threat they constitute towards his equanimity and his reclaimed self-ideal.[35]

Nina's story was the story of an emergent self, and of the neces-sary 'betrayal' of a false identity-for-the-other in commitment to that new self. Willems, on the other hand, enacts a flight from self and the suicidal 'rescue' of a self-ideal that is not, and cannot be, shared. His betrayals do not result in any new commitment, merely in loss. Brown and white are polarised in this novel, and this polarisation emphasises the impossibility of betrayal being a way to an alter-native commitment for Willems. When Willems violently and aggressively rejects Aissa ('It's all your doing. You . . .'), the narrator adds: 'She did not understand him – not a word. He spoke in the language of his people' (p. 285). Willems's use of Dutch is a means of dissociating himself from his earlier emotional and (presumably) Malay-speaking role with her. The brown/white polarity serves to express the polarisation of impulse and ideal, instinct and control; but it also stresses the isolation of the two individuals and their inability to understand each other; and, beyond this, there hovers the spectre of a more general human isolation. The separation and mutual unintelligibility of brown and white repeats the separation of men and women ('Who can tell what's inside their heads?' [p. 268]) and the unintelligibility of man to man ('Who could suspect, who could guess, who could imagine what's in you?' [p. 275]).

VIII

In Part V, the pattern is completed: having betrayed two father-figures, Hudig and Lingard, Willems now betrays his second 'wife'.

Part V begins, however, with Almayer, as at the start of *Almayer's Folly*, 'alone on the verandah of his house' (p. 291), musing and gazing on the river as the sun sets. This opening repeats much that is familiar from *Almayer's Folly*, but the narrative particularly focusses on self-deceiving idealisations: the fetishistic value attached to things or people, and the isolation such idealisation produces. It begins with an account of the Lingard and Co. 'office' in Sambir and with a criticism of 'the weakness of Almayer' (p. 299), who 'thought himself, by the virtue of that furniture, at the head of a serious business' (p. 300). Things are valued not for themselves but for their place in Almayer's idealisation: they are signs instead of a reality.[36] However, this particular fantasy did not last long: he 'found no successful magic in the blank pages of his ledgers' and 'the office became neglected then like a temple of an exploded superstition' (p. 320). This is juxtaposed to an account of Almayer's relationship with his daughter, Nina, which uses the same imagery: her cot stands 'looking like an altar of transparent marble in a gloomy temple' (p. 320), and Almayer watches over it 'like a devout and mystic worshipper' before the 'pure and vaporous shrine of a small god' (p. 320). At first, Almayer had sought refuge from his wife in his office, later 'he found courage and consolation in his unreasoning and fierce affection for his daughter' (p. 300). The parallel discloses the selfish motives beneath the idealisation: 'the impenetrable mantle of selfishness he wrapped round both their lives' (p. 300). This brief resumé of Almayer's career provides the context for the resolution of Willems's relations with Aissa and Joanna, which form the dramatic focus of Part V.[37]

Chapter 3 begins with the 'solitude and silence' that 'closed round' (p. 327) Willems after Lingard's departure. Willems dreams of escape 'down to the sea':

> There were ships there – ships, help, white men. Men like himself. Good men who would rescue him . . . take him far away where there was trade, and houses, and other men that could understand him exactly . . .   (p. 329)

This dream of 'understanding' signals his sense of alienation from Aissa and his sense of his 'incomprehensibility' to her. His continuation of the fantasy, however, brings him to an unexpected conclusion: 'He would swim out and drift away on one of those

trees. Anything to escape!' (p. 330). This desperate desire for escape
gives way to terrified thoughts of death: 'a terrible vision of
shadowless horizons where the blue sky and the blue sea met; or
a circular and blazing emptiness where a dead tree and a dead man
drifted together' (p. 330). The thought of death again has a disturbing effect on his egocentricity. He thinks of the world going on
after his death, and he wants 'to clasp, to embrace solid things'
(p. 331). The thought of their continuing existence gives them a
solidity he does not have, and there is a hint of sympathetic magic
in his apparent desire to infuse their solidity into his insubstantiality.

The desire to escape isolation and the fear of death find their
synthesis in Willems's desire to be remembered. The juxtaposition
of this wish to the re-appearance of Aissa produces an obvious
suspense. She is as isolated as Willems. She can't understand 'the
cause of his anger and of his repulsion' (p. 333). She can't understand
why he should want to hurt her 'who had wanted to show him the
way to true greatness, who had tried to help him' (p. 333). At the
same time, she 'did not know, and could not conceive, anything of
his – so exalted – ideals' (p. 333). They are mutually incomprehensible: 'surrounded each by the impenetrable wall of their aspirations
. . . out of sight, out of earshot of each other; each the centre of
dissimilar and distant horizons' (pp. 333–4). Willems's image of
Aissa and Aissa's image of Willems are quite unlike their respective
self-images: identity-for-the-other and identity-for-self do not
correspond.

Nevertheless, because of this feeling of isolation, combined with
his awareness of death and of cosmic indifference, Willems now
turns to Aissa, his heart 'softened with pity at his own abandonment' and his anger against her 'vanished before his extreme need
for some kind of consolation' (p. 337). He seeks a consolation, a
refuge, a means of forgetting; but he also wants to make a protest
against the 'merciless and mysterious purpose' (p. 337) of the universe. This time, however, the surrender to passion (like the magic of
Almayer's 'office') does not work:

He took her in his arms and waited for the transport, for the
madness, for the sensations remembered and lost; and while she
sobbed gently on his breast he held her and felt cold, sick, tired,
exasperated with his failure. . . . He stood still and rigid, pressing
her mechanically to his breast while he thought that there was
nothing for him in the world. He was robbed of everything; robbed

of his passion, of his liberty, of forgetfulness, of consolation. (pp. 338–9)

This is not, as Guerard has suggested, a sexual failure, but rather an emotional failure.[38] And it results from Willems's psychological contortions.

The account of Willems's 'solitude and silence' in Chapter 3 also drew attention to his sense of exclusion from lived time: 'Since Lingard had gone, the time seemed to roll on in profound darkness. All was night within him. All was gone from his sight' (p. 327). He has regained his old identity: he is 'a man possessed by the masterful consciousness of his individuality' (p. 327). But, behind this asserted identity is a terrible turmoil: he walks around 'with a set, distressed face, behind which, in his tired brain, seethed his thoughts' (p. 328). In addition, Willems experiences the psychological depredations of his spiralling attempts at self-evasion, which are suggested by various images of inanition: 'the deserted courtyards', 'the empty houses' (p. 327). In regaining his old identity, he has also created this inner emptiness and his sense of exclusion from lived time; and these feelings lie behind both the attempt to make contact and the failure to make contact: they simultaneously urge on and frustrate.

It is from these various problems that Joanna's re-introduction into the narrative promises to remove him. She seems to bring with her the possibility of escape not only from the island but also from isolation. She offers to bring him out of timelessness back into time: 'He seemed to struggle in the toils of complicated dreams where everything was impossible, yet a matter of course, where the past took the aspects of the future and the present lay heavy on his heart' (p. 347). She offers him recognition for his old identity: she retains the image of his 'lofty purity of character', and, accordingly, she sees in his face 'the aspect of unforgiving rectitude, of virtuous severity, of merciless justice' (p. 349). Willems could not achieve this identity-for-the-other with Aissa, nor can he now recapture the 'madness', the passionate transports, he used to feel with her. Joanna offers him an escape from his Sambir experiences: the tempting thought that the entire episode can be dissociated and forgotten. He tastes again the identity he had: 'He felt strong, reckless, pitiless, and superior to everything' (p. 349). And he begins to dream new plans of success and to create again a hopeful future for himself.

With this planned betrayal of Aissa, Willems hopes to return to his original position. He is still trying to evade the knowledge that deeds have consequences. But, in Willems's last transcendent vision, the reader is reminded of the four betrayals of the novel, even as Willems forgets them: 'He cared for nothing. He had forgotten Aissa, his wife, Lingard, Hudig – everybody, in the rapid vision of his hopeful future' (p. 356). The catastrophe that follows can be read as this 'evaded' past catching up with him – not just in the meeting of Joanna and Aissa, but in the echoes that come to Aissa's mind and prompt her action, echoes that have the status of ancestral wisdom and a father's commands:

> Hate filled the world, filled the space between them . . . hate against the man born in the land of lies and of evil from which nothing but misfortune comes to those who are not white. And as she stood, maddened, she heard a whisper near her, the whisper of the dead Omar's voice saying in her ear: 'Kill! Kill!'   (p. 359)[39]

In *Almayer's Folly*, the daughter and her lover 'betrayed' the father and escaped together into a new life. In *An Outcast of the Islands*, the double triad produces a different result: Willems betrays both fathers and both daughters, but the fathers finally win. Lingard 'kills' Willems by leaving him on the island, and Omar completes his earlier attempt on Willems's life through his daughter.

IX

Willems's lack of relation with his world and with himself could be classified, clinically, as schizoid. Laing supplies the following definition of the term at the start of *The Divided Self*:

> The term schizoid refers to an individual the totality of whose experience is split in two main ways: in the first place, there is a rent in his relation with his world and, in the second, there is a disruption of his relation with himself. Such a person is not able to experience himself 'together with' others or 'at home in' the world, but, on the contrary, he experiences himself in despairing aloneness and isolation; moreover, he does not experience himself as a complete person but rather as 'split' in various ways, perhaps as a mind more or less tenuously linked to a body, as two or more selves, and so on.[40]

Laing's subsequent account of 'schizoid' case-histories introduces the useful concept of ontological insecurity, and describes the experiences and consequences of that condition. According to Laing, the ontologically insecure person may (like Willems) lack the experience of his own temporal continuity, may feel himself 'split' in various ways, may feel the self as partially divorced from the body. It then follows, as Laing says, that a person whose experience of himself is of this order can no more live in a 'secure' world than he can be secure 'in himself' (p. 42). The whole 'physiognomy' of his world will be correspondingly different from that of a 'secure' individual, and, in particular, relatedness to others will be seen to have a radically different significance and function.[41] His 'low threshold' of security means that he constantly feels that his personal identity is threatened. This anxiety takes various forms and is countered by various strategies. Both these characteristic anxieties and the corresponding strategies are depicted in *An Outcast of the Islands*.

One form these anxieties take is what Laing terms the fear of engulfment:

> In this, the individual dreads relatedness as such, with anyone or anything or, indeed, even with himself, because his uncertainty about the stability of his autonomy lays him open to the dread lest in any relationship he will lose his autonomy and identity. (p. 44)

It is this fear that is behind Willems's treatment of his wife and his denial of her autonomy. But this also throws light on the start of Willems's relationship with Aissa. As Laing says: 'If a man hates himself, he may wish to lose himself in the other: then being engulfed by the other is an escape from himself' (p. 44). The image Laing uses to describe this self-experience is identical with the image used to describe Willems's 'surrender' to Aissa: 'The individual experiences himself as a man who is only saving himself from drowning by the most constant, strenuous, desperate activity'.[42] A second form this anxiety takes is what Laing calls petrification. Here the ontologically insecure individual is constantly in fear of being depersonalised by the other, and, for that reason, depersonalises the other. In both cases the basic anxiety is the fear of loss of autonomy, and, in response to that fear, the ontologically insecure person does to the other what he fears the other will do to him. The choice for him is always a choice between control and surrender.[43]

In the final stages of Willems's relationship with Aissa, his fear of loss of control is manifested in misogyny and paranoia. This becomes localised in an obsession with Aissa's eyes:

> . . . she can't move them till I stir, and then they follow me like a pair of jailers. They watch me; when I stop they seem to wait patient and glistening till I am off my guard – for to do something. To do something horrible.   (p. 271)

Aissa has, indeed, been watching over Willems, and Willems's fear of being watched could also be seen as the externalisation of his own sense of guilt at the betrayals he has perpetrated in the novel.[44] However, at this stage in the novel, his main fear is that he might return to his chaotic passionate 'self' with its dependence on Aissa. He fears being swamped (engulfment) or being turned into an appendage (petrification). In other words, he fears Aissa's autonomy. His response is to attempt to destroy that autonomy: he tries to depersonalise her and to seek isolation from her.[45] There is no middle way – no possibility of that genuine mutuality that Fairbairn calls 'mature dependence'.[46] Instead, the choice is either control or surrender, isolation or loss of self.

Paradoxically, this chosen isolation actually derives from a need for 'constant confirmation from others of his own existence as a person' (*D.S.*, p. 47). As Roussel notes:

> Even at the peak of his self-satisfaction Willems retains an almost obsessive need to be recognised by others. The power and position which he enjoys as Hudig's assistant and which define for him the meaning of his life are real to Willems only if he achieves a continuing affirmation of their reality. It is not enough that he himself is confident of his success; he must be constantly surrounded by an audience in which he can see it reflected . . . his audience provides the external ground necessary to establish his identity.[47]

Equally paradoxically, this strategy finally produces the loss of self against which it is intended as a defence. Ontological insecurity springs from an unachieved sense of separateness and autonomy, from a dependence on other people for a sense of self. In this same conversation with Lingard, Willems makes a statement that seems to contradict the idea that he is afraid of being watched: 'In the whole world there was only one man who had ever cared for me. Only one white man. You! Hate is better than being alone!' (p. 274).

As Laing suggests, the ontologically insecure individual needs to feel 'significant to someone', and being hated is preferable to being unnoticed.[48] Lingard has been that 'someone' to Willems: 'All his life he had felt that man behind his back, a reassuring presence ready with help, with commendation, with advice; friendly in reproof, enthusiastic with approbation; a man inspiring confidence by his strength, by his fearlessness, by the very weakness of his simple heart' (p. 281). When Lingard then disowns him, Willems states the precise psychological significance of this departure: 'He wanted to call back his very life that was going away from him' (p. 281). Appropriately, Lingard's departure is accompanied by imagery of death. Before his meeting with Willems, Aissa had expressed the fear that he would take away 'the light of her life and leave her in darkness': 'not in the stirring, whispering, expectant night in which the hushed world awaits the return of sunshine; but in the night without end, the night of the grave, where nothing breathes, nothing moves, nothing thinks – the last darkness of cold and silence without hope of another sunrise' (p. 249). When Lingard leaves, he seems to go 'straight into the past, into the past crowded yet empty, like an old cemetry full of neglected graves, where lie dead hopes that never return' (p. 282). And Willems is left, in an island-prison, in a monsoon that fills him with an 'insane dread': 'the dread of all that water around him, of the water that ran down the courtyard towards him, of the water that pressed him on every side' (p. 283). Willems experiences, imagistically, in his existential isolation after Lingard's departure, the engulfment of his identity against which he has tried to defend himself. This is what Laing calls the 'tragic paradox' of the schizoid character-structure, namely, 'the more the self is defended in this way, the more it is destroyed': 'The apparent eventual destruction and dissolution of the self in schizophrenic conditions is accomplished not by external attacks from the enemy (actual or supposed), from without, but by the devastation caused by the inner defensive manoeuvres themselves' (*D.S.*, p. 77).

This is what events on the island in Chapter 3 illustrate. Willems's main motivation for much of the novel has been the search for a refuge. Now he finally has a refuge in this island-prison. His initial experiences of this isolation are compounded of timelessness, futility, and a sense of the deadness of the world. This is the 'haunting sense of futility' and the inner impoverishment that Laing describes as the 'inevitable outcome' of the strategy of shutting-up the self and disowning participation with others.[49] Even Willems's dreams of escape are permeated by the deathliness of his experience, and his main activity, even in fantasy, is flight from 'the dread of his own dissolution into non-being' (*D.S.*, p. 77). The threat of his own death now enters all his experience: 'He could see and think of nothing else. He saw it – the sure death – everywhere. . . . It poisoned all he saw, all he did; the miserable food he ate, the muddy water he drank' (p. 331). At this point, in the face of this inner deadness, the progressive impoverishment of his inner life, what was before feared suddenly becomes vitally necessary. The world, which was threatening and filled with death, is now suddenly thought of as attractive and 'full of life' (p. 331). It is experienced as the locus of the life, reality, and solidity that he can no longer experience inside himself.[50] It is this need to get life and reality back inside himself that is behind Willems's desire to 'embrace solid things' (p. 331). But this strategy is bound to fail since the world has not lost its primarily threatening aspect. Instead of magically acquiring their solidity, he is reminded, by contrast, of his own original feeling of insubstantiality.

Nevertheless, at the thought of his physical dissolution, he seeks relation with others. To begin with, because the idea of death brings with it the thought that 'nobody would miss him; no-one would remember him' (p. 332), he wants 'someone' as a presence behind him, as Lingard was. Subsequently, he undergoes an overwhelming experience of existential isolation: 'he felt afraid of his solitude, of the solitude of his body, of the loneliness of his soul in the presence of this unconscious and ardent struggle' (p. 337). He now wants to escape into passionate self-forgetfulness, but the spiral of evasions has debilitated the inner world: the false-self system has sealed off access to the instinctive self. The result is, as Aaron Esterson says: 'if the identity is successfully established, no instinctual impulse is felt'.[51] When his attempt at passionate surrender fails, Willems is, as he says, 'a lost man' (p. 340). The gunshot that kills him is only a formality. His ontological insecurity has led him to a system of defences that work to produce the destruction of the self they were supposed to protect.

3

The Real Existence of Passions: *The Sisters* and 'The Rescuer'

Lingard's role in *An Outcast of the Islands* anticipates the creation of Marlow-as-narrator in 'Heart of Darkness' and *Lord Jim*: his struggle to understand and 'make sense' of Willems's actions provides a model for a narrative method which involves the reader through the narrator's questioning and allows the narrator to question his own values.[1] Conrad, however, did not pass smoothly from *An Outcast of the Islands* to 'Heart of Darkness' and *Lord Jim*. Most of 1896 and 1897 was taken up with work on two unfinished novels, *The Sisters* and 'The Rescuer'. In many ways, 'The Rescuer' is the missing link between *An Outcast* and *Lord Jim*.[2] Lingard, like Willems, experiences the disruption of his sense of himself as a result of his involvement with a woman. At the same time, Lingard, like Jim, betrays a bond of trust established with his Malay friends at the sudden intrusion of strangers from 'the white world'. In 'The Rescuer', Conrad explores directly the possibilities of Lingard's character, trying to find out how that model of male identity works. As Roussel says, 'Thematically, *The Rescue* is an investigation of the most obvious alternative to Willems's last vision. It examines the possibility that men can create and sustain a world of their own values.'[3]

With Willems, Conrad had reached the end of one particular road: an approach to 'identity' through the simple opposition of self-ideal and instinct. In subsequent works, the self-ideal becomes associated with ideas of 'honour' or 'duty', which in turn leads to the consideration of social commitment rather than just individualistic self-assertion.[4] In *The Sisters* and 'The Rescuer', the nature of this particular social commitment is not clearly developed. In both, there is a clash between the instinctive self of passion and a social self of duties, but these duties do not, at this stage, imply a consciously-

67

worked-out model of society: rather the passions are used to challenge bourgeois values. In *The Nigger of the 'Narcissus'*, Conrad presents his model of society, with the result that 'Heart of Darkness' and *Lord Jim* introduce a self-image that is based on a specific code of conduct. It is not, as with Lingard's, a romantic, personal code of conduct: it is a practical and established code that has certain social and political implications which are also explored. The self-image still incorporates an alterated identity, but that incorporated alterated identity is now institutionalised, and adherence to the code of conduct brings an escape from personal isolation. The code of conduct now seems to offer a solution to the dilemma discussed in Chapter 2: the choice between the isolation of an unshared ideal of self and the threat perceived in surrender to instincts.

In the period covered in this chapter, Conrad is engaged by the conflict between a buried, passionate self and an identity-for-self that is increasingly identified with ideas of honour and duty. Conrad explores that conflict by dramatising various kinds of betrayal: the betrayal of others through surrendering to passionate impulse; the different kinds of betrayal of oneself.

I

Conrad started work on *The Sisters* when he had finished *An Outcast of the Islands*, but he laid it aside after he had written about 10,000 words. According to Ford, in his introduction to the 1928 edition, *The Sisters* was to have been a novel about incest:

> He had that inhibition – that thwarted desire to write of the relationship between men and women. . . . And what he, curiously, desired to write of was incest. . . . The pensive Slav painter was to have married the older sister and then to have had an incestuous child by the other.
>
> I do not profess to know every detail of the plot of this story as it would finally have stood. . . . And of course in his shadowy and rather hurried projections of this forbidden story Conrad varied the narrative very often and I do not remember now all the variations. What comes to me as a sort of composite photograph is this: Stephen was to have met, fallen in love with and married the elder sister. The younger sister, failing in the religious vocation that her uncle the priest desired her to have was to come

to Paris and to stay with the young couple in Stephen's pavilion, the tyrannous character of her aunt being such that she could not live with the orange merchant and his wife. The elder sister proving almost equally domineering Stephen was to fall before the gentler charm of the younger. And the story was to end with the slaying of both the resulting child and the mother by the fanatic priest.[5]

Jocelyn Baines was very scornful of this suggestion, but these plot developments fit well with the schematic organisation of the existing text: Stephen and Rita share, alternately, the focus of the narrative; Rita's sister, Theresa, is provided as a potential complicating factor; Father Ortega, the uncle, is a very credible potential avenger.[6] And the narrative pattern of the lover of two sisters and an avenging father-figure occurs as the denouement of *Nostromo*. Ford is also precise about the nature of Conrad's interest in incest: 'I don't mean to say that he proposed to write of the consummation of forbidden desires, but he did not want to render the emotions of a shared passion that by its nature must be most hopeless of all.'[7] Given that Conrad was to go on to write in 'The Rescuer' of the hopeless, shared passion of Lingard and Mrs Travers, an interest in 'incest' as the epitome of hopeless passion does not seem so unlikely. Both narratives are centred on a passion that is prohibited from expression as a way of exploring the struggles of a passionate self to reach expression.

The Sisters begins by introducing its protagonist, the young painter Stephen. From the opening sentence, the fact of his exile is foregrounded:

> For many years Stephen had wandered amongst the cities of Western Europe. If he came from the East . . . yet it must be said he was only a lonely and inarticulate Mage, without a star and without companions.   (p. 19)

In the West, Stephen is rootless and isolated. He encounters, apparently, only the indifference of other people (p. 20), and he finds a world that is afraid of anything 'great', that imprisons possibilities within its narrow walls (pp. 21–2). In contrast to this is the Eastern world of Russia. It is evoked through memories of 'the limitless expanse' (p. 26) of its plains that Stephen crossed as a child and 'the great heaven' (p. 27) he stared up at as a baby. It is associated with home and early childhood, with 'dreamy memories and longings', and it is imbued with the physical sense of a mother's love: 'from his mother's arms, he scrutinised with inarticulate comprehension that vast expanse of the limitless and fertile blacklands nursing life in their undulating bosom under the warm caress of sunshine' (p. 28). This opposition of West and East, the opposition of an unreal, alienated world and an involved, passionate one can be read as an opposition between a disengaged ('European') false-self and a passionate, inner ('Eastern') self, comparable to Stendhal's opposition, in *Le Rouge et le Noir*, of provincial and Parisian modes of being in the persons of Mme de Renal and Mlle de la Mole. This is a variant on the 'choice of sides' motif in *Almayer's Folly* and *An Outcast*, and this new form of the opposition of 'West' and 'East' indicates one particular continuity between Conrad's Malayan and European novels.

Stephen's experience is replicated, in the last three chapters of the text, in the person of Rita. Rita and Stephen have striking similarities. Each is of peasant stock; each is an orphan; each lives in exile (in a multiple sense) in France. Rita is 'the wild girl of Basque mountains, transplanted into the heavy-scented but sordid atmosphere of the house in Passy', and now further transplanted into the 'ordered life' (p. 64) of the middle-class, Malagon household. Where Stephen experiences the unreality of a circumscribed 'western' life, Rita experiences the unreality of conventional, respectable, middle-class Paris life:

> The peaceful conventions of middle life, the conventions resembling virtues, made for Rita as if a shelter behind a respectable curtain that separated her from the real existence of passions. The pretty assumptions of selfish quietude gave to events an aspect of general benevolence, a polished surface of easy curves hiding the resounding emptiness of thoughts, the deadly fear of sincerity, the cherished unreality of emotions. . . . In the shallow stream Rita was carried away from year to year. . . . Listening, she was willing to forget the impressions of young days, the rugged landscapes, the rugged men, the strong beliefs, the strong passions.   (pp. 67–8)

Like Stephen, she lives in one world, but carries within her the memory of a more expansive and more passionate existence. For each of them, their homeland is the locus of reality, and their memories attest to a way of being that is not available to them in the present. Their status as exiles becomes a metaphor for a psychological state: their memories signify their potential for an alternative way of being and their desire for its realisation. It is significant too that each of them sees that lost reality in terms of passion. Their homeland is more real because it is more engaged and passionate. It stands in contrast to the 'unreality of emotions' of the middle-class urban life of their exile. Through these characters is presented both an image of disengagement from the bourgeois world, and an image of a repressed passionate self. At the same time, the complicated amalgam of fear and longings that accompanies that buried self is also evidenced. The passage quoted above concludes: 'She thought of them with love, with longing – sometimes with repulsion, often with scorn – now and then with rare lucidity that suggested fear, that swift fear of the unavoidable approaching in dreams' (p. 68). The words suggest both the inevitability of Rita's re-awakening, and the longing, repulsion, and fear that accompany that process. These brief observations also provide significant clues for an understanding of the behaviour of Edith Travers in 'The Rescuer' or Rita de Lastaola in *The Arrow of Gold*.

Rita, like Nina Almayer, is a prototype of Conrad's unawakened women who are faced with the challenge of their own awakening self, and struggle with the contradictory impulses that accompany it. Stephen, like Lingard, Willems or Jim, has an ideal image of himself – in Stephen's case, this is expressed in his ambition to be a painter. Presumably, as with Willems and the Lingard of 'The Rescuer', that self-ideal would have been challenged by a passionate awakening, when he and Rita were actually brought together. Chapter 1 draws attention to his quest for 'meaning' (p. 19), and Chapter 3 suggests that he is searching for 'the word that would give life, that would give shape, to the unborn longings of his heart'. The disappointment of that quest, juxtaposed to his return to Paris and the introduction of the Ortegas into the novel, suggests that his quest has been misdirected, and that a 'new principle' is about to emerge which will be related to the Ortegas rather than to his self-ideal.

Chapter 2 states that this self-ideal was the source of a lack of understanding between Stephen and his father, since his father had his own vision of Stephen's future ('He saw him uniformed, embroidered, bemedalled, autocratic, called Excellency' [p. 30]). The clash of identity-for-self and identity-for-the-other, however, is not explored further. Instead the narrative focusses on the guilt that Stephen subsequently feels when his parents die while he is abroad:

> He had abandoned those two loving hearts for the promise of unattainable things, for alluring lies, for beautiful illusions . . . he dispersed with frenzied renunciation the band of charming phantoms that had for so many years surrounded his life – and remained alone, humbled and appalled by the reality of his loss. (p. 35)

Like Jim, he has betrayed real people for phantoms: he has sacrificed others' love for himself to his own ambitions. It is also suggested that these ambitions will probably betray him in turn: 'He had paid an enormous price for the privilege of a hopeless strife!' (p. 38). Again, this issue is not examined: the different claims that are involved are not evaluated. They are merely juxtaposed – the claim of others and the claim of the self-ideal – in the muffled clash of father and son. And everything is overwhelmed by the sense of guilt and 'the reality' of loss (p. 35).

Other information about Stephen casts light on this area. Chapter 1 suggests that he sought a refuge 'from the reproach of his impotence in ardent work' (p. 22) – that is, from doubts about his own value in his self-ideal. Chapter 2 further suggests, by imaging his art as 'armour' (p. 35), that his self-ideal is in fact a defence-mechanism. And these suggestions are reinforced by Stephen's decision not to return home to Russia after his parents' death:

> Stephen . . . looked across space and time at the land of his birth. From afar it loomed up immense, mysterious – and mute. He was afraid of it. He was afraid of the silent dawn of life, he who sought amongst the most perfect expressions of matured thought the word that would fling open the doors of beyond.   (p. 37)

The effect of this passage – particularly the opposition of 'the silent dawn of life' to the 'doors of beyond' – is to undermine Stephen's quest, and to hint that his search for 'the word that would give life' to 'the unborn longings of his heart' (p. 43) is actually a flight; that what he flees is, significantly, 'the land of his birth' and 'the silent dawn of life'; and that what he is running towards is death.[8]

Stephen's memories of that Eastern world were dominated by a sense of the physical presence of a loving mother and the idea of being a child in 'his mother's arms' (p. 28). This closeness and intimacy seems to have been the dream from which he was rudely awakened, the home from which he was expelled into the world.[9] If this was the source of his 'dreamy memories and longings' (p. 28), it would explain both why his alternative reality is less definite – more dreamy and less passionate – than Rita's, and why the clash of father and son (which is what follows immediately in the text) is so muffled. Significantly, it dissolves into feelings of guilt and remorse. In Stephen's case, the alternative reality and the alternative way of being are pervaded by nostalgia for closeness to his mother, and the fears that accompany his buried self are oedipal as well as ontological.

These ontological fears, and the resulting defences, are evidenced in Stephen's doubts about his own value and the subsequent recourse to the 'armour of art'. But the 'armour of art' is not always an effective defence, and there are times when, as Willems found, defences work against the defender:

> He began to doubt his own aspirations. They presented themselves sometimes to him as a plot of the powers of darkness for the destruction of his soul. Then he would rush out of himself into the world. (p. 21)

The doubts, against which the self-ideal was asserted, undermine the self-ideal, and the self-ideal is experienced as something threatening and outside himself. At other places in the narrative, other defence-mechanisms also work against him. For example, it was mentioned earlier that Stephen felt he encountered only indifference in the West. But the images that were used to indicate that indifference can also be read as expressing Stephen's reification of others. The reader can choose between the stoniness of others' hearts towards Stephen or their petrification by him. An even clearer example is seen in the account of Stephen's decision to return to the city:

> He would withdraw into the repugnance he inspired to men and live there unembittered and pacific. He liked them well enough. Many of them he liked very much but he never felt the sense of his

own quality . . . as when in contact with the latent hostility of his kind.

The emphasis on unilateral hostility and the careful disclaimer of any reciprocal bitterness on Stephen's part are like Willems's claim that the 'evil' was always in other people and had nothing to do with him. It is obvious that the alienation described in the opening of the novel is, in fact, Stephen's own psychological condition. The unreal, alienated West is the West as experienced by Stephen, and Stephen's experience is permeated by the deadness of the false-self system. In contrast, memories of the East gesture towards another possibility: a buried self; a heavily defended, passionate inner self.

II

Conrad laid aside *The Sisters* in March 1896.[10] The first mention of 'The Rescuer' appears in a letter to Garnett of the same month, and Part I had been written and sent to London by 11 June 1896.[11] Conrad struggled with the novel till the summer of 1899. By that time he had completed the first four parts, which, later, after revision, made up about half of the final, published text. This revised version, *The Rescue*, was completed in 1919 and published in 1920. This chapter, however, will confine itself to the unpublished manuscript version, 'The Rescuer'.[12]

'The Rescuer' begins from the point at which *The Sisters* left off – with the deadness of the false-self system and the presence of a secret inner self. It starts with a long description of the 'narrow seas':

> The narrow sea, captive, sleeps profoundly; forgetting the free-
> dom of great winds that sweep round the globe; and wakes up
> now and then only to short-lived furious and foaming rages; to
> quick gales that stirring up its most intimate depths, are followed
> by long periods of exhausted repose; a repose which would re-
> semble death itself, were it not for the tender murmur exhaled.
> (p. 1)

This personified image of a passionate potential that is captive or dormant is proleptic of Lingard. A description of Lingard's lifeless, unchanging eyes ('as unconscious of the heart within the man as a

telescope is unconscious of the incomprehensible emotions within
the breast of an astronomer' [pp. 13–14]) re-states that lost contact
with one's innermost impulses, which the 'narrow seas' imaged, and
this connection is made explicitly later:

> He remained perfectly motionless, face down, looking at the sea,
> as if captivated by the play of the shifting and incomprehensible
> glimmers of fire low down under the gloomy surface of the water;
> . . . glimmers, as capricious and futile as the passing flashes of his
> own restless and fugitive ideas that could not in any way make
> clear to him the masterful depths of his own impulses, that pushed
> him here and there; that sent him on his careless and resolute way.
> (p. 45)

Lingard has no understanding of the forces within himself that
direct his actions: he was 'defenceless as a child before the shadowy
impulses of his own heart and the promptings of suggestive events
that wake up passions or illumine with a ray of unearthly light that
darkness with (*sic*) is the core of every human soul' (pp. 15–16). But
the implication is that the narrative will explore these hidden impulses and probe Lingard's inner 'core'.

The first part of 'The Rescuer' is occupied primarily with the
presentation of Lingard; his chief mate, Shaw; and the second officer
of the Travers's yacht, Carter. Lingard is depicted with characteristics that are already familiar from *An Outcast of the Islands*: his
simplicity, his pleasure in his own success, his good-natured egocentricity (pp. 14–16). In addition, there are reminders of his sense of his
own rightness and his need to control. But a new issue is also raised.
He replies angrily to Shaw at one point: 'Nobody has ever called me
a pirate – and nobody ever will' (p. 40). Yet the rumour that Shaw
reports suggests that precisely that name is given to Lingard among
the men Shaw knew in Singapore. Lingard's identity-for-self is clearly
at odds with his identity-for-the-other, and this lesion will be important later in his relations with Travers.

Shaw is, in some ways, a return to Willems's character-type. Like
Willems, he asserts his own superiority, respectability, and righteousness, and, as with Willems, this assertion reveals his fear of
his own unimportance, his insecurity, and his inability or unwillingness to face his own actions. To begin with, he asserts his superiority
as 'a deep water man' over these sailors of the narrow seas. Then he
asserts his superiority as a white man, a Christian, and a respectable

married man. But his shortcomings as a sailor are soon revealed, and the narrative then foregrounds his defensive strategies. He fails to see or hear Carter's boat approaching, and, when Carter arrives on board the brig, he tries to blame Carter for his own incompetence. Carter, by contrast, establishes his value straightaway in terms of this same code of sea-worthiness, by the seamanship he shows in approaching the brig and, again, in his description of where the yacht has run aground: 'Every word showed the minuteness of his observation, the clear vision of a seaman able to master quickly the aspect of a strange land and of a strange sea; the professional wide-awake state of mind of a man ever confronted by rapid changes of circumstances' (p. 61). It is on the basis of competent seamanship that Lingard likes and trusts Carter. Where Shaw prides himself on being 'all there', it is actually Carter who shows himself to have 'the professionally wide-awake state of mind'. As a result, it is Carter who is able to adapt to 'rapid changes of circumstance' (like Babalatchi in *An Outcast*), whereas Shaw eventually breaks down because of the rigidity of his sense of self, and the rigidity of his code of 'respectability'. The dismissive words Lingard addresses to Shaw, later in 'The Rescuer', prefigure Marlow's criticism of his audience in 'Heart of Darkness': 'I expect to be back in Singapore in three months at the latest, where you will be able to take your gear ashore on to a first-class european jetty and have shipping masters, hotel-keepers and police peons to look after you.' In each case, criticism is directed against those who will not risk encountering the un-known, whether within themselves or outside, but take refuge in an identity prescribed by the protecting framework of respectable society.[13] Conrad is visibly moving towards the location of values in 'seamanship' which he works out fully in *The Nigger of the 'Narcissus'*.

This first part also presents certain anticipatory parallels. The story of the French skipper and the woman from Bali, for example, establishes the strict code of honour of the Asians in the novel, and the crassness of Shaw's racist response, here as elsewhere, is used to steer the reader away from ethnocentric readings. The story also provides a reminder of Lingard's 'strange ideas of law', since, in the course of his narration, he tells Shaw that he was prepared then, for the first time, to make war on his own account. As the story of a sea-captain who is 'broken up' by a love affair with a woman, and as a story about the intrusion of a European that brings death to an Asian woman, Lingard's narrative is also proleptic of the outcome of his own adventure in 'The Rescuer' – particularly since it occurs shortly before Carter's boat arrives at the brig and sets the interests of Mrs Travers and Immada on a collision course.

There are other anticipations, in this first part, of Mrs Travers's role in the novel. Shaw immediately comments on Lingard's story: 'Women are the cause of a lot of trouble'. He and Lingard then begin a brief discussion of 'them old-time Greeks fighting for ten years about some woman', which introduces that archetype of the destructive woman, Helen of Troy:

> 'But to fight ten years. And for a woman!'
> 'I have read the tale in a book,' said Lingard . . . 'She was very beautiful.'
> 'That only makes it worse, sir – if anything. . . . Ten years of murder and unrighteousness! And for a woman. Would any body do it now? Would you do it sir?'

The answer to Shaw's question is implicit in their different reactions to the 'tale'; but the question itself remains in the air and is re-activated by the emphasis on the presence of a woman on board the stranded yacht. There is a strong intimation of what the 'decisive event' may turn out to be. There is also the first glimpse of Lingard's complex of conflicting loyalties. Lingard's initial response to Carter's story of the yacht-people is an affirmation of the 'objects and people to whom I have pledged my word, my strength, and my luck' (pp. 69–70) but this is followed, almost immediately, by an opposing pledge: 'I am a white man inside and out; I won't let white people – and an English lady too – come to harm if I can help it.' The terms in which Conrad describes Lingard's love for his brig suggest a further complication. His love for his ship is presented as an amalgam of possible kinds of love between a man and a woman: 'she was always precious – like old love; always desirable – like a strange woman; always tender – like a mother; always faithful like a favourite daughter of a man's heart' (pp. 14–15). Indeed, if Mrs Travers is associated with one female archetype, the destructive woman, Lingard's brig suggests another, the patient Griselda:

> His love for his brig was a man's love and was so great that it could never be appeased unless he called on her to put forth all her qualities and her power, to repay his exacting affection by a faithfulness tried to the very utmost extent of endurance. He wanted

to feel her patient, obedient, and ready, answering without fail and without hesitation to every perverse demand of his desire. (p. 96)

It is almost certain, even by this point in the novel, that the polymorphous feminine ideal embodied by the brig will be challenged for a place in Lingard's affections by at least one real woman, and that Lingard's own 'faithfulness' will also be severely tested.

III

Part II of 'The Rescuer' supplies the background to Lingard's actions: in particular, the commitments that Lingard had made before the intrusion of these Europeans. It also presents conflicting images of Lingard's secret self. Chapter 1 moves to Darat-es-Salam, 'The Shore of Refuge', where the Travers's yacht has run aground. The narrative emphasises (far more than it does in *The Rescue*) the history, the political situation, the colonial conflicts of the area. To begin with, the colonial picture is overshadowed by a nostalgic contrast of the heroic past and the deadly respectable present.[14] This contrast, involving the opposition of adventurer and trader, finds its resolution in Hassim, Immada and their Wajo companions, with whom the chapter ends:

> It is a common saying, among the Bugis race, that to be a successful traveller and trader a man must have some Wajo blood in his veins. And with those people trading which means also travelling afar is a romantic and an honourable occupation. The trader must possess an adventurous spirit and a keen understanding; he should have the fearlessness of youth and the sagacity of age; he should be diplomatic and courageous so as to secure the favour of the great and inspire fear in evildoers. These qualities naturally are not expected in a shopkeeper or a Chinaman pedlar; they are considered indispensable only for a man who, of noble birth and perhaps related to the ruler of his own country, wanders over the seas in a craft of his own and with many followers. (pp. 120–1)

Quite distinct from 'respectable traders' are romantic traders like Lingard or the particular kind of romantic trader represented by the

Wajo – who, with their 'adventurous spirit', their 'noble birth', and their combination of political and piratical functions, seem a latter-day equivalent to Homer's Odysseus. Indeed, they represent a similar stage of social development.

The narrative also formulates a contrast between the colonised and the coloniser. The most obvious difference between the two groups is that the colonised 'belong' where they are and the coloniser does not:

> They had been born, no doubt, on just such a coast; they have wandered all their life amongst just such dangers. Instinct and early training guide their efforts; they are spurred by the desire of life and liberty.   (p. 109)

This becomes the key to the psychological contrast between the two groups. The brown world is a world of instinct and of taking risks. It is directed by 'the desire of life and liberty'. The white world is the world not just of the alien, but of the alienated: it is a world of restraint and caution, directed by the fear of the 'pain of failure and disaster'.[15] This contrast between the world of the native and the world of the alien is also presented as the contrast between the world of the past and the world of the present:

> A laggard progress has come at last and it has changed everything except the sunshine. That is still undimmed, barbarous and crude – the sunshine of old days. . . . But civilisation stalks from island to island in the old sunshine; and where treads the foot of the greedy spectre there the song of fierce life dies out, to be replaced by a dreary mutter of laws and statistics.   (p. 112)

The system of contrasts recalls *The Sisters*: a respectable, dead, present of 'laws and statistics' and a passionate, lawless past. This is supported by both the narrative and metaphorical levels of this first chapter. On the narrative level, there is Hassim: the contradictory indications of poverty and wealth in his dress are explained when he is identified as a displaced prince, whose wealth and status existed in the past. On the metaphoric level, there is 'The Shore of Refuge' itself: 'Within, the vanquished reckon their losses. With their eyes fixed to seaward they remember the past or hope for better days' (p. 110). There is no lived present: reality is either in the past or to come. This 'nameless land of forests and silence', described initially largely by negatives, is a counterversion of the buried, passionate self. It represents the fear that perhaps the inner self is not an unalienated self of 'life and liberty', but is the self of fear and inanition that Willems discovered. 'The Rescuer' moves between three different conceptions of the repressed self: an instinctive passionate self of life and liberty; a dead self of emptiness and inanition; and (as the end of Part II suggests) a destructive self of explosive passion.

IV

The rest of Part II is devoted mainly to the character of Lingard. Chapter 1 had shown the bond between Hassim and Immada. Chapter 2 records a similar bond being formed between Lingard and Hassim: 'the gift of friendship that, sometimes, contains the whole good or evil of a life' (p. 131). This episode immediately raises certain questions: what will be the outcome of this 'gift of friendship'; will these bonds hold? The narrative approaches these questions through a consideration of Lingard's success. Success is part of both his identity-for-self and his identity-for-the-other, and his confidence derives from this. Although Lingard thinks in terms of 'luck', it is his strength, rectitude and certitude of success that matter:

> What he called his luck was something as impalpable but infinitely more real, the emanation of his strenght (*sic*) and his rectitude, that atmosphere of naive shrewdness, honesty and force he carried with him . . . as if every difficulty in the inward certitude of success could be nothing but an added favour of fate.[16]

However, another aspect of Lingard's emphasis on 'luck' is revealed by his recklessness, his need to gamble and take risks. The narrative refers to his 'inward exaltation' while he handled the brig 'with the concentrated and cool recklessness' of those rare moments 'in which his simple heart felt that there, at last, it had got life enough to satisfy its obscure craving for danger, contest and success' (p. 144), and this hints at the kind of personality-structure that requires danger in order to feel life intensely.

Part II also examines Lingard's imaginative and idealistic qualities, 'the romantic side of the man's nature', that 'responsive sensitiveness to the shadowy appeals made by life and death, which is the groundwork of a chivalrous character' (pp. 133–4), the qualities he shows, for example, during the sea-burial of the Malay crewman who was killed protecting him. These romantic qualities are subjected to scrutiny in the account of Lingard's rescue of Hassim and Immada from Wajo:

> It was the scene of an action he could not yet wholly see, but unseen he felt it all stirring and accomplished within the sudden awakening of his impulses. There was something to be done and he felt he would have to do it. It was expected of him. The sea expected it, the land expected it – men also. The story of war, of suffering; Jaffir's display of fidelity, the sight of Hassim and his sister, the night, the tempest, the coast under streams of fire all this made one inspiring manifestation of a life calling to him distinctly for interference. But above all it was himself[,] it was his longing, his obscure longing to mould his own fate in accordance with the whispers of his imagination awakened by the sights and the sounds, by the loud appeal of that night.   (pp. 156–8)

At first glance, this sounds like Lingard's 'responsive sensitiveness to the shadowy appeals made by life and death', 'the shadowy impulses' (p. 15) of Lingard's unknown inner depths responding to a 'decisive event' (p. 26). But other, more critical ideas are also present in this passage. For example, the statement that his experiences of the night 'made one inspiring manifestation of a life calling to him for interference' echoes Almayer's criticism of Lingard's apparent altruism in *An Outcast*.[17] In the same way, Lingard's sense that something is 'expected of him' demonstrates egotism rather than responsibility. Lingard's egotism, indeed, causes him to misread various signs. He misinterprets 'the weariness of men worsted in desperate strife, the stupor of safety after months of toil and danger' as silent trust, 'a proof of unbounded confidence to which he must respond in the fullest manner': 'It flattered him' (p. 158). But the flattery he experiences is, in fact, self-flattery: it supports his proud sense of his own power and the paternalistic, 'god-like' role that he has played in the earlier novels. This is the underlying significance of his decision to take up the political cause of Hassim and Immada:

> He would wake up the country! That was the fundamental and unconscious emotion on which were engrafted his need of action, the primitive sense of what was due to justice, to gratitude, to

friendship, the sentimental pity for the hard lot of Immada – poor child – the proud conviction that of all the men in the world, in his world, he alone had the means and the pluck 'to lift up the big end' of such an adventure.   (pp. 105–6)

Lingard's actions are designed to assert various ideals, but the basis of that assertion is his sense of his own superiority.

However, the secrecy required by the activities to which he now commits himself has a demoralising effect on him in relation to the community of European traders:

> Lingard had a subtle sense of solitude, the inward loneliness of a man who is conscious of having a dark side to his life. It hurt him. He needed the good fellowship of men who understood his work his feelings and his cares. . . . Before he had been many months engaged in his secret enterprise he began to feel unreasonably like an outcast. Nobody knew what he was doing but all the same everybody seemed to disapprove of it . . . He was afraid they suspected him of things of which he was incapable.   (p. 171)

Lingard, like Nostromo, has undertaken an action whose necessary secrecy undermines his identity. In Lingard's case, the situation is complicated by the fact that the secret action also involves the realisation of an inner self. Relative to the European traders, Lingard withdraws from an established identity to an unshared, secret self. Relative to Hassim and the Malays, Lingard is progressively realising that self as a new identity in their different world: 'The centre of his life had shifted about three hundred miles – from Singapore to the 'Shore of Refuge' – and when there he felt himself within the circle of another existence, governed by his impulse, nearer his desire' (p. 175). Almayer and Willems were dreamers whose dreams had little or no relation to reality, but Lingard is a successful and eminently practical ship's captain, and his prosaic preparations anchor his romantic dreams in a 'real world', and invest 'the unflagging ardour of his desire with a precise form' (pp. 187–8).

The concluding chapters of Part II, however, are full of doubts and equivocations about the possible outcome of Lingard's action and about the nature of the self of the dream. Belarab's settlement, the new centre of Lingard's life, at first sight suggests peace and prosperity, but there is already some internal dissension, and the allies Lingard's intrusion brings to the 'Shore of Refuge' are described as 'turbulent and untrustworthy' (p. 209). And Lingard seems to have released similarly turbulent passions within himself:

> It seemed to him that like one looking down into the crater of a quiescent volcano he had seen a sheet of glowing dull fire, the fire of smouldering passions underlying the sullen peace of the islands. . . . Then he told himself firmly that he must have a spark from that fire. Only a spark, no more, and then . . . A powerful and inexplicable emotion passed over him, and he fancied himself tossed about by a great wave of some warm sea.   (pp. 210–11)

There are other passages, that imply a less explosive but equally-destructive inner self. Wyndham and Jörgensen both advise Lingard against his undertaking and against getting involved in Malay politics or with Malays. Indeed, both men offer themselves as living warnings: 'I can speak English. I can speak Dutch, I can speak every cursed lingo of these islands – I can remember things that would make your hair stand on end – but I have forgotten the language of my own country' (p. 182). As in *An Outcast*, there is the fear of being lost forever in this 'other world'; and there is the same language of temptation and possession:

> And since this temptation that, perhaps no man on earth could be found to resist, the opportunity to make war and to make history, had been offered to him, the islands, the shallow sea, the men of the islands and the sea seemed to press on him from all sides with subtle and irresistible solicitation, they surrounded him with a murmur of mysterious possibilities, with an atmosphere lawless and exciting, with a suggestion of power to be picked up by a strong hand. They enveloped him, they penetrated his heart as does the significant silence of the forests and the bitter vastness of the sea. They possessed themselves of his thoughts, of his activity, of his hopes – in an inevitable and obscure way even of his affections.   (p. 187)

As in 'Heart of Darkness', the whisper of 'mysterious possibilities' enters the heart – and, perhaps, destroys. Jörgensen, in particular, is a constant admonition:

His taciturnity was as eloquent as the repeated warning of the slave at the feast. He demonstrated one way in which may end the romance of the illiterate who read it not in books but in their own life, one way in which prosaic fate deals with men who dream quickly and want to handle their dream in broad daylight. (p. 162)

When Lingard brings him back 'into the life of men' (p. 173), he creates an equivocal presence: he is a dead man brought back to life, but, at the same time, an image of death is placed at the centre of Lingard's new world in the form of the skeletal Jörgensen.[18] Jörgensen's 'new command', the beached *Emma*, reinforces this impression: 'the desolated emptiness of the decks', 'the stripped spars', 'the dead body of the dismantled little vessel that would know the life of the seas no more' (p. 214). The dead body of the *Emma* is another female figure to set against the polymorphous femininity of Lingard's brig.

V

In Part III, 'The Capture', the narrative returns to the atmosphere of stasis with which the novel began: the yacht is stranded on the sandbank, and time seems at 'a standstill' in 'the sameness of days upon that shallows' (p. 226). The complex balances of the situation have produced deadlock. The narrative now progresses through three significant confrontations: between Travers and Lingard; between Mrs Travers and Immada; between Lingard and Mrs Travers. These confrontations generate a series of probing questions about Tom Lingard, Mrs Travers and Mr Travers in turn.

Part III begins with the confrontation between Travers and Lingard. This confrontation, at first glance, is merely the clash of two men who are used to having their importance recognised in their own worlds:

> You want me to understand you are a great man. . . . But re-member you are very far from home, while I, here – I am where I belong. And I belong where I am. I am just Tom Lingard – no more, no less – wherever I happen to be.   (p. 218)

Lingard's tactical modesty – 'I am just Tom Lingard – no more, no less' – is, at the same time, a confident assertion of his identity. It rests on the accustomed recognition of that name and that identity within Lingard's world. It is as much a claim of greatness as Travers's expectation of deference that it answers. But Lingard's statement also raises the questions – who is Tom Lingard, and where does he belong? In answering these questions, the narrative re-appraises and clarifies not only Lingard's identity but the two separate worlds, subtended by these men, that confront each other in their encounter, and two versions of colonial discourse. Travers and his world are briefly sketched in:

> He was a man who possessed only imagination enough for his personal use just enough imagination to put him in motion, to quicken his ambition, his desire to rise, his craving for reputation. He had not enough of it to understand or even perceive anything or anybody under heaven, that was not connected immediately and absolutely with the upward evolution of his own self . . . He had travelled on beaten tracks, on the tracks of commerce, in the region of law and order, and he could not bring himself to admit anything else. (pp. 232, 240)

Travers's world of 'prudent', 'respectable' people, of 'conventional values' and 'law and order' is a world already familiar from *The Sisters*.[19] It is the alienated and circumscribed world of the European bourgeoisie which (in *The Sisters*) was set over against the world of the artist. That contrast is repeated here through the Shelleyan figure of the man whose ideas Travers exploits:

> It had so happened that some time before he had been thrown in contact with one of those men who are in the forefront of the race and yet remain obscure, one of those unknown guides of civilisation . . . They are like great artists a mystery to the many, appreciated only by the uninfluential few, wilfully neglected by the great who love ease. (pp. 234–5)[20]

The narrative foregrounds another aspect of Travers's character – his character-armour. The journey that he has undertaken is a compensatory action, designed 'to vindicate his importance' (p. 234) after a 'check' to his ambitions. And the same defence-mechanism is in operation in Travers's reaction to Lingard. The self-importance that he asserts through his 'dignified show of composure' and 'official verbiage' (p. 289) is produced by his fear of being seen as 'a nobody or a fool' (p. 278).[21] Lingard's lack of deference towards, and lack of recognition of, Travers constitutes a threat to Travers's sense of importance and, hence, to his sense of his own identity.[22]

More important, however, is the effect of this meeting on Lingard, and the threat it poses to Lingard's identity. Part III begins from the idea that Lingard now inhabits a reality that cannot be communicated to the world of his origins:

> In the shade of that quarter-deck, under the eyes of these strangers, he felt oppressively alone. What could he tell them? They could form no conception of his life, of his thoughts . . . He could tell them nothing – because he had not the means. Their coming at this moment of his life when he had wandered beyond that circle which race, memories, early associations, all the essential conditions of one's origin trace round every man's life, deprived him in a manner of the power of speech.   (pp. 219–21)

His first reaction is hatred, anguish, bafflement. He has spent two years creating for himself 'another existence, governed by his impulse, nearer his desire': he has given up his identity among the European adventurers for a more romantic identity among the Malays. Now the unexpected claim of the past makes his new existence seem as unreal and insubstantial as a dream. Lingard feels a 'desire to explain, to make clear, to secure belief', but, when he presents himself to Travers, Travers is too defended psychologically to be able to confirm him even in his well-established identity-for-the-other:

> [Lingard] had said all he dared to say – and he perceived with horror that he was not believed. This had not happened to him for years. It had never happened. He could not remember ever meeting a man who did not believe him. The bare mention of his name was enough to ensure confidence and he was so conscious of his local reputation that it was quite a shock to find there were people in the world who had never heard of him, who were disposed to ignore him. It bewildered him, as though he had suddenly discovered he was no longer himself.   (pp. 243–4)

Both Travers and Lingard receive a challenge to their sense of themselves in this confrontation. Travers's reaction is a hollow reassertion of his identity and the world that supports that identity.

Lingard's initial response is the temptation to destroy the world that fails to recognise him. But his underlying drive is the desire to be believed in and to be understood. This had motivated his attempt to communicate his identity to Travers, and, from this point on, this desire is the motive that impels the narrative of 'The Rescuer'. Mr Travers's nonrecognition undermines Lingard's identity-for-the-other, Mrs Travers's 'trust' opens him to the irruption from within of his hidden passionate self. The emotional climaxes of 'The Rescuer' will be Lingard's confession of his new identity-for-self to Mrs Travers and the final revelation to her of a passionate self. It is significant that the manuscript ends with Lingard's lengthy confession of himself to Mrs Travers – with that final expression of his shut-in-self.

VI

Lingard's identity-for-the-other is the identity established earlier among his fellow-adventurers. Lingard's commitment to Hassim and Immada, and his existence in the Malay world, represents a romantic dream-identity, that can perhaps best be interpreted as his identity-for-self. This identity is closer to, and governed by, a self-for-self of impulse and desire. This self-for-self is perceived, or represented, differently at different times: sometimes it suggests an attractive 'life and liberty'; at other times it is feared as either empty or explosive. The development of the novel is a move from the established social identity to the romantic, dream-identity, and this is conveyed by the novel's movement from the European to the Malay world, from the white to the brown world. The same movement occurs as a structural component in *Lord Jim*.

Mrs Travers makes a similar psychological journey in the course of 'The Rescuer'. She is first presented through the eyes of the Travers's travelling companion, the aristocratic Linares (D'Alcacer in *The Rescue*). He interprets her 'passive attitude' (p. 222), her lack of 'modulation of tone' or 'play of feature' as expressive of her general withdrawal from life: 'as though . . . a veil of an immense indifference stretched between her and the men, between her heart and the meaning of events, between her thought and the thoughts surrounding her weary surrender, between her eyes and the shallow sea that like her gaze appeared profound, stilled forever' (p. 228).[23] Linares's

memory of her in London brings out the desolation and disenchantment behind her disdainful indifference, and relates her passive
attitude to the conventionalities of upper-class London life. But the
key to her behaviour lies in her marriage to Travers:

> As a young girl – often reproved for her romantic ideas – she had
> dreams where the sincerity of a great passion appeared like the
> ideal, fulfillment and the only truth of life. Penetrating into the
> world she discovered that ideal to be unattainable because the
> world is too prudent to be sincere. Then she hoped that she could
> find the truth of life in ambition which she understood as a life-
> long devotion to some unselfish idea. . . . She married him
> [Mr. Travers], found him enthusiastically devoted to the nursing
> of his own career and had nothing to hope for now . . . the days
> went on rapid, brilliant, uniform, without a glimpse of sincerity or
> true passion, without a single true emotion.   (pp. 288–9)

This is the process by which the earlier romantic idealism of her self
of desire has given way to the indifference of her identity-for-the-
other. This throws light upon her unexpected reaction to the quarrel
between Lingard and Travers – 'something real at last . . . something
. . . genuine and human' (p. 251) – and her response to the arrival of
Hassim and Immada. After the sheltered, self-suppressing, passion-
less existence of her marriage, she has unexpectedly been brought in
contact with an alternative reality that corresponds to her earlier
romantic dreams, and she reveals 'a secret being within' (p. 266).
When Immada appears on board the yacht, Mrs Travers asserts
herself before her: 'with the maturity of perfection with the superiority of the flower over the leaf of the phrase that contains a thought
over the cry that can only express a primitive emotion'. From this
evolutionary model of colonial relations, Mrs Travers feels that 'immense spaces and countless centuries stretched between them'; but,
at the same time, 'she looked at her as when one looks into one's own
heart' (p. 269). What Mrs Travers sees, in this meeting with Immada,
is her own buried self of passion. This is precisely that use of the
'oriental' as 'a sort of surrogate and even underground self' that Said
has analysed:

> She envied for a moment the lot of that humble and obscure sister.
> Nothing stood between that girl and the truth of her sensations.
> She could be sincerely courageous, and tender and passionate and

– well – ferocious; why not ferocious? She could know the truth of terror – and of affection – absolutely, without artificial trammels, without the pain of restraint. Her heart was dilated by a momentary longing to know the naked truth of things; the naked truth of life and passion buried under a growth of centuries. (pp. 291–2)[24]

And, at this point, Lingard re-appears on the yacht, just as Jaffir appeared to him on board *The Flash* at the start of his two-year commitment to Hassim.

VII

In this third confrontation, Lingard and Mrs Travers are both forced to reassess their lives, but the reader is also aware of the complex network of hopes, impulses and commitments within which that reassessment takes place. The presence of the yacht on 'The Shore of Refuge' marked the intrusion of the white world into Lingard's secret existence. It challenged Lingard to situate his identity in relation to that world. As he says to Mrs Travers, 'It was like home coming to me when I wasn't thinking of it' (pp. 296–7). This unexpected 'home-coming' had sufficient force to pose a threat to his pledge to Hassim and Immada. When they appeared on board the yacht, it 'occurred to him that for the first time in two years or more he had forgotten, utterly forgotten these people's existence' (p. 260). Now, he returns to the fact of this pledge, and the possibility of betrayal that the intrusion of the yacht has come to imply (p. 302). Yet he has no illusions about the yacht-people:

When I was a boy in a trawler, and looked at you, yacht people, in the Channel ports you were as strange to me as the Malays here are strange to you. I am no nearer to your kind now than you are to that man and that girl [Hassim and Immada]. I left home sixteen years ago and fought my way all round the earth. I had the time to forget where I began. What are you to me? Do you know that if I was to die here this minute I would have no one in the whole big world to send a message to – no one – but these two. (p. 303)

A significant factor in the conflict between Travers and Lingard was that Lingard was not a 'gentleman'.[25] Class difference is as much of a barrier as 'racial' difference. Nevertheless, he has come back to the yacht, because of Mrs Travers and the possibility that she might believe in him.

In their earlier meeting on the yacht, the 'magic power' (p. 270) of Mrs Travers's voice and the enchanting effect of that voice on Lingard were described:

> He looked and listened with something of the stupor of a new sensation. And the sounds modulated, gentle and penetrating; the sounds escaping from her lips seemed to touch him everywhere, thrilled him from head to foot as though that enchanting voice had made its way into him.

As Parry observes, Lingard's 'implacable hostility to the rich' gives way to 'an erotic servitude feeding on his humble birth and her high rank'.[26] In this second meeting, it is Mrs Travers's turn to be enchanted: Lingard's story 'appealed to some reckless instincts within her and she became so charmed with what she heard that she forgot where she was' (p. 314). Linares had detected the 'subtle power of comprehension in her quietude' earlier, but this is not just a 'latent capacity for sympathy' (p. 225), it is the emergence of 'reckless instincts' and other 'impulses' in response to Lingard's story. The story Lingard tells fulfills the demands of both of her earlier romantic ideals: it has both 'the sincerity of a great passion' and 'devotion to some unselfish idea' (pp. 288–9). Where her perception of Immada had awakened in her 'a momentary longing to know the naked truth of things; the naked truth of life and passion' (pp. 291–2), Lingard's earlier conversation had stirred her bitter awareness of the pretences of her social life and social identity. Now Lingard's story has awakened the romantic needs that she had earlier suppressed after failing to find 'an object' and a 'way of expansion' (p. 312). In addition, Lingard gives her the new experience of 'a human soul' laid bare before her, the direct personal contact that is denied in her everyday life. But this direct personal contact raises the question that social conventions serve to mask, as Mrs Travers has the courage and honesty to realise:

> She was frank with herself. She considered him apart from social organization. She discovered he had no place in it. . . . Here was a human being and the naked truth of things was not so very far

from her notwithstanding the growth of centuries. Then it occurred to her that this man by his action placed her in a manner
also outside the pale of organized society. His confidence stripped
her at once of her position, wealth, rank – of her past. I am helpless. What remains? She asked herself.   (p. 324)

What does remain when 'social organization' is removed? What is
the nature and potential of the self, when the restrictions and safe-
guards of 'social organization' are stripped away? These are the
questions that are confronted again in 'Heart of Darkness'. There are
indications of an answer even in this incomplete novel, 'The
Rescuer'.

The 'growth of centuries' has an ambivalent force. While it implies
progress, that 'progress' has produced the 'complicated emotions'
(p. 258) that are the poor, European substitute for a life of passions.
At the same time, the status of this evolutionary discourse is itself
ambiguous: is it consistently focalised through Mrs Travers, or is it
sometimes underwritten by the narrative? The Malay world and
Lingard's dream-identity 'governed by his impulse, nearer his desire' (p. 175) are occasionally presented as if they marked a regression in evolutionary or psychological terms. In a cancelled passage,
Hassim and Immada are described as having 'the sincere vigour of
beings living on the morrow of creation, before human thought had
descended like a pall upon the reality of primitive emotions' (p. 290).
Elsewhere, Lingard's actions are sometimes likened to those of a
child. For example, when Shaw accused him of criminality, 'his pain
was simple profound and unjust like that of a child confronted by
the indignation of absurd elders' (p. 378). The possibility that this
romantic ideal is both a dream and regressive is important for an
understanding of the relations between 'The Rescuer', 'Heart of
Darkness' and *Lord Jim*. 'Heart of Darkness' re-opens the question of
'primitive emotions'; *Lord Jim* re-examines the romantic identity-for-
self. In subsequent works, Conrad separates out elements that are
combined in 'The Rescuer'.

In the closing chapter of Part III, Lingard tries to come to terms
with his new situation and the sets of conflicting loyalties. After his
confrontation with Travers, Lingard had felt the urge to destroy
Travers's world; now, in the exaltation that follows his confession of
himself to Mrs Travers, he experiences a destructive impulse towards the world of his romantic identity, and he imagines 'fighting

to extermination (nothing less would do) the people with whom he had been for two momentous years of his life on terms of close intimacy, trust, dependence and friendship' (p. 330). Where Willems betrayed his white allies for love of a brown woman, Lingard contemplates betraying his brown allies for love of a white woman. Indeed, he contemplates not just the betrayal but the extermination of his former allies, and the subsequent reported dialogue between Jörgensen and Tengga carefully places this impulse in the context of the attitudes of European colonisers towards subject-peoples.

However, in his meeting with Carter, Lingard re-affirms his sense of his separateness from 'kinship with his race' (p. 369). He identifies reality with 'the domain of his adventurous soul' rather than with the world of his origin, and he struggles to preserve 'the reality of two years of hard toil' (p. 370). One result of this commitment is that he is subject to contradictory emotions:

> He was humiliated by the distrust of which he was the object but it was also like a tribute to the enigma that lived within him. To the young man before him he turned with anger and sympathy. (p. 370)

Precisely because his 'real identity' is kept hidden, Lingard creates distrust in others, and this distrust is embodied in the gun that Carter carries. Lingard rationalises the situation:

> To leave his life to that youngster's ignorance seemed to redress the balance. . . . It was distasteful and bitter as an expiation should be. (p. 383)

But Carter is 'ignorant' because Lingard chooses to keep him ignorant. Lingard may feel 'humiliated' by his distrust, but he can argue that the distrust pertains to the false-self which is his representative in the real world. If the threat of Carter's gun expresses that distrust, it also gives substance to the real world. It marks a point of contact between the real world and Lingard's inner life, since it is a constant reminder of the threat the real world poses to the dream world. At the same time, the 'expiation' that it signifies to Lingard corresponds to the subjective guilt he feels in relation to the real world for his inauthenticity in it. However, as Part III has shown, Lingard is also under increasing pressure to reveal his secret identity.

VIII

Part IV begins with the confusion that Mrs Travers has caused within Lingard:

> A new power had come into the world, had possessed itself of human speech, had imparted to it a sinister irony of allusion. To be told that someone has 'a perfect knowledge of his mind' startled him and made him wince. It was cruel, since it made him aware that now he did not know it himself – that it seemed impossible for him ever to regain that knowledge.   (p. 411)

Lingard's guilty reaction to the suggestion that Hassim has 'a perfect knowledge of his mind' is an indication of the changed world which he now inhabits. It is not just that Lingard lacks 'perfect knowledge' of his own mind, but the divisions within him have affected his perception of the world. The world itself is split and language has acquired an ironic potential (as Razumov also discovers in *Under Western Eyes*). In this final section of the manuscript, Conrad delineates Lingard's initial confusion, his search for some guidance, his recognition of the powerful pull Mrs Travers exert on him, and the struggle within him as he tries to remain faithful both to the dream he shares with Hassim and Immada and to the passionate impulse he feels towards Mrs Travers. This section bears the title 'The point of honour and the point of passion', but the issue is not just the conflict between loyalty to Hassim and passion for Mrs Travers, but the contest between two worlds as to which is 'real'.

In Chapter 1, Lingard brings Mrs Travers off the yacht and back to his brig. As the yacht vanishes from sight in the darkness, the world implied by the yacht loses its reality. Even Mrs Travers becomes unreal and insubstantial – a mental event, 'a memory' (p. 406), rather than a person. But, when Lingard reaches the brig, he finds that a significant change has taken place there: 'Everything was as it had been perhaps but the world was not the same' (p. 411). A 'new power' has 'cast its spell' over every element of his world. The changes, in fact, are changes within Lingard himself. Chapter 2 makes clear that the 'new power' that has cast its spell over Lingard's life derives from the impulse which Mrs Travers has awakened within him. Chapter 2 begins with Lingard's ambivalent experience of this impulse:

> He would have to go in and talk to her. He wished to go in but the
> idea dismayed him. Of necessity he was not one of these men who
> have the mastery of expression who can set free in flowing speech
> their thoughts their sensations, their longings, their dreams. To
> liberate his soul was for him a gigantic undertaking – a matter of
> desperate effort and of doubtful success.   (pp. 413–14)

He experiences both desire and fear of his own desire, and he takes
refuge in ambiguity. It is not clear whether he wants to 'talk' to
Mrs Travers about the kidnapping of her husband or to 'liberate his
soul'. In the confusion he feels at the change that has taken place in
his world, he drifts in search of some guidance just as he did in *An
Outcast*. And it is a chance statement, overheard from one of the
crew of the yacht ('Under Providence he may serve her turn'), that
persuades him to open the door to the cabin where Mrs Travers
waits, and provides him with instructions for the first part of his
interview with her.[27]

It is not just Lingard, however, who experiences this conflict between two worlds. There has been a mutual intervention into each
other's existence 'from beyond the limits of the Conceivable' (p. 420),
and there is a conflict within Mrs Travers between the 'ordered
existences' (p. 429) of Travers's world and the 'lawless life' (p. 425)
offered by Lingard, between her social identity and her repressed
emotions. For Lingard, the removal from the yacht to the brig had
rendered the yacht and the events connected with it as insubstantial
as 'a vanished dream' (p. 406). For Mrs Travers, too, this journey has
deprived the world of the yacht of its reality. The description hinted
at a return to primal chaos, from which a new world might, perhaps,
emerge:

> At every stroke of the short sculls she felt the boat leap forward
> with her. The sea merged into infinity, as though the firmament
> and the waters separated since the day of Creation had on that
> night come together again.   (p. 406)

When she is in Lingard's cabin, she feels 'lost to her past and her
future alike' (p. 425): she feels outside of time, out of the temporal
continuity of her life.

Once she has seen something of 'the daily surroundings' of
Lingard's existence, she can understand better 'the meaning of his
inner life' (p. 425):

The red gleam of ambition burned within him of an ambition as subtle and commanding as a dream. He looked capable of great things, in his hallucination of misty greatness. The glamour and the pathos of a lawless life stretched over him like the sky is stretched over the sea down on all sides to an unbroken horizon. Within he moved very lonely dangerous and romantic. There was in him crime, sacrifice, tenderness devotion and the madness of a fixed idea.   (pp. 426–7)

Although she can appreciate Lingard's 'extravagant impulses' (p. 431), she fears this new world he has brought her into:

It seemed to her she had been dreaming till then. Now she was awakened and the awful thing was that the dream still went on. It had passed into waking life. But it was his dream. His dream in her life. His masterful dream the arbiter of the unknown, of the future, of fate.   (p. 429)

Accordingly, she hangs on to the idea of saving her husband and Linares as a defence against being possessed by the lawless reality of Lingard and by the lawless reality of passion:

She had been suddenly assailed (*sic*) by uncompromising realities but the sensation was as though she were about to grapple with hallucinations. . . . She could not appeal to the conventional sentiments of ordered existences of cautious existences untinged by the flames of strange desires and of uncommon illusions. She had to save the two men.   (p. 429)

She has no language for this world of human passion and no maps, and, like Lingard earlier, she fears being left alone in an alien world: 'It seemed to her that if she failed to preserve those two men she would be left alone on the earth, as alone as though they had been the only beings of her own kind and all the rest of mankind were strangers, more than strangers – creatures of another essence' (p. 430). Parry brilliantly delineates Mrs Travers's ways of protecting herself from the reality of Lingard's world 'by viewing its natural and human properties as the products of astonished western observation'.[28] Through the kind of narrative focalisation regularly used in the late fiction, the text proffers the 'articulations of the stranger from a dominant social order defending herself against the assaults of a foreign world she believes to be a negation of the norms and values that are her safety'.[29]

The dramatic focus of Part IV, however, is Lingard's attempt to remain loyal both to Hassim and Immada and also to Mrs Travers, to reconcile the claims of honour and of passion. Into this struggle go the self-divisions of Lingard and Mrs Travers. Mrs Travers argues for her husband but is drawn towards Lingard; Lingard struggles to remain faithful to both the dream-world he shares with Hassim and Immada, and the deeper impulse he feels for Mrs Travers.[30] The division of the chapter into mutually incomprehensible Malay and English conversations dramatises the split in Lingard: Hassim and Immada make their claim in Malay; Mrs Travers makes hers in English. But it is not through shared language or shared origins that Lingard feels a bond with Mrs Travers. The impulse that binds him to her operates on a deeper level than 'racial' or national loyalty. The passionate impulse is more powerful than 'the impulses of his extraordinary ambition and of his profound tenderness' (p. 436), which were the bases of the world he shared with Hassim and Immada and of the 'adventure which made him in his own sight, exactly what he was' (p. 446).

At this point, Lingard resembles Willems in his involvement with Aissa. There are suggestions of despair, possession, madness, and, as the passionate impulse carries him towards the betrayal of Hassim and Immada, the sense of vain struggle is conveyed by the same swimming/drowning imagery: 'He felt like a swimmer who in the midst of superhuman efforts to reach the shore perceives suddenly that the undertow is taking him to sea' (p. 444). As Lingard recognises: 'It was not these two men he had to save; he had to save himself' (p. 446). The echo (and reversal) of Mrs Travers's thought (p. 429) signals their conflicting interests. Lingard's entrance at the start of Chapter 4 recalls a similar entrance made by Willems in *An Outcast*:

> Lingard had rushed on deck with blind impetuousity. He reeled in the darkness as if robbed of his strenght (sic) by the poison of despair.   (p. 444)

Immada's comments on the effect of Mrs Travers's eyes on Lingard ('He looked into them and forgot to look at us', p. 450) also recall Willems's complaints about Aissa's eyes and her bewitchment of him. The obvious difference between Willems and Lingard is that

Lingard has reached this position despite his constant struggle to remain faithful, whereas Willems had no scruples about betraying his allies and his benefactors. Nevertheless, as in *An Outcast*, it seems that the self of impulse is to be feared rather than welcomed: it leads to 'madness' and possession rather than to 'life and liberty'.

This suggestion is reinforced and further elaborated by the final events of the manuscript. The departure of Lingard and Mrs Travers from Lingard's brig parallels their departure, at the start of Part IV, from the Travers's yacht, but, this time, it is Lingard's world that is being left behind. Lingard's departure from the brig also clearly figures a discarding of psychological defences: 'They fear the brig because when I am on board her, the brig and I are one. An armed man – don't you see?' (p. 465). The defences are discarded, in part, because they have already been breached:

> It is as though you had brought a curse for me in your yacht. Nobody believes me. . . . I am watched – on board my own ship. Watched. Mistrusted. Suspected. On board my own ship. Am I dreaming? Am I in a fever?   (pp. 467–71)

The intrusion of the white world challenged his identity-for-the-other, and the passionate impulse that Mrs Travers awakened has undermined his identity-for-self. Nevertheless, when he leaves the brig, he is conscious that he is also leaving his old identity: 'that he was saying goodbye to all the world, that he was taking a last leave of his own self, this very soul stripped of his illusion shuddered as though it had been standing naked and alone at the gate of Infernal Regions' (pp. 488–9). At the same time, he and Mrs Travers are penetrating deeper into the world of his 'dream', 'within the circle of another existence, governed by his impulse, nearer his desire' (p. 175).

The last five chapters of the manuscript are taken up with their journey towards the boundary-point, the reef that marks the entrance to the Shallows, and with the struggle within and between Mrs Travers and Lingard. The narrative moves steadily towards that other existence, that life of impulse, desire, passion. The 'low and threatening voice' of the Shallows, which, for Lingard, was 'forever mingled with the voice of his desire' (p. 511), evokes again the fearful side of passion, a reminder of the danger that is one of the conditions of that life. The reef is the image that dominates these last chapters. To begin with, it figures an impasse: 'the struggle of the

rocks forever overwhelmed and emerging with the sea forever vic-
torious and repulsed' (p. 522). Lingard reads 'the vain fury, the
helpless rage of that turmoil' as an image of 'the struggle within
himself': 'there was inspiration and despair in it' (p. 522). Then the
boat's negotiation of the reef is used to chart imagistically Lingard's
emotional adjustments to Mrs Travers.

At the decisive moment, when the boat reaches the reef, Lingard
decides to wake her:

> He turned into the creek leading into the lagoon . . . and it seemed
> to him that his life had commenced in that very moment. What
> went before did not count somehow. Now when he looked back
> he could not see anything he cared for beyond that night.
> (pp. 538–9)

In waking her, he has consciously committed himself to his passionate impulse towards her and denied his commitment to Hassim and
Immada.[31] But he has also committed himself to an illusion, as another reference to the reef makes clear: 'the sea would never rest and
the land would never give in' (p. 541). In context this acts as a
reminder of the different worlds of Lingard and Mrs Travers, and
testifies to the strength and hopelessness of his passion:

> There was a will in the sea; it was like a prisoner trying to break
> out and going at it blind, or like a man fighting for something
> dearer than life. He thought then it wanted something the land
> would not give up. Something it was mad after and would never
> get.   (p. 541)

The manuscript concludes with Lingard's 'confession' to her of his
secret existence. He describes his isolation:

> I was getting together my stake to play a game no man within
> these seas would dare even look at. And all without a word of
> cheer from a single human being. To whom could I speak even if
> I had dared? No-one would have understood what it had come to
> mean for me.   (p. 550)

Now, as throughout Part IV, he is waiting for some sign from her,
but she responds defensively to his revelations. She experiences him
as frighteningly powerful, and as a threat to her own existence:

The impetuous and deliberate passion in his life, his lust of conquest, his lust of generosity were like a triple wall encircling the
men she had to save. This was her task. She had to save them – to
satisfy her conscience and her pity; she had to defend something
else than her life – she had to defend its integrity against the
magnificence of this man's instincts.   (pp. 560–1)

She has to destroy 'the world of his creation' in order to regain her
own existence as 'reality'. Lingard's way of being is experienced not
as liberation from, but as a threat to, the compromises of her own
life, and his reality has, therefore, to be labelled a dream:

'Dreams' he ejaculated resentfully, were the years of work a dream;
was his toil and his anxiety and his forethought nothing but a
dream? Was Belarab a dream, and Tengga, and Sheif Daman?
Were the moments of profound delight at the thought of what he
could so, those moments when he did not seem to touch the earth
– were these the moments of a dream?   (pp. 581–2)

Part IV (and the manuscript as a whole) ends with Lingard returning
to her earlier affirmation of her belief in him:

You don't know what it was to me. For years I had been afraid to
whisper for fear that if I once opened my lips everything would
come out and be lost. You see the thing had grown within me, had
grown shut in; was getting bigger there . . . bigger every day,
mastering me and pent up so that sometimes I thought my breast-
bone would crack and my heart burst.   (p. 598)

The voyage that has ended in this confession of a 'shut in' self has
also been an exploration of various fears and dangers associated
with the self of passion. In addition, this exploration of passion has
involved – for both Lingard and Mrs Travers – a choice of sides.
Lingard had to choose between his identity-for-self (an heroic, romantic self-image that is associated with his bond with Hassim
and Immada) and this passionate impulse towards Mrs Travers.
Mrs Travers has been faced with a choice of sides between the
'ordered existence' of Travers, the safe world of her disillusionment,
or the lawless life of the adventurer, that is closer to her original
romantic ideals. It resembles the choice embodied in *The Sisters*.
    On 22 November 1898, Conrad wrote to Mrs Bontine, describing

his difficulties with 'The Rescuer'. His attempt 'to tell romantically a love story in which the word love is not to be pronounced' felt like 'courting disaster deliberately': 'Add to this that an inextricable confusion of sensations is of the very essence of the tale, and you may judge how much success, material or otherwise, I may expect.'[32] This 'inextricable confusion' no doubt played a part in Conrad's decision to abandon 'The Rescuer'. The narrative was too rich thematically: in subsequent works, Conrad was to explore separately issues which were intermingled in 'The Rescuer'.

4

The Brotherhood of the Sea: *The Nigger of the 'Narcissus'*, 'Heart of Darkness' and *Lord Jim*

In his 'personal remembrance' of Conrad, Ford suggested how Conrad's boyhood reading of Marryat's novels about 'the frigate warfare of Napoleonic times' had shaped his response to his own career in the merchant navy:

> In the seventies and eighties of last century Conrad by dint of experience found in that service . . . the tradition of Marryat's frigates. It was fidelity to an ideal, the ideal of the British merchant service.[1]

Marryat's *Peter Simple* is quite explicit about this ideal.[2] Captain Savage, for example, takes advantage of a storm in the Bay of Arcason to tell the first lieutenant, Falcon:

> The consequence of any carelessness or neglect in the fitting and securing of the rigging will be felt now; and this danger, if we escape it, ought to remind us how much we have to answer for if we neglect our duty. The lives of a whole ship's company may be sacrificed by the neglect or incompetence of an officer when in harbour.   (I. 242)

Later, when the storm abates, Mr Chucks, the boatswain, draws a similar moral from the incident: 'Private feelings . . . must always be sacrificed for the public service' (I. 247). *The Nigger of the 'Narcissus'* introduces this ideal code of conduct, in fully articulated form, into Conrad's fiction. Conrad's moral and psychological exploration is grounded in, and derives its value system from, what is essentially

101

a political vision. The ship is presented as a paradigmatic organic society – and issues of egotism and altruism, of true and false claims of kinship, are examined within that ideological framework. The interaction between psychological exploration and political vision determines the course of Conrad's subsequent novels: 'Heart of Darkness', *Lord Jim* and *Nostromo*, from different angles, test the ideal code of conduct to the limits.

I

The Nigger of the 'Narcissus' tells the story of the journey of the 'Narcissus' from Bombay to London. In particular, it focuses on the problems that arise *en route* from a storm and from the demoralising presence on board of a dying West Indian sailor, James Wait. From his first appearance, Wait's function in the novella is clear. The chief mate is calling the roll, and Conrad's description gives this roll-call the quality of a rite of passage. Each man is called into individual existence for a moment, before he surrenders this individuality and becomes part of the crew:

> As the chief mate read out a name, one of the men would answer: 'Yes, sir!' or 'Here!' and, detaching himself from the shadowy mob of heads visible above the blackness of starboard bulwarks, would step barefooted into the circle of light, and in two noiseless strides pass into the shadows on the port-side of the quarter-deck. . . . The last man had gone over, and there was a moment of silence while the mate peered at his list – 'Sixteen, seventeen,' he muttered. 'I am one hand short, bo'sun,' he said aloud. The big west-countryman at his elbow, swarthy and bearded like a gigantic Spaniard, said in a rumbling bass:- 'There's no one left forward, sir. I had a look around. He ain't aboard, but he may turn up before daylight.' 'Ay. He may or he may not,' commented the mate, 'can't make out that last name. It's all a smudge . . . That will do, men. Go below.' The distinct and motionless group stirred, broke up, began to move forward.
>
> 'Wait!' cried a deep, ringing voice.   (pp. 15–17)

From the start, Wait uses ambiguity to disrupt and control. 'Wait' as a command challenges the power-structure of the ship, and it is as a command that the chief mate, at this moment, has to understand the word.[3] When Wait subsequently explains that he is supplying the smudged name, he further increases his control of the situation. Wait's arrival immediately disrupts the organisation of the ship and threatens to overthrow the ship's system of control.

The first chapter indicates another threat to the power-structure of the ship. Belfast's story of the officer and the tar-pot asserts class solidarity against the 'human solidarity' affirmed by the narrative.[4] Belfast's ideological position is attacked, during the course of the narrative, in and through the person of Donkin. Donkin, with his ability to 'conquer the naive instincts of that crew' (p. 12) is represented as manipulating the crew by establishing a false kinship with them, and the crew's reaction to Donkin's appeal for clothes provides the key to their response to Wait later: 'The gust of their benevolence sent a wave of sentimental pity through their doubting hearts. They were touched by their own readiness to alleviate a shipmate's misery' (p. 12). This 'latent egoism of tenderness' (p. 138), which Wait will also exploit, is established from the start as potentially subversive of the discipline and the power-structure of the ship.

However, as Conrad wrote later, 'the problem that faces them is not a problem of the sea, it is merely a problem that has arisen on board a ship where the conditions of complete isolation from all land entanglements make it stand out with a particular force and colouring'.[5] The problem, in fact, is how to exist 'within sight of eternity'.[6] James Wait is the centre of 'the ship's collective psychology'.[7] Conrad uses him to explore the mechanisms people employ to avoid direct awareness of their own mortality and the errors into which this self-deception leads them. Throughout the narrative, Wait plays on the crew's unacknowledged fear of death. In the first half of the narrative, he takes control over the crew by asserting his illness:

> It was just what they had expected, and hated to hear, that idea of a stalking death, thrust at them many times a day like a boast and like a menace . . . he paraded it unceasingly before us with an affectionate persistence that made its presence indubitable and at the same time incredible. . . . Was he a reality – or was he a sham. (p. 36)

The oppositions here are neither contradictory nor mystificatory.[8] They delineate precisely the 'bind' by means of which Wait controls the crew – which the reader experiences, in turn, through the indeterminacies of the text. They both believe in his illness and suspect that he is only pretending illness to avoid work – and Wait encourages this suspicion. He controls them not through their belief, but through their doubt – and through the resulting ambiguity of their response: 'we oscillated between the desire of virtue and the fear of ridicule; we wished to save ourselves from the pain of re-morse, but did not want to be made the contemptible dupes of our sentiment' (p. 41). In addition, the episode where Donkin appealed for clothes has prepared the reader to recognise that their concern for Wait is not altruistic but egoistic. They are 'tender' towards him because of the thought of their own death. Equally, it is because of their own fear of death that, later, they will want to believe that he is not really dying. Because they cannot face the fact of their own mortality, and cannot acknowledge their own fear of death, they are vulnerable to being controlled through those unacknowledged fears.[9] Wait, however, is not only equivocating with the crew, he is also equivocating with himself. The doubt that he creates in the crew also functions as a means of defence: it allows him to feel that he is only pretending to be dying. This explains his puzzling friendship with Donkin, who accuses him of pretending illness to avoid work. Donkin's accusations are reassuring for Wait, because they reinforce his desire to believe that he is only pretending illness. In fact, Wait is pretending to be pretending to die, and the second level of pretence is intended to deceive himself.

This emerges clearly from Wait's reaction to Podmore. Podmore, like Donkin, has been shown to represent a threat to the hierarchy of the ship. In part, this is because his religion gives him allegiances and duties outside the power-structure of the ship, but he is also represented as a threat because of his personality. Podmore behaves 'like a conceited saint unable to forget his glorious reward' (p. 32). Where Wait aims at power through illness and uncertainty, Podmore asserts his power through religious certainty. When Podmore tries to 'save' Wait by preaching to him of eternal punishments, he touches on the fear of death in Wait that Wait has been avoiding through his pretences. Wait's reaction is to assert his fitness. In the second part of the narrative, Wait brings about a second crisis in the ship: this time by asserting he is well, when he is obviously dying. Once again, Wait's method of fleeing from his own fear of death affects the rest of the crew, and, again, this is because he plays on the same fear in them:

He was demoralising. Through him we were becoming highly humanised, tender, complex, excessively decadent: we understood the subtlety of his fear, sympathised with all his revulsions, shrinkings, evasions, delusions. (p. 139)

As in Jim's identification with Gentleman Brown, some repressed or unacknowledged aspect of self is brought into action.

This false (egoistic) solidarity is set against the real (altruistic) solidarity of 'the brotherhood of the sea':

Night and day the head and shoulders of a seaman could be seen aft by the wheel, outlined high against sunshine or starlight, very steady above the stir of revolving spokes. The faces changed, passing in rotation. Youthful faces, bearded faces, dark faces; faces serene, or faces moody, but all akin with the brotherhood of the sea. (p. 30)

With this image, Conrad offers his solution to the problem he has confronted: the individual escapes solitariness and the negating power of death by commitment to the group. The actions of the individual have value by maintaining the survival of the group: the survival of the group reciprocally gives value to the actions of individuals.[10] This true solidarity is displayed by the crew in the other test they face: the storm in Chapter 3. The storm is, symbolically, a death and a resurrection. What saves the ship is the loyalty and solidarity of the crew. They work together selflessly within the power-structure of the ship; and it is significant that James Wait is out of sight for most of this section of the narrative: 'We hardly gave a thought to Jimmy and his bosom friend. There was no leisure for idle probing of hearts' (p. 53).

Wait represents the burden of self – the tangle of fears and desires, self-doubts and self-questionings. This is the source of the crew's betrayal of themselves and their betrayal of their duty to the ship. Conversely, service of the ship is represented as offering a protection against this burden.[11] The ideal code of conduct is asserted against the darkness of the self just as, in both title and narrative, the whiteness of the *Narcissus* is poised against the black sailor, Wait. In 'Heart of Darkness', Conrad breaks through the protection of oxymoron and antithesis that *The Nigger of the 'Narcissus'* proliferates in order to go further into the darkness.

II

'Heart of Darkness' was written in 1898. It is based on Conrad's experiences in the Congo, but it is far more than 'experience pushed a little (and only very little) beyond the actual facts of the case' (p. xi), which is what Conrad asserts in the 'Author's Note'.[12] It can be read as an account of colonialism that reveals the massive gap between statement and practice – between what Conrad called 'the vilest scramble for loot that ever disfigured the history of human conscience' and the philanthropic words that were used to cover it.[13] It is also a psychological exploration, but, as in *The Nigger of the 'Narcissus'*, the psychological exploration is located in a political context.

'Heart of Darkness' begins with a yawl becalmed in the Thames Estuary. As the sun sets, an unnamed narrator evokes 'the great spirit of the past upon the lower reaches of the Thames' (p. 47). The speech begins like a eulogy: 'It had known and served all the men of whom the nation is proud, from Sir Francis Drake to Sir John Franklin, knights all, titled and untitled – the great knights-errant of the sea' (p. 47). This patriotic rhetoric would have seemed comfortingly familiar to the original readers in *Blackwood's Magazine*, but it is presented only to be subverted. It ends with more doubtful praise: 'Hunters for gold or pursuers of fame, they had all gone out on that stream, bearing the sword and often the torch, messengers of the might within the land, bearers of a spark from the sacred fire' (p. 47). Every word is cunningly weighted: greed and pride are the implied motives for exploration; the sword (rather than the torch of religion and learning) is the dominant characteristic.[14] And Marlow's first words – 'this also . . . has been one of the dark places of the earth' (p. 48) – lead into a speech that continues this subliminal criticism. Marlow's account of the Roman colonisation of Britain implies and conceals criticism of contemporary imperialism. The unnamed narrator's 'hunters for gold or pursuers of fame' are close relations of Marlow's readily-identifiable 'Romans':

> Perhaps he was cheered by keeping his eye on a chance of pro-
> motion to a fleet at Ravenna by-and-by, if he had good friends in
> Rome and survived the awful climate. Or think of a decent young
> citizen in a toga – perhaps too much dice, you know – coming out
> here in the train of some prefect, or tax-gatherer, or trader even, to
> mend his fortunes.   (pp. 49–50)

More important, Marlow undermines the easy ethnocentricity of his readers by the reminder that the 'sand-banks, marshes, forests, savages' (p. 49) feared by the Romans were to be found in the Thames basin. Marlow's historical fantasy destabilises the imperialist discourse of 'savage' and 'civilised', just as his first words challenged the imperialist rhetoric of 'darkness' and 'light'.[15] 'Savages' clearly says more about the non-comprehension of the observer – his fear and his need to feel superior – than it does about the observed.

Marlow adopts a dual strategy against his audience at this stage. He makes repeated efforts to bring home to them the meaning of being colonised. For example, his description of his life in England before he went to the Congo concludes: 'I was loafing about, hindering you fellows in your work and invading your homes just as though I had got a heavenly mission to civilise you' (pp. 51–2). At other times, he takes pains to deny any reflection upon English imperialism. For example, immediately after making critical statements about the Roman colonisation of Britain, Marlow disclaims any intention of comparing Roman and English colonisers: 'Mind, none of us would feel exactly like this. What saves us is efficiency' (p. 50). But, in the context he has described, 'efficiency' is morally irrelevant. His subsequent generalisation about colonialism makes this clear – just as it emphasises that it is modern and not first-century colonisation that is in his mind:

> The conquest of the earth which mostly means the taking it away from those who have a different complexion or slightly flatter noses than ourselves, is not a pretty thing when you look into it too much.   (p. 50)

Again, however, he ends with a disclaimer which seems to excuse English colonisers:

> What redeems it is the idea only. An idea at the back of it; not a sentimental pretence but an idea; and an unselfish belief in the idea – something you can set up, and bow down before, and offer a sacrifice to . . .   (pp. 50–1)

Marlow trails off at the end of this statement, because the image he has used derives from (and evokes memories of) Kurtz and his practices. Kurtz had set himself up as a god for others to 'bow down before, and offer a sacrifice to'. Marlow's subsequent narration is

motivated by the memory of Kurtz's activities rather than by belief
in the 'idea' that redeems imperialism, which is what his listeners
might reasonably expect from this introduction. It is a heuristic
narration, driven by Marlow's desire to understand his own experience, but, once the narrative begins, the search is not for an
idea to redeem colonialism but for something to redeem human
existence.[16]

III

In the early stages of the journey, the colonial theme is foregrounded.
In Brussels, Marlow's aunt asserts the idea of colonisation as a civilising mission. She 'talked about weening those ignorant millions
from their horrid ways' (p. 59). Marlow, in reply, ventures to hint
'that the company was run for profit' (p. 50). Marlow's aunt is easily
dismissed: she lives in the unreal world of appearances, by which
bourgeois women are kept in ignorance of the economic bases of
their position. The reader is not allowed this ignorance: how the
company makes its profit is soon revealed. The French steamer
introduces the machinery of repression and exploitation: at every
port it lands 'soldiers and custom-house officers' (p. 60). Civilising
the Africans means making them slaves and working them till they
die, and the soldiers and agents who supervise this 'heavenly
mission' are as exploited as the Africans. The men on the French
warship are 'dying of fever at the rate of three a day' (p. 62); the
agents are struck down by various tropical diseases; while the 'great
man' who runs the company back in Brussels has 'his grip on the
handle-end of ever so many millions' (p. 56).

Once the journey has reached Africa, the experience of 'the merry
dance of death and trade' (p. 62) overwhelms Marlow. The journey
becomes a descent, in search of meaning, from the surface world of
Brussels to the Central Station of the traders, and then on to the Inner
Station of Mr Kurtz: 'a weary pilgrimage amongst hints for nightmares' (p. 62). The 'heart of darkness' is the centre of Africa; the
heart of Kurtz; the atavistic element of the self that the narrative
explores. The narrative, accordingly, superimposes a number of
parallel and overlapping journeys: Marlow's physical journey from
London to the Congo; Marlow's moral journey in his confrontation
with the wilderness and with the workings of imperialism; and the

psychological journey undertaken by Marlow, his audience, and the reader. Marlow's narrative can be read as a quest; a *katabasis*; an inverted pilgrim's progress; a Buddhist teaching story; a Faustian pact.[17] The narrative of the journey is constructed in three sections based on three questions articulated by the text: whether there is any redeeming idea behind colonialism; what becomes of the mercenary in the wilderness; and what becomes of the moral man in the wilderness.

The Swedish captain introduces the second structural question: what becomes of the mercenary in the wilderness. Marlow heads inland, impelled by his comment: 'It is funny what some people will do for a few francs a month. I wonder what becomes of that kind when it goes up country?' (p. 63). At his first stop, the Brussels world (and its values) are definitively placed in the person of the immaculately-dressed chief accountant with his orderly account books: 'In the great demoralization of the land he kept up his appearance. That's backbone. His starched collars and got-up shirt-fronts were achievements of character' (p. 68). The ironic tone suggests that, if this is achievement, then it is a very limited one; and, as the narrative progresses, it becomes clear that his efficiency and neatness are based on a lack of humanity. This is most chillingly revealed in his response to the sick man whose bed has been placed in his office: '"The groans of this sick person," he said, "distract my attention. And without that it is extremely difficult to guard against clerical errors in this climate"' (p. 69).

The dissociation that takes place in Brussels is harder to disguise here. As Marx put it, the 'profound hypocrisy and inherent barbarism of bourgeois civilisation lies unveiled before our eyes', when we turn 'from its home, where it assumes respectable forms, to the colonies, where it goes naked'.[18] At the Central Station itself, the veil is almost completely dropped. Under their languid pretences, the 'pilgrims' have only one strong feeling – greed, and, from this greed, they have created their world of 'back-biting and intriguing' (p. 73). At the same time, their fetish, the ivory, seems powerless against the power of the wilderness. Their greed becomes absurd in the face of imminent death.

Against this background, the mention of Kurtz holds out a hope. The agent tells Marlow that Kurtz is 'an emissary of pity, and science, and progress' (p. 79). He is one of the 'new gang – the gang of virtue' (p. 79). The next stage of Marlow's pilgrimage is impelled by a new question: 'I was curious to see whether this man, who had come out equipped with moral ideas of some sort, would climb to the top after all and how he would set about his work when there' (p. 88). Unlike the 'pilgrims', Kurtz apparently believes in the idea that Marlow's aunt voiced earlier. Marlow overhears the manager quoting Kurtz: 'Each station should be like a beacon on the road towards better things, a centre for trade . . . but also for humanising, improving, instructing' (p. 91). Kurtz's painting, however, of 'a woman, draped and blindfolded, carrying a lighted torch' (p. 79) suggests the conclusion to Marlow's quest long before he meets Kurtz. The dissociation that occurs in Brussels – asserting the civilising mission while engaging in barbarism – reappears in Kurtz. There is his 'gift' (p. 113), his powerful and eloquent voice, and there are his deeds. There is his seventeen-page report, 'a beautiful piece of writing' (p. 118), full of noble words and appeals to altruistic sentiments, and there is the single practical suggestion, scrawled as a 'postscriptum': 'Exterminate all the brutes' (p. 118). In the freedom of the Inner Station, Kurtz's idealism has broken open to reveal the will-to-power it concealed. This is the implication of Marlow's comment on the report:

> The opening paragraph . . . in the light of later information, strikes me now as ominous. He began with the argument that we whites, from the point of development we had arrived at, 'must necessarily appear to them (savages) in the nature of supernatural beings – we approach them with the might as of a deity,' and so on, and so on. 'By the simple exercise of our will we can exert a power for good practically unbounded,' etc. etc.   (p. 118)

Kurtz, like Lingard, is a man who plays at being God. But he is, ultimately, not strong enough to withstand the temptations of the position:

> There was something wanting in him – some small matter which, when the pressing need arose, could not be found under his magnificent eloquence . . . the wilderness had found him out early, and had taken on him a terrible vengeance for the fantastic invasion. I think it had whispered to him things about himself which he did not know, things of which he had no conception till he took counsel with this great solitude – and the whisper had proved irresistibly fascinating.   (p. 131)

In the 'great solitude' of the jungle, Kurtz has found no source of restraint either outside or inside himself. In the exercise of his power, he has opened himself to other forces within: 'the heavy, mute spell of the wilderness . . . seemed to draw him to its pitiless breast by the awakening of forgotten and brutal instincts' (p. 144). Yet there remain essential differences between Kurtz and the 'pilgrims'. He is a man of good intentions who has betrayed his ideals through the will-to-power that was implicit in them. Furthermore, in his death, if he does not actually redeem himself, he nevertheless marks his distance from the traders. 'The horror! The horror!' (p. 149) is a very different kind of statement from the manager's criticism of Kurtz's practices as an 'unsound method' (p. 137) of trade.[19] Whatever its exact significance, Kurtz's statement is in the realm of moral discourse. As Marlow says:

> Better his cry – much better. It was an affirmation, a moral victory paid for by innumerable defeats, by abominable terrors, by abominable satisfactions. But it was a victory! That is why I have remained loyal to Kurtz to the last, and even beyond.   (p. 151)

This determines Marlow's choice of Kurtz in his 'choice of nightmares' (p. 138). But it is important to remember that it is a choice of *nightmares*.[20] It is a bond partly forced on him by the chance that they were both recommended by the same people in Europe, but that bond continues through Marlow's quest for Kurtz because of Marlow's rejection of the values of the traders.

IV

Marlow compares his journey up the Congo to 'travelling back to the earliest beginnings of the world' (p. 92). This can be related to the late-Victorian fear of the white man's deterioration in the colonies and to the corresponding psychological theories about 'white man's reversion', based on a racialist reading of Darwin. At the same time, this comparison is also proleptic of a confrontation with an atavistic component of the self.[21] On a number of occasions, Marlow refers to the Congo as a place where 'anything can be done' (p. 91): it is an area where the self is free to express and realise itself unhindered by laws and social controls. Conrad had already considered the idea of a self free from the conditioning and controls of Western society in

The Sisters and 'The Rescuer'. In 'Heart of Darkness', this line of psychological speculation produces Marlow's discovery of 'forgotten and brutal instincts . . . gratified and monstrous passions' (p. 144): 'We are accustomed to look upon the shackled form of a conquered monster, but there – there you could look at a thing monstrous and free' (p. 96). Marlow's discovery of these powerful impulses within the self brings with it the urgent need for some source of resistance:

> Let the fool gape and shudder – the man knows and can look on without a wink. But he must . . . meet that truth with his own true stuff – with his own inborn strength. Principles won't do. Acquisitions, clothes, pretty rags – rags that would fly off at the first good shake. No; you want a deliberate belief.   (p. 97)[22]

The traders are 'hollow men': the inadequacy of their fetish, the ivory, has already been shown. Kurtz's disciple, the Russian 'harlequin' (p. 122), survives untouched by the wilderness because he is one of those who is 'too much of a fool to go wrong' (p. 116). Kurtz's idealism cannot withstand the temptation of the will-to-power inscribed within it. Marlow's 'deliberate belief' now becomes the focus of narrative interest.

At the Central Station, Marlow reacted against the 'backbiting and intriguing' world of the 'pilgrims': 'It was as unreal as everything else – as the philanthropic pretence of the whole concern, as their talk, as their government, as their show of work' (p. 78). Against this unreality, Marlow located himself in his work: 'In that way only it seemed to me I could keep my hold on the redeeming facts of life' (p. 75). He goes on: 'I don't like work – no man does – but I like what is in the work, – the chance to find yourself. Your own reality – for yourself, not for others – what no other man can ever know' (p. 85). Work is a way of experiencing his own reality, his self-for-self. However, as he journeys from the Central Station to the Inner Station, the significance of work changes. It becomes not so much a way of experiencing his own inner reality as a way of protecting himself from external reality:

> I had no time. I had to keep guessing at the channel. . . . When you have to attend to things of that sort, to the mere incidents of the surface, the reality – the reality, I tell you – fades. The inner truth is hidden – luckily, luckily.   (p. 93)

Even so, the work Marlow recommends is not just any work. The work of the traders, for example, does not offer a 'surface-truth' (p. 97) that might provide protection against reality. The book Marlow finds, *An Inquiry into Some Points of Seamanship*, provides a clue to the distinction Marlow is making:

> Not a very enthralling book; but at the first glance you could see there a singleness of intention, an honest concern for the right way of going to work, which made these humble pages, thought out so many years ago, luminous with another than a professional light. The simple old sailor . . . made me forget the jungle and the pilgrims in a delicious sensation of having come upon something unmistakably real. (p. 99)

Seamanship involves 'a singleness of intention' and 'an honest concern for the right way of going to work'.[23] As in *The Nigger of the 'Narcissus'*, it embodies a code of conduct that transcends the concerns of the self:

> The earth for us is a place to live in, where we must put up with sights, with sounds, with smells, too, by Jove! – breathe dead hippo, so to speak, and not be contaminated. And there, don't you see? your strength comes in, the faith in your ability for the digging of unostentatious holes to bury the stuff in – your power of devotion, not to yourself, but to an obscure, back-breaking business. (p. 117)

In contrast to the individualism of the traders and the flawed moral idealism of Kurtz, Marlow's 'deliberate belief' implies a true altruism, a devotion 'not to yourself, but to an obscure, back-breaking business'.

In addition, this code of seamanship offers solidarity, brotherhood, kinship – a sense of community that contrasts with the 'great solitude' (p. 131) of Kurtz's struggle with the wilderness. This was already implied during the first stage of Marlow's journey on board the 'little sea-going steamer': 'Her captain was a Swede, and knowing me for a seaman, invited me on the bridge' (p. 62). The death of Marlow's helmsman produced a more explicit assertion:

> Perhaps you will think it passing strange this regret for a savage who was no more account than a grain of sand in a black Sahara.

Well, don't you see, he had done something, he had steered; for months I had him at my back – a help – an instrument. It was a kind of partnership. He steered for me – I had to look after him, I worried about his deficiencies, and thus a subtle bond had been created, of which I only became aware when it was suddenly broken.   (p. 119)

And, at the end of Chapter 2, it is as a 'brother sailor' (p. 123) that Kurtz's disciple approaches Marlow.

The disciple functions as a variant of Marlow.[24] He is the owner of Towson's *Inquiry*; he relates to Marlow in terms of 'the brotherhood of the sea'; and he, too, has formed a bond with Kurtz. Marlow, however, 'did not envy him his devotion to Kurtz': 'to me it appeared about the most dangerous thing in every way he had come upon so far' (p. 127). It is Marlow, in the end, who engages with the threat embodied in the bond with Kurtz. For Marlow, Kurtz represents the evil potential of unbridled human instinct and appetite: 'I saw him open his mouth wide – it gave him a wierdly voracious aspect, as though he had wanted to swallow all the air, all the earth, all the men before him' (p. 134).

Kurtz, like Willems earlier, embodies a fear of the uncontrolled and appetitive aspects of instinctive behaviour, and Marlow confronts this aspect of the self when he struggles with Kurtz:

If anybody had ever struggled with a soul, I am the man . . . his intelligence was perfectly clear. . . . But his soul was mad. Being alone in the wilderness, it had looked within itself, and, by heavens! I tell you, it had gone mad. I had – for my sins, I suppose – to go through the ordeal of looking into it myself.   (pp. 144–5)

Marlow is like the narrator of Poe's story, 'A Descent into the Maelström': he sees into the abyss, but he has the means whereby to prevent himself from falling in.[25]

V

In the last section of Chapter 3, Marlow returns to Europe:

I found myself back in the sepulchral city resenting the sight of people hurrying through the streets to filch a little money from each other. . . . Their bearing, which was simply the bearing of commonplace individuals going about their business in the assurance of perfect safety, was offensive to me like the outrageous flauntings of folly in the face of a danger it is unable to comprehend.   (p. 152)

The same tone of hostility has made itself heard, during the course of the narrative, in some of Marlow's addresses to his audience:

You can't understand. How could you? – with solid pavement under your feet, surrounded by kind neighbours ready to cheer you or to fall on you, stepping delicately between the butcher and the policeman, in the holy terror of scandal and gallows and lunatic asylums.   (p. 116)

He is critical of their complacency, protected, as they are, by social conventions and institutions from experiencing the full force of their own appetites: the policeman provides an external check; the butcher is an essential part of the process that dissociates food from the killing of animals. In this world, issues need not be faced because the 'inner truth' is concealed.[26]

Yet this explains only part of Marlow's bitterness of tone. His meeting with Kurtz's 'Intended' explains the rest. The 'Intended' asks to hear Kurtz's last words, because she wants something 'to live with' (p. 161), but Marlow has already stated that 'No eloquence could have been so withering to one's belief in mankind as his final burst of sincerity' (p. 145). Marlow opts for the 'saving illusion' (p. 159): he betrays himself and his sense of truth to protect the 'Intended' and her idealistic 'woman's world'.[27] Marlow's exploration of the 'heart of darkness' ends in this complex compromise: the maintaining of an illusion with a clear awareness of its illusory nature at the expense of his own honesty and truth. Indeed, this meeting forces a double 'choice of sides' upon Marlow. He experiences not only the superimposition of the 'Intended's' 'I have survived' upon Kurtz's 'summing up whisper of his eternal condemnation' (p. 157), but also the opposition of the 'Intended' to Kurtz's African mistress (p. 160). Where the 'Intended' is associated with light, death, insubstantiality (pp. 156–7), the African woman is identified with the 'fecund and mysterious life' of the 'wilderness'; she is, as it were, 'the image of its own tenebrous and passionate soul' (pp. 135–6). Marlow's descent into the self has uncovered fearful appetites and instincts; it has revealed the inadequacy of both mercenary values and of individual idealism; and it has shown the ideal code of conduct as merely a survival-strategy. His journey ends with the bitter choice of the illusion of idealism over the truth and life of instinct. Where 'The Rescuer' embodied Lingard's desire to live in a domain 'governed by his impulse, nearer his desire' (p. 175), and enacted his struggle to express and realise that buried self, 'Heart of Darkness' uncovers appetites and instincts that it prefers to suppress.

VI

Conrad started work on *Lord Jim* before he wrote 'Heart of Darkness', but 'Heart of Darkness' was completed in 1899, whereas *Lord Jim* was not finished until 1900.[28] The two works are very closely connected, and indeed can be seen as, in some ways, complementary. Conrad wrote to Meldrum about *Lord Jim*: 'It has not been planned to stand alone. *H of D* was meant in my mind as a foil, and *Youth* was supposed to give the note.'[29] Where 'Heart of Darkness' explores the instinctive self, *Lord Jim* separates the ideal code of conduct and the self-ideal in order to explore the self-deception of the self-ideal. *Lord Jim* goes back to the theme of Conrad's first two novels – the self in the dream, but, this time, the character's self-ideal is based on ideas of heroism and selflessness. More significantly, *Lord Jim* separates what was mingled and confused in the figure of Lingard. As C. F. Burgess notes, 'Jim is subject to two codes, the code of the craft, and a highly personal code of his own devising which has to do with his romantic vision of himself as "a man destined to shine in the midst of dangers" '.[30] Jim has been taught a code of seamanship, that, as *The Nigger of the 'Narcissus'* made clear, includes ideas of responsibility and duty that are both practical rules and social laws. At the same time, Jim acts according to a romantic vision of himself. As Paul Wiley noted, Jim's 'habit of living in a mental world of romantic adventure which exceeds the possibilities of the milieu in which he is placed' means that he resembles 'more than any other early characters of Conrad' such characters as Madame Bovary and Frederic Moreau.[31] In the first half of *Lord Jim*, Jim is judged in terms of the ideal code of conduct that he has betrayed, but judgement is complicated because he is also being judged, particularly by himself, in terms of his romantic self-ideal; in the second half of the novel, Jim is apparently allowed to redeem himself and to realise this self-ideal; but, in the final pages, this ideal itself is judged and evaluated.

Lord Jim was to have been concerned solely with the episode on board the *Patna*: it would have been the story of the crew deserting a ship they think is going to sink. Paul Wiley observes:

> Had the story ended with his leap from the *Patna*, [Jim] would have remained only a more sensitive and well-meaning example of inner weakness which results in the double betrayal of the self and of other men.[32]

In the novel, the *Patna* episode becomes the crucial action that colours and influences a whole life. It leaves Jim with a public fact that conflicts with his private image of himself, and the first half of the novel depicts Jim's consciousness of the lesion between identity-for-self and identity-for-the-other, or, rather, Jim's struggle 'to save from the fire his idea of what his moral identity should be' (p. 81). This personal drama, however, is intermeshed with Jim's betrayal of the ideal code of the sea, and it is only by disentangling the two that the drama of the self-ideal can be appreciated. In the second half of the novel, Jim cuts himself off from the sea and the 'white world' which has witnessed his failure. Jim's retirement to Patusan is the equivalent of the move, in the second half of 'The Rescuer', towards 'The Shore of Refuge', except that 'The Shore of Refuge' was associated with both the instincts and romantic idealism. Having explored an area of instincts in 'Heart of Darkness', Conrad concentrates on romantic idealism in *Lord Jim*.[33] As Robert Secor suggests, the events of Patusan 'are all wish fulfillments of the romantic consciousness' and 'the whole Patusan episode can be seen as an externalisation of Jim's inner world'.[34] What Dickens did unconsciously with the Brownlow–Maylie world of *Oliver Twist*, Conrad does consciously with the world of Patusan: Patusan is a romantic escape-world in which the dream is allowed to come true so that the dream, and the corresponding self-ideal, can be evaluated.[35]

The narrative of *Lord Jim* falls into three sections, each of which is focussed on a particular, critical decision: the first decision occurs on board the training ship, where, in an anticipatory parallel to the main action, Jim's failure to live up to his self-ideal and also his evasion of the knowledge of that failure are both displayed; the second decision occurs on board the *Patna*, when Jim leaves the ship; the third decision takes place in Patusan, when Jim is confronted with Gentleman Brown. *Lord Jim* begins with a brief description of Jim – his deceptively good appearance 'spotlessly neat, apparelled in immaculate white' (p. 3) – and a brief account of his life as a water-clerk. This account ends with a mystery: why does this popular and respectable-looking water-clerk keep giving up good jobs for inadequate reasons? The only clue is the thematic concern with 'Ability in the abstract' and the capacity to 'demonstrate it practically' (p. 3): 'He was a seaman in exile from the sea, and had Ability in the abstract, which is good for no other work but that of a water-clerk' (pp. 4–5). The rest of the first chapter is taken up with an account of Jim's boyhood that leads up towards the incident on the training ship. This analepsis elaborates on that opposition of 'abstract' and 'practical'. Jim is a parson's son who turned to the sea 'after a course of light holiday literature' (p. 5):

> He saw himself saving people from sinking ships, cutting away masts in a hurricane, swimming through a surf with a line; or as a lonely castaway, barefooted and half-naked, walking on uncovered reefs in search of shell-fish to stave off starvation. He confronted savages on tropical shores, quelled mutinies on the high seas, and in small boat upon the ocean kept up the hearts of despairing men – always an example of devotion to duty, and as unflinching as a hero in a book.   (p. 6)

Like Emma Bovary, Jim is full of romantic illusions derived from a reading of romantic literature. More specifically, his identity-for-self is constructed through the light literature he has been reading, but this identity is confronted with consciously anti-romantic experiences: Jim's sea-life is a counter-version of the 'sea-life of light literature'.[36] He does not save 'people from sinking ships', he does not keep up the hearts of his companions 'in a small boat upon the ocean', he is far from being 'an example of devotion to duty'.

The incident on board the training ship is proleptic of Jim's future career. Jim dreams heroic dreams from his station 'in the fore-top': 'and often from there he looked down, with the contempt of a man destined to shine in the midst of dangers, at the peaceful multitude of roofs' (p. 6). But, while he dreams these dreams, he fails to take part in a real rescue, and this juxtaposition of imagined success and actual failure provides a further clue to the mystery of Jim's behaviour. It reveals Jim's elevated self-ideal and prefigures Jim's failure to live up to that ideal on board the *Patna*. More important, it demonstrates Jim's psychic processes. Jim is immobilised by real danger (p. 7), but then, like Willems, preserves his self-ideal through a series of self-deceiving manoevres:

> The tumult and the menace of wind and sea now appeared very contemptible to Jim. . . . It seemed to him he cared nothing for the gale. He could affront greater perils. He would do so – better than anybody. . . . When all men flinched, then – he felt sure – he alone would know how to deal with the spurious menace of wind and seas. (pp. 8–9)

Once he achieves this posture of contempt for the 'menace of wind and sea' (and for the real hero of the incident), his self-ideal is safe.

The second stage of the narrative begins in Chapter 2 with the start of Jim's nautical career: after two years of training he went to sea, and 'entering the regions so well known to his imagination, found them strangely barren of adventure' (p. 10). Jim has not found the adventurous existence he had imagined; at the same time, because of his romantic expectations, he has missed the reward that might be gained from 'the prosaic severity of the daily task' (p. 10). Jim's pursuit of romance is a betrayal of reality. Jim's imaginative involvement in a fantasy-world in support of his heroic identity-for-self entails a psychic withdrawal from the real world, and re-inforces the lesion between identity-for-self and identity-for-the-other.

Jim's response to the only threatening experience of his sea-career up to this time, the storm at sea, is not at all reassuring about 'the fibre of his stuff' (p. 10). As in the incident on board the training ship, he experiences 'the anger of the sea' (p. 10) as a 'sinister violence of intention' aimed specifically at him and is overwhelmed by it. Accordingly, when he is 'disabled' by a falling spar, his disablement seems more psychological than physical. The accident breaks through the protective barrier of his fantasy world, and the sudden experience of reality plunges him into 'an abyss of unrest' (p. 11). Jim's subsequent, desperate desire for 'escape' finds its object in the East.

In the hospital, Jim breathes in 'the bewitching breath of the Eastern waters' with its 'suggestions of infinite repose' (p. 12). The temptation embodied by the East is explored through an analysis of the two kinds of white men Jim meets in the town: the dreamers and the idlers. The 'dreamers' are adventurers (like Lingard), who 'appeared to live in a crazy maze of plans, hopes, dangers, enterprises, ahead of civilisation, in the dark places of the sea' (pp. 12–13). The idlers – officers, like Jim, 'thrown there by some accident' – had now 'a horror of the home service, with its harder conditions, severer view of duty, and the hazard of stormy oceans'. They were 'attuned to the eternal peace of Eastern sky and sea' and 'in all they said – in their actions, in their looks, in their persons – could be detected the soft spot, the place of decay, the determination to lounge safely through existence' (p. 13). Jim's decision to take a berth as chief mate of the *Patna* identifies him with this second group. He evidently chooses the diminished danger of this existence, because of the fear he experienced when confronted by the storm at sea. In addition, the sense of security he now experiences, 'the great certitude of unbounded safety and peace' (p. 17), becomes the ground for 'the adventurous freedom of his thoughts' (p. 21):

> At such times his thoughts would be full of valorous deeds: he loved those dreams and the success of his imaginary achievements. They were the best parts of life, its secret truth, its hidden reality. (p. 20)

Jim has arranged his life in such a way that his identity-for-self is a secret self that is deliberately prevented from realisation in order to protect it from challenges from reality. By the same process, his actions in the real world are regarded as irrelevant to his true identity: 'the quality of these men did not matter; he rubbed shoulders with them, but they could not touch him; he shared the air they breathed, but he was different' (pp. 24–5). Unfortunately, the universe is not 'a safe universe' (p. 17), and this withdrawal of identity-for-self into a fantasised world becomes a severe handicap: fantasising becomes the dominant mode of being and prevents effective intervention in the real world. This was evident in Jim's response to the accident on board the training ship. It is even more obvious when the *Patna*, with its 800 passengers, runs into something at night. Jim is at last faced with that test of his fibre which he has so far missed, and his failure presents him with a fact that contraverts his long-held identity-for-self.

At this point, the narrative jumps a month to the time of the trial. This temporal dislocation conceals what has happened from the reader, and Conrad takes advantage of our ignorance to mislead us: Jim describes how one of the passengers clung to him 'like a drowning man' (p. 90); Marlow suggests that 'the incident was as completely devoid of importance as the flooding of an ant-heap' (p. 93). Both images suggest that the ship sank, and that the passengers drowned, so that Jim is judged as if he were responsible for the deaths of the pilgrims. The narrative method emphasises the situation that faced Jim when he jumped. Morally, it is irrelevant whether the passengers survived: Jim's action is what matters not the consequences. Jim has betrayed his social responsibility, and betrayed the code of conduct of the sea, by day-dreaming while on watch and by deserting the ship, leaving the passengers to drown.[37]

As far as the Inquiry is concerned, the judgement on Jim is a foregone conclusion: 'There was no incertitude as to facts – as to the one material fact, I mean' (p. 56). The Inquiry is interested in only 'the superficial how' not 'the fundamental why' (p. 56), and Jim is manifestly guilty. Similarly, there is no doubt that Jim has failed to live up to the ideal code of the sea.[38] But both of these judgements are irrelevant to Jim's experience of the problem. As Ian Watt has pointed out, Jim does not feel guilt at his failure to live up to the code of the sea, but shame at failing to live up to his sense of himself.[39] Jim's experience at the Inquiry involves not a questioning of his identity-for-self, but rather a sense of entrapment as he attempts to reconcile his identity-for-self with the facts of the case:

> This had not been a common affair, everything in it had been of the utmost importance, and fortunately he remembered everything . . . his mind positively flew round and round the serried circle of facts that had surged up all about him to cut him off from the rest of his kind: it was like a creature that, finding itself imprisoned within an enclosure of high stakes, dashes round and round, distracted in the night, trying to find a weak spot, a crevice, a place to scale, some opening through which it may squeeze itself and escape. (p. 31)

Jim is suddenly in the position where he has to bring identity-for-self and identity-for-the-other into line. Instead, he finds his secret self shut in by the facts, since he cannot present the facts in such a way as to tally with his heroic self-image. At the same time, he is unwilling to surrender that identity-for-self by allowing it to be challenged by the facts.

This is presented more clearly in Jim's conversation with Marlow in the Malabar Hotel. Having failed to find confirmation of his identity-for-self in the public confession of the Inquiry, Jim tries again in his private confession to Marlow. Marlow, however, is aware of the conflict within him: 'He would be confident and depressed all in the same breath, as if some conviction of innate blamelessness had checked the truth writhing within him at every turn' (p. 79). He knows that Jim is 'trying to explain' (p. 92) away the discovery he has made about himself, and that he is using various 'artful dodges to escape from the grim shadow of self-knowledge' (p. 80). The outcome of Jim's struggle is never in doubt:

> I could see in his glance darted into the night all his inner being carried on, projected headlong into the fanciful realm of recklessly heroic aspirations. . . . With every instant he was penetrating deeper into the impossible world of romantic achievements. (p. 83)

The conversation between Marlow and Jim begins with Jim's assertion of his own blamelessness. He cannot face his father again, not because he feels guilty, but because he 'could never explain' and his father 'wouldn't understand' (p. 79). Indeed, Jim shows no sense of guilt at his action, but only regret for the 'lost opportunity': 'My God! what a chance missed!' (p. 83). Jim's subsequent account of his 'jump' reveals how he has achieved this sense of 'blamelessness': '"I had jumped . . ." He checked himself, averted his gaze . . . "It seems", he added' (p. 111). He has dissociated the part of himself that motivated the jump, and he has made it into something external to himself 'as though he had not acted but had suffered himself to be handled by the infernal powers who had selected him for the victim of their practical joke' (p. 108). Like Willems, he seeks to place the blame for his actions outside himself – if not on 'the infernal powers', then at least on his companions: 'It was their doing as plainly as if they had reached up with a boat-hook and pulled me over' (p. 123).

Nevertheless, he cannot escape from the fact of the 'jump'. He realises that it is an irrevocable act: 'There was no going back. It was as if I had jumped into a well – into an everlasting deep hole' (p. 111).

For Jim, as for Willems earlier, the threatened loss of the identity-for-self is experienced as, literally, a fate worse than death, and Jim, like Willems, plays with the idea of suicide (p. 129). Jim's response, however, is to re-assert his identity-for-self: hence his presence at the Inquiry. If he did not act heroically on board the *Patna*, he has found a response to that failure that allows him to act according to his elevated sense of his own identity – even though this response brands him with an identity-for-the-other sharply at odds with his identity-for-self. By this manoeuvre, however, Jim seeks to transform his failure into a moral and psychological challenge: it is now his duty to 'wait for another chance' (p. 139) to prove himself.

At the same time, however, Jim has not completely regained his former sense of himself. As Marlow is aware, there is another kind of struggle taking place within him:

> He was not speaking to me, he was only speaking before me, in a dispute with an invisible personality, an antagonistic and insep-arable partner of his existence – another possessor of his soul. (p. 93)

There is not just a lesion between identity-for-self and identity-for-the-other, there is also now a repressed aspect of self that asserts itself against the apparently successfully maintained heroic self-image. The clearest indication of this repressed aspect of self comes, during the Inquiry, in the incident involving the yellow dog outside the court-room. Jim's immediate reaction to the words 'Look at that wretched cur' (p. 70) not only reveals his awareness of how others regard him but is also a sign of Jim's own secret doubts about his own worth. The 'inseparable partner' (p. 93) of his existence is a much less glamorous sense of himself than his heroic identity-for-self, and the stimulus and accompaniment to his continued assertion of that heroic identity is not so much self-confidence as self-doubt.

VII

If the focus of the novel is Jim's inner life, the narrative interest is not so much the presentation of that inner life as the drama of Marlow's intense probing of it; and most of the first part of *Lord Jim* is taken up with Marlow's private investigation. It is also important to notice that where Jim is concerned primarily with his idealised self-image, Marlow's main interest is the threat that Jim's failure poses to the larger community who live by the code of the sea.

Marlow's initial interest in the case arises from Jim's deceptive appearance:

> There he stood, clean-limbed, clean-faced, firm on his feet, as promising a boy as the sun ever shone on; and, looking at him, knowing all he knew and a little more too, I was as angry as though I had detected him trying to get something out of me by false pretences. He had no business to look so sound. I thought to myself – well, if this sort can go wrong like that . . .   (p. 40)

Jim's appearance challenges Marlow's faith in his own judgement; more specifically, it threatens Marlow's sense of professional competence: 'I would have trusted the deck to that youngster on the strength of a single glance, and gone to sleep with both eyes – and, by Jove! it wouldn't have been safe' (p. 45). Marlowe's involvement with Jim springs, in part, from their membership of 'an obscure body of men held together by a community of inglorious toil and by fidelity to a certain standard of conduct' (p. 50). Jim's infidelity is a threat both to that sense of 'community' and to the idea of 'the sovereign power enthroned in a fixed standard of conduct' (p. 50). Jim's failure suggests that there might be temptations that that 'fixed standard' might not be strong enough to withstand, and Marlow's definition of 'the instinct of courage' shows how directly personal that threat is:

> I don't mean military courage, or civil courage, or any special kind of courage. I mean just that inborn ability to look temptations straight in the face – a readiness unintellectual enough, goodness knows, but without pose – a power of resistance . . . an unthinking and blessed stiffness before the outward and inward terrors, before the might of nature, and the seductive corruption of men. (p. 43)

There is an obvious continuity between Marlow's concern with 'courage' in *Lord Jim* and his search for 'inborn strength' (p. 97) in 'Heart of Darkness'. It is not just a question of Marlow's trust in Jim's appearance, it is also a question of Marlow's trust in himself. The idea of 'brotherhood' turns back on Marlow: Jim's failure raises the possibility of weaknesses in himself: 'From weakness that may lie hidden, watched or unwatched, prayed against or manfully scorned, repressed or maybe ignored more than half a lifetime, not one of us is safe' (p. 43).

This area is explored through Captain Brierly, one of the assessors at the Inquiry. Brierly is a crack skipper, who has done the kind of things Jim dreams of doing: 'He had saved lives at sea, had rescued ships in distress' (p. 57). His identity-for-the-other recalls the earlier description of Jim's identity-for-self. He is successful and 'acutely aware of his merits': he had 'never in his life made a mistake, never had an accident, never a mishap, never a check in his steady rise', and he seemed to be 'one of those lucky fellows who know nothing of indecision, much less of self-mistrust' (p. 57). But that word 'self-mistrust' reverberates through the account of his suicide, which takes place a week after the trial. Brierly, like Marlow, experiences Jim's failure both as a threat to 'the brotherhood of the sea' and as a threat to his own self-confidence:

> We aren't an organised body of men, and the only thing that holds us together is just the name for that sort of decency. Such an affair destroys one's confidence. A man may go pretty near through his whole sea-life without any call to show a stiff upper lip. But when the call comes . . . Aha! . . . If I . . .   (p. 68)

Jim's failure allows self-doubt to enter his unreflective self-confidence: Jim forces Brierly to face, for the first time, the possibility of inadequacy.

Brierly also provides an illuminating parallel to Jim by reason of his sense of superiority, his immaculate appearance, and this subtle flaw. The nature of the flaw is suggested in Brierly's words: 'the *only* thing that holds us together is just the *name* for that sort of decency' (p. 68). Ian Watt has drawn attention to the significance of these two words: Brierly, like Jim, lives for a self-image that incorporates an alterated identity.[40] Brierly has seen that self-image reflected in the consciousness of others: Jim has yet to experience that alignment of identity-for-self and identity-for-the-other. Nevertheless, the personality-structure is basically the same, as will be revealed with the arrival of Gentleman Brown in Patusan. Brown has the same effect on Jim as Jim has on Brierly: he represents a secret fear and a secret guilt, the self-mistrust that is part of a personality constructed on identification with an alterated identity. He speaks to that 'inseparable partner' (p. 93), that repressed aspect of Jim's self, that Marlow detected earlier.

Another part of Jim's effect on Brierly springs from the ambiguity of Jim's moral position. Jim's action in deserting the *Patna* links him with the ship's other officers, but he refuses to accept the identity-for-the-other that the action implies. This disturbs Brierly's framework of beliefs just as Willems's incomplete rascality, evidenced by his refusal to act guiltily, undermined Lingard's. For Marlow, on the other hand, Jim's decision to face the Inquiry demonstrates 'a kind of courage' (p. 66) and represents 'a redeeming feature in his abominable case' (p. 68). This idea is explored in Marlow's next two encounters: with the French lieutenant and with Chester.

It was the French lieutenant who actually brought the *Patna* into harbour. He presents an image of heroism that is diametrically opposed to the self-image of Jim's heroic dreams. Where Jim's appearance is precisely that of a certain kind of hero in boys' adventure-romances – 'an inch, perhaps two, under six feet, powerfully built and . . . spotlessly neat, apparelled in immaculate white' (p. 3) – the French lieutenant's appearance is distinctly 'unheroic':

> He was a quiet, massive chap in a creased uniform sitting drowsily over a tumbler half-full of some dark liquid. His shoulder-straps were a bit tarnished, his clean-shaved cheeks were large and sallow; he looked like a man who would be given to taking snuff. (p. 138)[41]

There is also a significant difference in their attitude to fear, as Marlow's narration suggests:

> 'The fear, the fear – look you – it is always there.' . . . He touched his breast near a brass button on the very spot where Jim had given a thump to his own when protesting that there was nothing the matter with his heart . . . 'Given a certain combination of circumstances, fear is sure to come.' (p. 146)

The French lieutenant acknowledges his fear and lives 'with that truth' (p. 146). Jim is unable to handle his fear, in part at least, because he feels it is inconsistent with the heroism to which he aspires, and his declaration of fearlessness involves a dramatic gesture whose very nature as a dramatic gesture suggests the inauthenticity of the heroism it is intended to assert. The French lieutenant's self-effacing, laconic manner ('One does what one can' – p. 140) shows up Jim's self-dramatisation. Further, as the French lieutenant goes on to explain, there is a world of difference between acknowledging one's fear and allowing one's fear to dictate a dishonorable course of action:

> I contended that one may get on knowing very well that one's courage does not come of itself. . . . But the honour . . . that is real – that is! And what life may be worth when . . . the honour is gone . . . I can offer no opinion.   (p. 148)

The French lieutenant's code of honour rejects Jim as firmly as the code of the sea. If Jim is to be 'redeemed', it cannot be in terms of either of these codes.

Marlow's meeting with Chester provides a different perspective on Jim's position. Chester's values are clearly contrasted with those of the French lieutenant and those of Jim. In contrast to Jim's illusions, he represents a 'realism' that is a cynical, amoral selfishness.[42] The fact that Jim has taken 'to heart' (p. 162) his disgrace in the Inquiry is, for Chester, a failing on Jim's part, and his view of Jim's lost master's certificate is characteristically reductive: 'What's all the to-do about? A bit of ass's skin' (p. 161). Chester repeatedly asserts that Jim is 'no good' (p. 161), but it is precisely because of this that he is interested in him for one of his own projects. Chester's interest in Jim spurs Marlow on to rescue him (p. 174), just as Chester's appraisal of him paradoxically serves to save him from the French lieutenant's evaluation of him. The French lieutenant and Chester represent opposite poles but, from their opposed positions, they agree in defining Jim as 'no good'. Marlow's task is to find a *tertium quid*, a middle way between these extremes, to match his sense that there is more to Jim than either Chester or the French lieutenant can perceive.

VIII

Chapter 15 begins with Marlow's rescue of Jim, which echoes Lingard's rescue of Willems from his suicidal drift:

I caught sight of Jim leaning over the parapet of the quay. Three native boatmen quarrelling over five annas were making an awful row at his elbow. He didn't hear me come up, but spun round as if the slight contact of my finger had released a catch. 'I was looking,' he stammered.   (p. 170)

Marlow, initially, provides Jim with a refuge in which to come to terms with himself. The imagery used to describe this struggle again recalls Willems: Jim, like Willems, experiences the collapsing, up-rooting, and undermining of his world, and the overwhelming of his sense of identity by external reality, despite which he struggles to find some way to continue living like 'a swimmer fighting for his life' (p. 18). By Chapter 17, Jim seems to have succeeded. The first clue to Jim's 'solution' is supplied by his response to Marlow's offered help. He is, at first, unresponsive to Marlow's concern with 'the material aspect of his position' (p. 182), but when Marlow draws attention to the trust his help implies, Jim immediately latches on to this as psychological support: ' "You have given me confidence," he declared, soberly' (p. 185). Jim is keen to read Marlow's material assistance as a sign of faith in his identity-for-self, while Marlow is at pains to disclaim any such intention. It is significant that, as this conversation with Marlow continues, Jim talks not, as earlier, of the need for another chance to prove himself, but of a desire to begin again with a 'clean slate' (p. 185). Jim is once more trying to deny responsibility for his 'jump', and this explains the difficulties he experiences in the next phase of his life (before he goes to Patusan). Jim acts as if Marlow had, indeed, given him a 'clean slate', whereas the truth is that Jim cannot escape from public knowledge of his past: 'It was almost pathetic to see him go about in sunshine hugging his secret, which was known to the very up-country logs on the river' (p. 198). It is not surprising that Jim's past constantly rises up before him to confront him. The problem, however, is not so much that others reject him because of his past, but that Jim himself is unable to live with the idea that others know 'his secret'.[43] His repeated flights emphasise the lesion between his identity-for-self and his identity-for-the-other: Jim's identity-for-the-other includes the fact of his failure on board the *Patna*, while his identity-for-self denies that fact. Jim has not come to terms with his past actions. He cannot reconcile those actions with his self-image, and he is trying to 'bury' the conflict rather than resolve it.

Marlow now realises that he 'had given him many opportunities, but they had been merely opportunities to earn his bread' (p. 202), whereas what Jim wants is the opportunity to realise his self-ideal. At this point, Marlow approaches Stein, who has lived a life of adventure, 'rich in generous enthusiasms, in friendship, love, war – in all the exalted elements of romance' (p. 217). Stein represents a shift in the narrative perspective from a way of thinking that rejects Jim as a failure to a way of thinking that is more sympathetic towards him – or, more specifically, a shift from the code of the sea to Romanticism.[44] Stein accepts that reality falls short of the ideal, of the dream, but he also accepts the validity of the dream:

> A man that is born falls into a dream like a man who falls into the sea. If he tries to climb out into the air as inexperienced people endeavour to do, he drowns – *nicht wahr?* . . . No! I tell you! The way is to the destructive element submit yourself, and with the exertions of your hands and feet in the water make the deep, deep sea keep you up. (p. 214)

Less metaphorically, he advises Marlow that the way 'to be' is to 'follow the dream, and again to follow the dream – and so – *ewig – usque ad finem*' (p. 215). Instead of asking Jim to modify his identity-for-self in the light of his past failures, Stein counsels the maintenance of that identity-for-self and perseverance in attempting to realise it. What matters is not loyalty to a code of conduct, but fidelity to a dream, and past failures do not invalidate a dream (p. 217). At this point, the narrative moves to Patusan.

IX

Brierly's advice for Jim had been 'Let him creep twenty feet underground and stay there' (p. 219). Patusan is, from one angle, a grave for Jim: the story of Jewel's mother prompts Marlow to observe that 'once before Patusan had been used as a grave for some sin, transgression, or misfortune' (p. 219). From another angle, Patusan offers Jim the 'clean slate' for which he had asked: 'He left his earthly failings behind him and that sort of reputation he had, and there was a totally new set of conditions for his imaginative faculty to work upon' (p. 218). The imagery of the grave is also cancelled out by the description of the moon that casts its light over Marlow's first account of Patusan: the full moon, rising behind the hills, floats up the sky 'as if escaping from a yawning grave in gentle triumph' (p. 221).[45] Jim, in Patusan, is re-born into the conditions of heroic existence. Marlow affirms at the outset that Jim 'had achieved greatness' (p. 225), even if that affirmation is somewhat modified when he adds, later, 'greatness as genuine as any man ever achieved' (p. 244). Jim attains the heroic achievements he had sought – the 'conquest of love, honour, men's confidence' (p. 226) – although, again, Marlow immediately begins a subtle undermining of the 'heroic' by describing the adventurers and traders who first visited Patusan. Their 'heroic' deeds were motivated by a desire for pepper, and Marlow comments on the difficulty of believing that 'mere greed could hold men to such a steadfastness of purpose, to such a blind persistence in endeavour and sacrifice' (pp. 226–7). From the start of Jim's exploits in Patusan, Marlow's commentary provides an ironising, questioning frame.

The conditions of Jim's new life are 'utter insecurity for life and property' (p. 228). This is in sharp contrast to the security Jim thought he had found on board the *Patna*: a sense of security that provided the basis for Jim's escapes into heroic fantasy. In Patusan, he has been given 'a refuge at the cost of danger' (p. 230). He has made 'a jump into the unknown' (p. 229).[46] But the life of risks that Jim has chosen allows him no time for fantasy. This is partly because Jim's life in Patusan is itself the fulfillment of a fantasy: the conditions of Jim's life are consciously those of popular heroic romance. Where Jim's sea-life was a counter-version of the heroic sea-life of popular fiction, Jim's life in Patusan is a self-conscious version of popular colonial romance. The silver ring that Jim is given by Stein as a talismanic token and Doramin's pistols (which were the present Doramin had received from Stein in exchange for the ring) are precisely, as Jim says, 'like something you read of in books' (pp. 233–4). Similarly, Doramin and Dain Waris are, as Jim also says, 'like people in a book' (p. 260). The story of Jim's relations with Doramin's family forms a tightly plotted adventure-romance: there is Jim's friendship with Dain Waris which repeats Stein's friendship with Doramin, and there is the pathetic irony of the involvement of the silver ring and the pistols in the description of Jim's death. The first part of Marlow's account of Patusan is organised by two romantic stories: the story of the assault on Sherif Ali's stronghold and the story of Jim's love for

Jewel. This second story, in particular, is presented as a self-conscious version of a stereotyped romance pattern. Marlow begins, 'We have heard so many such stories', and this, apparently, is 'a story very much like the others' (p. 275). Later, he links 'their romance' to an older romance pattern: 'they came together under the shadow of a life's disaster, like knight and maiden meeting to exchange vows amongst haunted ruins' (pp. 311–12). It is hardly necessary for Marlow to say, as he does, that 'Romance had singled Jim for its own' (p. 282).

These two stories, the war-story and the love-story, have a common thematic element: trust. Jim describes his relationship with Jewel as 'a trust' (p. 304). His steadfastness during the attack on Sherif Ali's stronghold was because 'those people had trusted him implicitly' (p. 268). And trust continues to provide the bond in his day-to-day life in Patusan: 'Look at these houses; there's not one where I am not trusted' (p. 246). Jim's identity-for-self now corresponds to his identity-for-the-other. He has followed his dream, and his dream has been realised in Patusan. Nevertheless, there is still a small, niggling doubt. He tells Marlow: 'I must feel – every day, every time I open my eyes – that I am trusted – that nobody has a right – don't you know?' (p. 247). What begins as an affirmation of his achievement changes gradually into a revelation of his continuing insecurity. If the people of Patusan need him and trust him, he, in turn, needs their trust: 'all these things that made him master and made him a captive, too' (p. 247). The need to feel trusted expresses a need for reassurance about his trustworthiness, and Jim's tentative affirmation 'that nobody has a right' is a reminder why he feels this need. Even if nobody else in Patusan knows of Jim's past failures, Jim does: Jim's need to feel that others trust him springs from his own awareness that he has betrayed such trust in the past.

Although Patusan has offered Jim a 'clean slate' and has given him the chance to realise his heroic self-image, there is still a part of himself that is not satisfied. The 'clean slate' has its own drawbacks:

'Is it not strange,' he went on . . . 'that all these people, all these people who would do anything for me, can never be made to understand? Never! . . . If you ask them who is brave – who is true – who is just – who is it they would trust with their own lives? – they would say, Tuan Jim. And yet they can never know the real, real truth . . . ' (p. 305)

He has realised his heroic self-image, but he feels disappointed. He wants not just confirmation of his self-image, but a confirmation that acknowledges his past failure. He wants his past to be fully lived down, not just concealed, as it is in Patusan. For all his regained self-confidence, that concealed past remains as a potential source of guilt and insecurity, an unexorcised doubt about himself, and it marks a continuing gap between his own sense of himself and his identity-for-the-other. Jim has successfully established his false-self system but the buried conflict over which it has been built continues to make itself felt. Jim experiences not the inanition of the false-self system (as Willems did) but guilt at its falseness and at his own inauthenticity.

This is enacted in the narrative through dealings with the 'white' world. If Jim's existence in Patusan corresponds to the false-self system, his awareness of his past and of the larger 'white' world functions as an involuntary awareness of another mode of being, associated with feelings of shame and guilt: the shame of his failure on board the *Patna* to live up to his self-ideal; the guilt connected with that failure which he has never confronted; and the further guilt that arises from that evasion – an existential guilt about his own inauthenticity. Jewel's fears of the 'white' world, Jim's awareness of his past failure, and this complex knot of guilt and shame all find their focus in the confrontation with Gentleman Brown. Brown is the catalyst whose presence precipitates Jim's unresolved conflicts.

X

Brown is 'a latter-day buccaneer' (p. 352) who arrives in Patusan in search of provisions after stealing a Spanish schooner. Brown is, in some ways, a parodic version of Jim. There is, to begin with, the similarity of their titles: 'Gentleman Brown' and 'Tuan Jim'.[47] Through this similarity, the problematic nature of Brown's asserted gentility subtly subverts Jim's status in Patusan. More important, Brown (like Jim) constructs his identity around a sense of his own pre-eminence: he has 'a blind belief in the righteousness of his will against all mankind' (p. 370), and this belief is enacted in his response to the inhabitants of Patusan. After the repulse of his attempt to approach the settlement, Brown is displayed in Coriolan mood 'working himself into a fury of hate and rage against those people who *dared* to

defend themselves' (p. 359). The basis of Brown's character, however, is merely 'intense egoism' (p. 344), whereas Jim is motivated by
'a sort of sublimated, idealised selfishness' (p. 177). His egoism finds
expression in aggression, ruthlessness, 'and a vehement scorn for
mankind at large and for his victims in particular' (pp. 352–3). Brown
assures himself of his own 'superiority' by his degradation and
humiliation of others:

> He would rob a man as if only to demonstrate his poor opinion of
> the creature, and he would bring to the shooting or maiming of
> some quiet, unoffending stranger a savage and vengeful earnest-
> ness fit to terrify the most reckless of desperadoes.   (p. 353)

The combination of differences and similarities between Jim and
Brown forces the reader to discriminate between their assertions of
their self-images. It is a distinction comparable to the earlier distinction between real and sham courage, that was enforced by the French
lieutenant, and the later distinction between different kinds of 'steadfastness of purpose' (p. 227), that was encouraged by Marlow's
reference to seventeenth-century adventurers and traders. Marlow's
account of Brown's death-bed emphasises Brown's self-image (his
'illusion of having trampled all the earth under his feet' – p. 384), but
also shows that Brown was doubly self-deceived by exposing more
vulnerable sides to him, which are not part of that self-image. It
raises the possibility that following the dream might be at the expense of other aspects or potentialities of self, that might be more
valuable.

Jim and Brown, in other respects, stand at 'opposite poles of that
conception of life which includes all mankind' (p. 381). Brown's
immediate response to Jim is one of antipathy (p. 380). For Brown,
Jim represents decency, order, 'duty', 'responsibility'. In his exchanges
with Brown, Jim asserts the identity he has achieved in Patusan, but
the whole purpose of Brown's speech is to break through that asserted identity and to disclose a bond between himself and Jim.
Brown's words are designed to play on any guilt or insecurity Jim
might feel:

> 'And what do you deserve,' I shouted at him, 'you that I find
> skulking here with your mouth full of your responsibility, of
> innocent lives, of your infernal duty? . . . I came here for food. . .
> . And what did *you* come for?'   (p. 382)

A series of questions, directed against Jim's stance of moral superiority, insinuates that Brown is Jim's moral equal, if not his superior. Brown seeks to establish a bond between himself and Jim in order to short-circuit Jim's will and gain ascendancy over him:

> There ran through the rough talk a vein of subtle reference to their common blood, an assumption of common experience; a sickening suggestion of common guilt, of secret knowledge that was like a bond of their minds and of their hearts. (p. 387)

Like Wait in *The Nigger of the 'Narcissus'*, he seeks control by activating a repressed and denied aspect of the other's self.[48]

For Jim, this meeting with Brown represents the return of his past and of the shame associated with his desertion of the *Patna*. It also signifies the re-emergence of an unresolved conflict and the reappearance of doubts about his own worth. It is not just that Brown's words play on Jim's submerged feelings about the *Patna*, but, in himself, Brown also represents the white world 'out there' where Jim 'did not think himself good enough to live' (p. 385). The linking of Jim's decision in relation to Brown with his earlier action on board the *Patna* reinforces the idea that Jim's crisis in Patusan is the re-emergence of the earlier conflict rather than a completely new problem. This is evident in the treatment of Jim's betrayal of the people of Patusan. When he tells his Patusan audience that 'their welfare was his welfare, their losses his losses, their mourning his mourning' (p. 392), he asserts an identity (in both senses of the word) that, since Brown's arrival, is no longer true. In narrative terms, Jim has other interests which are, in fact, more powerful: his consciousness of the 'white' world and the *Patna* intrude upon his performance in the world of Patusan. Like Lingard in 'The Rescuer', Jim betrays his eastern commitments at the call of this white world. In psychological terms, Jim has been permitted to realise his identity-for-self as his identity-for-the-other in Patusan, but his betrayal of the people of Patusan now reveals what that identity denied:

> He had retreated from one world, for a small matter of an impulsive jump, and now the other, the work of his own hands, had fallen in ruins upon his head. . . . Everything was gone, and he who had been once unfaithful to his trust had lost again all men's confidence. (pp. 408–9)

Gentleman Brown serves to expose the falseness of Jim's false-self system, and the radical self-doubt that underlies it.

Jim's response to this catastrophe is presented with striking ambiguity. Jim accepts responsibility for the deaths that result from his misjudgement, but that acceptance of responsibility is also an attempt to 'prove his power in another way and conquer the fatal destiny itself' (p. 410). Jim's acceptance of responsibility apparently pays for his error of judgement in Patusan, as well as his earlier failure on board the *Patna*.[49] However, this acceptance of responsibility is, at the same time, an assertion of Jim's heroic self-image: it is, in fact, one of the few ways left in which that self-image can be asserted since the world Jim had created for it has been destroyed. And the way in which that self-image is asserted maintains the fictional mode of the false-self system: Jim's death is the summation of the romance-pattern that shapes the second half of the novel. In his death, Jim recovers for himself the romance world to which his identity-for-self belongs. As Doramin stands to execute him with Stein's pistol, the romance-motifs suddenly cluster together:

> People remarked that the ring which he had dropped on his lap fell and rolled against the foot of the white man, and that poor Jim glanced down at the talisman that had opened for him the door of fame, love, and success. (p. 415)

In his death, either Jim has found the opportunity for complete self-realisation or he has made a romantic gesture that forever saves him from confronting himself.

At this point, Marlow introduces a different consideration. Having apparently accepted the conventions and values of adventure-romance for his account of Jim's life in Patusan, Marlow now suddenly shifts the terms of reference and brings the 'frame' into the picture:

> we can see him, an obscure conqueror of fame, tearing himself out of the arms of a jealous love at the sign, at the call of his exalted egoism. He goes away from a living woman to celebrate his pitiless wedding with a shadowy ideal of conduct. (p. 416)

In this opposition of the 'shadowy ideal of conduct' ('like an Eastern bride') and the 'living woman', Jewel, Marlow introduces a radical challenge to Jim's values. Even if Jim's action has redeemed his betrayal of the trust of the people of Patusan, the same action deepens his betrayal of Jewel's trust in him. He has betrayed the 'living woman' for 'a shadowy ideal': he has valued Jewel's love less than the demands of his own self-image and his 'exalted egoism'. Conrad explores this issue further, in the character of Charles Gould, in his next novel, *Nostromo*.

5

The Betrayal of Land-entanglements: *Nostromo* and *The Secret Agent*

In *The Nigger of the 'Narcissus'*, Conrad had developed a model of society, that was presented through one particular small society: the crew of a ship. In 'Heart of Darkness', Conrad had held in painful tension the ideal code of the sea and what he felt to be the terrifying potentialities of human nature. In *Lord Jim*, that ideal code and the solidarity it implies were tested against the difficulties of knowing another person or even one's own truth.[1] In the two novels that are the subject of this chapter, *Nostromo* and *The Secret Agent*, Conrad explores the political implications of his organicist model. In these novels, to use Kirschner's terms, Conrad turns from consideration of 'the self in the dream' to 'the self in society'.[2] Conrad observed that *The Nigger of the 'Narcissus'* was not primarily concerned with 'a problem of the sea': 'it is merely a problem that has arisen on board a ship where the conditions of complete isolation from all land entanglements make it stand out with a particular force and colouring'.[3] In *Nostromo*, what had before been seen as an aesthetic advantage is now perceived to be an ideological limitation. Conrad realises that the problem of values cannot be solved by creating a model that ignores 'land entanglements': the ship has to come into port; the forces of trade and money, the power of what Conrad calls 'material interests', have to be brought into the picture.[4] The organicist model is now brought into the interplay of 'material interests' which *The Nigger of the 'Narcissus'* had explicitly excluded. Critics have tended to ignore the fact that Nostromo, like Jim, is 'a seaman in exile from the sea', yet this is the key to Nostromo's behaviour, to his exalted sense of his own identity, and to one of the novel's principle thematic concerns.[5] Nostromo attempts to bring the code of the sea ashore, and his fate then reveals the relevance and usefulness of that code in a capitalist society. The ideal code of conduct is strained beyond breaking-point, and *The Secret Agent*, with its bitter ironies and its vision of an atomised society, is the product of the thorough disillusionment that follows.

I

Nostromo, written between May 1903 and September 1904, is probably Conrad's most complex and tightly organised novel. Throughout the novel, there are constant shifts in time, place, point-of-view. There are echoes, anticipations, a complex patterning of affinities and contrasts.[6] The technical mastery that Conrad displays in *Nostromo* is necessitated by the nature of his thematic concerns: the innumerable intersecting forces that create the historical event, that are involved in the processes of historical and social change. As Arnold Kettle has argued, form and technique in *Nostromo* are directed to the solution of the multitude of problems connected with trying to convey political and social movement on various levels – 'conscious, unconscious, semi-conscious' – and trying to show 'the almost infinite inter-relatedness of character and character, character and background'.[7] Accordingly, in *Nostromo*, the psychology of the characters is inseparable from the social processes in which they are enmeshed. In a letter to Ernst Bendz, Conrad wrote:

> I will take the liberty to point out that *Nostromo* [*sic*] has never been intended for the hero of the Tale of the Seaboard. Silver is the pivot of the moral and material events, affecting the lives of everybody in the tale. That this was my deliberate purpose there can be no doubt. I struck the first note of my intention in the unusual form which I gave to the title of the First Part, by calling it 'The Silver of the Mine', and by telling the story of the enchanted treasure on Azuera, which, strictly speaking, has nothing to do with the rest of the novel. The word 'silver' occurs almost at the very beginning of the story proper, and I took care to introduce it in the very last paragraph, which could, perhaps, have been better without the phrase which contains that key-word.[8]

'Silver' constitutes the centre of the novel: it operates on both the personal and the social level. And any attempt to analyse the individual psychologies of characters has to come back to the fact of the 'silver' and to the material conditions that the 'silver' points towards. In Irving Howe's words:

Between one man and another falls the silver shadow of the San Tomé mine. . . . Becoming a symbol as large and inclusive as Zola's mine, it forces the reader to see private drama as public struggle.[9]

The first chapter serves as an illustration. It describes the scene of the novel and conveys information about the past of Sulaco in order to create a solid social and historical world, but this mimetic surface is fractured by figurative language that draws attention to underlying meanings – there is a constant shifting from semic to symbolic code.[10] The first paragraph counterbalances commerce and the 'temple' of nature within the context of colonial exploitation, and the implications of this opposition are reinforced in the subsequent association of 'evil and wealth' in the story of the 'two wandering sailors' and the 'forbidden treasures' (p. 4) of the Azuera peninsula. In addition, just as Jim's experience on the training ship acted as an anticipatory parallel to his behaviour on the *Patna*, so the story of these two sailors acts as a parallel, and prototype, for various other characters in the novel:

> The two gringos, spectral and alive, are believed to be dwelling to this day amongst the rocks, under the fatal spell of their success. Their souls cannot tear themselves away from their bodies mounting guard over the discovered treasure.   (p. 5)

They provide parallels, most obviously, to Gould and Nostromo, 'the two racially and socially contrasted men, both captured by the silver of the San Tomé mine' (p. xix).

II

In *Nostromo*, Conrad presents character and action in a fragmented, multi-perspectival fashion.[11] Nostromo himself is first introduced, in the words of Captain Mitchell, as an 'invaluable fellow', 'a fellow in a thousand' (p. 12). His 'force of character' (p. 13) is confirmed in his relations with the *cargadores*. However, by the end of the first part of the novel, he still remains a shadowy figure, in the background or just out of focus, recognised by various signs – 'his black whiskers and white teeth' (p. 13) or his revolver and 'silver-grey mare' (p. 124). The catalogue of titles presented near the end of the first section is a deliberate tease:

The circle had broken up, and the lordly Capataz de Cargadores, the indispensable man, the tried and trusty Nostromo, the Mediterranean sailor come ashore casually to try his luck in Costaguana, rode slowly towards the harbour.   (p. 130)

Each phrase 'describing' Nostromo represents one aspect of his social identity, and each is qualified by the point-of-view it represents. The catalogue of titles signals a mystery: it draws attention to the lack of deeper insight into Nostromo. The titles, however, also contain the solution to the mystery. Nostromo, like Jim, has a romantic conception of himself, and he lives only to have that self-image reflected back to him. Nostromo, however, does not seek confirmation of an identity-for-self, but rather he has constructed an identity-for-self through identification with his alterated identity.

One of the questions raised in Part I concerns Nostromo's motivation:

'The fellow is devoted to me, body and soul!' Captain Mitchell was given to affirm; and though nobody, perhaps, could have explained why it should be so, it was impossible on a survey of their relation to throw doubt on that statement.   (p. 44)

Captain Mitchell offers an explanation for Nostromo's behaviour, but the narrator problematises the explanation by raising the spectre of doubt. Another explanation is suggested by Teresa Viola in Chapter 4:

He has not stopped very long with us. There is no praise from strangers to be got here. . . . That is all he cares for. To be first somewhere – somehow – to be first with these English.   (p. 23)

Decoud makes a similar analysis: he remarks with surprise that 'the only thing he seems to care for' is 'to be well-spoken of' (p. 246). It is not until Chapter 8 that Nostromo's own view of his actions is provided:

The old Englishman who has enough money to pay for a railway? . . . I've guarded his bones all the way from the Entrada pass down to the plain and into Sulaco, as though he had been my own father. . . . And I have sat alone at night with my revolver in the Company's warehouse time and again by the side of that other

Englishman's heap of silver, guarding it as though it had been my own. (p. 125)

The tone could easily be bitter, but it is not: the narrator takes care to indicate that Nostromo makes these remarks 'carelessly' (p. 125). Nostromo accepts the situation he describes: this speech is the equivalent of those passages where Gould expresses his faith in 'material interests'. Nostromo, like Jim, has an idealised self-image, and this self-image incorporates an ideal code that includes the idea of service. Nostromo is a 'sailor come ashore' (p. 130), and he has transferred the idea of community (and of service to the community) from the ship to the town.

A further perspective is provided by his name: his loyalty of service has been rewarded with the substitution of 'Nostromo', which is Captain Mitchell's mispronunciation of 'nostro uomo' (our man), for his real name Gian' Battista.[12] 'Nostromo' expresses both a recognition of Gain' Battista's loyal service and the suggestion of his exploitation and appropriation by those he serves. These suggestions are confirmed at the start of Chapter 6:

> Clearly he was one of those invaluable subordinates whom to possess is a legitimate cause of boasting. Captain Mitchell plumed himself upon his eye for men – but he was not selfish – and in the innocence of his pride was already developing that mania for 'lending you my Capataz de Cargadores' which was to bring Nostromo into personal contact, sooner or later, with every European in Sulaco. (p. 44)

'Possess' and 'lending' bring out the reification implicit in Mitchell's attitude towards Nostromo. In *Lord Jim*, Conrad presented a character with a self-ideal, who was unable to live up to the ideal code of conduct of the sea, but was allowed a second chance to realise that self-ideal so that the self-ideal could itself be questioned. In *Nostromo*, the intertwining of ideal code and self-ideal serves a different purpose. With *Nostromo*, Conrad has realised that the values associated with the ideal code of conduct, particularly ideals of loyalty and service, do not apply when they are brought ashore: values derived from an organicist model of society cannot be applied to a society whose basis is individual assertion and the clash and competition of different interests. In such a society, ideals of service merely mean collusion in one's own exploitation.

In Part I of *Nostromo* ('The Silver of the Mine'), this meaning is implicit in the text. On the one hand, there is Nostromo's fidelity: on the other hand, there is the Costaguana society which the narrative constructs. After Guzman Bento's period of tyrannical rule, there followed a period of even greater suffering, cruelty, and corruption: 'a brazen-faced scramble for a constantly diminishing quantity of booty': 'Thus it came to pass that the province of Sulaco' had become 'one of the considerable prizes of political career' (p. 116). Mrs Gould's early travels in Costaguana produce a similar impression:

> In all these households she could hear stories of political outrage; friends, relatives, ruined, imprisoned, killed in the battles of sense-less civil wars, barbarously executed in ferocious proscriptions, as though the government of the country had been a struggle of lust between bands of absurd devils let loose upon the land with sabres and uniforms and grandiloquent phrases.   (p. 88)

This 'scramble' for booty and these 'bands of absurd devils let loose upon the land' are reminiscent of 'Heart of Darkness': Conrad's experience of colonialism in the Congo seems to underlie his picture of the recent past in Costaguana; and a similar, though more sophis-ticated, disenchantment inheres in the novel's picture of the political processes of neo-colonialism.[13] The narrative begins with Ribiera's flight to Sulaco, after his defeat in the battle of Socorro. The 'local authorities of Sulaco had fled for refuge to the O.S.N. Company's offices' (p. 12), while Captain Mitchell 'went back in his gig to see what could be done for the protection of the Company's property': 'That and the property of the railway were preserved by the Euro-pean residents' (p. 14). It is made clear later that the Europeans are protecting the property of the steamship company and the railroad because these represent the infra-structure of trade – that is, the more efficient communications that open up the country to Euro-pean exploitation. It is also implied that the 'local authorities' take refuge in the Company's offices, in part, because Don Vincente's government is controlled and financed by English and American money.

Chapter 5 begins with an analepsis to Don Ribiera's previous visit, eighteen months earlier, to initiate the building of the railroad. It shows Don Ribiera at the lunch-party on board one of the O.S.N. Company ships, sitting 'smiling urbanely between the representa-tives of two friendly foreign powers' who 'had come with him from

Sta. Marta to countenance by their presence the enterprise in which the capital of their countries was engaged' (p. 34). The lunch-party links Don Vincente Ribiera and the aristocratic 'Blanco' party, who are the official political leaders, with the San Tomé mine, the steamship company, and the railroad, the 'material interests of all sorts' (p. 116) that actually run the country:

> The chairman of the railway . . . had been kept busy negotiating with the members of Don Vincente's Government – cultured men, men to whom the conditions of civilised business were not unknown. (pp. 36–7)

In Chapter 8, when the narrative returns to that lunch-party again, that phrase 'the conditions of civilised business' is decoded. The intervention of General Montero comically subverts the 'civilised' discourse between the politicians and the representatives of 'material interests'. Where Ribiera had described the railroad as a 'progressive and patriotic undertaking' (p. 34), and the 'representative of two friendly foreign powers' (p. 34) had expressed concern about the 'development' (p. 37) of the Occidental Province, Montero offers to drink to 'the health of the man who brings us a million and a half of pounds' (p. 120) and produces an appalled silence until Don José Avellanos translates Montero's crass honesty into the correct 'civilised' language with 'a short oration, in which he alluded pointedly to England's good-will towards Costaguana' (p. 121). As in 'Heart of Darkness', Conrad is very conscious of the gap between official language and the political reality it is intended to mask. The lunch-party is, it becomes clear, a tactical manoeuvre on the part of the railroad company, an appeal to patriotic sentiment as a way of acquiring rights of way cheaply and easily:

> It had happened that some of the surveying parties scattered all over the province had been warned off with threats of violence. In other cases outrageous pretensions as to price had been raised. . . . Since he was met by the inimical sentiment of blind conservatism in Sulaco he would meet it by sentiment, too, before taking his stand on his right alone. The Government was bound to carry out its part of the contract with the board of the new railway company, even if it had to use force for the purpose. But he desired nothing less than an armed disturbance in the smooth working of his plans . . . and so he imagined to get the President-

Dictator over there on a tour of ceremonies and speeches. . . . After all he was their own creature – that Don Vincente.   (pp. 37–8)

In such a context, Nostromo's ideal of service and loyalty is clearly out of place.

It is, perhaps, significant that Captain Mitchell, Nostromo's boss, is also an old sailor – 'having spent a clear thirty years of his life on the high seas before getting what he called a "shore billet" ' (p. 112). As a former sea-captain, Mitchell is more ready to accept, without questioning, the loyalty Nostromo offers. At the same time, Mitchell's characteristic mental condition in this 'shore billet' – 'utterly in the dark, and imagining himself to be in the thick of things' (p. 112) – sounds a number of warning bells. From beginning to end, Mitchell has no understanding of the complex political processes in which he plays a part.[14] It is also significant that Giorgio Viola, Nostromo's other patron, 'like the great Garibaldi, had been a sailor in his time' (p. 25). The implications of Viola's nautical past are reinforced by his more prominent part as 'one of Garibaldi's immortal thousand' (p. 20):

His austere, old-world Republicanism had a severe, soldier-like standard of faithfulness and duty, as if the world were a battle-field where men had to fight for the sake of universal love and brotherhood, instead of a more or less large share of booty.
(p. 313)

Viola embodies a standard of selfless devotion to an ideal, 'the spirit of self-forgetfulness, the simple devotion to a vast humanitarian idea' (p. 31). However, this idealism is presented as out-of-date and out of touch with reality. Monygham sees him as 'a rugged and dreamy character, living in the republicanism of his young days as if in a cloud' (p. 319), and this view is shared by the narrator, who describes Viola as 'full of scorn for the populace, as your austere republican so often is' (p. 16). His political integrity removes him from an active role in political life in Costaguana, and his 'liberalism of heroic action' has, in Irving Howe's words, declined into 'a dream of lost fraternity'.[15] Both Mitchell and Viola implicitly warn that Nostromo's way of being in the world might be based on a false or out-dated model of the world. The ideal code of the sea, when brought ashore, might, like Viola's Garibaldianism, be no more than 'a dream of lost fraternity'.[16]

III

In Part II ('The Isabels'), Nostromo is seen principally through the eyes of Decoud. Decoud thinks he has 'discovered a complete single-ness of motive behind the varied manifestations of a consistent char-acter' (p. 275): Nostromo 'was made incorruptible by his enormous vanity, that finest form of egoism which can take on the aspect of every virtue' (p. 300). Nostromo is 'a man for whom the value of life seems to consist in personal prestige' (p. 243), and his own com-ments confirm this. He tells Teresa Viola that a 'good name' is 'a treasure' (p. 257); and he reveals to Monygham what he expects to gain from the task of removing the lighter full of silver from the harbour: 'They will talk about the Capataz of the Sulaco Cargadores from one end of America to another' (p. 259).[17] Nostromo, indeed, would rather die than fail in this task: just as Gould would rather destroy the mine than surrender it, Nostromo asserts that he would rather scuttle the lighter and 'let the sea have the treasure' than 'give it up to any stranger' (p. 267). Other comments reveal more of the personality-structure that lies behind this concern with reputation. For example, he tells Viola: 'It concerns me to keep on being what I am: every day alike' (p. 253). This assertion of consistency is clarified by a later explanation, to Decoud, of his conception of integrity: 'Since it was the good pleasure of the Caballeros to send me off on such an errand, they shall learn I am just the man they take me for' (p. 267). For Nostromo, 'being what I am' does not involve some idea of truth to his own instincts or impulses. It does not involve an introspective inquiry into the relationship between identity-for-self and identity-for-the-other. It involves only the maintenance of his identity-for-the-other. His behaviour is determined not by his own wishes but by his sense of what is expected from him:

> I don't care for cards but as a pastime; and as to those girls that boast of having opened their doors to my knock, you know I wouldn't look at any one of them twice except for what the people would say.   (p. 297)

Thus he tells Decoud of a day he spent alone on the Isabels because he had no money and 'did not want to go amongst those beggarly people accustomed to my generosity': 'It is looked for from the Capataz de Cargadores, who are the rich men, and, as it were, the *caballeros* amongst the common people' (p. 297). Nostromo is doubly self-alienated. He has not only interiorised 'the other's view' of himself as his identity-for-self but also internalised the class-divisions of Costaguana: his political support for the *caballeros* is accompanied by an analogous construction of his own position relative to other members of his own class.

The removal of the lighter-load of silver, which occupies Part II of *Nostromo*, simultaneously reveals and challenges the bases of Nostromo's identity. The first problem Nostromo encounters is that his society does not work according to the values upon which his identity is constructed. Decoud writes of him:

> He is more naive than shrewd, more masterful than crafty, more generous with his personality than the people who make use of him are with their money. At least, that is what he thinks himself with more pride than sentiment.   (p. 248)

Nostromo's awareness of his collusion in his own exploitation is, to begin with, a source of pride, but it has the potential for a different emotion and estimation, and events in Part II effectively conspire to bring about this change. There is his last meeting with Teresa Viola. When he argues that a 'good name' is 'a treasure', she takes his metaphorical language and asserts its literal meaning in order to confront his idealism with the material values of their society: 'They have been paying you with words' (p. 257). Her evaluation of Nostromo in precise market terms (as a commodity with a certain exchange-value) has already been given. She thinks he is 'an absurd spendthrift of these qualities which made him so valuable': 'He got too little for them' (p. 254). Accordingly, when Nostromo refuses to fetch a priest for her and gives priority to saving the silver, she tells him to 'Get riches at least for once': 'you indispensable, admired Gian' Battista, to whom the peace of a dying woman is less than the praise of people who have given you a silly name – and nothing besides – in exchange for your soul and body' (p. 256). As a result, Nostromo leaves the Viola household 'baffled by this woman's dis-paragement of this reputation he had obtained and desired to keep' (p. 257). Nostromo then receives a second shock to his value-system when he encounters Monygham. When he reveals what he expects to gain from this mission ('they will talk about the Capataz of the Sulaco Cargadores from one end of America to another'), Monygham, like Teresa Viola, undermines his idealism with more material considerations:

I hope you have made a good bargain in case you come back safe from this adventure . . . for taking the curse of death upon my back, as you call it, nothing else but the whole treasure would do. (p. 259)

There is evidence, however, that Nostromo has already begun to question his values and is beginning to think of his labour as a commodity rather than as service. When Decoud remarked on Nostromo's 'peculiar talent when anything striking to the imagination has to be done' (p. 226), he was surprised by Nostromo's response: 'He said quite moodily, "And how much do I get for that, señor?" ' (p. 226). And later, on board the lighter, when Decoud reflects upon 'the way men's qualities are made use of, without any fundamental knowledge of their nature' (p. 265), Nostromo echoes his analysis of reification and exploitation: 'Those gentlefolk do not seem to have sense enough to understand what they are giving one to do' (p. 280). As Irving Howe notes, Nostromo's growing sense of personal betrayal is accompanied by 'the dawning realisation of distinct class interests and sharpening class antagonisms'.[18]

When Nostromo wakes from his fourteen-hour sleep, he wakes 'with the lost air of a man just born into the world' (p. 411):

The Capataz of the Sulaco Cargadores had lived in splendour and publicity up to the very moment, as it were, when he took charge of the lighter containing the treasure of silver ingots. . . . But this awakening in solitude . . . amongst the ruins of the fort had no such characteristics. . . . The necessity of living concealed some- how, for God knows how long, which assailed him on his return to consciousness, made everything that had gone before for years appear vain and foolish, like a flattering dream come suddenly to an end. (p. 414)

His identity has been based on 'certain simple realities, such as the admiration of women, the adulation of men, the admired publicity of his life' (p. 42). His present solitude and the need for concealment deprive him of those 'realities': he has lost the audience on which his reputation and his identity are based, and he loses the sense of the reality of his past existence. In his attempt to understand his posi- tion, he fixes 'upon the clear and simple notion of betrayal' to account for the dazed feeling of 'having inadvertently gone out of his existence on an issue in which his personality had not been taken into account' (pp. 419–20). He re-appraises his past and realises the extent of his own exploitation:

> His fidelity had been taken advantage of. He had persuaded the body of Cargadores to side with the Blancos against the rest of the people . . . he had been made use of by Father Corbelán for negotiating with Hernandez. . . . All these things had flattered him in the usual way. . . . And at the end of it all – Nostromo here and Nostromo there – where is Nostromo? Nostromo can do this and that – work all day and ride all night – behold! he found himself a marked Ribierist for any sort of vengeance Gamacho, for instance, would choose to take.   (p. 417)

This realisation of his own exploitation involves a new perception of the world in which he has lived, a perception of that world as a world motivated by self-interest:

> [Decoud] was the only one who cared whether he fell into the hands of the Monterists or not. . . . And that merely would be an anxiety for his own sake. As to the rest, they neither knew nor cared. What he had heard Giorgio Viola say once was very true. Kings, ministers, aristocrats, the rich in general, kept the people in poverty and subjection; they kept them as they kept dogs, to fight and hunt for their service.   (p. 415)

Now, when Nostromo places his ideal of service within this society of self-interest, he finds that the status and identity it gives him is that of a rich man's 'dog', and, in the bitterness of mood that marks this stage of the narrative, he constantly returns to this negative self-evaluation.

This negative self-image is not, however, primarily directed at himself, but rather at those who have exploited him. Nostromo is not a Willems, drifting slowly towards suicide. Instead, his realisation of the loss of his old identity brings with it the intimation of a basis on which his new identity can be built:

> He felt the pinch of poverty for the first time in his life. . . . He remained rich in glory and reputation. But since it was no longer possible for him to parade the streets of the town, and be hailed

with respect in the usual haunts of his leisure, this sailor felt himself destitute indeed. (p. 415)

With the loss of his ability to enjoy the 'treasure' of reputation, Nostromo feels, for the first time, his lack of material reward. Together with his new sense of 'the selfishness of all the rich people' (p. 416), this points the direction his character will take. With his new understanding of the nature of the social world he inhabits, the selfishness of the rich now provides the model for his own identity. Nostromo is confirmed in this tendency through his subsequent meeting with Monygham. At first, Monygham seems to show some personal interest in him (pp. 433–4), but Monygham is 'in the pursuit of his idea' (p. 434), and, in the course of that pursuit, reveals to Nostromo that Gould would have been quite happy if Sotillo had captured the silver: 'And the Capataz, listening as if in a dream, felt himself of as little account as the indistinct, motionless shape of the dead man' (p. 435). Instead of confirming Nostromo's old identity-for-self, Monygham confirms his more recent apprehension of the unreality of his former life. In addition, Hirsch's corpse provides a symbolic gloss to the encounter: Hirsch has already paid with his life for Monygham's 'idea', and Nostromo realises that what has happened to Hirsch might have happened to him. He is forced to reconsider his evaluation of his mission ('Is it for an unconsidered and foolish whim that they came to me, then?' – p. 435), and that revaluation involves a re-appraisal of how his employers regarded him: 'Had I not done enough for them to be of some account . . . ?' (p. 435). Nostromo keeps returning to this question: where he had thought his service had made him 'of some account', he now feels that he was being treated like a dog.

Monygham's response to Nostromo during this meeting confirms that impression. His attitude towards Nostromo is purely instrumental:

Nostromo's return was providential. He did not think of him humanely, as of a fellow-creature just escaped from the jaws of death. The Capataz for him was the only possible messenger to Cayta. (pp. 431–2)

He feels grateful for 'the chain of accident which had brought that man back where he would be of the greatest use' (p. 431). This

second dialogue between Monygham and Nostromo relates ironically to their first. Earlier, Monygham had challenged Nostromo
to look after his own interests; now Monygham seeks to make use
of Nostromo himself, and Nostromo asserts self-interest against
him:

> You fine people are all alike. All dangerous. All betrayers of the
> poor who are your dogs. . . . A poor man amongst you has got to
> look after himself . . . you do not care for those that serve you.
> (pp. 453–4)

Nostromo's stance on self-interest is justified by his new understanding of the operations of Costaguana society:

> He understood well that the doctor was anxious to save the San
> Tomé mine from annihilation. He would be nothing without it. It
> was his interest. Just as it had been the interest of Señor Decoud,
> of the Blancos, and of the Europeans to get his Cargadores on their
> side.   (p. 455)

The idea of self-interest has now replaced the concept of service, but
Nostromo's adoption of individualism as a principle of action is
accompanied by a new awareness of his class-position. One of the
divisions in the 'Captain Fidanza' of the final part of the novel is
between the individualism that directs his economic behaviour and
the solidarity with his own class that has replaced his earlier fidelity
to his 'superiors'.[19]

There is another division within Nostromo which is foregrounded
in the final chapters. When he returned to Sulaco, he had felt 'com-
municative' (p. 434), but this impulse had been frustrated in the
unsatisfactory encounter with Monygham. He had then considered
Captain Mitchell and Giorgio Viola, in turn, as possible confidants,
but he had come to the conclusion that there was 'no-one to understand; no-one he could take into the confidence of Decoud's fate, of
his own, into the secret of the silver' (p. 469). The secret of the silver
adds the guilt of Decoud's death to the guilt he already feels about
turning down Teresa Viola's last request, but Nostromo handles this
by reasserting his old identity:

> First a woman, then a man, abandoned each in their last extremity,
> for the sake of this accursed treasure. It was paid for by a soul lost

and by a vanished life. The blank stillness of awe was succeeded
by a gust of immense pride. There was no-one in the world but
Gian' Battista Fidanza, Capataz de Cargadores, the incorruptible
and faithful Nostromo, to pay such a price.   (p. 502)

Through this manoeuvre, the betrayals about which he has felt guilty,
become signs of his superiority; at the same time, through his new
appreciation of exchange-value, the burden of guilt becomes the
price he has paid to take possession of the silver. Although the
manoeuvre is apparently successful, insofar as his old identity is
accepted and confirmed by the world which he inhabits, that success
has its psychological price. The reality of secret betrayals sits uneas-
ily with an identity-for-the-other of fidelity. Nostromo has regained
his former identity, or, rather, 'Nostromo, the miscalled Capataz de
Cargadores,' has made for himself, under his rightful name, 'another
public existence, but modified by the new conditions' (p. 527). However, the secret supply of silver which is the material basis of his new
identity is also the symbol of what he denies in order to assert that
identity; and his new identity, even though it is under 'his rightful
name', is a false-self system:

> Nostromo had lost his peace; the genuineness of all his qualities
> was destroyed. He felt it himself, and often cursed the silver of San
> Tomé. His courage, his magnificence, his leisure, his work, every-
> thing was as before, only everything was a sham.   (pp. 523–4)

Accordingly, Nostromo lives in fear lest light will fall on the 'secret
spot' of his life – 'that life whose very essence, value, reality, con-
sisted in its reflection from the admiring eyes of men' (p. 525).
Because his identity comprises an alterated component, Nostromo
still needs 'the admiring eyes of men', but, because his identity is
constructed over a guilty secret, he also fears the 'eyes of men'. This
contradiction is enacted in the split between Nostromo's 'public
existence' as the successful Captain Fidanza and his nocturnal life on
the Great Isabel, the site of both his hidden treasure and his secret
love. And it gradually becomes clear that, despite the apparently-
successful maintenance of his false-self system, Nostromo secretly
regards himself as a thief for having taken the silver. This is how he
describes himself to Giselle, after he has confessed to her about the
silver ('Do not forget that you have a thief for your lover' – p. 544),
and it is this identity that is, ironically, fixed upon him by his death.

When Giorgio Viola shoots him, he thinks he has shot Ramirez: 'Like a thief he came, and like a thief he fell' (p. 554). Although Viola has made a mistake in that he has shot Nostromo rather than Ramirez, he has not made a mistake in that he intended to shoot the man who was visiting Giselle. Indeed, Nostromo was doubly a thief: both as Giselle's lover and as the slave of the silver.

Nostromo begins with an identity based on the ideal code of the sea, which incorporates ideas of service and assumes an organic community. This is an identity which, viewed from another angle, colludes in its own exploitation in the radically different society of Sulaco. He then moves to an identity which is split between a false-self system (a public self of courage, fidelity, incorruptibility) and an inner awareness of betrayals and corruption. Nostromo's initial identity is inappropriate for the kind of society he inhabits: it leads to his collusion in his betrayal by others. Nostromo's reconstructed identity betrays others through its inauthenticity, but it also betrays Nostromo himself. In this process, Nostromo is both involved in and identified with the changes taking place in Sulaco. Like Sulaco, he has 'fallen under a curse' (p. 470). As with Sulaco, external prosperity is not accompanied by inner peace. When Nostromo tried to reveal his secret to Giselle, he discovered that he 'had not regained his freedom': 'The spectre of the unlawful treasure arose, standing by her side like a figure of silver, pitiless and secret, with a finger on its pale lips' (p. 542). The communication, for which he had longed, is denied him. As with Jim, a spectral female figure intrudes between him and 'a living woman'; and his death completes, and emblematises, the sacrifice of the personal to 'material interests'.

IV

The story of Charles Gould presents with equal clarity the sacrifice of personal life to material interests, but this time from the perspective of the mine-owner rather than the wage-labourer.[20] Part I shows Gould's deepening involvement in the San Tomé mine and displays the motives behind that involvement. Gould Senior repeatedly warns his son against this 'tainted' inheritance but, ironically, the repeated warnings serve only to arouse his interest, and, when Gould Senior dies, Charles Gould returns to take over the mine:

These two young people remembered the life which had ended wretchedly just when their own lives had come together in that splendour of hopeful love which to the most sensible minds appears like a triumph of good over all the evils of the earth. A vague idea of rehabilitation had entered the plan of their life. . . . It had presented itself to them at the instant when the woman's instinct of devotion and the man's instinct of activity receive from the strongest of illusions their most powerful impulse. The very prohibition imposed the necessity of success. It was as if they had been morally bound to make good their vigorous view of life against the unnatural error of weariness and despair.   (p. 74)

Charles Gould's interest in the mine is stimulated by his father's letters warning him against it, but the impulse to work the mine derives from his love for Mrs Gould – that 'strongest of illusions' the 'splendour of hopeful love'. The mine is the site for the contest between two different attitudes to life: the 'despair' of Gould Senior and the hope of Mr and Mrs Gould. It is to justify their hopeful view of life that the Goulds commit themselves to the mine: the mine must be a success to prove Gould's father wrong both in his advice and in his unhappiness. Accordingly, as Suresh Raval suggests, Gould's story can be read as a re-writing of *Lord Jim* 'in the arena of socio-economic historical forces': Gould, like Jim, constructs an heroic identity for himself on the denial of past failure; but Gould also ignores the 'politico-economic' reality of the mine for his plot of familial and national regeneration.[21]

In the 'Author's Note', Conrad describes Gould as 'the Idealist-creator of Material Interests' (p. xix). Gould's idealism is manifested, in part, in his 'idealistic view of success' (p. 67): 'The mine had been the cause of an absurd moral disaster; its working must be made a serious and moral success' (p. 66). After his father's misery, he 'could not have touched it for money alone' (p. 74). Gould's idealism is also manifested in the hopes he has for the mine:

What is wanted here is law, good faith, order, security. Anyone can declaim about these things, but I pin my faith to material interests. Only let the material interests once get a firm footing, and they are bound to impose the conditions on which alone they can continue to exist. That's how your money-making is justified here in the face of lawlessness and disorder. It is justified because the security which it demands must be shared with an oppressed people. A better justice will come afterwards.   (p. 84)

Mrs Gould's survey of Costaguana provides some justification for this hope: 'on all the lips she found a weary desire for peace' and a dread of 'administration without law, without security, and without justice' (p. 88). By the end of Part I, Gould's dream seems to have been fulfilled. The mine has become 'a power in the land' (p. 110). It seems to have established prosperity, security, stability, but, since the novel began with the fall of the Ribiera government, this sense of stability is obviously deceptive. There are also worrying indications of another effect the mine has on Costaguana:

> The material apparatus of perfected civilization which obliterates the individuality of old towns under the stereotyped conveniences of modern life had not intruded as yet; but over the worn-out antiquity of Sulaco ... the San Tomé mine had already thrown its subtle influence. It had altered, too, the outward character of the crowds on feast days on the *plaza* before the open portal of the cathedral, by the number of white ponchos with a green stripe affected as holiday wear by the San Tomé miners.   (pp. 96–7)

These green-and-white liveries are the sign of more significant changes that have been brought about in Sulaco by the mine. The green-and-white liveries and silver accoutrements, which spread through the country like a stain, indicate the growing power and influence of the mine in the running of the country, but also, as in the passage above, the changes the mine is making on the level of individual psychology. The passage begins with the prospect of loss of 'individuality' as one corrollary of 'perfected civilisation': it ends with the image of the miners in the uniform of the mine.

Gould's own story is a paradigm of the deleterious effects of 'material interests' on individual psychology. Part II begins with Gould's changing role in Costaguana. Once the mine is established, Gould finds himself drawn into Costaguana politics in order to protect the interests of the mine:

> The extraordinary development of the mine had put a great power into his hands. To feel that property always at the mercy of unintelligent greed had grown irksome to him. ... In the confidential communications passing between Charles Gould, the King of

Sulaco, and the head of the silver and steel interests far away in California, the conviction was growing that any attempt made by men of education and integrity ought to be discreetly supported. (p. 143)[22]

The result of these 'confidential communications' is that 'the Ribierist party in Costaguana took a practical shape under the eye of the administrator of the San Tomé mine' (p. 143), but these efforts to protect the interests of the mine backfire:

> The ignorant were beginning to murmur that the Ribierist reforms meant simply the taking away of the land from the people. Some of it was to be given to foreigners who made the railway.   (p. 195)

Montero now leads a 'military revolt in the name of national honour' (p. 145), with the support of a Monterist press 'cursing in every issue the "miserable Ribiera", who had plotted to deliver his country, bound hand and foot, for a prey to foreign speculators' (p. 145). 'Material interests' have brought not security and stability but the opposite. The mine, from being the victim of corruption, has become the centre of corruption: it has provided both the justification for the revolt and its target.

A similar change takes place within Charles Gould. Decoud suggests that Gould's idealism involves a dangerous loss of contact with reality and, in particular, with his own feelings and desires:

> He cannot act or exist without idealizing every simple feeling, desire, or achievement. He could not believe his own motives if he did not make them first a part of some fairy tale.   (pp. 214–15)

As Berthoud and Hawthorn have pointed out, Gould's initial idealisation and self-deception related to his family's role in the history of Costaguana.[23] He tells his wife, 'we Goulds are no adventurers' (p. 64), and he has, accordingly, an ideal conception of the public function of the mine that is comparable to Nostromo's conception of service; but, as the mine involves him more and more in political processes, he is forced to admit 'that he was an adventurer in Costaguana, the descendant of adventurers' (p. 365). As the narrative proceeds, Charles Gould, like Nostromo, is forced to re-appraise his self-conception. More important, however, is the process by which he is gradually taken over by what he has idealised: the 'material interests' that twine 'about the weary heart of the land' (p. 166) also twine about the heart of Charles Gould. They affect both his relationship with his wife and his relationship with himself. Decoud notes Gould's 'subtle conjugal infidelity' (p. 365): 'The San Tomé mine stands now between these two people' (p. 239). An exchange between Gould and his wife shows the accuracy of Decoud's analysis and the damage that has been done to their relationship:

> She raised her eyes and looked at her husband's face, from which all sign of sympathy or any other feeling had disappeared. 'Why don't you tell me something?' she almost wailed.
> 'I thought you had understood me perfectly from the first,' Charles Gould said, slowly. 'I thought we had said all there was to say a long time ago. There is nothing to say now. There were things to be done. We have done them; we have gone on doing them.' (p. 207)

As Raval notes, Gould's fatalism here is in striking contrast to the hopefulness with which he and his wife set out on this venture, but what is emphasised is the lack of reciprocity between the couple. The scene ends with Mrs Gould's reflections on the effect of the mine on their relationship:

> The fate of the San Tomé mine was lying heavy upon her heart. . . . It had been an idea. She had watched it with misgivings turning into a fetish, and now the fetish had grown into a monstrous and crushing weight. It was as if the inspiration of their early years had left her heart to turn into a wall of silver-bricks, erected by the silent work of evil spirits, between her and her husband. (pp. 221–2)

The mine has corrupted their marriage just as it has corrupted Costaguana. In addition, just as the ideals of imperialism were transformed into idols in 'Heart of Darkness', so Gould's idealistic attempt to align capitalism with morality is represented as both fetish and fairy-tale.[24]

Marx suggested that the contradiction between the actual socialisation of production and the fragmentation of property among a multitude of private interests 'distorts human society into a society ruled by things . . . an alien world of . . . powerful institutions, gigantic fetishes'.[25] This aspect of 'material interests', the condition of alienation, is evident in the further exploration of Gould's characteristic taciturnity:

> The impenetrability of the embodied Gould Concession had its surface shades. To be dumb is merely a fatal affliction; but the King of Sulaco had words enough to give him all the mysterious weight of a taciturn force.   (p. 203)

That ironic reference to Gould as 'the embodied Gould Concession' accurately describes both the extent and the way in which he has been depersonalised. He has been taken over by the mine he 'owns' and has become merely the instrument of its expression: he has become 'the might and majesty of the San Tomé mine in the person of Charles Gould' (p. 204), the representative of an economic force among other economic forces.[26] Irving Howe provides a fitting epitaph for him: 'If ever a man has fetishized the production of commodities, if ever a man has surrendered his self to his social role, it is Charles Gould.'[27]

The final section of the novel completes the picture of the development of 'material interests'. The mine has become the ruler of Sulaco 'lording it by its vast wealth over the valour, the toil, the fidelity of the poor' (p. 503), and various voices join in a chorus challenging Gould's belief that 'material interests' would bring 'law, good faith, order, security' (p. 84). Monygham warns Antonia that 'material interests will not let you jeopardize their development for a mere idea of pity and justice' (p. 509); similarly, when Mrs Gould asks 'Will there never be any peace?', he tells her that there is 'no peace and no rest in the development of material interests': they 'have their law, and their justice' but 'it is founded upon expediency and is inhuman' (p. 511).[28] Mrs Gould herself now sees 'the San Tomé mountain hanging over the Campo, over the whole land, feared, hated, wealthy; more soulless than any tyrant, more pitiless and autocratic than the worst Government, ready to crush innumerable lives in the expansion of its greatness' (p. 521). Her own life with Charles Gould has been the first victim. He has been 'incorrigible in his devotion to the great silver mine . . . in his hard, determined service of the material interests', but his 'devotion' and 'service' have been at the expense of her 'young ideal of life, of love, of work' (p. 522). The San Tomé mine has come between them, just as the 'spectre of the unlawful treasure' (p. 542) rose between Nostromo and Giselle.

V

In *Nostromo*, Conrad explored, through Nostromo, the ideal code of conduct and the social model on which the ideal code was based. He brought the ship to shore and discovered that the concept of an organic society, which ship-life had supplied and supported, was not applicable: instead of a community organised towards a common end, there was only the clash of conflicting interests. At the same time, through Gould, he examined the attempt to align capitalism and morality. In *Nostromo*, Conrad presented the clash of interests largely on the national and international socio-economic level, although, as Berthoud points out, the action is framed by Nostromo's relationship with the Viola family and by Gould's relationship with his wife to show how personal, domestic life is affected by these larger forces.[29] In *The Secret Agent*, the personal and domestic is foregrounded, but, as Hillis Miller observes 'to explore the meaning of this novel' is 'to approach as close as possible to the dark heart of Conrad's universe'.[30] In part, this 'darkness' is metaphysical: it is an apprehension of a reality that resists human plans and formulations, the reality that is 'usually hidden behind the façade of meanings which has been spread over the world', the reality which Marlow had encountered in 'Heart of Darkness' and Decoud had faced in the Golfo Placido in *Nostromo*.[31] But the darkness is also related to the novel's vision of society.[32] The narrative constructs the picture of a society that is atomised, and this vision springs from the failure of the organicist model in *Nostromo* and from Conrad's conviction that 'material interests' could not provide a viable alternative.

The 'Author's Preface' suggests what originally attracted Conrad to the Greenwich bombing: he describes it as 'a blood-stained inanity of so fatuous a kind that it was impossible to fathom its origin by any reasonable or even unreasonable process of thought' (p. x). Conrad, nevertheless, rises to the challenge, and his narrative interpretation of the incident provides an 'origin', but it is an interpretation which also emphasises the resistance of reality to rational control. The explosion is produced by the intersection of various independent plans – in particular, by the collision of Vladimir's plan (to provoke more repressive legislation through an 'anarchist' bombing) with the plans of Winnie Verloc and her mother to safeguard Stevie's future. As a result, both plans dramatically misfire. Vladimir's efforts produce the explosion he required, but lead to his own repatriation; Winnie's scheme ends in the death of the brother she has tried to protect. As Hillis Miller has observed, the plot of *The Secret Agent* is 'a chain reaction, a sequence of disenchantments started by M. Vladimir's demand that Verloc create a sensational anarchist demonstration': 'One by one these characters are wrested from their complacency and put in a situation which is outside everything they have known.'[33] In the course of the narrative, almost all of the characters are forced to change their view of themselves or their view of the world.

The key link in this chain is Verloc. The novel begins with him 'dwelling secure in the consciousness of his high value' (p. 248), and his walk through Knightsbridge gives off a sense of security and well-being. As the Assistant Commissioner says later, Verloc 'had come to regard his services as indispensable': Vladimir's reception 'was an extremely rude awakening' (p. 219). For Verloc the final link in the chain is his murder, which discloses and invalidates another of the assumptions upon which he has constructed his world. The narrative prior to the murder plays ironically with the gap between Verloc's view of his relations with his wife and the reader's knowledge of Winnie's true feelings. At bottom, he believes that he is 'loved for himself' (p. 251): he is ignorant of the 'contract' (p. 251) that Winnie has made. Because he does not understand his wife's position, Verloc literally invites death upon himself. As Guerard pointed out: 'Verloc rather than his wife takes the initiative in each important step towards his murder.'[34] Verloc begins by 'asserting the claims of his own personality' as a husband: 'Do be reasonable, Winnie. What would it have been if you had lost me?' (p. 234). Then he asserts his professional identity: 'There isn't a murdering plot for the last eleven years that I haven't had my finger in' (p. 238). This proud assertion of his professional achievements derives from (and compensates for) the sense of humiliation he re-experiences as he recalls his meeting with Vladimir: it is, indeed, addressed to Vladimir rather than to Winnie. Winnie sees only the man who killed Stevie, boasting about himself. Finally, blind to what is going on inside Winnie, and still trusting in her love for him, Verloc invites her towards him using the 'peculiar tone' which was 'intimately known to Mrs Verloc as the note of wooing' (p. 262). Verloc's use of the codes of their marriage is ironically set against Winnie's exultant realisation that Stevie's death frees her from her 'contract', and Verloc's domestic security is shattered as unexpectedly as his professional self-confidence had been by Vladimir.

It is Winnie, however, who is the thematic and compositional centre, as the 'Author's Preface' indicates:

> At last the story of Winnie Verloc stood out complete from the days of her childhood to the end. . . . The figures grouped about Mrs Verloc and related directly or indirectly to her tragic suspicion that 'life doesn't stand much looking into'.   (pp. xii–xiii)

Repeated references to her 'air of unfathomable indifference' (p. 5) and her 'unfathomable reserve' (p. 6) establish her as an enigma within the novel's hermeneutic code. In Chapter 8, she receives her first 'shock', when her mother announces her plan to move to the charity cottages, and this prompts her first departure from 'that distant and uninquiring acceptance of facts which was her force and her safeguard in life' (p. 153). The death of Stevie is an even greater shock for her: 'the most violent earthquake of history could only be a fair and languid rendering' (p. 255) of it. Winnie's life has been 'a life of single purpose and of noble unity of inspiration' (p. 242): she has sacrificed her own happiness to try and provide 'security' for her brother. With Stevie's death, she suddenly realises:

> There was no need for her now to stay there, in that kitchen, in that house, with that man – since the boy was gone for ever. No need whatever. . . . But neither could she see what there was to keep her in the world at all.   (p. 251)

Where Verloc had his sense of identity shaken by his interview with Vladimir, Winnie has suffered a much greater loss with the death of Stevie: it takes away not only the reason for her 'contract' with Verloc, but also the 'single purpose' of her life. Winnie loses the 'safeguard' of her 'uninquiring acceptance of facts' (p. 153), and is forced, at last, to look into 'things'. The result is that she passes 'from the most complete innocence to the most shattering knowledge of what lies beyond the world'.[35]

Winnie's first reaction to Stevie's death is to feel herself 'a betrayed woman' (p. 241), and she focuses that sense of betrayal on Verloc:

> It was not death that took Stevie from her. It was Mr Verloc who took him away. She had seen him. She had watched him, without raising a hand, take the boy away.   (pp. 246–7)

The narrative, however, does not explore her sense of betrayal. Instead, Winnie's subsequent reactions are presented in relation to the system referred to and used elsewhere in *The Secret Agent*: the criminal anthropology of Cesare Lombroso.[36] Conrad uses Lombroso's typology not just for Stevie, but also for Ossipon, the Professor and Winnie. The 'maddening thought' that Verloc took Stevie away 'to murder him' (p. 246) goes round and round in Winnie's head, until Verloc releases it by mentioning the park where Stevie died. The name acts as the trigger for the repressed emotion. The repressed visualisation of Stevie's death comes into her consciousness, and the 'maddening thought' reaches its conclusion:

> Her face was no longer stony. Anybody could have noted the subtle change on her features, in the stare of her eyes, giving her a new and startling expression; an expression seldom observed by competent persons under the conditions of leisure and security demanded for thorough analysis.   (pp. 260–1)

Winnie has 'gone raving mad – murdering mad' (p. 262), and that madness is represented by her taking on Stevie's features: 'the resemblance of her face with that of her brother grew at every step, even to the droop of the lower lip, even to the slight divergence of the eyes' (p. 262). The resemblance to Stevie signifies that, under pressure, Winnie reverts to type, and that reversion is emphasised by the addition of new details (in particular the strabismus) which feature in Lombroso's description of 'degenerates'. Furthermore, as Hunter has noted, the narrative alludes to Lombroso's theories in its explicit linkage of Winnie's crime with atavism:

> Into that plunging blow . . . Mrs Verloc had put all the inheritance of her immemorial and obscure descent, the simple ferocity of the age of caverns, and the unbalanced nervous fury of the age of barrooms.   (p. 63)[37]

This last word is also a reminder that Winnie, as the daughter of a 'licensed victualler', would already be marked down, as far as Lombroso was concerned, as a likely degenerate and 'born criminal'. In fact, Winnie corresponds precisely to the sub-group of 'born criminals' that Lombroso calls 'mattoids'. In 'Criminal Anthropology', Lombroso describes this group 'whose lunacy has so long concealed itself behind an habitual calm' until it suddenly emerges in the form of 'transitory madness'.[38] The 'unfathomable reserve' that has consistently characterised Winnie can be read as this 'habitual calm': certainly, the depiction of Winnie's sudden 'transitory madness' fits exactly with Lombroso's account. If Conrad's use of Lombroso's typology in his representation of Winnie suggests a lack of interest in exploring individual psychology in *The Secret Agent*, it can also be seen as a readiness to use the discourses of contemporary science as discourse rather than as a system of belief to which Conrad himself is committed. This has important implications for Conrad's later fiction.

VI

The cab-ride through South London in Chapter 8, which takes Winnie's mother on her final journey to the almshouses, is also the occasion for Stevie's horrified insight into the struggle for existence of the urban poor. 'Bad world for poor people' is the sentence he finally produces to express his 'sense of indignation and horror at one sort of wretchedness having to feed upon the anguish of the other – at the poor cabman beating the poor horse in the name, as it were, of his poor kids at home' (p. 171). The expression of indignation, however, is not enough for Stevie. He seeks some practical solution, and, in his 'guileless trustfulness' (p. 173), he suggests going to the police. The narrator observes that he had 'formed for himself an ideal conception of the metropolitan police as a sort of benevolent institution for the suppression of evil' (p. 172). Winnie, 'guiltless of all irony', tries to put him right by defining their real function: 'They are there so that them as have nothing shouldn't take anything away from them who have' (p. 173). By drawing attention to her lack of ironic intention, the narrator discloses the statement's ironic potential: Winnie's innocent definition ('untroubled by the problem of the distribution of wealth' – p. 173) enters the ironic discourse of the novel and presents the police as the protectors of the interests of the propertied classes. This chimes with Verloc's view of himself (as police and embassy spy) as the protector of 'opulence and luxury':

> All these people had to be protected. Protection is the first necessity of opulence and luxury. They had to be protected; and their horses, carriages, houses, servants had to be protected; and the

source of their wealth had to be protected in the heart of the city and the heart of the country; the whole social order favourable to their hygienic idleness had to be protected against the shallow enviousness of unhygienic labour.   (p. 12)

In a manner that is characteristic of *The Secret Agent*, the passage turns upon itself as it proceeds, and the initial implicit opposition of propertied and propertyless is subverted by an alternative binary coding, 'idleness' and 'labour'.[39]

As Hillis Miller has pointed out, the 'vision of society' that informs *The Secret Agent* is not (as in Stevenson's *The Dynamiter*, for example) that of 'a stable civilisation' under threat from political extremists.[40] The 'whole social order' is exposed to subversive irony, while, as Jeremy Hawthorn argues: 'Far from constituting a special political target, the "anarchists" in *The Secret Agent* are in effect treated as *symptomatic* of the society in which they are resident'.[41] Furthermore, while it satirises the 'anarchists', the narrative often incorporates their views. It is significant, for example, that the source of Conrad's narrative-interpretation of the bombing (in terms of *agents provocateurs* and the attempted manipulation of the Government) derives, as Norman Sherry has shown, from anarchist accounts and not from official sources.[42] In particular, the Professor's stated aim – to 'destroy public faith in legality' (p. 81) – precisely describes the effect of the novel's representation of the police.

The novel's representation of the police can be explored fruitfully through the figure of Chief Inspector Heat. Heat makes his first appearance in Chapter 5 when he accidentally encounters the Professor. At the end of this confrontation, he is described as stepping out 'with the purposeful briskness of a man . . . conscious of having an authorized mission on this earth and the moral support of his kind' (p. 96). For a moment, it seems as if the metropolitan police might inherit the role played earlier by the merchant navy. The 'moral support of his kind' sounds very like the idea of 'solidarity' celebrated in earlier novels. But, when Heat recalls this meeting with the Professor, during his interview with the Assistant Commissioner in Chapter 6, the police are shown in a very different light:

The encounter did not leave behind with Chief Inspector Heat that satisfactory sense of superiority the members of the police force get from the unofficial but intimate side of their intercourse with the criminal classes, by which the vanity of power is soothed, and

the vulgar love of domination over our fellow-creatures is flattered as worthily as it deserves.   (p. 122)

Instead of selfless devotion to duty and to an ideal code of conduct,
this is the same 'vanity of power' and 'love of domination' as motivates the Professor ('He was a moral agent – that was settled in his
mind. By exercising his agency with ruthless defiance he procured
for himself the appearances of power and personal prestige'; p. 81).
When Heat feels discomforted by the Assistant Commissioner's questioning, the narrator's commentary again conjures up this phantom
resemblance between the police and the merchant navy:

A man must identify himself with something more tangible than
his own personality, and establish his pride somewhere, either in
his social position, or in the quality of the work he is obliged to do,
or simply in the superiority of the idleness he may be fortunate
enough to enjoy.   (pp. 116–17)

To begin with, this sounds like Marlow's advocation, in 'Heart of
Darkness', of 'devotion, not to yourself, but to an obscure, back-
breaking business' (p. 117), but the sentence traces a slow trajectory
from the hint of Marlovian values through the disconcerting implications of 'pride' and 'social position' to arrive at 'superiority' of
'idleness'. The metropolitan police can be seen as another parodic
version of 'the brotherhood of the sea', and the trajectory to superiority of 'idleness' firmly locates this parody within 'the whole social
order' implied in Verloc's Kensington vision.

The police act as a representative institution in *The Secret Agent*, in
much the same way as Dickens uses the Court of Chancery in *Bleak
House* and the Circumlocution Office in *Little Dorrit*. Heat's concern
for his 'reputation' provides a key to the nature of this institution.
When Heat was first introduced, there was an analepsis to an earlier
meeting with the Assistant Commissioner: 'He was strong in his
integrity of a good detective, but he saw now that an impenetrably
attentive reserve towards this incident would have served his reputation better' (p. 86). The sentence moves from the inner-directed
concept of 'integrity' to the other-directed concern with 'reputation',
from an internalised code of conduct to an individual's investment
in their identity-for-the-other; and it suggests that 'reputation' might
have more importance to Heat than moral integrity. The Assistant
Commissioner, however, has a 'mistrust of established reputations':

His memory evoked a certain old fat and wealthy native chief in the distant colony whom it was a tradition for the successive Colonial Governors to trust and make much of as a firm friend and supporter of the order and legality established by white men; whereas, when examined sceptically, he was found out to be principally his own good friend, and nobody else's. Not precisely a traitor, but still a man of many dangerous reservations in his fidelity, caused by a due regard for his own advantage, comfort and safety.   (p. 118)

Heat's conduct in his second interview with the Assistant Commissioner fully justifies the Assistant Commissioner's mistrust. Heat is keen to arrest Michaelis in connection with the explosion:

It was perfectly legal to arrest that man on the barest suspicion. It was legal and expedient on the face of it. . . . Moreover, besides being legal and expedient, the arrest of Michaelis solved a little personal difficulty which worried Chief Inspector Heat somewhat. This difficulty had its bearing upon his reputation, upon his comfort, and even upon the efficient performance of his duties. (pp. 121–2)

This passage follows a now-familiar pattern, as it slides from legality through expedience to what best serves Heat's own 'advantage, comfort and safety'. Heat is keen to arrest Michaelis partly out of jealousy for Michaelis's 'reputation' and partly to direct attention away from Verloc, who has been the source of information on which Heat's own 'reputation' has been built. At the same time, if Heat has 'reservations in his fidelity', the Assistant Commissioner has reservations of his own. Michaelis is his wife's friend's protégé, and if Michaelis were to be connected with the explosion, there would be repercussions in his own social and domestic life. Where Heat is concerned with safeguarding his 'reputation', the Assistant Commissioner seeks to maintain domestic peace. The exchange between them, unknown to either participant, represents a clash of different interests, and the investigation is not so much the operation of justice as the intersection of those interests. The novel presents a world in which, in Leavis's words, 'the different actors or lives' are 'as insulated currents of feeling and purpose'.[43] The Verlocs have shown this on the domestic level, the investigation of the bombing generalises that familial experience. Through these domestic and institutional examples, the novel constructs its image of a fragmented society.

In *The Secret Agent*, Conrad is not interested in psychological exploration as he was in his earlier novels. He makes ambivalent and ironic use of a typology derived from Lombroso for certain characters, while, for the others, he has returned to his earlier idea of the direct or indirect assertion of power as the basis of individual identity. Accordingly, most of the characters are constructed in terms of egotism, vanity, self-interest. However, as Richard Curle noted, character is 'subordinate to the unity of the book as a whole'; and this construction of character is a constituent part of Conrad's picture of a society, characterised by atomised individuals and the clash of individual interests, which is the basis of the novel's political vision.[44] *The Secret Agent* embodies a vision of London comparable to Engels's, where the crowded city streets presented what he saw as the starkest revelation of the essence of capitalism: 'the unfeeling isolation of each in his private interest . . . the dissolution of mankind into monads, of which each one has a separate principle and a separate purpose'.[45]

6

Independence and Community: *Under Western Eyes* and 'The Secret Sharer'

In *Under Western Eyes*, Conrad deals again with the world of anarchists and revolutionaries that he had touched upon in *The Secret Agent*, but, now he starts from the explicit premiss that acts of terrorism can be seen as a desperate response to an oppressive society.[1] Haldin's successful assassination attempt is described as 'characteristic of the moral corruption of an oppressed society' (p. 7). As Berthoud has shown, the precise significance of 'moral corruption' is dramatically revealed at that moment, during Haldin's dialogue with Razumov, when he suddenly breaks down and weeps (p. 22): this collapse is 'more than a delayed reaction to the physical shock of the explosion; it is a result of the strain of moral conflict – of being obliged to act in defiance of his deepest feelings'.[2] In this respect, Haldin's career is proleptic of Razumov's: Razumov, too, is forced to act 'in defiance of his deepest feelings' as a result of the 'moral corruption of an oppressed society'. As Conrad says, in 'Autocracy and War', the psychology of individuals 'reflects the general effect of the fears and hopes of its time'.[3] The aftermath of the assassination precipitates a crisis in Razumov's life: he is forced to re-examine his own identity, and the process forces him to consider his relations to the opposed political forces in the society he inhabits. In *Under Western Eyes*, Conrad returns to the theme of his earliest fiction: the search for identity carried out through a sequence of betrayals. Indeed, *Under Western Eyes* can be seen as the culmination of that thematic concern: this is Conrad's final treatment of 'his central story of betrayal and self-punishment', but the treatment also involves the knowledge (that was made explicit in *Nostromo*) of 'the unavoidably political nature of human life'.[4]

I

Conrad's model for *Under Western Eyes* was quite obviously Dostoevsky's *Crime and Punishment*. Michael Holquist has described how *Crime and Punishment*'s narrative of 'Raskolnikov's various attempts to forge an identity for himself' is constructed:

> In the first part Raskolnikov murders two women: then, in the next five parts, everyone (including Raskolnikov) tries to figure out the crime; in the sixth part Raskolnikov confesses. . . . In the epilogue he repents of the crime . . . and has a mystical experience; the novel ends with the narrator's assertion that 'here begins a new story'.[5]

As this suggests, there are two radical discontinuities in Raskolnikov's psychological history: first, when he murders the two women; secondly, in the epilogue, when he undergoes a mystical experience. In each case, one conception of self is lost and replaced by another: the man who murdered the pawnbroker '*in that act* got rid of the self Raskolnikov conceived himself to be before the act of murder'.[6] In committing the murders, Raskolnikov is, simultaneously, both murderer and victim. Subsequently, he is obliged to take up a new role to replace his lost identity, and again it has a dual nature: he now becomes both criminal and detective.[7] By Part VI, Raskolnikov concludes that his identity is merely that of a criminal, but then, in the epilogue, his mystical experience destroys that identity just as his earlier sense of himself was destroyed with the murder of the two women. Conrad follows a similar pattern, though within a significantly different framework of ideas, in *Under Western Eyes*.[8] The two 'radical discontinuities' in Razumov's psychological history are brought about by his initial betrayal of Haldin to the czarist authorities and by his final betrayal of himself to the revolutionists. Like Raskolnikov's mystical experience at the end of *Crime and Punishment*, Razumov's final act of self-betrayal provides him with a completely unexpected identity.

Under Western Eyes begins by exploring Razumov's identity as a student in St Petersburg. It notes that Razumov 'was easily swayed by arguments and authority', and, in response, has adopted a defensive strategy: 'With his younger compatriots he took the attitude of an inscrutable listener, a listener of the kind that hears you out intelligently and then – just changes the subject' (p. 5). This strategy has resulted in a certain reputation for profundity and a misleading identity-for-the-other: 'By his comrades at the St. Petersburg University, Kirylo Sidorovitch Razumov, third year's student in philosophy, was looked upon as a strong nature – an altogether trustworthy man' (p. 6). The narrative next establishes the nature of the society Razumov inhabits: it is 'an oppressed society' (p. 7), with an autocratic ruler and a pervasive police presence; it is a society in which students, in particular, are liable to be suspected of subversion. Razumov's response has been to remain distant from the political conflicts:

> Razumov was one of those men who, living in a period of mental and political unrest, keep an instinctive hold on normal, practical, everyday life . . . he shrank mentally from the fray as a good-natured man may shrink from taking definite sides in a violent family quarrel. (pp. 10–11)

The simile is significant. Razumov tries to lead his life apart from the politics of his society largely because of his own lack of family:

> The word Razumov was the mere label of a solitary individuality. There were no Razumovs belonging to him anywhere. His closest parentage was defined in the statement that he was Russian. Whatever good he expected from life would be given to or withheld from his hopes by that connexion alone. (pp. 10–11)

Razumov's lack of family has led him to construct an identity-for-self which does not exist in the present but is projected on to the future. In this, he resembles Willems in *An Outcast of the Islands* and Jim in *Lord Jim*. Razumov's immediate goal is the silver medal for the prize essay, but this is merely a step towards his long-term goal: he sees himself as 'a celebrated old professor, decorated, possibly a Privy Councillor, one of the glories of Russia' (p. 13). Razumov pursues this altered identity, ultimately, because of ontological insecurity: as he puts it 'a celebrated professor was a somebody' (p. 13).

Because of his lack of family, Razumov is a completely isolated individual. Indeed, he might almost be seen as the psychological equivalent of the atomised social world that Conrad presented in *The Secret Agent*:

He was aware of the emotional tension of his time; he even responded to it in an indefinite way. But his main concern was with his work, his studies, and with his own future.   (p. 10)

In the course of the novel Razumov progresses from this position of isolation to making a choice of sides. At the same time, through his relationship with Nathalie Haldin, Razumov's progress can also be seen as an education of feelings. This indicates the continuity between *Under Western Eyes* and later novels like *Chance* and *The Arrow of Gold*, while it also points to a significant difference between *Under Western Eyes* and earlier works like *Lord Jim* and *The Secret Agent*. The first step in Razumov's progress is the revelation that his apparent aloofness from the political conflicts of his society is an illusion. In reality, Razumov is a supporter of autocracy insofar as his future identity is predicated upon 'the stability of the institutions which give rewards and appointments' (p. 11). Far from being sympathetic towards the revolutionaries, Razumov's self-interest, at the start of the novel, directs him towards conservatism. This emerges clearly with the arrival of Haldin in his room.

Haldin's first speech (p. 15) draws attention to the deceptive identity-for-the-other that Razumov has acquired among his fellow-students, and subsequent exchanges constitute a bitter comedy of misunderstanding that dramatises the lesion between Razumov's identity-for-self and his identity-for-the-other:

> Razumov had listened in astonishment; but before he could open his mouth Haldin added, speaking deliberately, 'It was I who removed de P—— this morning.'
>
> Razumov kept down a cry of dismay. The sentiment of his life being utterly ruined by this contact with such a crime expressed itself quaintly by a sort of half-derisive mental exclamation, 'There goes my silver medal!'
>
> Haldin continued after waiting a while –
>
> 'You say nothing, Kirylo Sidorovitch! I understand your silence.'   (p. 16)

Haldin's irruption into Razumov's life is like Willems's stepping off the path of virtue or Jim's jump from the *Patna*. It is a fact that threatens his steady progress to the fulfillment of his self-ideal:

Razumov, of course, felt the safety of his lonely existence to be permanently endangered. This evening's doings could turn up against him at any time as long as this man lived and the present institutions endured.   (p. 11)

Razumov's isolated existence has been brought into the play of political forces, or, more accurately, its concealed relation to those political forces has been disclosed. He knows enough about the nature of his society to understand what his identity-for-the-other would be, as regards the authorities, if Haldin were caught:

Everybody Haldin had ever known would be in the greatest danger. Unguarded expressions, little facts in themselves innocent would be counted for crimes. Razumov remembered certain words he said, the speeches he had listened to, the harmless gatherings he had attended.   (p. 20)

The self-interest that had dictated an unacknowledged, and perhaps unconscious, support for the autocracy now directs him to assist Haldin to escape in an attempt to recover the conditions upon which his future-projected identity depends for its fulfillment.

Guerard has commented perceptively on the process by which the failure of this attempt to help Haldin leads to Razumov's decision to betray him: in particular, he notes how Razumov's 'egoism and fear create the doctrinal commitment which alone can rationalize the betrayal'.[9] When Razumov is unable to rouse the drunken Ziemianitch, he converts his frustration into a political analysis. The beating which Razumov, in his fear and frustration, gives Ziemianitch enacts a 'longing for power to hurt and destroy' that finds political expression in ideological support for the 'stern hand' of autocracy (p. 31). Razumov's earlier, unconscious reliance on the institutions of autocracy is replaced by an asserted commitment to autocracy. But this illiberalism springs from a desire for self-preservation: he hates Ziemianitch ('the peasant incapable of action') and Haldin ('the idealist incapable of perceiving . . . the true character of men') because they endanger him.

Accordingly, his thought processes take him steadily towards the decision to betray Haldin as the only way out of the situation:

He walked slower and slower. And indeed, considering the guest he had in his rooms, it was no wonder he lingered on the way. It was like harbouring a pestilential disease that would not perhaps take your life, but would take from you all that made life worth living – a subtle pest that would convert earth into a hell. (pp. 31–2)[10]

By means of these metaphors, Razumov depersonalises Haldin in order to minimise the act of betrayal he contemplates. At the same time, while he is consciously moving towards this decision, another part of his mind intuits the bond that has been established between them. He has a 'morbidly vivid vision' of Haldin lying on his bed, 'as if dead, with the back of his hands over his eyes' (p. 32). Where Dostoevsky used the detective story, Conrad has recourse to motifs from Gothic fiction to trace his protagonist's search for identity: the double, the diabolic pact or diabolic possession. Ironically, it is the betrayal of Haldin that will truly 'convert earth into hell' for Razumov. This 'vision' of Haldin haunts Razumov, and Haldin's phantasmal appearances always occur at significant junctures in the narrative – like the appearances of Bertha Mason in *Jane Eyre* or the ghost in *Villette*.[11] Haldin's subsequent phantasmal appearance in the snow (pp. 36–7), just as Razumov reaches the decision to betray him, represents the guilt (and, by implication, the bond) that Razumov feels but is not yet ready to acknowledge. The appearance of the phantom serves as counterpoint to, and commentary on, the rationalisations by which Razumov persuades himself to betray Haldin:

> Betray. A great word. What is betrayal? They talk of a man betraying his country, his friends, his sweetheart. There must be a moral bond first. All a man can betray is his conscience. And how is my conscience engaged here; by what bond of common faith, of common conviction, am I obliged to let that fanatical idiot drag me down with him? (pp. 37–8)

Razumov's rhetorical question formulates one of the 'enigmas' with which the narrative will engage: 'What are the respective claims of self-interest, social duty and common humanity.'[12]

Indeed, even as he plans to betray Haldin, Razumov is momentarily taken by the idea of 'rushing to his lodgings and flinging himself on his knees by the side of the bed with the dark figure stretched on it': 'to pour out a full confession in passionate words that would stir the whole being of that man to its innermost depths; that would end in embraces and tears; in an incredible fellowship of souls' (pp. 39–40). This introduces into the narrative the motif of confession: Razumov's desire to confess signifies his need to reduce the gap between inner and outer world, and to bring closer together identity-for-self and identity-for-the-other. Razumov's first confession, and first attempt to align identity-for-self with identity-for-the-other, is his betrayal of Haldin to the authorities. This confession, however, does not produce the desired results. Razumov finds himself defending Haldin and feeling remorse towards Ziemianitch. More important, he also has the first intimation that his betrayal of Haldin will not clear his own name. The General twice reveals the suspicion that he feels. At the end of Razumov's confession, he observes: 'And you say he came in to make you this confidence like this – for nothing – *à propos des bottes*' (p. 48). Later, in response to a remark from Prince K——, he asks Razumov whether he often indulges 'in speculative conversation' (p. 48). Razumov has made an incomplete confession to the General, but, even so, his attempt to clear himself has succeeded only in drawing himself to the attention of the authorities.

When Razumov returns to Haldin, he experiences an urge to make a second confession: a 'diabolical impulse to say, "I have given you up to the police", frightened him exceedingly' (p. 55). As their conversation proceeds, a 'mocking spirit' (p. 56) enters Razumov, and their final meeting takes on some of the colouring of a dialogue between Mephistopheles and Faust: Razumov 'avoided with difficulty a burst of Mephistophelian laughter' (p. 60), and the scene ends with Haldin's sudden disappearance as the clock sounds midnight. The effect on Razumov of Haldin's intrusion and the fact of Razumov's betrayal of Haldin are both presented by reference to the Gothic; but, above all, the Gothic coloration serves to convey the impression of unconscious forces driving Razumov. It is in this scene that Razumov begins the ironic double-talk that becomes his characteristic mode. (He comments on his 'interview' with Ziemianitch: 'It was satisfactory in a sense. I came away from it much relieved' – p. 56.) Razumov's equivocation signals his uneasy sense of the falseness of his position and his awareness of the gap between his identity-for-self and his identity-for-the-other. The equivocation expresses the simultaneous desire to reveal himself and to conceal himself. There is a conflict within Razumov (as there was within

Raskolnikov) between a conscious desire to conceal himself and an unconscious pressure to reveal the truth. One result of this conflict is Razumov's disguised confession to Haldin:

> There are secrets of birth, for instance. . . . And there are secret motives of conduct. A man's most open actions have a secret side to them. . . . For instance, a man goes out of a room for a walk. Nothing more trivial in appearance. And yet it may be momentous. He comes back – he has seen perhaps a drunken brute, taken particular notice of the snow on the ground – and behold he is no longer the same man.   (p. 59)

This elliptical account of his own actions testifies to the pressure to confess that he experiences; and, before Haldin leaves, Razumov feels impelled to clarify his political position also: 'What have I to look back to but that national past from which you gentlemen want to wrench away your future' (p. 61).

After the betrayal of Haldin, Razumov awakes into a world that seems 'without significance or interest' (p. 68). The lamp which had been the 'beacon of his labours' has become merely 'a cold object of brass and porcelain' (p. 68). His notes and books have become 'a mere litter of blackened paper' (p. 68). The project which gave his life meaning has disappeared, and things have become merely 'dead matter'. Razumov experiences himself as similarly dull, lifeless, inert: he finds himself 'going through all the motions mechanically' (p. 68). Razumov's work was directed towards the realisation of his identity-for-self, but Haldin's intrusion into his life has made him aware of political uncertainties in the outside world which he had been ignoring:

> The true Razumov had his being in the willed, in the determined future – in that future menaced by the lawlessness of autocracy . . . and the lawlessness of revolution. The feeling that his moral personality was at the mercy of these lawless forces was so strong that he asked himself seriously if it were worth while to go on accomplishing the mental functions of that existence which seemed no longer his own.   (pp. 77–8)

Razumov has been forced to realise the limit of his own will. He has been forced into awareness of the otherness of other people (and of their connectedness with himself), and his initial reaction is a sense of fear at their power over him. This is the first breach in the wall of his egoism, and the first result, after his Sartrean experience of 'nausea', is a paranoid fear of others.

At the same time, Razumov's feeling that 'his moral personality' is 'at the mercy of these lawless forces' is justified by subsequent experiences. He soon learns that Haldin's influence on his life does not end with the removal of Haldin from it. Not only is he now suspected by the authorities; but he learns, from a fellow-student, that Haldin had often expressed 'a warm appreciation' (p. 74) of his character. He discovers that he 'had been made a personage without knowing anything about it' (pp. 82–3). He has become the victim of a 'conspiracy of mistaken judgement taking him for what he was not' (p. 82). His inside knowledge of Haldin and his family (p. 74), and the police-search of his rooms, serve only to confirm this false identity. Kostia's response is presumably typical: 'A man doesn't get the police ransacking his rooms without there being some devilry hanging over his head' (p. 81). Razumov is made to feel that his 'solitary and laborious existence had been destroyed' (p. 82): he had lived with a strong sense of his isolation, but, like Heyst, he has been compelled to recognise his connectedness with other people. For most of the novel, Razumov lives in the nightmare world apprehended by Heyst, where identity-for-self is at odds with identity-for-the-other.

Haldin's continuing influence on Razumov's life is also manifested in a more intimate way. At one o'clock, half-an-hour after Haldin had been arrested, Razumov has a curious experience: 'He heard himself suddenly saying, "I confess", as a person might do on the rack. "I am on the rack", he thought' (p. 65). Similarly, the following evening, when Razumov is lying on his bed 'his hands under his head', he finds himself thinking, 'I am lying here like that man' (p. 70). Again, when he is being interviewed by Councillor Mikulin, Razumov 'beheld his own brain suffering on the rack – a long, pale figure drawn asunder horizontally with terrific force in the darkness of the vault, whose face he failed to see' (p. 88). Razumov's continuing awareness of Haldin is readily interpretible as guilt at his betrayal of the trust put in him. Guerard has commented on the effect of the betrayal of Haldin on Razumov:

For the remainder of the novel Razumov is always on a rack; or on the two racks of fear and guilt. There are times when it is difficult to distinguish between the two, and if the analysis of guilt is more impressive, the dramatisation of fear is more exciting.[13]

Razumov's guilt in relation to Haldin mixes with his fear for himself, and these mixed emotions are expressed through an identification with Haldin. The long, pale figure 'whose face he failed to see' (p. 88) could be either himself or Haldin. By such means, Haldin comes to suggest a repressed part of Razumov, a part of Razumov that has been split off and denied.

In Part I, with the arrival of Haldin in his room, Razumov's progress towards the identity he seeks for himself is halted. Haldin's arrival involves him in the play of political forces from which he had tried to remain aloof. Once he has become involved, he realises that, between 'the lawlessness of autocracy' and 'the lawlessness of revolution' (p. 77), the conditions for the fulfillment of his self-ideal are no longer available to him. At the same time, Haldin's arrival forces him to confront the gap between his identity-for-self and his identity-for-the-other. He feels himself 'misunderstood' (p. 87) by the revolutionists and 'mistrusted' by the authorities: with both groups there is a gap between identity-for-self and identity-for-the-other. With both groups also there are areas of guilt which prevent full revelation of himself: in relation to the revolutionists, there is his betrayal of Haldin and his ideological difference from them; in relation to the authorities, there are the 'unguarded expressions' and 'the speeches he had listened to, the harmless gatherings he had attended' (p. 20), which the authorities would regard with suspicion. Razumov is, like Nina in *Almayer's Folly*, caught between two sides, to neither of which he fully belongs. At the same time, there is pressure on him, from outside, to align himself clearly with one or the other. More important, there is pressure also, from within himself, to 'confess' and to bring into accord his sense of himself and his identity-for-the-other. Furthermore, since his original identity-for-self – a self-ideal projected into the future – is no longer viable, he also has to forge a new identity for himself and find a new basis for that identity.

II

In Part II, Conrad changes the narrative perspective. The language teacher's account of Razumov, based on Razumov's diary, is now replaced by the language teacher's own impressions of Razumov in Geneva. The most important effect of this change is that it removes direct access to Razumov's inner thoughts and feelings. As Guerard writes:

> Through the second and much of the third part the reader has no certain knowledge that Razumov, welcomed in Geneva as the late Haldin's friend and associate, is actually a police spy. The motives for his presence might as plausibly be inward ones: a self-destructive tempting of fate; a compulsion to confront those most likely to destroy him; even, an unconscious effort to appease guilt through re-enactment of the crime.[14]

Indeed, the concealment of Razumov's status as police-spy both procures sympathetic attention from the reader and provokes an intense interpretative activity that registers the complexity of Razumov's motivation. To quote Guerard again:

> By delaying as long as he does the formal revelation that Razumov is Mikulin's agent, Conrad preserves a sympathy that would (with a more abrupt procedure) have been lost. We must see Razumov suffer before we see, nakedly, this second of his crimes. And the 'deceptive' impression that Razumov is obeying a psycho-moral compulsion is not deceptive at all.[15]

For example, in Part III, Razumov teases Peter Ivanovitch: 'if you only knew the force which drew – no, which *drove* me towards you!' (p. 228). Again, Guerard is a perceptive guide:

> Razumov is thinking of Councillor Mikulin. But the reader is likely to think of a generalized self-destructiveness, and the reader not Razumov would be right. That *is* the hidden motive, hidden even from him. Thus Razumov, in his 'satanic' game of suggesting yet concealing a second and truer meaning from Peter Ivanovitch, stumbles with unconscious irony upon a third and truest one.[16]

For most of Part II, Razumov is absent from the narrative, but various preparations are made for his re-entrance. The most obvious preparation relates to Nathalie Haldin. She is emotionally and politically close to her brother, but entirely ignorant of 'his Petersburg

comrades' (p. 115). Indeed, where her mother had 'seen the experiences of her own generation, its sufferings, its deceptions,
its apostasies too' (p. 140), her political idealism is based upon
innocence and inexperience. As a result, her 'unconsciously lofty
ignorance of the baser instincts of mankind left her disarmed before
her own impulses' (pp. 142–3); and she is 'very capable of being
roused by an idea or simply by a person' (p. 102).

In Chapter 3, Nathalie receives a letter from Haldin, referring to
'unstained, lofty and solitary existences' (p. 135). Nathalie explains:

> These are the words which my brother applies to a young man he
> came to know in St Petersburg. An intimate friend, I suppose. It
> must be. His is the only name my brother mentions in all his
> correspondence with me.   (p. 135)

Haldin's misreading of Razumov's character, combined with
Nathalie's ignorance and trust, prepares the way for Razumov's
acceptance in Geneva: the misinterpretation that had created
Razumov's false identity in St Petersburg is at work again. On a first
reading, when Razumov's arrival in Geneva seems to be his answer
to Mikulin's question at the end of Part I ('Where to?' – p. 99), it
seems that Razumov is unable to escape from Haldin's mistake, that
he is trapped by this identity-for-the-other. The revelation that he
has been sent as a spy intensifies the sense of his entrapment: he is
not just experiencing the conflict between the false identity Haldin
has created for him and his guilt at betraying Haldin, but, as a
further turn of the screw, his very presence in Geneva, that forces
him to experience this conflict, is not an escape from the Russian
authorities but is controlled by those authorities. Razumov has replaced the false identity and the betrayal imposed upon him by
Haldin with a consciously-adopted false identity and a second, open-
eyed betrayal. In other words, Razumov has moved from an unconscious lesion between identity-for-self and identity-for-the-other to
an awareness of that lesion and a conscious assertion of that false
identity. The sense of isolation that accompanied the original lesion
has now been intensified, and the burden of guilt has immeasurably
increased.

Something of this is glimpsed through Nathalie's misinterpretation of Razumov's anguished response to the mention of Haldin's
name:

You should have seen his face. He positively reeled. He leaned against the wall of the terrace. Their friendship must have been the very brotherhood of souls! (p. 172)

The reader's knowledge of the real relationship between Haldin and Razumov provides some insight into the horror implied by Razumov's reaction. In addition, Nathalie's phrase 'the very brotherhood of souls' ironically echoes Razumov's earlier thoughts, when he had imagined making a full confession to Haldin (p. 40). Moreover, there is a sense in which there is a 'fellowship of souls' between Haldin and Razumov, and this is suggested by those images which present Haldin as Razumov's 'double' or 'secret sharer'. These images, and the corresponding guilt felt by Razumov, affirm the 'human solidarity' which Razumov feels but has not yet consciously recognised.

The language teacher's response to Razumov is similarly (though less directly) shaped by Haldin's misinterpretation, and contains a similar double irony. After his first meeting with Razumov, he observes:

It occurred to me that his clean-shaven, almost swarthy face was really of the very mobile sort, and that the absolute stiffness of it was the acquired habit of a revolutionist, of a conspirator everlastingly on his guard against self-betrayal in a world of secret spies. (p. 187)

Razumov is indeed 'on his guard', but not because he is a revolutionist. And that reference to 'self-betrayal' opens up a complex area. The self-betrayal that Razumov consciously fears is the disclosure of his 'true' identity to the revolutionists – that is, his identity as the betrayer of Haldin and the intended betrayer of the Geneva group – but, on another level, the concealment of this identity is itself a betrayal of himself. Towards the end of Part II, the language teacher tells Razumov that 'a curse is an evil spell' and that 'the great problem' is 'to find the means to break it' (p. 194). The language teacher uses this idea of a 'curse' to explain the problems of Russians generally, but it has an obvious and specific relevance to Razumov: since the intrusion of Haldin into his life, it is as if Razumov has been under 'an evil spell'. Razumov has to break away from the torture of the false identity which Haldin's action seems to have fixed on him. He had asked himself earlier, 'Must one kill oneself to escape this visitation?' (p. 32). Part II suggests another possibility with Tekla's story of the journeyman lithographer who betrayed revolutionary secrets under police-torture. She comments on his guilty isolation:

> He ought to have trusted in his political friends when he came out of prison. He had been liked and respected before, and nobody would have dreamed of reproaching him for his indiscretion. (p. 155)

This story echoes Razumov's betrayal of Haldin and looks forward to the outcome of Razumov's story: just as she nursed the lithographer after his release from prison, she will nurse Razumov at the end of his life. Peter Ivanovitch's account of his escape conveys a similar message:

> He had become a dumb and despairing brute, till the woman's sudden, unexpected cry of profound pity, the insight of her feminine compassion discovering the complex misery of the man under the terrifying aspect of the monster, restored him to the ranks of humanity.   (p. 124)

Both stories have a clearly proleptic function: Razumov too will be brought back 'to the ranks of humanity', from which he is at present excluded, through 'feminine compassion'.[17] And only by betraying himself will Razumov be able to find himself.

III

Part III returns to Razumov's perspective. At the end of Part I, he had been under suspicion from the czarist authorities and had been keen to establish an identity-for-the-other as a loyal and law-abiding subject: in Part II, he was responding to the suspicions of the revolutionists; and, in Part III, he is anxious to establish and maintain his false-self system, his 'identity' as a revolutionist.

Part III consists largely of a series of meetings: Razumov's interview with Madame de S—— (which re-introduces the Gothic motifs used earlier); his two conversations with Peter Ivanovitch; and a third meeting with Sophia Antonovna. The conversations with Peter Ivanovitch are represented as 'a duel' (p. 229). Razumov feels that

Peter Ivanovitch is 'waiting behind his spectacles' (p. 228) for him to give himself away. Peter Ivanovitch's impenetrability – 'masked by the dark blue glasses' (p. 205) and by his expression of 'meditative seriousness' (p. 206) – is matched against Razumov's taciturnity. At the end of his second conversation, after he has succeeded in maintaining his false identity, Razumov undergoes a 'bizarre' self-experience 'as though another self, an independent sharer of his mind, had been able to view his whole person very distinctly indeed' (p. 230). This is clearly more than a sense of guilt at betraying Haldin. It expresses a self-division, and the dynamics of that self-division are revealed by Razumov's response. He asks himself, 'Is it possible that I am but a weak creature after all?' (p. 230). What Razumov sees as strength – 'moral resistance . . . moral endurance' (p. 230) – is his conscious effort to assert a false identity and to have this false identity accepted as his identity-for-the-other. His 'weakness' is the return of the repressed or denied aspects of himself: the rebellion within himself against the maintenance of the false-self system. These repressed aspects of himself reveal themselves in the compulsions to 'self-betrayal' that Razumov continually experiences:

> All day long he had been saying the wrong things. It was folly, worse than folly. It was weakness; it was this disease of perversity overcoming his will.   (p. 253)

It is significant, then, that, at the very moment when Razumov seems to have succeeded in establishing his false identity, he undergoes this vivid apprehension of self-division.

Razumov's subsequent, unexpected meeting with Sophia Antonovna is a repetition of the test he has just undergone with Peter Ivanovitch. Sophia Antonovna, however, poses a greater threat: with Peter Ivanovitch, Razumov was duelling with a sham; with Sophia Antonovna, his falseness is set against her 'true stuff'. He 'could not despise her as he despised all the others' (p. 242).[18] At first, Sophia Antonovna misinterprets Razumov. Like the others, she is deceived because of her own preconceptions:

> He flings out continually these flouts and sneers. . . . And what for, pray? Simply because some of his conventional notions are shocked, some of his petty masculine standards.   (p. 248)

She initially misinterprets him, because she interprets him from the stand-point of her own feminism. The main part of her 'investigation', however, involves questioning him about his actions on the morning of the assassination. For his replies, Razumov appropriates Haldin's experiences: he mentions the falling snow, the narrow side-street, the inclination to 'lie down on the pavement and sleep' (p. 17), even the absence of the *dvornik* that had featured in Haldin's account earlier. Razumov's narrative ends: 'The stairs were dark. I glided up like a phantom' (p. 257). His choice of the word 'phantom' carries the subliminal suggestion that he has not just appropriated Haldin's experiences but also, in the course of this narration, identified himself with Haldin. This is reinforced by his reaction to the end of his own narration: 'He checked himself, passed his hand over his forehead, confused, like a man who has been dreaming aloud' (p. 257). His trance-like state also testifies to a tendency to lose his grip on himself – to lose the conscious control of his actions that is a necessary part of his assertion of a false identity.

Despite this lapse, however, Razumov feels confident enough of his success in maintaining his false identity to indulge in the kind of ironic statements that he had made to Peter Ivanovitch. He assures her, for example, that his conduct 'was dictated by necessity' and by the sense of 'retributive justice' (p. 261). She assumes he is referring to the assassination, when he is actually referring to his present role as police-spy against the revolutionists. But there are also moments, during their conversation, when he is discomfited. For example, when she asserts that death 'is not a shameful thing like some kinds of life', he feels 'something stir in his breast, a sort of feeble and unpleasant tremor' (p. 260). And Razumov's triumph in his successful deception contrasts unfavourably with Sophia Antonovna's manifest sincerity and integrity.

With the arrival and intervention of Nikita, Razumov's sense of safety and security fades. He feels that he is under suspicion once more, and he becomes impatient because the suspicion that he faces from the revolutionists repeats the suspicion he encountered earlier from the authorities: 'He had spoken such words before. He had been driven to cry them out in the face of other suspicions' (p. 268). As a result of this repetition, he feels himself trapped in 'an infernal cycle' (p. 268), and this sense of entrapment finds expression in a new image: 'The choking fumes of falsehood had taken him by the throat – the thought of being condemned to struggle on and on in that tainted atmosphere' (p. 269). Their suspicion of him reflects and activates his own awareness of his inauthenticity. Like Jim, he is oversensitive to the casual remarks of others, and his defensive reaction to assumed attacks reveals the guilt that is consciously denied. His sense of entrapment – and this sensation of 'choking' in a 'tainted atmosphere' – can thus be seen to express his inner experience of the false-self system.[19]

The second part of Sophia Antonovna's 'investigation' involves questioning Razumov about Ziemianitch. Razumov had decided not to mention Ziemianitch in his confession to Mikulin ('To mention him at all would mean imprisonment for the "bright soul", perhaps cruel floggings, and in the end a journey to Siberia in chains' – p. 48). The relief he feels now that he is at last able to confess to some knowledge of him is suggested by the 'savage delight' he takes 'in the loud utterance of that name, which had never before crossed his lips audibly' (p. 274). This bears witness to the pressure he experiences from the concealments forced on him by the parts he is playing. Ziemianitch, like Razumov, has fallen victim to appearances. By his suicide, he has confirmed the false impression that he had betrayed Haldin, and he has released Razumov from some of the burden of suspicion. Razumov's sense of security, however, is short-lived:

> Had his own visit to that accursed house passed unnoticed? It was barely possible. Yet it was hardly probable. . . . But the letter did not seem to contain any allusion to that. Unless she had suppressed it.   (pp. 277–8)

Razumov desires 'perfect safety' (p. 278), but this representation of his thought-processes shows that the source of his insecurity is within himself: it springs, not from external causes, so much as from his own fears that, in turn, derive from his repressed awareness of guilt.

Part III ends with Razumov wandering through Geneva, and this self-absorbed wandering is expressive of his inner state. He had intended to write a report to Mikulin in order to fulfil his role as police-spy, but he 'then had forgotten all about it' (p. 288). He reflects:

> That incorrigible tendency to escape from the grip of the situation was fraught with serious danger. . . . What was it? Levity, or deep-seated weakness? Or an unconscious dread?   (p. 288)

That word 'weakness' is a reminder of his earlier lapse. It sounds again the opposition of 'strength' and 'weakness' (recurrent in Part

III) that figures the conflict between Razumov's conscious attempt to play the part he has been given and his involuntary resistance to it, the conflict between the false-self system and denied aspects of himself. Razumov's wanderings and forgetfulness indicate his unconscious flight from the role to which he has consciously committed himself. Part III concludes with Razumov at last finding a safe place to write his report. He assures himself: 'There can be no doubt that now I am safe' (p. 291). But the place of security is an island, and Razumov's position on this island emblematises his isolation.[20] This isolation stands in significant contrast to the bonds Razumov will discover and acknowledge in Part IV.

IV

Part IV begins with a striking analepsis: it returns to the discussion with Mikulin (which was interrupted at the end of Part I) to supply information withheld during the course of Parts II and III. In particular, it reveals the process by which Razumov came to accept the role of police-spy. It starts with a reminder of the psychological crisis that was precipitated by the irruption of Haldin into his life: 'The Revolution had sought him out to put to a sudden test his dormant instincts, his half-conscious thoughts, and almost wholly unconscious ambitions' (p. 294). Razumov was brought to self-conscious awareness of the problematics of his own identity through Haldin. In Part IV, the conversation with Mikulin brings Razumov 'to the test of another faith' as he is forced to 'defend his attitude of detachment' (p. 294). Mikulin makes it clear that Razumov's aloofness, which was misinterpreted by Haldin, is also open to misinterpretation by the authorities: 'abstention, reserve, in certain situations, come very near to political crime' (p. 294). Razumov's enforced awareness of his identity-for-the-other is experienced by him, alternately, as entrapment or potential understanding. If he feels trapped by the consciousness of other's interpretations and misinterpretations of him, he can also feel attracted by the possibility of aligning identity-for-the-other with identity-for-self through confession: 'To be understood appeared extremely fascinating' (p. 297).

To begin with, however, he tries to escape from this opposition by flight into psychosomatic illness: 'something in the nature of a low fever, which all at once removed him to a great distance from the perplexing actualities, from his very room, even' (p. 298).[21] When he recovers from this illness, he discovers that things are 'changed, subtly and provokingly in their nature' (p. 298). If he stays at home, he suffers, alternately, from apathy and from rages (pp. 298–9). If he goes out, he is assailed by a sense of guilt: 'whenever he went abroad he felt himself at once closely involved in the moral consequences of his act' (p. 299). Haldin has become 'a moral spectre infinitely more effective than any visible apparition of the dead' (pp. 299–300). He is particularly troubled by his new sense of being the object of others' attention.[22] He feels that, through his association with Haldin, 'the eye of the social revolution was on him' (p. 301), and he has a similar sense of being watched by the authorities: at one point, he hallucinates 'the eyes of General T—— and of Privy-Councillor Mikulin side by side fixed upon him' (p. 302). He begins to suspect that 'he no longer belonged to himself' (p. 301); and, in the end, he can enjoy neither work nor rest, neither solitude nor 'intercourse with his kind': 'Everything was gone. His existence was a great cold blank' (p. 303). Once he has reached this point, it comes as no surprise that, when he receives the summons from Mikulin, he goes to him with 'the eagerness of a pursued person welcoming any sort of shelter' (p. 304). Haldin has pursued him both through the guilt Razumov feels at his betrayal and through the false position that Haldin has placed him in. Councillor Mikulin was 'the only person on earth with whom Razumov could talk, taking the Haldin adventure for granted': 'And Haldin, when once taken for granted, was no longer a haunting, falsehood-breeding spectre' (p. 304).

Once Razumov has returned to Mikulin, Mikulin has other resources for gaining control over him. Mikulin believes that 'Things and men have always a certain sense, a certain side by which they must be got hold of if one wants to obtain a solid grasp and a perfect command' (p. 307). The collocation of 'things' and 'men' is a sign of the instrumental view of Razumov that Mikulin takes ('that tool so much finer than the common base instruments' – p. 307), and that instrumental view of Razumov is ironically contrasted with the means Mikulin uses. In Razumov's case, the 'certain side' by which he can be controlled is his sense of isolation, and Mikulin exploits this to the full: 'The obscure, unrelated young student Razumov, in the moment of great moral loneliness, was allowed to feel that he was an object of interest to a small group of people of high position' (pp. 307–8). Even Prince K——, his natural father, is persuaded to play a part in this scheme: 'The sudden embrace of that man . . . was a revelation to Mr Razumov of something within his own breast' (p. 308). Here, however, Mikulin overplays his hand. That 'revelation' of 'something within his own breast' is the start of a different process that will eventually bring about the failure of Mikulin's plans. Razumov's unexpected emotional responsiveness to his father looks forward to his later reaction to Nathalie Haldin. The emotional manipulation, which Razumov experiences in Russia, is replaced by genuine emotional interest in Geneva. In both instances, Razumov reveals the emotional need that is the corrollary of his isolated position. Initially, however, Razumov's desire to escape from his 'great moral loneliness' (p. 307) serves only to place him in a position of even greater falseness as a police-spy among the revolutionaries in Geneva, whereas his emotional response to Nathalie brings about not only his integration into a community but his re-location within his own body.[23]

Part IV focuses on two important meetings: Razumov's first meeting with Nathalie Haldin and his first meeting with Haldin's mother, which comes about when Razumov goes to the Haldin house to tell them the story of Haldin's arrest. He intends to retell this story as an assertion of his false identity, but what happens at the Haldin house is not what he had expected. His meeting with Mrs Haldin represents 'the revenge of the unknown': he finds, after meeting her, that he cannot 'shake off the poignant impression of that silent, quiet, white-haired woman' (p. 340). He tries to get rid of his response by denying it: 'He had felt a pitying surprise. But that, of course, was of no importance. Mothers did not matter' (p. 340). His next change of mood, however, shows exactly how much mothers do matter as 'the old anger against Haldin reawakened by the contemplation of Haldin's mother':

> And was it not something like enviousness which gripped his heart, as if of a privilege denied to him alone of all the men that had ever passed through this world? It was the other who had attained to repose and yet continued to exist in the affection of that mourning old woman.   (p. 341)

When Haldin had appeared in Razumov's room, he had observed that Razumov's lack of family was one of the factors that had influenced him in his decision to turn to Razumov for help (p. 19). Razumov's unspoken response had been: 'Because I haven't that,

must everything else be taken away from me?' (p. 26). Part I explored the identity that Razumov tried to create for himself in the
absence of family ties; in Part IV, that absence of family is redefined
as a need for love.

As Razumov tries to flee from Mrs Haldin, he runs into Nathalie,
and her 'presence in the ante-room was as unforeseen as the
apparition of her brother had been' (p. 341). The implications of this
comparison are immediately spelt out:

> It was she who had been haunting him now. He had suffered that
> persecution ever since she had suddenly appeared before him in
> the garden of the Villa Borel with an extended hand and the name
> of her brother on her lips.   (p. 342)

The imagery of 'haunting', which has so far been related to Haldin,
is now associated with Nathalie and with Razumov's emotional
response to her. At this point, the only clue to the nature of that
response is the observable change in Razumov that this meeting
with Nathalie produces:

> He raised his face, pale, full of unexpressed suffering. But that
> look in his eyes of dull, absent obstinacy, which struck, and
> surprised everybody he was talking to, began to pass away. It
> was as though he were coming to himself in the awakened con-
> sciousness of that marvellous harmony of feature, of lines, of
> glances, of voice.   (p. 342)

The suggestion is that Razumov is ceasing to assert his false identity
and that he is experiencing the emergence of some new principle.
This is re-inforced in the subsequent dialogue between Razumov
and Nathalie, in the course of which Razumov is drawn progressively through various acts of self-definition towards full confession.
He talks of his lack of parents and describes himself as 'a breast
unwarmed by any affection' (p. 344). He reveals some of the truth of
Haldin's fate: 'your brother meant to save his life – to escape'
(p. 349). He tells Nathalie that 'in the last conversation he held as a
free man he mentioned you both':

> Of you he said that you had trustful eyes. . . . It meant that there
> is in you no guile, no deception, no falsehood, no suspicion –
> nothing in your heart that could give you a conception of a living,

acting, speaking lie, if ever it came in your way. That you are a predestined victim. (p. 349)

Razumov's words contain not only another veiled self-portrait ('a living, acting, speaking lie'), but they also acknowledge the temptation he has experienced to exploit Nathalie's innocence. Truth emerges through the lies of the false-self system, as the language teacher's comments on this speech suggest:

> The convulsive, uncontrolled tone of the last words disclosed the precarious hold he had over himself. He was like a man defying his own dizziness in high places and tottering suddenly on the very edge of the precipice. (p. 349)

As the dialogue continues, Razumov proceeds through half-disguised confessions (p. 353) to his final, silent admission of guilt as he 'pressed a denunciatory finger to his breast with force, and became perfectly still' (p. 354).

Chapter 4 elaborates on this silent self-denunciation with extracts from Razumov's written confession. Razumov records how 'Victor Haldin had stolen the truth of my life from me, who had nothing else in the world' (p. 359). He describes the emotions he consequently felt towards Haldin's mother and sister ('I believed that I had in my breast nothing but an inexhaustible fund of anger and hate for you both' – p. 358), and his surprising discovery:

> Hate or no hate, I felt at once that, while shunning the sight of you, I could never succeed in driving away your image. . . . It is only later on that I understood – only today, only a few hours ago. What could I have known of what was tearing me to pieces and dragging the secret for ever to my lips. You were appointed to undo the evil by making me betray myself back into truth and peace. (p. 358)

This process, by which Razumov moves from 'anger and hate' to love, is accompanied by a second process. He tells Nathalie how, after the news of Ziemianitch's suicide, the 'strength of falsehood seemed irresistible': 'I embraced the might of falsehood, I exulted in it' (p. 360). But Nathalie's influence has drawn him from this life of falsehood ('the truth shining in you drew the truth out of me' – p. 361) and freed him from the suffocation of the false-self system: 'as

I write here, I am in the depths of anguish, but there is air to breathe at last' (p. 361). Razumov now realises 'In giving Victor Haldin up, it was myself, after all, whom I have betrayed most basely' (p. 361). In betraying Haldin, he not only lost the possibility of realising his former identity-for-self, he also initiated the process which ended in his assertion of a false identity, his employment of a false-self system. Nathalie Haldin has made him 'betray' himself back into 'truth and peace' (p. 358). Her truth and her trust in him have led him to make this confession, which destroys the false-self system he has deployed in Geneva.

To complete the process, Razumov feels he now has to make a formal confession to the revolutionists. With this confession, he will at last 'escape from the prison of lies' (p. 363): he will have established a true identity with one of the two sides of the polarised Russian world of the novel. Just as Razumov's dialogue with Nathalie Haldin was a re-play of his earlier betrayal of her brother, other events from that evening when he betrayed Haldin are echoed in this concluding section of the novel. Thus he sets off, at midnight, for the house of Julius Laspara, 'the facts and the words of a certain evening in his past . . . timing his conduct in the present' (p. 362). His full and public confession is followed by the penance of his deafening by Nikita and his crippling by the tram, but this is not the end of Razumov's story. The truth that he thought would kill him, in some sense, saves him. He asks the revolutionists to observe that he could have remained silent: 'Today, of all days since I came amongst you, I was made safe, and today I made myself free from falsehood, from remorse – independent of every single human being on this earth' (p. 368). His confession frees him from falsehood, but, rather than granting him independence from 'every single human being on this earth', it actually brings him into relation with others, and Razumov, who has been characterised by his absence of family, now finds kin. When he is run down by the tram, Tekla runs forward to claim him: 'This young man is a Russian, and I am his relation' (p. 371).

His confession also earns him the respect of the revolutionists, and he acquires a place in their community: some of the revolutionists 'always go to see him when passing through' (p. 379). Sophia Antonovna offers a final judgement upon him:

There are evil moments in every life. A false suggestion enters one's brain, and then fear is born – fear of oneself, fear for oneself.

Or else a false courage – who knows? Well, call it what you like; but tell me, how many of them would deliver themselves up deliberately to perdition (as he himself says in that book) rather than go on living, secretly debased in their own eyes? . . . It was just when he believed himself safe and more – infinitely more – when the possibility of being loved by that admirable girl first dawned upon him, that he discovered that his bitterest railings, the worst wickedness, the devil work of his hate and pride, could never cover up the ignominy of the existence before him. There's character in such a discovery.   (p. 380)

Guerard seems to have missed this aspect of the novel's conclusion. He suggests that Razumov's act of betrayal, 'carrying him out of one solitude and into another' compels him to destroy himself at last.[24] But Razumov has not merely been carried 'out of one solitude and into another': at the end, he escapes from solitude into community. Through the assertion of his independence from others, he finds an integrity that becomes the basis for a true relation to others. But to understand the significance of this assertion of independence, it is necessary to place it in the context of Razumov's initial identification with an alterated identity and his subsequent suffering from 'ideas of reference'. Hawthorn observes that 'Razumov confesses his betrayal and faces the revolutionaries much as Jim refuses to try to escape his fate'.[25] But Razumov's final confession has none of the ambivalence of Jim's end: when Jim faces Doramin, he is still caught up in the drama of his self-ideal; when Razumov confesses to the revolutionists, he frees himself from that dependence on others' views of himself that was part of his isolated existence, but, in doing so, he discovers another kind of dependence on others.

Through Razumov, Conrad rediscovers and re-affirms a concept of community and 'human solidarity'. As Guerard notes:

The energizing conflict derives from the fact that Razumov, this sane conservative scorner of visionaries and servant of law and victim of revolutionary folly, is (when he informs on Haldin) dramatized as committing a crime; he has violated the deepest human bond.[26]

If Razumov's betrayal of Haldin to the authorities were not assumed to be a 'crime', the rest of the novel would be morally meaningless. Gekoski clarifies the point: 'Why is Razumov tormented by his deci-

sion to turn Haldin in to the police? Unlike Jim, he has not contra-
vened the law; he has obeyed it'.[27] The answer is that the narrative
assumes bonds of human solidarity which transcend the laws of a
given society: in attempting to keep within the latter, Razumov
breaks the former. It should also be noted that, after discovering the
impossibility of clearing his name with the czarist authorities, it is
with the revolutionists that Razumov finally makes his peace.

V

The conflict of legality and personal loyalty figured in another work
written in this period. After a visit from Captain Marris in October
1909, Conrad wrote three stories set in South East Asia: 'The Secret
Sharer', 'A Smile of Fortune' and 'Freya of the Seven Isles'. The first
of these, 'The Secret Sharer', was written in less than a month during
late November and early December of that year. At that time, Conrad
had taken up and set aside *Chance*, had completed *The Secret Agent*
and *A Personal Record*, and had almost completed *Under Western
Eyes*.[28] 'The Secret Sharer' tells how Leggatt, the mate of the *Sephora*,
kills a member of the crew during a storm and is put under arrest by
his captain. He escapes and swims to another ship, whose captain is
the unnamed narrator of the story. This captain is a young man, who
has just been given his first command, and feels himself to be both 'a
stranger to the ship' and 'somewhat of a stranger' to himself.[29]

The opening of the story emphasises the narrator's sense of isolation as the new captain of a strange ship, and the captain's state of
mind is closely connected with Leggatt's arrival on board. The narrator has set no anchor-watch, and, as a result, a rope-ladder has
been left hanging over the side. It is this rope-ladder that saves
Leggatt (p. 110). As Guerard points out, the narrative insists upon
the captain's responsibility for 'the dangling ladder' and, hence, for
Leggatt's arrival on board.[30] The captain, however, does not consciously decide to conceal the fugitive, but, as soon as he sees Leggatt,
he feels that 'a mysterious communication was established' (p. 99)
between them. The implications of this 'mysterious communication'
are then drawn out through the accidental similarity of their appearance, when the captain provides the naked Leggatt with his spare
sleeping-suit, a suit 'of the same greystripe pattern as the one I was
wearing' (p. 100).

On the basis of this accidental physical resemblance, Leggatt is repeatedly described as the captain's 'double' or 'other self', and the narrative, more than once, constructs a mirror-image:

> He rested a hand on the end of the skylight to steady himself with, and all that time did not stir a limb, so far as I could see. . . . One of my hands, too, rested on the end of the skylight; neither did I stir a limb, so far as I knew.   (p. 103)[31]

Leggatt's criminal status is the most problematic part of this identification. Leggatt's crime has various mitigating circumstances, but, nevertheless, Leggatt, like Jim, has transgressed the ideal code of conduct of the sea. He has also transgressed the moral and criminal codes of society. The story, however, is not primarily concerned with the precise nature of Leggatt's offence, nor with the exact degree of his guilt. Leggatt is more important as the embodiment of the captain's original feeling of being 'a stranger' to himself. He represents what Hewitt calls 'that fear that there are parts of himself which he has not yet brought into the light of day'.[32] These are parts of himself which might interfere with the realisation of what he calls 'that ideal conception of one's own personality every man sets up for himself secretly' (p. 94). What matters, then, is not so much the nature of Leggatt's crime as the fact that the captain has a possibly criminal 'secret sharer' – and the relationship between the captain's 'ideal conception' of himself and other aspects of himself 'not yet brought into the light of day' which that fact figures.

As a result of Leggatt's presence on board ship, the captain leads a life of sharp anxieties and sudden concealments. His nerves begin to go, and his men regard his strange behaviour with suspicion: they assume that he is either mad or drinking. The captain himself realises how his anxieties about Leggatt impair his ability to command:

> I was not wholly alone with my command: for there was that stranger in my cabin. Or rather, I was not completely and wholly with her. Part of me was absent. That mental feeling of being in two places at once . . .   (p. 125)

As a result, orders which should spring to his lips without thinking do not come: his awareness of his 'other self' intervenes. As the narrator's mental state deteriorates, this feeling of duality is pushed to the point where he begins to fear for his sanity. To begin with, his 'confused sensation of being in two places at once' (p. 111) is set against his endeavour to function as captain of the ship. The climax of this mental torment occurs when, on the fourth day, the steward enters the captain's cabin, but the expected discovery of Leggatt does not occur: 'An irresistible doubt of his bodily existence flitted through my mind. Can it be, I asked myself, that he is not visible to other eyes than mine?' (p. 130).

On the character-level, 'The Secret Sharer' 'dramatises a human relationship and individual moral bond at variance with the moral bond to the community implicit in laws and maritime tradition'.[33] The situation resembles Jim's relationship with Gentleman Brown or the initial stage of Razumov's relationship with Haldin. In each case, there is, to a greater or lesser extent, 'the act of sympathetic identification with a suspect or outlaw figure, and the ensuing conflict between loyalty to the individual and loyalty to the community'.[34] It could be argued that the captain's unconventional behaviour, which allowed Leggatt to board the ship, implied flaws or weaknesses in the captain which the identification with Leggatt both clarifies and further exemplifies. On the symbolic level, Leggatt's presence on board the ship can be seen to represent the captain's guilty awareness of aspects of himself that do not correspond to his role as captain. The captain's self-division prevents his satisfactory fulfillment of the role and alarms the crew. More precisely, it is not so much self-division that is the captain's problem as self-consciousness in the role rather than the automatic performance of the role.[35] By the end of the narrative, with the departure of Leggatt from the ship, the captain has, apparently, overcome his initial feeling of 'strangeness' and can feel confident of his ability to command. The conclusion of the story can then be interpreted as dramatising the splitting-off of that 'secret self' – those parts of him that do not correspond to the 'ideal conception' that the narrator has of his own personality – to achieve the satisfactory performance of the role.

Guerard offers a reading of the conclusion in terms of the captain's self-integration:

> The story moves from his sense of being stranger to his ship, and to himself, to a final mature confidence and integration: 'And I was alone with her. Nothing! no-one in the world should stand now between us, throwing a shadow on the way of silent knowledge and mute affection, the perfect communion of a seaman with his first command'.[36]

However, this reading encounters a difficulty: in psychological terms 'the positive end of the introspective experience is incorporation not separation and split'.[37] That is, Guerard finds it difficult to reconcile what he regards as a 'positive end' with the process by which that end has been achieved. This difficulty, however, can be resolved using Guerard's own suggestion of a distance between Conrad and the narrator. He comments on the captain's loyalty to Leggatt: 'Leggatt must be hidden from the captain's own crew. And he must be kept hidden from the captain of the *Sephora* (with his fidelity to the law) on the following day.'[38] Then he points out that the narrator refers slightingly to Captain Archbold's 'obscure tenacity', 'immaculate command', and sense of 'pitiless obligation' (pp. 118–19), whereas these qualities are presented positively, elsewhere in Conrad's work, in relation to the ideal code of the sea.[39] It is wrong to assume, therefore, 'that Conrad unequivocally *approves* the captain's decision to harbour Leggatt'.[40] Indeed it is quite possible that Conrad was distanced from – and, indeed, critical of – his narrator.

On this reading, 'The Secret Sharer' offers another of Conrad's studies of sea-captains and the problematics of command. It could be compared with 'Typhoon' or 'The Shadow-Line', but the most useful comparison is with *The Nigger of the 'Narcissus'*: what *The Nigger of the 'Narcissus'* treated from the view-point of the crew, 'The Secret Sharer' examines from the view-point of the new captain. In each case, Conrad presents the conflict between 'the burden of self' and the ideal code of the sea, but, where *The Nigger of the 'Narcissus'* presented a paradigm, 'The Secret Sharer' is more ambivalent. That ambivalence can be seen from a comparison of James Wait and Leggatt. Both can be read, symbolically, as the embodiment of the burden of self, but, where Wait dies and is buried at sea, Leggatt is very much alive at the end of 'The Secret Sharer'. The captain imagines Leggatt's existence after he leaves the ship – 'I saw myself wandering barefooted, bareheaded, the sun beating on my dark poll' (p. 138) – and the story ends with Leggatt 'a free man, a proud swimmer striking out for a new destiny' (p. 143). If this were Leggatt's story, it would be tempting to read this conclusion as the liberation of the repressed self. However, since it is the captain's story, this conclusion has to have a different significance. The story shows the captain becoming aware of, and splitting-off, an aspect of himself that will prevent him from performing the role of captain, from achieving that alterated identity. The ambivalence of the conclusion is to be explained by Conrad's awareness of the personal cost of such a split: what is lost is 'a free man, a proud swimmer', a vivid image of existential life.[41]

In *Under Western Eyes*, Razumov moves from ontological insecurity and identification with an alterated identity to an assertion of self unhindered by ideas of reference; he progresses from withdrawal and a sense of isolation to integration within a community; and it is a community, that is not constructed hierarchically as it was in *The Nigger of the 'Narcissus'* but is represented in terms of non-hierarchical human interactions. Similarly, in 'The Secret Sharer', although the story ends with the captain splitting off the unsuitable aspects of himself and fulfilling the role of captain, this conclusion is not a simple assertion of the ideal code of conduct of the sea. Leggatt's continuing existence on land signifies Conrad's awareness of (and interest in) other psychological possibilities outside that ideological framework. *Under Western Eyes* and 'The Secret Sharer' mark the end of one line of thought, but they also contain hints of what is to follow. 'The Secret Sharer' might, indeed, be read as 'an allegory of Conrad's future development', as Hewitt suggests, but only if it is recognised that it does not end with the suppression of that aspect of self associated with Leggatt: in his later fictions, Conrad becomes, like Leggatt, 'a free man, a proud swimmer striking out for a new destiny' (p. 143).[42]

7

The Wisdom of the Heart:
Chance and *Victory*

The seeds of the positive vision of Conrad's late novels are present in *Nostromo* in the figure of Mrs Gould.[1] The narrator observes of her:

> The wisdom of the heart having no concern with the erection or the demolition of theories any more than with the defence of prejudices, has no random words at its command. The words it pronounces have the value of acts of integrity, tolerance, and compassion. (p. 67)

The 'wisdom of the heart', precisely because it is not concerned with 'the erection or the demolition of theories', becomes a possible refuge for Conrad's radical scepticism.

I

Nostromo was completed on 30 August 1904. On 21 December 1904, in a letter to J. B. Pinker, Conrad indicated his return to work on *The Rescue* and mentioned 'the new novel' which was 'simmering within' him.[2] This was presumably *Chance*, which Conrad seems to have begun writing during 1905. He set it aside during 1906, while he wrote *The Secret Agent*, and took it up again in 1907. At this point, it seems still to have been a sea-story; indeed, in a letter to Pinker (20 December 1909), Conrad describes it as 'a Malay sea tale'.[3] He returned to it in July 1910 and again in May 1911, when he at last found a way to finish it. He wrote to Pinker on 2 June 1913:

> You who know the inner history of that novel will understand why I had more trouble than enough with it. It was written in 1907 [i.e. the opening chapter] and the rest of the novel in 1911–12. And it did not belong to that novel – but to some other novel which will never be written now I guess.[4]

Chance, indeed, begins as if it were going to be a novel about sailors and the sea.[5] It is perhaps because the opening of the novel reinforces these expectations, that a number of critics have misread it. *Chance*, however, is not really a sea-story – though much of it takes place at sea. Neither Powell nor Captain Anthony is the central figure: unusually (in terms of readers' expectations from Conrad), the central position is taken by a female character, Flora de Barral. R. L. Mégroz provided an honourable early exception to the general critical tendency to read the novel from a male-centred position:

> The whole book is the story of Flora, injured deeply in childhood, attracting by her psychic condition a kind of cyclic repetition of experience. If the story had been mainly about Roderick Anthony, we should need to know more about his childhood. We are told only just enough to make us understand that his romantic behaviour is caused by a psychic condition similarly established in youth.[6]

The earliest criticism tends to have been more sensitive to the narrative method and its significance than later criticism has been.[7] Henry James, for example, in a generally negative review of the novel, compared its succession of narrators to 'the successive members of a cue from one to the other of which the sense and the interest of the subject have to be passed on together, in the manner of the buckets of water for the improvised extinction of a fire' with, of course, a certain quantity of 'sense' and 'interest' being spilt by the way.[8] James's criticism, in fact, indicates the precise significance of the narrative method in *Chance*: the succession of narrators constitutes, in effect, a series of witnesses. Marlow both recounts and explores the testimonies of these various witnesses to try and produce a coherent account just as the detective does in a classic detective story.[9] Marlow constructs a narrative by induction from the details presented to him. Conrad thus develops what Guerard, putting the cart before the horse, called 'the Faulknerian device of narration through speculative commentary'.[10] Conrad's model for the narrative-method of *Chance* is not Henry James but rather Edgar Allan Poe or Arthur Conan Doyle. At the same time, unlike the classic detective story, Marlow's narrative interpretation constantly shades into uncertainties and indeterminacies.

The narrative of *Chance* is structured by three mysteries. There is, first of all, 'the affair of the purloined brother' (p. 148), which is solved by Flora's account (at the end of Part I) of her relations with Anthony. Part II then opens with 'the mystery of the vanishing Powell' (p. 258), which is solved by Flora again at the end of Part II. This operates as a frame-story for Part II: within it there is the inset-story which is the focus of interest for most of the second part – namely 'that psychological cabin mystery of discomfort' (p. 325), the strained relations of Flora and Captain Anthony on board the *Ferndale*. Through all of this, Marlow occupies the position of the detective, and the unnamed primary narrator is effectively assigned the position of client or confidant. In Part II, for example, Marlow reports back to him in much the way that a detective might report back to his client or Marlow's contemporary, Sherlock Holmes, might have reported back to Dr Watson:

> 'I suppose,' he said . . . 'that you think it's high time I told you something definite. I mean something about that psychological cabin mystery of discomfort . . . '
> 'You are going to confess now that you have failed to find it out,' I said in pretended indignation.
> 'It would serve you right if I told you that I have. But I won't. I haven't failed. I own though that for a time I was puzzled. However, I have now seen our Powell many times under the most favourable conditions – and besides I came upon a most unexpected source of information. . . . I'll admit that for some time the old-maiden-lady-like occupation of putting two and two together failed to procure a coherent theory. I am speaking now as an investigator – a man of deductions.   (pp. 325–6)

Although there is an attempted murder in *Chance*, the mysteries which Marlow investigates are not so much mysteries about events as mysteries about processes. As the narrator says (with a change of metaphor and literary allusion), Marlow is 'the expert in the psychological wilderness' (p. 311), tracking the psychological causes of events by the smallest of signs.

In *Chance*, as in a detective story like Poe's 'Murders in the Rue Morgue', a succession of narrators presents a succession of partial views that are presented as partial views: the different points of view produce various subjective interpretations of events. Hough complains that this intricate introduction with multiple narrations 'seems to promise a more complex and many-sided mode of apprehension than the book actually affords': 'It is not, for instance, the prelude to a complex way of presenting character and situation through several different visions, as it might be in Henry James'.[11] However, Conrad's aim was not, as Moser similarly assumes, to present 'the action filtered through several intervening planes of consciousness'.[12] Conrad was not interested, in *Chance*, in consciousness and the objects of consciousness, but in psychology and in the self-conscious handling of narrative. Marlow, like Poe's Dupin, attempts to resolve the contradictions between the accounts of the various 'witnesses', to fill in the blanks and gaps in the narrative, and to produce a 'coherent theory' (p. 396) based on the information supplied to him. At the same time, Conrad does not share the faith in the power of reason of either Poe or Conan Doyle, and, accordingly, his presentation of his 'investigator' is significantly different from theirs: where they underwrite their investigator's ratiocination, Conrad, by various means, distances himself from Marlow and maintains a certain detachment from Marlow's narrative interpretation. One of those means is to emphasise the literary self-consciousness that was always potentially present in the classic detective-story.[13]

Some of the critical dissatisfaction with *Chance* can also be traced to a misreading of Conrad's authorial strategy in relation to Marlow – and to a corresponding sense of disappointment with Marlow. Moser, for example, criticises *Chance* by comparing it with *Lord Jim*. But the difference between these two novels – a difference in technique rather than in quality – is obvious, when the different role given to Marlow in each narrative is considered. Moser offers an accurate and sensitive description of Marlow's role in *Lord Jim*:

> Marlow, as the narrator of *Lord Jim*, contributes meaning in several ways. In the first place, he gives the reader a sense of actuality. After all, he knew Jim better than any one else did. He was there. More important, however, Marlow acts as Jim's interpreter because . . . he has a more subtle mind than Jim and can see implications that Jim cannot. Marlow is important in his own right, too. He adds a new moral dimension because Jim's dilemma becomes his own. Finally, Marlow acts as an interviewer who brings together and comments upon the testimony of more than a dozen secondary observers of Jim.[14]

In *Chance*, Marlow fulfils only the last of these roles. As for the others, it would be hard to argue, for example, that Marlow gives the reader 'a sense of actuality'. Certainly, if he does, it is not because he knew Flora de Barral and Captain Anthony better than anyone else. Marlow frequently asserts how limited his direct contact with them has been. He meets Flora on only three occasions – though, admittedly, on the second and third occasion, she is the source of important information. He has never met Captain Anthony, yet he spends the last half of the novel discussing and analysing Anthony's character and behaviour. As in *Lord Jim*, Marlow acts as an interpreter, but, in *Chance*, that interpretation is undercut by Marlow's acknowledged lack of direct contact with the central characters. His narration has a tentative, speculative, hypothetical character even more obviously than it had in 'Heart of Darkness'. As Marlow says, just before Flora gives her account of her elopement with Captain Anthony:

> The trouble was that I could not imagine anything about Flora de Barral and the brother of Mrs Fyne. Or if you like, I could imagine *anything* which comes practically to the same thing.   (p. 210)

Hough describes how a picture of Flora de Barral is built up 'with fragments of narrative by Fyne and Mrs Fyne, observations and surmises by Marlow, scenes, fragments of scenes, glimpses, guesses', and he concludes that it is handled, 'as far as the sheer machinery is concerned, with immense technical assurance'; yet there is 'a slightly disturbing sense of being kept at a remove, or rather several removes, from the actuality'.[15] Again, Hough's criticism provides its own answer. In talking of 'the actuality' in a non-problematical way, Hough fails to see that the problematical status of 'actuality' is the ground of Conrad's narrative. Marlow, indeed, answers Hough's criticism and offers his own justification for *Chance*'s narrative method: 'Dark and, so to speak, inscrutable spaces being met with in life, there must be such places in any statement dealing with life' (p. 101). *Chance* is grounded in indeterminacy, in the ultimate unknowableness of things, and Conrad's narrative-strategy is to use Marlow in order to register this aspect of reality. Marlow presents fiction as fiction, not as 'actuality'. John Palmer observes, of *Chance* and *Victory*, that 'these later novels brings into the foreground the metaphysical and epistemological skepticism which had always been in the background of Conrad's fiction'.[16]

At the same time, Conrad has changed Marlow's character. Moser describes Marlow in *Lord Jim* as having 'a more subtle mind than Jim' and as being able to see implications that Jim cannot. The

Marlow of *Chance* lacks the subtlety, sensitivity and intensity of the Marlow of *Lord Jim*. Indeed, as a number of critics have observed, this Marlow can be trivial, long-winded, and even obtuse.[17] The Marlow who comments on the Fynes' rescue of Flora that it had never occurred to them that 'the simplest way out of the difficulty was to do nothing and dismiss the matter as no concern of theirs' (p. 95) sounds very different from the Marlow who involved himself in the fate of Jim or the Marlow who allied himself with Kurtz.[18] This Marlow's verbal presentation of himself lacks the moral sense and moral responsibility of earlier Marlows. In addition, when he asserts that 'no one, I imagine, is anxious' to take 'stock of the wares' of their mind if it can be avoided (p. 136), he not only articulates the refusal to analyse and introspect that is characteristic of him in this novel, but he also points towards what has been seen as another flaw in *Chance* – that Marlow as narrator is not personally involved in his narration as he was in 'Heart of Darkness' and *Lord Jim*.[19]

This Marlow does not live up to the expectations created by earlier Marlows, but, as William York Tindall wisely observes:

> We too may dislike Marlow and his manner or method, but we must not blame Conrad for a dramatic revelation of middle-aged nostalgia or the discursive insistency that seems its accomplice.[20]

Moreover, while this Marlow lacks the self-questioning and self-exploration that characterised him in 'Heart of Darkness' and *Lord Jim*, there is an interaction of a different kind between him and his tale: Marlow's obtuseness, while unattractive and even irritating, is, nevertheless, generally functional. This can be seen particularly clearly in relation to his much-criticised statements about women. It is not necessary to ascribe these comments to assumed misogynistic feelings in Conrad.[21] Conrad consistently distances himself from Marlow through his use of the anonymous narrator, who regularly challenges Marlow's statements.[22] By this means, Marlow's misogyny becomes not a leakage into the novel from Conrad's subconscious but rather one of the novel's semantic elements: Marlow's misogyny is put into significant interaction with other elements in the novel as part of the novel's analysis of the position of women, and as part of the novel's exploration of human sexuality. As Gary Geddes puts it: 'Through this by-play between Marlow and the narrator, a kind of dialectic or ironic counterpoint is established, which allows for the clarification of important issues in the novel.'[23] By contrast, some of the critical insensitivity to Conrad's use of Marlow in *Chance* seems to derive from the naive expectation that Marlow should be Conrad's mouthpiece or, at least, should act as an authoritative guide through the narrative.[24]

Moser argued that Conrad's art, in *Lord Jim*, 'lies in the way he carefully qualifies each narrator's analysis of Jim and shows clearly that the truth about Jim must be the sum of many perceptions'.[25] In the same way, in *Chance*, Marlow's comments are held in significant tension with other elements of the novel as part of the novel's production of meaning. As Frances Cutler noted, this places a particular responsibility on the reader:

> The older novel, the simplification of life, gave us the creative process achieved, the decision handed down. . . . But with Conrad we actually enter into the creative process: we grope with him through blinding mists, we catch at fleeting glimpses and thrill with sudden illuminations . . . we, the listeners, not only share in the creation, but verily 'confirm and complete' these stories, whose aim is the search itself and not its ending.[26]

II

Although the opening chapter was originally going to introduce a different narrative, it nevertheless sounds a note that is repeated in the story of Flora de Barral. When young Powell fails to find an officer's berth after gaining his certificate, he 'didn't think himself good enough for anybody's kinship' (p. 8). This is the ironic prelude to his meeting with his namesake and the unexpected acquisition of 'kin': the older Powell encourages Captain Anthony to draw the wrong conclusion from the coincidence of names, and, in doing so, plays the part of 'a sort of good uncle' (p. 22) to the younger man. Indeed, young Powell adds: 'he had done more for me that day than all my relations put together ever did' (p. 22). Flora de Barral, too, is oppressed by 'youthful hopelessness' (p. 9). Even more than Powell she experiences no recognition of her 'right to live' (p. 9) and is made to think of herself as worthless: what for Powell is a brief and passing phase of his development is a much more deeply ingrained part of Flora de Barral's experience of herself and the world. And 'kinship' plays an important role in Flora's story too.

Flora is introduced through Marlow's account of his first meeting with her, when he saw her walking dangerously near the edge of a quarry. Later, Flora reveals that what seemed like recklessness was, in fact, an attempt to commit suicide. But Marlow's account already hints at Flora's suicidal tendencies:

> Had she given occasion for a coroner's inquest the verdict would have been suicide. . . . They would never be able to understand that she had taken the trouble to climb over two post-and-rail fences only for the fun of being reckless. Indeed even as I talked chaffingly I was greatly struck myself by the fact. (p. 45)

This incident establishes Marlow's imperceptiveness, but the significance of Flora's reply might also be missed by the reader: 'She retorted that, once one was dead, what horrid people thought of one did not matter' (p. 45).[27] This is more than just a response to Marlow's banter: it expresses Flora's desire to escape from her sense of other people's low opinion of her. This, in turn, suggests both her lack of a sense of personal worth and her identification with her alterated identity. In the course of tracing Flora's development through the narrative, Conrad rejects the model of identity based on identification with an alterated identity; he confronts the underlying ontological insecurity; and, having recognised that insecurity, moves towards another basis for identity. Moser comments on *Chance*:

> We must conclude, then, either that Conrad's fundamental attitude towards women and love has changed, or else that Conrad hopes that it has changed. . . . That is, in 1913 either a new Conrad was born or else the old Conrad began to write love stories, the intended meanings of which ran counter to the deepest impulses of his being.[28]

This chapter will try to demonstrate that it was indeed 'a new Conrad' that was born in this last phase of his writing career, but that this new Conrad, far from being imposed upon 'the deepest impulses' of the old, in fact grew out of that earlier self. To do so, this chapter will concentrate on two aspects of *Chance*: the presentation of Flora de Barral's psycho-sexual development, and the novel's exploration of human sexuality.

After Flora's disappearance from the Fyne household, Marlow is informed of her background. He learns, in particular, about her childhood in Brighton, where, before her father's fall, she 'was stared at in public places as if she had been a sort of princess' (p. 90). Flora's position, at this stage, is directly comparable to young Powell's immediately after he gained his certificate, when, as he puts it, he 'would not have called the Queen his cousin' (p. 8). With the news of her father's impending financial failure, however, Flora is subjected to the experience that determines most of the events of the novel.[29] Marlow presents this experience as the rape and desecration of her child's consciousness:

> Her last sleep, I won't say of innocence . . . but I will say: of that ignorance, or better still, of that unconsciousness of the world's ways, the unconsciousness of danger, of pain, of humiliation, of bitterness, of falsehood. An unconsciousness which in the case of other beings like herself is removed by a gradual process of experience and information, often only partial at that, with saving reserves, softening doubts, veiling theories . . . her unconsciousness was to be broken into with profane violence, with desecrating circumstances like a temple violated by a mad, vengeful, impiety. (p. 99)

This trauma, from which it takes Flora the rest of the novel to recover, is brought about by Flora's governess. The governess was scheming to bring about a marriage between Flora, as the heir to the de Barral fortune, and her 'nephew', 'Mr Charley'. With the fall of de Barral's financial empire, the governess sees her own schemes collapsing also. In particular, Marlow surmises, she foresaw the end of her relationship with 'Mr Charley' (p. 103). The governess's 'envenomed rage' draws on all the disappointments and repressions of her existence, but the form it takes is influenced particularly by the jealousy she felt while encouraging Flora's relationship with 'Mr Charley'. Now that her schemes have fallen through, she is 'very determined that there should be no more of that boy and girl philandering' and 'angry with herself for having suffered from it so much in the past' (pp. 105–6). Her jealousy, her self-suppression in pursuit of her scheme, and her consciousness of her age and its implications for her relationship with 'Mr Charley', Marlow suggests, combine in a compensatory assertion of herself against Flora – 'a little fool who would never in her life be worth anybody's attention' (p. 105). She takes revenge for all her disappointments by presenting Flora with this image of herself. She tells the child that there was nothing in her 'apart from her money, to induce any intelligent person to take any sort of interest in her existence' (p. 119). The effect on Flora is, understandably, devastating. Marlow remarks:

> Even a small child lives, plays and suffers in terms of its conception of its own existence. Imagine, if you can, a fact coming in suddenly with a force capable of shattering that very conception itself. (p. 117)

This 'fact' has all the more force because of its source: the governess 'had been the wisdom, the authority, the protection of life, security embodied and visible and undisputed' (p. 117). Geddes accurately registers that the governess's revenge shatters Flora's conception of herself, but fails to recognise what this actually involves.[30] It deprives Flora of security and of any sense of her own worth. It destroys her sense of her own identity and her sense of her relationship to the world around her. Marlow describes it as 'a mark on her soul, a sort of mystic wound, to be contemplated, to be meditated over' (pp. 118–19).

This traumatic event is the climax of Marlow's account of Flora's childhood. In the next stage of her 'pilgrimage' (p. 210), various events combine, accidentally, to reinforce the sense of her own worthlessness that Flora received from this incident. For example, though the Fynes rescue Flora, various aspects of their character and household work against Flora's recovery from her trauma. The incident of the barking dog reveals qualities in the Fynes that explain how their rescue of Flora continued the psychological damage done to her. The Fynes refuse to allow Marlow to let the dog into the house, and Marlow observes: 'I might indeed have saved my breath, I knew it was one of the Fynes' rules of life, part of their solemnity and responsibility, one of those things that were part of their unassertive but ever present superiority' (p. 142). The Fyne children have the same sense of superiority: they were 'at the same time solemn and malicious, and nursed a secret contempt for all the world' (p. 154). Marlow's restrained account of Flora's visit ('The rest of that day she spent with the Fyne girls who gave her to understand that she was a slow and unprofitable person'; pp. 224–5) prompts the reader to imagine the effect of this attitude of superiority on the insecure Flora. It is, however, not just the Fynes' sense of superiority that is psychologically damaging for Flora: another of the Fynes' characteristics also has its effect. In his account of the incident of the barking dog, Marlow observed that the Fynes were 'strangely consistent in their lack of imaginative sympathy' (p. 143), and it is precisely this 'lack of imaginative sympathy' that characterises their relationship with Flora. Marlow gives full credit to the Fynes' sense of responsibility, but he is not blind to their limitations:

> Mrs Fyne was unflinching in her idea that as much truth as could be told was due in the way of kindness to the girl, whose fate she feared would be to live exposed to the hardest realities of unprivileged existences. She explained to her that there were in the world evil-minded, selfish people. . . . These two persons had been after her father's money. The best thing she could do was to forget all about them.   (p. 139)

The mis-match of 'unflinching' and 'kindness' provides the clue: it is not just that Mrs Fyne's explanation reinforces the idea that Flora is worthless in herself and that only her father's money made her of interest to others, but also that the absence of emotional responsiveness to Flora tacitly transmits the same message. Marlow deduces that 'at no time did she think the victim particularly charming or sympathetic': 'It was a manifestation of pure compassion, of compassion in itself, so to speak, not many women would have been capable of displaying with that unflinching steadiness' (p. 140) The repetition of 'unflinching' and Marlow's steely irony together convey his judgement. What Flora needs is a personal, emotional response to reassure her of her worth, but Mrs Fyne offers her a detached and undemonstrative, purely abstract 'compassion'. It is not surprising that Flora responds with the question: 'Mrs Fyne, am I really such a horrid thing as she has made me out to be?' (p. 140).

One particular difficulty that Mrs Fyne fails to negotiate is Flora's association of her own worth with the question of her father's criminality. Through the governess's attack on both of them, Flora's sense of her own worth has become entangled with her evaluation of her father. She tells Mrs Fyne that the governess called her father 'a cheat and a swindler', and begs to be assured that 'it isn't true' (p. 140). Mrs Fyne's response does nothing to still Flora's anxieties:

> Mrs Fyne restrained her, soothed her, induced her at last to lay her head on her pillow again, assuring her all the time that nothing this woman had had the cruelty to say deserved to be taken to

heart. The girl, exhausted, cried quietly for a time. It may be she had noticed something evasive in Mrs Fyne's assurances. (p. 140)

If Mrs Fyne's evasiveness about de Barral's criminality is registered by Flora, it would serve to undermine Mrs Fyne's other 'assurances'. But, even if Flora has not registered this evasiveness, when Mrs Fyne does tell the truth about de Barral's criminality, the disclosure undoes earlier assurances. The truth of the governess's description of de Barral lends authority to her attack on Flora. Mrs Fyne leaves this linkage intact partly through 'lack of imaginative sympathy' and partly because she herself, in some sense, believes in that linkage – as her reaction to Flora's elopement with Captain Anthony suggests.[31]

Kirschner compares the next stage of Flora's pilgrimage to Jim's career as a water-clerk:

Flora's career after her father's conviction somewhat recalls Jim's retreat. Just as Jim felt he had forfeited men's confidence, Flora has suffered the ultimate feminine defeat by being persuaded that she is incapable of inducing 'any intelligent person to take any sort of interest in her existence'. Like Jim, she revolts vicariously: despite the overwhelming evidence, she refuses to accept the verdict against her father and becomes obsessed with the idea of his innocence.[32]

There is a superficial resemblance between Flora's career, with its succession of posts, and Jim's career, with its succession of jobs. But Jim is fleeing from a fact that challenges his image of himself, and it is this that motivates his sudden departure from each job. Flora, on the other hand, is not 'fleeing from a fact'. She does not leave because her employers seem to have found out about her past. She leaves each post for a different reason, and the succession of posts represents not a flight from guilt but rather a continuing process by which Flora's ontological insecurity is reinforced. As Geddes says, the important difference between the character relations in *Chance* and *Lord Jim* is that 'in *Chance* we are interested not so much in each character's opinion or corresponding problem as in his emotional response to Flora and her needs'.[33] Her life with her relations in Limehouse, her job as an old lady's companion, her post in the German merchant's family represent a succession of conditioning environments, each of which in different ways reinforces Flora's sense of worthlessness. Marlow's account of the Limehouse family makes this abundantly clear:

> I could imagine easily how the poor girl must have been bewildered and hurt at her reception in that household – envied for her past while delivered defenceless to the tender mercies of people without any fineness either of feeling or mind, unable to understand her misery, grossly curious, mistaking her manner for disdain, her silent shrinking for pride. . . . After the trial her position became still worse. On the least occasion and even on no occasions at all she was scolded, or else taunted with her dependence.
> (pp. 163–4)

Marlow describes these recurrent rows as 'scenes which, in their repetition, must have had a deplorable effect on the unformed character of the most pitiful of de Barral's victims' (p. 165). Marlow presents three different kinds of effect this environment must have had on Flora's 'unformed character'. First of all, there is the confusing effect of being misinterpreted and misunderstood: the environment offers no positive reinforcement of Flora's sense of herself. Secondly, Marlow suggests ways in which this environment actively attacks Flora:

> Of the two girls in the house one was pious and the other a romp. . . . The pious girl lectured her on her defects, the romping girl teased her with contemptuous references to her accomplishments. (p. 164)

Between them, these 'two girls' mount a pincer attack on any remnant of self-esteem Flora might have. Thirdly, there is the way in which this environment proliferates double-binds. The father, in particular, deploys the double-bind as deftly as Raskolnikov's mother.[34] When he comes to the Fynes' house to collect Flora, after her flight from Limehouse, he delivers a homily to her which furnishes a striking example of his skill:

> Ingratitude was condemned in it, the sinfulness of pride was pointed out – together with the proverbial fact that it 'goes before a fall'. There were also some sound remarks as to the danger of nonsensical notions and the disadvantages of a quick temper. It

sets one's best friends against one. 'And if anybody ever wanted friends in the world it's you, my girl.'   (p. 169)

He expresses aggression through submission, pride through humility, threats in the language of concern. More particularly, his reference to a 'fall' plays on the fact of her father's downfall, while comparison with the incident which provoked Flora's flight exposes the binds created by those injunctions against ingratitude and pride:

> Flora on one occasion had been reduced to rage and despair, had her most secret feelings lacerated, had obtained a view of the utmost baseness to which human nature can descend – I won't say *à propos de bottes* as the French would excellently put it, but literally *à propos* of some mislaid cheap lace trimmings for a nightgown.   (p. 165)

Marlow elaborates: 'both the word convict and the word pauper had been used a moment before Flora de Barral ran away' (p. 167). Flora has had her father's position and her own thrown at her, her 'most secret feelings' have been lacerated, and now her pain is described as pride, and she is expected to show gratitude for the treatment to which she is subjected. To cap it all, in that final sentence, she is reminded of her isolation and her powerlessness; she is reminded that she has to accept this treatment because she has no other option ('He was the only protector she had'); and her sense of being unloveable is unerringly targetted. Marlow speculates on the effect of this environment on her:

> It was as though Flora had been fated to be always surrounded by treachery and lies stifling every better impulse, every instinctive aspiration of her soul to trust and to love. It would have been enough to drive a fine nature into the madness of universal suspicion – into any sort of madness.   (pp. 174–5)

Flora's experiences with the old lady and with the German merchant's family repeat this process. The old lady is like the Fynes. She is well-meaning and far from malicious, but she too lacks the necessary 'imaginative sympathy'. Her advice to Flora echoes Mrs Fyne's: 'The only way to deal with our troubles, my dear child, is to forget them' (p. 179). Like Mrs Fyne, she fails to realise the nature of Flora's 'troubles': Flora is not merely upset by her father's imprisonment and her own isolation, but her sense of her own worth has been destroyed, and this cannot be remedied by forgetting. The old lady also reveals the selfishness that underlies this advice. She goes on: 'I do hope the child will manage to be cheerful. . . . At my age one needs cheerful companions' (p. 179). She is thinking of her own needs, not Flora's; and Flora's employment is terminated, not by Flora, but by the old lady:

> She had discovered that Flora was not naturally cheerful. When she made efforts to be it was still worse. The old lady couldn't stand the strain of that. And then, to have the whole thing out, she could not bear to have for a companion any one who did not love her.   (p. 179)

In the context of Flora's elopement with Captain Anthony, Flora's ability to love is a matter of some importance. At the same time, Flora is quite likely to have interpreted her failure as a companion in the light of the governess's earlier attack upon her, so that, where the old lady feels that Flora did not love her, Flora herself is likely to have felt that the old lady had discovered that Flora was unloveable.

If her experiences with the old lady confirmed Flora in this idea, her experiences with the German family would confirm her in the idea of the untrustworthiness of other people. The German husband takes an interest in Flora, and she thinks him 'sympathetic – the first expressively sympathetic person she had ever met' (p. 181). As Marlow notes, Flora is 'too innocent, and indeed not yet sufficiently aware of herself as a woman' (p. 181) to understand the true nature of his interest in her:

> She was so innocent that she could not understand the fury of the German woman. For, as you may imagine, the wifely penetration was not to be deceived for any great length of time. . . . The man with the peculiar cowardice of respectability never said a word in Flora's defence. He stood by and heard her reviled in the most abusive terms, only nodding and frowning vaguely from time to time. It will give you the idea of the girl's innocence when I say that at first she actually thought this storm of indignant reproaches was caused by the discovery of her real name and her relation to a convict . . . even in London, having had time to take a reflective

view, poor Flora was far from being certain as to the true inwardness of her violent dismissal.   (pp. 181–2)

Flora's betrayal by this man – both through his attempt to take
advantage of her sexually and through his subsequent failure to
defend her – confirms her sense of the untrustworthiness of others.
At the same time, the wife's jealous abuse of Flora confirms Flora's
sense of her own lack of worth, particularly since she is too innocent
to appreciate the true nature of the situation, but, instead, misreads
the situation in relation to her own guilty awareness of her father's
identity.

It is curious that, at this point, Marlow applies to Flora the formula
he earlier applied to Jim: she 'felt the shame but did not believe in the
guilt of her father' (p. 182), just as Jim 'made so much of his disgrace
while it is the guilt alone that matters' (p. 177). The governess linked
de Barral's guilt with the idea of Flora's own worthlessness, and
Flora's experiences in Limehouse and Germany have reinforced that
link. Her father's guilt has become a metonymy for her sense of her
own worth. Jim denied his guilt in order to protect his self-image:
Flora denies her father's guilt not so much to protect her self-image
as to maintain some minimal self-esteem. The alternative for her is
the suicide that Part I constantly hints at. For example, after her
experience in Germany, if it had not been for the stewardess who
'took charge of her quietly in the ladies saloon' without asking
questions, 'it is by no means certain she would ever have reached
England': the 'quiet, matter-of-fact attentions of a ship's stewardess'
were 'enough to dissipate the shades of death gathering round the
mortal weariness of bewildered thinking which makes the idea of
non-existence welcome so often to the young' (pp. 182–3). The stewardess's rescue of Flora from her suicidal impulses provides another
interpretative context for Captain Anthony's elopement with her.

The final chapter of Part I returns to the East End, and goes over
the main points of the narrative. There is a reminder of the initial
trauma and its continuing effects: Flora's 'abominable experience
with the governess had implanted in her unlucky breast a lasting
doubt, an ineradicable suspicion of herself and of others' (p. 232).
Marlow elaborates upon this later:

She could not help believing what she had been told; that she was
in some mysterious way odious and unloveable. It was cruelly

true – *to her*. . . . Only other people did not find her out at once.
(p. 263)

Flora imagines herself to be 'odious and unloveable', and she expects to find this confirmed in her relations with others: if it is
not immediately confirmed, then she feels it is only a matter of
time before she is found out. She comments on Mrs Fyne: 'I know
she hates me now. I think she never liked me. I think nobody
ever cared for me. I was told once nobody could care for me; and I
think it is true' (p. 232). What she says about Mrs Fyne is true, and
what she says about her own experience of the world is also true;
but her conclusions about herself are another matter. As Marlow
observes:

> The world had treated her so dishonourably that she had no
> notion even of what mere decency of feeling is like. . . . And she
> had nothing to fall back upon, no experience but such as to shake
> her belief in every human being.   (pp. 236–7)

Flora's account of the incident with the Fynes' dog shows how even
apparently trivial details have had the effect of confirming her low
opinion of herself and of others. She did not jump over the cliff, in
case the dog jumped after her, but, immediately afterwards, the dog
deserted her: 'I really did think that he was attached to me. What did
he want to pretend for, like this?' (p. 203). She had been made to feel
that 'not even that animal cared for her in the end' (p. 203).

This was the context for Flora's relationship with Captain Anthony.
Flora, at the time of their meeting, was 'a girl who had come to the
end of her courage to live' (p. 220): 'with one foot in life and the other
in a nightmare', she was 'inert and unstable, and very much at the
mercy of sudden impulses' (p. 223). It was this combination of inert-
ness and instability, and her liability to 'sudden impulses', that led to
her elopement with him. Marlow describes her emotional state on
what turned out to be the eve of their elopement:

> That dread of what was before her which had been eating up her
> courage slowly in the course of odious years, flamed up into an
> access of panic, that sort of headlong panic which had already
> driven her out twice to the top of the cliff-like quarry. She jumped
> up saying to herself: 'Why not now? At once! Yes. I'll do it now –
> in the dark!'   (p. 229)

In her rush to the quarry, she accidently runs into Captain Anthony, who interprets her presence in the garden as keeping the appointment she had suggested. Her suicidal impulse now gives way to inertia, and Anthony takes 'charge of her' (p. 182) just as the stewardess had done on her journey from Germany.

The elopement immediately raises certain questions. The account of Flora's desertion by the Fynes' dog had already intimated her need for love (p. 203). Now Marlow and Fyne attempt to decide whether need or love characterises Flora's relationship with Anthony. Fyne has no doubts: 'She doesn't care a bit about Anthony, I believe. She cares for no one. Never cared for anyone' (p. 243). Marlow finds it less easy to decide, but, as the chapter progresses, he also begins to express doubts about Flora's ability to love:

> I suppose affections are, in a sense, to be learned. If there exists a native spark of love in all of us, it must be fanned while we are young. Hers, if she ever had it, had been drenched in as ugly a lot of corrosive liquid as could be imagined.   (p. 244)

This, however, has to be set against the impression Marlow had of Flora at the start of the chapter. Marlow's account began with an evocation of the East India Dock Road, which had stressed 'its immeasurable poverty of forms, of colouring, of life' (p. 204). At first glance, this seemed an appropriate setting for Flora, dressed in the black dress which Mrs Fyne had given her:

> It accentuated the slightness of her figure, it went well in its suggestion of half-mourning with the white face in which the unsmiling red lips alone seemed warm with the rich blood of life and passion.   (p. 205)

This last detail breaks out of the overall impression of lifelessness to suggest a potential in Flora that her relationship with Captain Anthony might yet develop.

The other important element in this chapter is the account it gives of Flora's relationship with her father, which will become a major obstacle to Flora's self-realisation. Flora has her own view of her father's history:

> She was used to reproaches, abuse, to all sorts of wicked ill usage. . . . Otherwise inexplicable angers had cut and slashed and tram-

pled down her youth without mercy – and mainly, it appeared, because she was the financier de Barral's daughter and also condemned to a degrading sort of poverty through the action of treacherous men who had turned upon her father in his hour of need. And she thought with the tenderest possible affection of that upright figure. . . . She seemed to feel his hand closed round hers. (pp. 228–9)

Because of her own mistreatment since de Barral's fall, she has created this fantasy of a loving father. More than that, she has come to identify with her father – on the grounds that both of them have suffered from the treachery of the world. She sees her father as 'a victim' (p. 242) like herself. It is not quite true to say, as Kirschner does, that 'despite the overwhelming evidence, she refuses to accept the verdict against her father'.[35] As Marlow observes:

It seems that for the last six months. . . . Flora had insisted on devoting all her spare time to the study of the trial. She had been looking up files of old newspapers, and working herself up into a state of indignation with what she called the injustice and the hypocrisy of the prosecution. Her father, Fyne reminded me, had made some palpable hits in his answers in Court, and she had fastened on them triumphantly.   (p. 197)

Flora is obviously predisposed to discover her father's innocence, because of the equivalence, created by the governess, between de Barral's innocence/guilt and Flora's worth/worthlessness. This identification, however, produces certain difficulties. While she needs to believe in her father's innocence, she knows how he is regarded generally. Her belief in her father's innocence accordingly problematises her being-in-the-world: it creates a lesion between her identity-for-self and her identity-for-the-other, because of the gap between her view of her father and others' view of him. The change of her name to 'Miss Smith' is expressive of this lesion between identity-for-self and identity-for-the-other. Captain Anthony offers her a way out of the trap she has created for herself. When she tells him that her name is not 'Miss Smith', he replies: 'That's all one to me. Your name's the least thing about you I care for' (p. 223). Anthony, unknowingly, utters the magic formula that will release Flora from her poisoned sleep: he has expressed a readiness to accept Flora for herself; he has expressed a sense of Flora's worth that, if it is not accompanied by a belief in de Barral's innocence, is yet innocent of a belief in de Barral's guilt. Anthony's assertion side-steps Flora's 'ideas of reference'.

It is significant that Flora's attitude towards her father is dominated by a concern with others' views of him. Her assertion of his innocence in the face of the world's judgement of his guilt, and her sense of shame rather than guilt in relation to her own position, are directly comparable to Jim's assertion of his self-ideal in *Lord Jim*, but with the important difference that what took place there *within* Jim is now divided between two characters – and that, where Jim rescued his self-ideal at the expense of both himself and others, in *Chance*, the self-ideal is relinquished in the pursuit of psychological integration and psycho-sexual maturity.

III

Part II begins by reconsidering Flora's elopement with Captain Anthony. Marlow states explicitly what had been implicit in the earlier account of Flora's elopement: namely that Anthony's forceful nature had swept her along (p. 264). His incursion into her life is both liberating and bewildering:

> Ever since Anthony had suddenly broken his way into her hopeless and cruel existence she lived like a person liberated from a condemned cell by a natural cataclysm . . . not absolutely terrified, because nothing can be worse than the eve of execution, but stunned, bewildered – abandoning herself passively. (pp. 330–1)

Despite this bewilderment, the potential liberation of Flora by Captain Anthony is clearly suggested by the image of 'her soul awakening slowly from a poisoned sleep' (p. 332). But Flora's awakening is not the immediate awakening of fairy tale: it is a lengthy process, complicated by various misunderstandings between herself and Anthony – and by the presence of her father on board the *Ferndale*.

In Chapter 1, Marlow returns to the question raised at the end of Part I: whether Flora loves Anthony. He begins his answer by reference to Anthony's impetuosity:

> She could not have spoken with a certain voice in the face of his impetuosity, because she did not have time to understand either

the state of her feelings, or the precise nature of what she was
doing. (p. 262)

Later, in his more detailed account of Anthony's early discussions
with Flora, Marlow imagines Flora thinking 'that he had never given
her time, that he had never asked her! And that, in truth, she did not
know' (p. 330). Flora's passivity and her ignorance about the nature
of her feelings for Anthony contribute to their misunderstanding of
each other that almost destroys their relationship.

The main source of that misunderstanding, however, is the advice
that Fyne gives Anthony at the end of Part I: 'I told him it was a
shame. . . . A shame to take advantage of a girl's distress' (p. 251).
Fyne sees Anthony's motive in running off with Flora as sexual
opportunism, and he warns him against taking sexual advantage of
her. Fyne's warning initiates Anthony's misreading of his relationship with Flora: it leads, in the first instance, to his decision to control
and inhibit his feelings for her. This self-inhibition, in turn, is experienced by Flora as an emotional withdrawal on Anthony's part:
she is described as 'missing Anthony's masterful manner, that something arbitrary and tender' which, 'after the first scare, she had
accustomed herself to look forward to with pleasurable apprehension' (p. 374). Inevitably, she reads his withdrawal as confirmation of
her low self-esteem:

> It was all over. It was as that abominable governess had said. She
> was insignificant, contemptible. Nobody could love her.   (p. 335)

She feels a sense of isolation (p. 336), alienation (p. 337), and betrayal:

> It was a rejection, a casting out; nothing new to her. But she who
> supposed all her sensibility dead by this time, discovered in her-
> self a resentment of this ultimate betrayal.   (p. 342)

That 'resentment', however, is an indication of the growth that is just
beginning to take place within her. Ironically, Anthony reads Flora's
acceptance of his decision as confirmation of Fyne's interpretation of
her motives. He thinks 'with mournful regret not unmixed with
surprise': 'That fellow Fyne has been telling me the truth. She does
not care for me a bit!' (p. 342). He even misunderstands her words,
when she does find the courage to offer herself to him: ' "Neither am

I keeping anything back from you." She had said it. But he in his blind generosity assumed that she was alluding to her deplorable history' (pp. 343–4). He interprets her assertion of her emotional openness to him as a reference to her frankness about her past.

In the state of isolation created by these mutual misunderstandings, Flora turns her thoughts and feelings again towards her father. Marlow observes that in 'the distrust of herself and of others she looked for love, any kind of love, as women will': 'And that confounded jail was the only spot where she could see it – for she had no reason to distrust her father' (pp. 353–4). From the start, however, it is clear that Flora's image of her father bears little relation to the reality. As she leaves the prison with him, her 'half-mournful, half-triumphant exultation' suddenly subsides, as she realises he was 'different': 'there was something between them, something hard and impalpable' (p. 355). She now begins to remember the past more clearly, and to adjust her image of it, as she re-interprets those aspects of him that have not changed:

> He bent on her that well-remembered glance in which she had never read anything as a child, except the consciousness of her existence. And that was enough for a child who had never known demonstrative affection. But she had lived a life so starved of all feeling that this was no longer enough for her.   (p. 358)

During the course of their cab-journey, Flora comes to feel that he was 'almost a stranger' (p. 366). The disappointment of her expectations and his resistance to her plans for him throw her back again to her negative self-evaluation; and, by the time the cab reaches the *Ferndale*, she has made a resolution:

> 'If he bolts away,' she thought, 'then I shall know that I am of no account indeed! That no one loves me, that words and actions and protestations and everything in the world is false – and I shall jump into the dock.'   (p. 370)

De Barral, however, does follow her on board the *Ferndale*, and now, to the misunderstandings of Flora and Anthony, are added the tensions between Flora and her father, and the life-and-death struggle between Anthony and de Barral. Conrad recreates the kind of triangular relationship that had recurred in his early fiction – in *Almayer's Folly* and *An Outcast of the Islands*. De Barral's particular conditions of existence, his years in prison, have intensified that 'certain repugnance' which Marlow suggests even the 'usual, normal father' experiences at 'parting with his daughter' (p. 371). As for Flora, Kirschner argues that she clings to her father because, 'however pathological his feeling for her, it is not humiliating': 'she is wanted without pity or generosity, for herself alone'.[36] This is corroborated by Flora's own view of her relationship to the two men:

> She did not want to quarrel with her father, the only human being that really cared for her, absolutely, evidently, completely – to the end. There was in him no pity, no generosity, nothing whatever of these fine things – it was for *her*, for her very own self, such as it was, that this human being cared.   (p. 380)

Flora is right about the pity and generosity that are components of Anthony's attitude and feelings towards her, but she has misunderstood his other feelings for her. Conversely, her belief that her father loves her for herself needs some qualification. Marlow comments on the 'terrible simplicity' of de Barral's 'fixed idea', and adds darkly: 'for which there is also another name men pronounce with dread and aversion' (p. 377).

While Flora's relationship with her father and her father's jealousy of Anthony are foregrounded, other emotions, emotions less apparent but no less powerful, are experienced by Flora and Anthony, and these produce their sense of 'being tormented' (p. 380). The major source of the 'torment' on board the *Ferndale* is the emotional and sexual frustration of Flora and Anthony. It is emphasised that Flora and Anthony are each yearning for the other. After Anthony had decided not to 'take advantage' (p. 251) of Flora, Flora concealed her tears, because she 'felt bound in honour to accept the situation for ever and ever unless . . . ' (p. 341). Similarly, when de Barral arrives on board, Anthony's consciousness of the false situation is tinged by his desire for a different relationship with Flora: 'That man's coming brought him face to face with the necessity to speak and act a lie; to appear what he was not and what he could never be, unless, unless – ' (p. 350). As the parallel suggests, each, for different reasons, is waiting for the other to make the first move: Anthony will not make any demands – or even reveal his love for Flora – unless Flora approaches him first, and Flora will not do that, because she does not believe that she is loveable. As Marlow says, she 'beat him at his own honourable game' but 'it was as if they both had taken a bite of

the same bitter fruit' (pp. 341–2). This impasse resembles that created by James in *The Spoils of Poynton*, where Fleda Vetch will not
express her love for Owen Gereth, until he voluntarily breaks his
engagement with Mona Brigstock, even though Fleda knows that
Owen does not have sufficient strength of character to break the
engagement, unless she encourages him.[37]

In addition, Flora and Anthony also endure the strain of the 'thorough falseness' of their position (p. 374): they are officially husband
and wife, but their marriage has not been consummated. The novel
emphasises the physicality of their frustration. For example, early in
Part II, the shipkeeper observes Captain Anthony showing Flora
round the *Ferndale*:

> He saw the captain put his hand on her shoulder, and was prepar-
> ing himself with a certain zest for what might follow, when the
> 'old man' seemed to recollect himself, and came striding down all
> the length of the saloon.   (p. 266)

Similarly, after de Barral has gone to bed on his first night on board
the *Ferndale*, the conversation between Flora and Anthony ends with
a powerful, physical sense of self-restraint:

> He saw she was swaying where she stood and restrained himself
> violently from taking her into his arms, his frame trembling with
> fear as though he had been tempted to an act of unparalleled
> treachery.   (p. 375)

Because of his misunderstanding of the situation, Anthony regards
the expression of his feelings towards Flora as 'treachery': conversely,
Flora regards Anthony's self-restraint (through her misreading of
his motives) as the 'ultimate betrayal' (p. 342).

Both Guerard and Moser are critical of this impasse and its resolution.[38] *The Spoils of Poynton*, however, offers an instructive comparison. In both works, the impasse created between the central
characters is not resolved by those characters but by the third figure
in the triangle: in James's work, Mona Brigstock forces Owen Gereth
into marriage; in Conrad's work, de Barral finally tries to kill
Captain Anthony. But de Barral's attempted poisoning of Captain
Anthony does not, of itself, break the impasse. It merely creates the
circumstances in which the impasse can be broken: the scene in the
saloon attracts Flora's attention and draws her in. Furthermore, as

Marlow tentatively suggests, 'just then the tension of the false situation was at its highest' (p. 426): Flora 'had arrived at the very limit of her endurance as the object of Anthony's magnanimity' (p. 427), and Anthony has arrived at a similar crisis:

> To the innocent beholder Anthony seemed at this point to become physically exhausted. My view is that the utter falseness of his, I may say, aspirations, the vanity of grasping the empty air, had come to him with an overwhelming force, leaving him disarmed. (p. 429)

Anthony's impulse is to give up the struggle with de Barral and to renounce his claim on Flora: 'You are free. I let you off since I must' (p. 429). Flora's response is quite different: when she arrives 'at the very limit of her endurance', she feels herself being pushed back into 'that moral loneliness, which had made all her life intolerable' and then, 'in that close communion established again with Anthony', she felt 'as on that night in the garden – the force of his personal fascination' (p. 428). As a result, Flora has the strength to reject Anthony's offer to give her up:

> 'But I don't want to be let off,' she cried. . . . 'You can't cast me off like this, Roderick. I won't go away from you.'   (p. 430)

This climactic confrontation is the occasion for something that has not happened so far on board the *Ferndale*: Flora and Anthony engage each other in dialogue without any of the constraints that have characterised their ship-board relationship. Also, as Kirschner points out, when Flora asserts herself in this way, she is not aware of de Barral's attempt to poison Anthony.[39] Her response does not spring from the attempted murder, but from all the circumstances which the narrative has recorded, and it is not a reasoned response but, explicitly, 'a cry . . . from her heart' (p. 429). It is this cry, which marks Flora's release from her 'poisoned sleep' (p. 332), that finally breaks the impasse. As Hough observes, this is 'the true greatness of the latter half of the book': 'a greatness which consists in the piled-up sense of emotional incomprehension, of solitude and strain; in the splendid peripeteia, almost melodramatic, by which the strain is resolved; and the immense flooding current of generous release, far more than a conventional happy ending, in which even Mr Powell comes ultimately to be included'.[40]

When de Barral was released from gaol, Marlow speculated about the effects of imprisonment: 'One has a notion of a maiming, crippling process; of the individual coming back damaged in some subtle way' (p. 352). This speculation is confirmed by the subsequent portrayal of de Barral. As Daniel Schwarz notes, one effect of de Barral's imprisonment is that every place in which he lives becomes a prison.[41] When he is told by Flora that the cab which has collected him from the gaol is taking him to the *Ferndale*, he reacts like 'some wild creature scared by the first touch of a net falling on its back' (p. 365). And, as he expects, the *Ferndale* becomes a prison to him with Captain Anthony as 'the jailer' (p. 307). These prison images express what Marlow presents as one of the effects of de Barral's actual imprisonment – his self-imprisonment within his own obsessions. In addition, as Schwarz suggests, Conrad uses de Barral's physical imprisonment as a trope for 'more subtle kinds of imprisonment', as 'an apt metaphor for kinds of psychological confinement'.[42] Where Flora's refuge for her father is experienced by him as a second imprisonment, Anthony's rescue of Flora has also ended in imprisonment. It is not just that de Barral's obsession leads to his 'guardianship' (p. 377) of Flora, but Flora's own psychological state is as imprisoned and self-imprisoning as her father's. If Anthony's earlier actions had 'liberated' her 'from a condemned cell' (p. 330), his withdrawal from her has returned her to it. And, by this process, Anthony has imprisoned himself as well as Flora. For Anthony and Flora, 'imprisonment' aptly expresses the way in which they are psychologically constricted as a result of determining factors in their pasts as well as the knot of their present relationship. In particular, for both of them, 'imprisonment' ultimately signifies the entrapment of sexual energy.

Through that involuntary cry 'from her heart', Flora finally expresses her love for Anthony and breaks the impasse that the novel has carefully constructed. In *Chance*, the old model of identity (identification with an alterated identity) is rejected: it is replaced by the idea of integration around a new principle which operates 'through sexuality – the force of unconscious nature – and not through the medium of ideas'.[43] By the end, Flora has achieved self-realisation by way of self-fulfilment in love. Marlow concludes that she 'was now her true self' (p. 442), but this does not mean that she has completely shaken off her earlier insecurity. When Marlow hints to her that she might marry Powell, she asks, 'Do you think it is possible that he should care for me?' (p. 446), and, for that moment, her voice was 'the very voice of the Flora of old days, with the exact intonation', showing 'the old mistrust, the old doubts of herself, the old scar of the blow received in childhood' (pp. 445–6). As Geddes says, Flora is 'doomed to have the spectre of self-doubt perpetually near at hand'.[44] Apart from that, however, her account of her relationship with Captain Anthony reveals a woman completely fulfilled; like Jane Eyre with Rochester, she can claim 'I loved and I was loved, untroubled, at peace, without remorse, without fear' (p. 444). And this fulfilment has also 'transformed' her view of the world: the most familiar things appeared 'lighted up with a new light, clothed with a loveliness I had never suspected' (p. 444). This new conception of herself and the world contrasts significantly with her earlier idea of herself as 'odious and unloveable' (p. 63) and her view of the world as 'piled-up matter without any sense' (p. 337).

IV

Marlow has three sources of information about Captain Anthony: Mrs Fyne, Powell, and Flora. Of these, Mrs Fyne is unreliable, Powell is allegedly limited, and Flora is presumably the most trustworthy. Mrs Fyne is unreliable as a witness partly because of her lack of contact with her brother: 'She had not seen him for fifteen years or thereabouts, except on three or four occasions for a few hours at a time' (p. 155). But she is unreliable also because her sense of superiority colours her perception of her brother:

> I should have liked him to have been distinguished – or at any rate to remain in the social sphere where we could have had common interests, acquaintances, thoughts.   (p. 185)

Her description of 'the Liverpool relations' (p. 185) as 'some distant relations of our mother's people' (p. 184) is significantly different from Anthony's reference to them as 'very nice, cheery, clever girls' (p. 219). Not only are his words considerably warmer than hers, but they also seem to imply a contrast between these 'girls' and his sister. Powell is limited as a witness through his inexperience: as Marlow observes, 'for us who didn't go to sea out of a small private school at the age of fourteen years and nine months', it is difficult to understand 'the extent, the completeness, the comprehensiveness of his inexperience' (p. 308). He is limited also (at least, according to

Marlow) by the simplicity of his character: 'He's one of those people who form no theories about facts. Straightforward people seldom do. Neither have they much penetration' (p. 261). As a result of this simplicity, Marlow alleges, the 'inwardness of what was passing before his eyes was hidden from him' (p. 426).

Marlow himself has never met Captain Anthony: the nearest he comes to meeting him is when he stands outside the Great Eastern Hotel with Flora, while Fyne and Anthony have a conversation inside. Marlow's account of Anthony is accordingly more self-consciously constructed and more obviously tentative, explorative, and hypothetical than his account of Flora. Indeed, Marlow's comments often serve to raise questions rather than supply answers:

> I sat down on the porch and, maybe inspired by secret antagonism to the Fynes, I said to myself deliberately that Captain Anthony must be a fine fellow. Yet on the facts as I knew them he might have been a dangerous trifler or a downright scoundrel. He had made a miserable, hopeless girl follow him clandestinely to London. (p. 193)

Marlow simultaneously asserts and withdraws interpretations of Captain Anthony's behaviour:

> I don't know why I imagined Captain Anthony as the sort of man who would not be likely to take the initiative; not perhaps from indifference but from that peculiar timidity before women which often enough is found in conjunction with chivalrous instincts, with a great need for affection and great stability of feelings. (p. 208)

In this instance, while Marlow's ideas about Anthony's 'chivalrous instincts' are consistent with the account he gives of Anthony in Part II, his suggestion that Anthony would 'not be likely to take the initiative' is immediately contradicted by Flora's version of her meetings with Anthony. Marlow's narration insists on the part that surmise and speculation play in its generation: though he aims at a 'coherent theory' (p. 326), he produces a self-conscious fiction.

Hewitt's complaint that, in *Chance*, Conrad avoids 'the painful awareness of the darker side of even our good feelings', reveals a curious insensitivity to the text.[45] The opening chapters raise a number of questions about Anthony's flight with Flora de Barral – in particular, how this flight has come about and how to evaluate the behaviour of Flora and Anthony respectively. According to Flora's account, Anthony appealed to her on the grounds of their common isolation: 'You told me you had no friends. Neither have I. Nobody ever cared for me as far as I can remember' (p. 224). Kirschner interprets this to mean 'You are too poor to refuse me, even if I am not good enough for anyone else.'[46] Marlow himself suggests that Flora's isolation and helplessness constituted a particular attraction to Anthony: 'her misery was his opportunity and he rejoiced while the tenderest pity seemed to flood his whole being' (pp. 223–4). As Kirschner says: 'Flora appeals to Anthony precisely because she is less secure than he; if he is her material opportunity, she is his psychological one.'[47] Marlow's more elaborate analysis supports this reading:

> It was obvious the world had been using her ill. And even as he spoke with indignation the very marks and stamps of this illusage of which he was so certain seemed to add to the inexplicable attraction he felt for her person. It was not pity alone, I take it. It was something more spontaneous, perverse and exciting. It gave him the feeling that if only he could get hold of her, no woman would belong to him so completely as this woman.   (p. 224)

Anthony combines pity for Flora's 'ill-usage' with exultation at the opportunity that Flora's position affords him. Indeed there is more than just an ambivalent emotional response to Flora's powerlessness, there is a suggestion of excitement at the power that Flora's powerlessness gives him.[48] Anthony's response to Flora is not very different from her relation's threatening reminder that 'if anybody ever wanted friends in the world it's you' (p. 169): his pity for her contains a similar desire to possess and control her. Fyne warned him that it was 'a shame to take advantage of a girl's distress' (p. 251). From this angle, Fyne's interpretation of the situation was not so much wrong as oversimple: if Anthony does not take sexual advantage of Flora, he nevertheless aims, at some level, to take psychological advantage of her. Conrad had explored, in 'Heart of Darkness' and through the figure of Lingard in *Almayer's Folly*, *An Outcast of the Islands* and 'The Rescuer', the will-to-power as a component of apparently altruistic behaviour. In *Chance*, he transfers this analysis from a colonial to a sexual context.

At the start of Part II, relations between Anthony and Flora on board the *Ferndale* are presented externally through the eyes of the shipkeeper and Powell. Then Marlow announces that he has a new and 'unexpected source of information' (p. 325), and his analysis now deepens. He begins by characterising Anthony's life before he met Flora as 'a life of solitude and silence – and desire', and he uses this new insight to explain Anthony's 'violent conquest' and 'eager appropriation' of her (p. 328). Leavis describes Anthony's relationship with Flora as 'a variant of the Heyst–Lena situation': 'while each needs, neither knows, the other, and the nature and circumstances of the rescue leave each exquisitely and inhibitingly scrupulous about taking advantage of the other's helplessness or chivalry'.[49] If Anthony, in his solitude and in his rescue of Flora, anticipates Heyst; as a man of 'desire', he recalls Lingard of 'The Rescuer', particularly since, like Lingard, he is also capable of self-sacrifice:

> If Anthony's love had been as egoistic as love generally is, it would have been greater than the egoism of his vanity – or of his generosity, if you like – and all this could not have happened. . . . But it was a love born of that rare pity which is not akin to contempt because rooted in an overwhelmingly strong capacity for tenderness. . . . At the same time I am forced to think his vanity must have been enormous.   (p. 331)

Marlow locates Anthony's self-denying decision partly in his tenderness and partly in his self-ideal, and he connects this self-ideal to the relationship between Anthony and his father:

> He certainly resembled his father, who, by the way, wore out two women without any satisfaction to himself, because they did not come up to his supra-refined standard of the delicacy which is so perceptible in his verses. That's your poet. He demands too much from others. The inarticulate son had set up a standard for himself with that need for embodying in his conduct the dreams, the passion, the impulses the poet puts into arrangements of verses, which are dearer to him than his own self – and may make his own self appear sublime in the eyes of other people, and even in his own eyes.   (p. 328)

According to Marlow, Anthony (like Jim) is capable of sacrificing himself and others, for what is ultimately an ideal image of self. He elaborates upon this idea by presenting Anthony as thinking of his love for Flora as something more than love, as it is generally understood:

More? Or was it only something other? Yes. It was something other. More or less. Something as incredible as the fulfillment of an amazing and startling dream in which he could take the world in his arms – all the suffering world – not to possess its pathetic fairness but to console and cherish its sorrow.   (pp. 347–8)

An act of appropriation is disguised and displaced by an ideal of cherishing. At the same time, Anthony magnifies himself in order to embrace the world, while he abstains from embracing Flora, the 'living woman' who actually requires some show of personal warmth. Anthony has created an idealised self-image, which disguises the nature of his own desires and denies the reality of others.

Both Anthony and Flora are presented as shaped (and, indeed, damaged) by their respective fathers. For Marlow, the source of Anthony's self-denying decision is to be found in the cast of mind exemplified in his father's poetry: the father 'could only sing in harmonious numbers of what the son felt with a dumb and reckless sincerity' (p. 332). Carleon Anthony represents a certain 'supra-refined standard' (p. 328), which Marlow gives short shrift:

> There are several kinds of heroism and one of them is idiotic. It is the one which wears the aspect of sublime delicacy. It is apparently the one of which the son of the delicate poet was capable. (p. 328)

However, Marlow also insists on the split within Carleon Anthony between a refined public identity and a tyrannical private one, between ideals and performance:

> The late Carleon Anthony, the poet, sang in his time, of the domestic and social amenities of our age with a most felicitous versification, his object being, in his own words, 'to glorify the result of six thousand years' evolution towards the refinement of thought, manners, and feelings'. . . . But in his domestic life that same Carleon Anthony showed traces of the primitive cave-dweller's temperament. (p. 38)

Marlow's insistence on the gap between Carleon Anthony's idealisation of the 'domestic . . . amenities' and his actual exhaustion of two wives has a further significance: Carleon Anthony and Captain

Anthony are based on Coventry Patmore and his sea-captain son, Milnes Patmore, and Coventry Patmore is best-known as the author of 'The Angel in the House'.[50] Through Carleon Anthony and his son, Conrad produces a critique of 'chivalrous love' (p. 332) and its idealisation of women. He uses them to explore a particular male attitude to women and a particular sense of 'masculinity'. The split in Carleon Anthony between a theoretical idealisation of women and an actual mistreatment of women is less obvious in Roderick Anthony, but, nevertheless, still present. Marlow points to this split in his analysis of Roderick Anthony's feelings immediately after his marriage and, again, in his decision not to 'take advantage' of Flora:

> Possessed by most men's touching illusion as to the frailness of women and their spiritual fragility, it seemed to Anthony that he would be destroying, breaking something very precious inside that being. In fact nothing less than partly murdering her. (pp. 332–3)

Flora, who was initially damaged by the governess's 'desecration' of her, is now subjected to further damage through Anthony's fear of desecrating her – and Anthony, who fears to harm her, causes her more harm through his illusions about 'the frailness of women'.

Anthony's course of action causes suffering not just to Flora, but also to himself. Anthony underestimates the force of his desire, and he suffers a conflict between the strength of that desire and the restraint that he has imposed upon himself. The frustrations produced by this decision turn Anthony from an elevated sense of himself to a low estimation of himself:

> He had rushed in like a ruffian; he had dragged the poor defenceless thing by the hair of her head, as it were, on board that ship. It was really atrocious. Nothing assured him that his person could be attractive to this or any other woman. And his proceedings were enough in themselves to make any one odious. (pp. 396–7)

This echoes Flora's belief 'that she was in some mysterious way odious and unloveable' (p. 263). Even more striking, however, is his feeling that, instead of rescuing Flora, he 'had dragged the poor defenceless thing by the hair of her head' on board the ship, since the image recalls the description of Carleon Anthony as showing 'traces of primitive cave-dweller's temperament' (p. 38). The Roderick

Anthony who set out with refined and delicate ideals now feels that his behaviour belongs to the opposite end of the evolutionary spectrum, and he has begun to recognise that his rescue of Flora has something of the quality of a capture. Marlow sums up his behaviour as 'trying to act at the same time like a beast of prey, a pure spirit and the "most generous of men" ' (p. 415). And these divisions in Anthony, by implication, derive from a false idea of women and a false concept of masculinity. Anthony is betrayed by his idealism; by a false concept of masculinity that is a part of that idealism; by his underestimation of the power of sexual desire; and by an insecurity that is the basis upon which everything else is constructed.

Kirschner has argued that the 'main theme' of the novel is 'the role of women', with 'Flora de Barral's story a case in point'.[51] And it is true that, if Flora is presented as a victim, she is also presented specifically as a female victim. Mrs Fyne comments on Flora's enforced return to her father's relations that she had 'never had such a crushing impression of the miserable dependence of girls – and of women' (p. 172). This is, of course, the moral that the feminist Mrs Fyne would be expected to draw from Flora's experiences, but even Marlow finds himself forced to agree: 'It was very true. Women can't go forth on the high roads and by-ways to pick up a living even when dignity, independence or existence itself are at stake' (p. 172). Flora was initially traumatised by her governess's mistreatment of her, but she is subsequently trapped by her gender.

There is, however, more to the novel's involvement with feminism than its presentation of Flora de Barral. Kirschner has shown how an understanding of the central thematic importance of the role of women provides the key to the narrative method:

> During the first third of the novel, while we catch only a brief glimpse of Flora, the conflict that keeps the story going lies between Marlow and the militant feminist, Mrs Fyne.[52]

Kirschner interprets this conflict as a conflict resolved in and through the plot. He sees Marlow as engaged in 'male sabotage of Mrs Fyne's attempt to prevent Flora being a woman'.[53] He makes Marlow effectively into a second Basil Ransom in contest with another Olive Chancellor, intervening in Flora's life in order to save her 'from Mrs Fyne's feminist clutches'.[54] But this reading gives Mrs Fyne a prominence in the plot that she does not have. Since the narrative begins with Flora's flight from the Fyne household and continually stresses the subsequent alienation of Mrs Fyne and Flora, there is no suggestion that Mrs Fyne's feminism is likely to trap Flora. Indeed, the conflict between Marlow and Mrs Fyne is more important structurally. As Kirschner notes, after the first chapter, 'Flora's story unfolds to the accompaniment of a running fire on women by Marlow'.[55] More precisely, Flora's story 'unfolds' between the theoretical feminism of Mrs Fyne and the misogyny of Marlow, a dialogue that problematises the position of women within the narrative.

Conrad's use of the figure of the governess falls into this pattern. The governess is a recurring figure in nineteenth-century fiction concerned with the position of women.[56] Although her role in the plot of *Chance* is vastly different from her role in *Jane Eyre* or *Agnes Grey*, nevertheless, Conrad's presentation of her embodies attitudes familiar from those earlier appearances. Conrad emphasises, as much as Charlotte Brontë, the self-repression that is part of the governess's life. Marlow refers to 'the years, the passionate, bitter years, of restraint' (p. 120), that the governess has endured. He presents her as 'a woman as avid of all the sensuous emotions which life can give as most of her betters' (p. 104), but her life has been 'like living half strangled' (p. 120). It is one of the ironies of *Chance* that, in the disappointment and frustration of her desire for a fuller existence, the governess almost ruins Flora's life.

There are similar subtleties in Conrad's handling of Mrs Fyne. James's Olive Chancellor considered men in general as so much in the debt of the opposite sex 'that any individual woman had an unlimited credit with them; she could not possibly overdraw the general feminine account'.[57] Mrs Fyne's views are very similar:

> No consideration, no delicacy, no tenderness, no scruples should stand in the way of a woman (who by the mere fact of her sex was the predestined victim of conditions created by men's selfish passions, their vices and their abominable tyranny) from taking the shortest cut towards securing for herself the easiest possible existence. (p. 59)

Marlow is critical of Mrs Fyne's feminism on two grounds. First of all, he asserts that it was 'not political . . . not social' but 'a practical individualistic doctrine' (pp. 58–9). Secondly, he is critical of her 'complete ignorance of the world, of her own sex, and of the other kind of sinners' (p. 66). If her individualistic feminism makes her

seem a version of Olive Chancellor, her impracticality and ignorance
of the world recall rather James's Miss Birdseye, the type of the
theoretical, gullible, naive reformer. At the same time, Mrs Fyne's
particular kind of feminism is quite clearly the product of her own
particular past. As Marlow observes, 'Mrs Fyne wasn't the daughter
of a domestic tyrant for nothing' (p. 62). Mrs Fyne, like Captain
Anthony, is what she is because of what her father was.

As the novel progresses, Marlow is brought to examine his own
ideas about men and women.[58] When he contemplates the 'cabin
mystery' of the estrangement of Flora and Anthony, he remarks: 'I
must confess at once that it was Flora de Barral whom I suspected'
(pp. 326–7). Then he continues:

> In this world as at present organized women are the suspected
> half of the population . . . the part falling to women's share being
> all 'influence' has an air of occult and mysterious action, some-
> thing not altogether trustworthy like all natural forces which, for
> us, work in the dark because of our imperfect comprehension.
> (p. 327)

For a moment, Marlow acknowledges that the roles assigned to men
and women are cultural rather than 'natural'. For a moment, he
acknowledges a fear of women and relates that fear both to the role
socially assigned to women and to the limits of male comprehension.
He even considers the possible relationship between man's fear of
woman and his attempt to assert 'mastery' over her:

> He had dealt with her masterfully. But man has captured electric-
> ity too. It lights him on his way, it warms his home, it will even
> cook his dinner for him – very much like a woman. But what sort
> of conquest would you call it? He knows nothing of it. He has got
> to be mighty careful what he is about with his captive. And the
> greater the demand he makes on it in the exultation of his pride
> the more likely it is to turn on him and burn him to a cinder.
> (p. 327)

For a moment, Marlow tentatively and obliquely explores his own
misogyny and the implications of the contemporary, social organisation of male/female relations. It is, perhaps, significant then that, at
the end of the novel, after all his detective work, deduction and
speculation, Marlow acts to help Flora again. He not only acciden-

tally rescues her from suicide at the start, but he also intervenes, quite consciously, in her relationship with Powell. For all the limitations of his character, Marlow alone in the novel has sufficient 'sympathetic imagination', and sufficient understanding of Flora, to be able to act consciously and effectively to her advantage.

V

Conrad started work on *Victory* in April 1912 and had completed the manuscript version in May/June 1914.[59] Like *Chance*, *Victory* looks back to *Nostromo*: in particular, the relationship of Heyst and his father has discernible affinities with that of Gould and his father – or, for that matter, with the relationship of Captain Anthony and Carleon Anthony. In each case, the son has effectively inherited a curse from his father: a philosophy of detachment, the San Tomé mine, or a concept of masculinity.

Geddes has argued that *Victory* needs to be seen 'as a continuing exploration of the aesthetic and philosophical concerns given shape in *Chance*'.[60] *Victory*, like *Chance*, is grounded in scepticism. In *Chance*, that scepticism was embodied in the narrative technique; in *Victory*, scepticism is all-pervasive. Heyst provides the focus for the novel's scepticism: he is both a source of scepticism and the object of the novel's own sceptical narrative strategies. Heyst articulates the novel's epistemology: 'There is a quality in events which is apprehended differently by different minds or even by the same mind at different times' (p. 248). He recognises both 'the untruth of appearances' (p. 267) and the importance of appearances: 'Appearances – what more, what better can you ask for? In fact, you can't have better. You can't have anything else' (p. 204). But Heyst's articulation of the novel's philosophical bases does not grant him a privileged position: Heyst's scepticism is itself subjected to the scepticism that pervades the novel. Heyst's philosophical position is challenged, in particular, by a psychological exploration of his character, and he takes his place in the novel's thematic opposition of detachment and action, reason and passion, scepticism and 'the wisdom of the heart'.

In Part I, Heyst is presented by means of an unnamed narrator who has no privileged access to the inner man. Indeed, he observes that 'from the first there was some difficulty in making him out' (p. 6), and draws attention to the reserve, the courtesy, the gentlemanliness that serve to mask Heyst's thoughts and character. Various attempts to 'make him out' are exemplified by the succession of labels attached to him: 'Enchanted Heyst' (p. 7); 'Hard Facts' (p. 8); 'Heyst the Spider' (p. 21); 'Heyst the Enemy' (p. 24). These different perspectives on Heyst both encourage the reader to penetrate his appearances and suggest the impossibility of any such attempt.[61] They establish his shifting identity-for-the-other, but provide no clue to his identity-for-self. Laskowsky has noted how the scientific observation with which the novel begins ('There is, as every schoolboy knows in this scientific age, a very close chemical relation between coal and diamonds' – p. 3) relates to this presentation of Heyst's identity. The fact that carbon exists in different allotropic forms foregrounds the question of appearance and essence: more particularly, it suggests that Heyst might exist merely as a succession of identities-for-the-other and that his 'real self' may never be revealed.[62] This accords with the contents of a letter to Warrington Dawson (20 June 1913), which Conrad wrote while working on *Victory*:

> If you tell me that I am a shallow person thinking of forms and not of essence, I will tell you that this is all we have got to hold on to – that form is the artist's (and scientist's) province, that it is all we can understand (and interpret or represent) and that we can't tell what is behind.[63]

This view is implicit in the narrative-technique of Part I: Heyst's observable characteristics are reported by a narrator who is clearly dependent on the reports of other observers, each of whom has made his judgement on the basis of limited information and in line with his own prejudices and passions.

The first important event in Part I, Heyst's rescue of Morrison, has a different significance. The narrator observes:

> It was about this time that Heyst became associated with Morrison on terms about which people were in doubt. Some said he was a partner, others said he was a sort of paying quest, but the real truth of the matter was more complex.   (p. 10)

There is a 'real truth' to this relationship, and the narrative proceeds to offer it. Heyst rescues Morrison as the result of an irresistible sympathetic impulse. Morrison, in return, is overcome by the thought of his inability to repay him, until he hits upon the notion 'of inviting Heyst to travel with him in his brig and have a share in his trading ventures up to the amount of his loan' (p. 18). Out of delicacy of feelings, Heyst agrees 'in order to put an end to the harrowing scene in the cabin' (p. 19). As Leavis says, Heyst's 'combined generosity, indifference, and inexperience of mutuality in personal relations' make him unable to resist being drawn into Morrison's trading ventures.[64] Perhaps the most significant part of his account of this incident is the narrator's later observation:

> The Swede was as much distressed as Morrison; for he under-
> stood the other's feelings perfectly. No decent feeling was ever
> scorned by Heyst. But he was incapable of outward cordiality of
> manner, and he felt acutely his defect.   (p. 18)

Heyst's rescue of Morrison acts as an anticipatory parallel to the main event of Part I, his rescue of Lena, and this particular comment looks forward to the difficulties Heyst experiences in relation to Lena on the island.

Heyst's rescue of Morrison, however, is not just an anticipatory parallel to his rescue of Lena, but rather, as Gurko suggests, the first rescue creates the context for the second.[65] Other characters' percep-tion of the first incident conditions their perception of the second. Heyst is trying to live at a distance from others, but, like Razumov, he has ignored the fact that his appearances in the world will, nev-ertheless, be interpreted by others: his elusiveness does not save him from acquiring an identity-for-the-other. Indeed, his unawareness is all the more dangerous. After his rescue of Morrison, for example, his identity-for-the-other is distinctly unflattering: 'A rumour sprang out that Heyst, having obtained some mysterious hold on Morrison, had fastened himself on him and was sucking him dry' (p. 20). Schomberg, in particular, has taken pains to circulate a negative image of Heyst: 'a Heyst fattened by years of private and public rapines, the murderer of Morrison, the swindler of many sharehold-ers, a wonderful mixture of craft and impudence, of deep purposes and simple wiles' (p. 156). Moreover, his rescue of Morrison hints that, despite his conscious desire for solitude, Heyst might be uncon-sciously impelled to escape that solitude. In other words, besides the implied lesion between Heyst's identity-for-self and his identity-for-the-other, there is a further division between Heyst's identity-for-self and another denied aspect of himself. One result of Morrison's

rescue, then, is the revelation of Heyst's illusions: his illusions about
his relationship with the world and his illusions about his own
nature. His rescue of Morrison, like his rescue of Lena, is a self-
betrayal in a double sense: he betrays the code of detachment which
is the 'abiding illusion' (p. 18) of his existence and, in doing so,
betrays (discloses) a denied aspect of himself.

The major event of Part I is Heyst's flight with Lena. This is
presented, not directly, but through Davidson's investigation of the
mystery of Heyst's disappearance from Sourabaya. By this method,
the reader is involved in Davidson's attempts to understand Heyst
('This startling fact did not tally somehow with the idea Davidson
had of Heyst' – p. 42). At the same time, Davidson himself acts as a
'reflector' to provide clues to Heyst's behaviour and character. For
example, Davidson's concern for Heyst prompts an observation on
the 'capacity for sympathy in these stout placid men' (p. 43). This, in
turn, suggests a possible motive for Heyst's flight with Lena, particularly in the light of Heyst's sympathetic impulse towards
Morrison. Davidson's spontaneous response to Zangiacomo's poster
reinforces this interpretation:

> Davidson felt sorry for the eighteen lady-performers. He knew
> what that sort of life was like, the sordid conditions and brutal
> incidents of such tours.   (p. 38)

All these hints prepare for Davidson's conclusion that Heyst's flight
'was in its essence the rescue of a distressed human being' (p. 51).
However, the difference between the views of on-lookers and the
'more complex' truth of Heyst's relationship with Morrison should
make the reader wary of accepting this statement as a complete
account of the incident.

VI

In Part II, Heyst's flight with Lena is presented from Heyst's view-
point. Part II begins with an analepsis to describe Heyst's mental
state when he arrived at Schomberg's hotel:

> Heyst was disenchanted with life as a whole. His scornful tem-
> perament beguiled into action, suffered from failure in a subtle
> way unknown to men accustomed to grapple with the realities of

common human enterprise. It was like the gnawing pain of use-
less apostasy, a sort of shame before his own betrayed nature.
(p. 65)

This surprising being-for-himself is to some extent explained in a
further analepsis (in Chapter 3) to Heyst's relations with his father,
'thinker, stylist, and man of the world' (p. 91). Heyst had lived with
him from the age of eighteen to twenty-one; and three years of such
companionship 'at that plastic and impressionable age' were bound
'to leave in the boy a profound mistrust of life' (p. 91). As a result of
this 'mistrust of life', Heyst decided to 'drift'. He saw drifting as a
'defence against life' (p. 92):

> It was the very essence of his life to be a solitary achievement,
> accomplished not by hermit-like withdrawal with its silence and
> immobility, but by a system of restless wandering, by the detach-
> ment of an impermanent dweller amongst changing scenes. In this
> scheme he had perceived the means of passing through life with-
> out suffering and almost without a single care in the world –
> invulnerable because elusive.   (p. 90)

Heyst's disenchantment 'with life as a whole' (p. 65), his sense of
apostasy and his feeling that he has 'betrayed' his own nature are
now explained. Certain details in Part I have also acquired a fuller
meaning, retrospectively, by being provided with this context. (For
example, Heyst's comment, on his rescue of Lena, that he had allowed himself 'to be tempted into action': p. 54.) In addition, there is
the dramatic irony that this consciousness of apostasy and self-
betrayal (occasioned by his rescue of Morrison) is the prelude to his
rescue of Lena; and there is the further irony that his belief that he
has betrayed himself by involving himself with Morrison reveals his
deep misunderstanding of his true nature.

It is this issue that now dominates the narrative. One of the effects
of his 'apostasy' is a sense of 'failure' from not living up to his own
code of behaviour, and that sense of failure has caused Heyst to see
himself in a new way. His failure to remain detached from the
world, paradoxically, has made him conscious of his own isolation:

> Not a single soul belonging to him lived anywhere on earth. Of
> this fact – not such a remote one, after all – he had only lately
> become aware. . . . And though he had made up his mind to retire

from the world in hermit fashion, yet he was irrationally moved
by this sense of loneliness which had come to him in the hour of
renunciation.   (p. 66)

This contradiction in Heyst's character points to a conflict between
the rationalist scepticism, derived from his father, by which he has
tried to live, and an irrational, emotional aspect of him that resists
that scepticism. It is this other aspect of Heyst that is now called into
operation. Heyst is described as 'temperamentally sympathetic'
(p. 70), and his sympathetic temperament responds to the situation
of Zangiacomo's Ladies Orchestra: 'Heyst felt a sudden pity for
these beings, exploited, hopeless, devoid of charm and grace' (p. 70).
This generalised sympathetic emotion becomes focused on Lena,
when he sees her being mistreated by Mrs Zangiacomo, and,
responding to 'the same sort of impulse which years ago had made
him cross the sandy street of the abominable town of Delli' (p. 71)
to address Morrison, he crosses the room to her.
    Up to this point, Heyst's rescue of Lena corresponds to the im-
pression given in Part I: 'in its essence the rescue of a distressed
human being' (p. 51). In Chapter 2, however, the narrative moves
away from the parallel with Morrison and registers a significant
difference between the two rescues which the phrase 'human being'
had obscured:

He was the same man who had plunged after the submerged
Morrison. . . . But this was another sort of plunge altogether, and
likely to lead to a very different kind of partnership.   (p. 77)

The sexual dimension, which is intimated in this passage, comes to
the fore in the rest of the chapter as Heyst's response to Lena becomes something more complex than merely sympathy. Lena's voice
had stirred 'unexpressed longings' (p. 75) deep in Heyst's heart, now
he experiences 'the awakening of a tenderness, indistinct and confused as yet, towards an unknown woman' (p. 82). The narrator
continues, in the eliptical, coded language characteristic of the
novel's treatment of their relationship, that Heyst 'had no illusions
about her; but his sceptical mind was dominated by the fulness of his
heart' (p. 83). Heyst's behaviour at Schomberg's hotel is governed by
this new principle, and the scene is set for a conflict between his
habitual scepticism and his newly awakened 'heart'.[66]

At this point, the narrative shifts to Schomberg and to Schomberg's view of Heyst's flight with Lena. Schwarz notes that the 'doubling of characters' is an organisational principle in *Victory*.[67] Davidson has already acted as a reflector on Heyst, and now Schomberg is used in the same way. To begin with, there are certain obvious narrative parallels between the two: both have an interest in Lena; and both have to find a way of dealing with Jones, Ricardo and Pedro. But these narrative parallels generate other, subtler parallels between Heyst and Schomberg – or the teasing suggestion of possible parallels – by means of which various issues are raised for consideration. For example, Schomberg's dealings with Jones and Ricardo expose certain weaknesses in his character, and, in particular, the difference between the identity that he asserts and his true nature: 'The consciousness of his inwardly abject attitude towards these men caused him always to throw his chest out and assume a severe expression' (pp. 122–3). This is 'the Lieutenant-of-the-Reserve bearing by which he tried to keep up his self-respect before the world' (p. 119). This compensatory behaviour is seen most clearly in Schomberg's relations with his wife: he has bullied her to compensate for his own fears and anxieties; he has mistreated her in order to establish a 'manly' and superior image of himself.[68] But this strategy has worked against himself: he feels now that the crushed and demoralised Mrs Schomberg is 'no fit companion for a man of his ability' (p. 119). And, when Jones and Ricardo challenge the false identity that he asserts, he feels the need for a woman's passionate response to reassure him of his 'manliness': 'What he needed was a pair of woman's arms which, flung round his neck, would brace him up for the encounter. Inspire him, he called it to himself' (p. 120).

By juxtaposing the narrator's account of Schomberg's feelings to the translation of those feelings into Schomberg's own idiom, Conrad economically discloses Schomberg's self-delusion: he displays the verbal strategy by which Schomberg muffles and masks the precise nature of his need. But the strategy has implications that go beyond the psychology of a particular individual. That word 'inspire' expresses the man's need for reassurance from a woman in a way that fits it back into patriarchal attitudes. Instead of openly acknowledging male vulnerability and emotional need, this formulation presents the man as active and the woman as the passive inspiration of male action.

Through Schomberg, Conrad initiates an examination of 'masculinity', which is continued in his subsequent presentation of Heyst. There are repeated references to Schomberg's 'manliness' and to Heyst's 'martial' and 'masculine' appearance, and these play ironically on the difference between that appearance and the inner man.[69] In Schomberg's case, the difference between the identity he asserts and the fear that lies behind it is explicitly acknowledged: Schomberg hides 'a timid disposition under his manly exterior' (p. 104). Heyst's case is more complex:

> At that epoch in his life, in the fulness of his physical development, of a broad martial presence, with his bald head and long moustaches, he resembled the portraits of Charles XII, of adventurous memory. However, there was no reason to think that Heyst was in any way a fighting man. (p. 9)

This raises the possibility that Heyst's 'martial presence' is as much a sham as Schomberg's asserted 'manliness'. Also, that reference to Charles XII is, perhaps, not quite as straightforward as it seems: Charles XII was not only an active military campaigner, but also a confirmed bachelor. Another character introduced in Part II, the woman-hating 'Mr Jones', develops this part of the novel's open-ended exploration of 'masculinity'. Mr Jones, like Schomberg, acts as a reflector on Heyst, and the reader is encouraged to explore the similarities and differences between the two men. Where Heyst's relationship to Schomberg problematises 'manly' appearance, his relationship with Jones interrogates 'gentlemanly' lack of emotional display. In addition, the reader cannot ignore one of Mr Jones's most prominent characteristics: his fear and hatred of women. As Ricardo cheerfully reports, 'He funks women' (p. 160).[70]

VII

Part III falls into two halves: the first five chapters are devoted to Heyst and Lena, the second five present the first stage of Heyst's confrontation with Jones and Ricardo. The anticipated arrival of Jones and Ricardo hangs over the first five chapters and gives a poignancy to the attempts of Lena and Heyst to come to terms with each other.

Chapter 1 begins, however, by returning to Heyst's relationship with his father: the earlier account of Heyst's father is now amplified and Heyst's father's beliefs, in particular, come in for more extensive treatment. He is described as the 'destroyer of systems, of hopes, of beliefs', the 'bitter contemner of life' (p. 175). Heyst's 'mistrust of life' (p. 91) and his corresponding effort to make his life 'a masterpiece of aloofness' (p. 174) are now more readily understandable. His father told him, 'Look on – make no sound' (p. 175), and Heyst has attempted to do this. He adopted a 'scheme' to avoid attachment by 'a system of restless wandering' (p. 90). The words 'scheme' and 'system' indicate the rationalistic basis of Heyst's *modus vivendi*, but they also point to an inconsistency in Heyst's response. He has erected a 'system' in an attempt to live according to his father's anti-systemic scepticism. There is a further and more important inconsistency in Heyst's position. His father detected Heyst's incomplete detachment and contempt for the world, and advised him, therefore, 'to cultivate that form of contempt which is called pity' (p. 174). The narrative has already shown how Heyst's 'pity' has worked against his aimed-at detachment, but it now foregrounds a fundamental contradiction in his relations with his father. This is evidenced in his response to the obituary notices at his father's death. Heyst reads them 'with mournful detachment', but suddenly: 'He became aware of his eyes being wet. It was not that the man was his father. For him it was purely a matter of hearsay which could not in itself cause this emotion' (p. 175). Geddes draws attention to the revealing contradiction in the phrase 'mournful detachment'. In the passage as a whole, Heyst's emotional response is juxtaposed to his conscious, rational attitude, and this juxtaposition confirms that his rationalist self-image is at odds with his true nature.[71]

His attitude towards his father's house and furniture has the same implication. His attachment to them sharply contradicts his stated beliefs:

It seemed as if in his conception of a world not worth touching, and perhaps not substantial enough to grasp, these objects familiar to his childhood and his youth, and associated with the memory of an old man, were the only realities, something having an absolute existence. He would never have them sold, or even moved from the places they occupied when he looked upon them last. When he was advised from London that his lease had expired, and that the house, with some others as like it as two peas, was to be demolished, he was surprisingly distressed.   (p. 176)

Hodges has written perceptively of the series of ironic contradictions in Heyst's relationship with his father.[72] He notes the contradiction between the origin and the content of Heyst's father's philosophy. The basis of that philosophy was not a rational analysis of the conditions of life, but an emotional response of disillusionment and regret. Heyst's father began as a romantic, eager for all experience, 'covetting all the joys, those of the great and those of the humble, those of the fools and those of the sages' (p. 91). But, when life did not meet his extravagant demands, he became disillusioned and sceptical. There is, then, a contradiction between the elder Heyst's theory of observation and detachment, which he impresses upon his son, and the conditions of his own life, which was marked by emotional turmoil. As Hodges points out, this contradiction is exposed in 'one incisive, ironic sentence':

> 'Look on – and make no sound,' were the last words of the man who had spent his life in blowing blasts upon a terrible trumpet which had filled heaven and earth with ruins, while mankind went on its way unheeding.   (p. 175)[73]

Heyst's father's teachings about human relationships are also in conflict with their own father–son relationship: it is because of the strength of Heyst's bond with his father that his father's teachings have such a firm grip on him. This is the basis of Heyst's self-deceptions. It is also, as Hodges points out, self-perpetuating: the longer he remains aloof and sceptical, the stronger grows his attachment to his dead father, because, while he remains aloof, the world seems unreal to him and his father's memory is the one thing that retains force and solidity.[74] At the same time, the shadowy unreality that is his experience of the world reinforces the scepticism his father gave him. There is, then, a deep contradiction in Heyst's sense of 'apostasy'. He feels that he has betrayed his father and his father's advice, but that feeling of betrayal is itself interwoven with an emotional response to his father and his childhood that is inconsistent with the values Heyst feels he has betrayed.

Even after he has rescued Lena, Heyst is still clearly under his father's influence, and the continuing influence of Heyst's father is signified by regular references to his portrait: 'Primarily the man with the quill pen in his hand in that picture you so often look at is responsible for my existence. He is also responsible for what my existence is, or rather has been' (p. 195). This influence is also evident in Heyst's comments. For example, he sums up his relationship with Morrison:

> I had, in a moment of inadvertence, created for myself a tie. How to define it precisely I don't know. . . . I only know that he who forms a tie is lost. The germ of corruption has entered into his soul. (pp. 199–200)

However, while he asserts his old beliefs and his old, sceptical, detached identity in this way, Heyst's words conflict with his feelings towards Lena, who 'gave him a greater sense of his own reality than he had ever known in all his life' (p. 200). Does Heyst's relationship with Lena represent the 'germ of corruption' entering into his soul or release from his father's inhibiting influence? This is the question that is explored through the psychological drama of Parts III and IV. Heyst's relationship with Lena involves him in a conflict between his old identity and a new principle or, rather, it makes manifest the contradictions within Heyst between his sceptical and detached identity-for-self and his repressed emotions. Though the relationship begins as Heyst's rescue of Lena from Schomberg, it turns into Lena's struggle to rescue Heyst from the inhibiting influence of his father.

As Leavis observes, Heyst at the start of Part III, 'finds himself committed to the establishment of a mutuality that is alien to the habit of a life-time'.[75] He feels uneasy at the discrepancy between his 'scheme' and the necessities of his own nature, between his sense of himself and this sympathetic impulse that contradicts it. He also feels both afraid and perplexed at the prospect of trying to relate to Lena. When they first arrive at Heyst's house, Lena stands still, staring fixedly at it:

> 'Don't you want to go in?' he asked, without turning his head to look at her. 'The sun's too heavy to stand about here.' He tried to overcome a sort of fear, a sort of impatient faintness, and his voice sounded rough. 'You had better go in,' he concluded. (p. 183)

Heyst's fear at having to acknowledge the otherness of another person expresses itself as impatience or brusqueness. There is a gap between what Heyst feels and the way he presents himself to Lena that has important consequences for both of them. At the same time, Heyst has great difficulty understanding either Lena or his own response to her: 'In the intimacy of their life her grey, unabashed gaze forced upon him the sensation of something inexplicable reposing within her; stupidity or inspiration, weakness or force – or simply an abysmal emptiness' (p. 192). Heyst is aware of 'the profound effect those veiled grey eyes produced', but 'whether on his heart or on his nerves, whether sensuous or spiritual, tender or irritating, he was unable to say' (p. 193). He feels that he does not know Lena, or how to live with her, or even the precise nature of his own feelings.

Heyst's involvement with Morrison disclosed not only an aspect of Heyst at odds with his identity-for-self, but also a further split between his identity-for-self and his identity-for-the-other. The discussion about Morrison that takes place between Heyst and Lena in Part III returns to these divisions. Heyst tells Lena that the 'people in this part of the world went by appearances, and called us friends, as far as I can remember' (p. 204). Heyst's irony about 'appearances', however, rebounds on himself. He learns from Lena how his relationship with Morrison was actually regarded by the world he inhabited (p. 208). Heyst had sought to remain elusive and undefined. Once he discovers how he was defined, the shock of this discovery never leaves him: 'The power of calumny grows with time. It's insidious and penetrating. It can even destroy one's faith in oneself – dry-rot the soul' (p. 362). Indeed, Heyst uses this discovery to explain his inability to act against Jones and Ricardo:

> Do you know what the world would say? . . . It would say . . . that I – the Swede – after luring my friend and partner to his death from mere greed of money, have murdered these unoffending shipwrecked strangers from sheer funk. That would be the story whispered – perhaps shouted – certainly spread out, and believed. (pp. 361–2)

Schomberg's malice has done for Heyst what Haldin's admiration accidentally did for Razumov: in both cases, a false identity has been given currency in the world. Heyst, like Razumov, is made aware of the gap between identity-for-self and identity-for-the-other, but,

where Razumov is eventually able to break through that false identity and bring identity-for-self and identity-for-the-other into line,
Heyst feels unable to escape. He feels, instead, that the false identity
will damage his own sense of himself. What lies behind this, of
course, is the further division between his identity-for-self and his
true self. When Lena reported to him Schomberg's version of his
relationship with Morrison, he replied: 'So that's how the business
looked from outside! . . . Strange that it should hurt me!' (p. 208).
Again Heyst's surprise at his own response draws attention to the
self-deception that has been part of the construction of that identity-
for-self.

Heyst's 'system of restless wandering' (p. 90) has obvious affinities with what Laing describes as the unembodied or disembodied
self.[76] Heyst's courteous and ironic manner, the 'faint playfulness of
manner and speech' like 'a habit one has schooled oneself into'
(p. 204), is clearly an analagous strategy: both are ways of living in
the world without committing oneself, attempts to remain elusive
and undefined, and both operate in the novel as parts of a false-
self system. Certainly, Heyst's experience of the world resembles
Laing's account of the experience of the world produced by the false-
self system:

> If the individual delegates all transactions between himself and
> the other to a system within his being which is not 'him', then the
> world is experienced as unreal, and all that belongs to this system
> is felt to be false, futile, and meaningless.[77]

Similarly, Laing's account of the effects of the false-self system on
the individual's powers to act – 'the gates of action are not in the
command of the self but are being lived and operated by a false self'
– casts a suggestive light on Heyst's difficulties with Lena (and, later,
with Jones and Ricardo).[78] As Conrad puts it in his 'Author's Note':
'Heyst in his fine detachment had lost the habit of asserting himself'
not 'the courage of self-assertion, either moral or physical, but the
mere way of it, the trick of the thing' (p. x). Heyst is hampered in his
relations with others because, before he can relate to them, he has to
struggle within himself against his false-self system. Laing's comments on attempts to break through the false-self system by acts of
commitment can be compared to Heyst's feelings in relation to
Morrison and Lena: 'Once commit itself to any real project and it
suffers agonies of humiliation – not necessarily for any failure, but

simply because it has to subject itself to necessity and contingency.'[79]

Lena, in her attempts to relate to Heyst, runs into the barrier of his false-self system, in the form of his defensive system of ironic courtesy, but she is also assisted by an impulse within him which is in conflict with those defences. As he expresses it: 'when one's heart has been broken into in the way you have broken into mine, all sorts of weaknesses are free to enter – shame, anger, stupid indignations, stupid fears' (p. 210). Heyst's negative description of the process indicates the struggle taking place within him and the resistance of his false-self system to the new principle. Heyst's words express precisely the 'agonies of humiliation' at being subjected to 'necessity and contingency': 'All his defences were broken now. Life had him fairly by the throat . . . all his cherished negations were falling off him one by one' (p. 222). Despite his resistance, Heyst seems to be advancing towards release from his false-self system, but, at this point, Ricardo and Jones arrive on the island.

VIII

Chapters 3, 4 and 5 of Part III offer an economic, dramatic representation of the first stage of Lena's relationship with Heyst on the island. It soon becomes clear that, whatever adjustments have taken place, Heyst has not broken through his detached manner. Whatever he feels for Lena, he 'could not help being temperamentally, from long habit and from set purpose, a spectator still' (p. 185). The narrative presents Lena's reading of this detached manner as a lack of interest in her:

> She felt in her innermost depths an irresistible desire to give herself up to him more completely, by some act of absolute sacrifice. This was something of which he did not seem to have an idea. He was a strange being without needs.   (p. 201)

Here is, also, the first hint of that displacement of erotic feeling into idealistic self-sacrifice, which will be Lena's final response to Heyst's shut-upness. Her immediate response is a sense of insecurity: she worries that Heyst will 'grow weary of the burden' (p. 209) of their relationship. This feeling of insecurity is not helped by the way in which Heyst talks about his relationship with Morrison: 'Funny position, wasn't it. The boredom came later, when we lived together on board his ship' (p. 199). Heyst, in his ironic, detached reflections, is insensitive to the likely effect of his words upon Lena. Heyst is insensitive to the implications of his speech and to the significance of her reactions, because he is, generally, insufficiently aware of her 'otherness'. Lena, for her part, is unaware that there might be a difference between what Heyst says and what he feels.

Lena's sense of insecurity is ultimately derived from her sense of lack of worth. She responds to Heyst's banter, at one point, by saying: 'It looks as if you were trying to make out that I am disagreeable. . . . Am I? You will make me afraid to open my mouth presently. I shall end by believing I am no good' (p. 187). Lena's sense of lack of worth has a social and moral basis. The clearest indication of the social basis occurs, in Chapter 9, when Heyst is looking for his revolver. Lena assures him that she has 'touched nothing in the house' except what he gave her, and Heyst immediately understands the implications of this 'disclaimer of a charge which he had not made': 'It was what a servant might have said – an inferior open to suspicion' (pp. 253–4). During their conversations at Schomberg's hotel, Lena told Heyst of her working-class childhood 'in the north of London, off Kingsland Road' (p. 191) as well as of her present difficulties, trapped between the cruelty of the Zangiacomos and the sexual harassment of Schomberg. She responded to his initiative in talking to her by imposing on him the burden of rescuing her (p. 80). This demand was indicative of her desperation, but it was influenced by what she took to be his 'friendliness' (p. 78). Heyst talked to her 'with the ease of a man of the world speaking to a young lady in a drawing-room' (p. 74), and Lena admired his 'quiet, polished manner':

> She had never seen anything like that before . . . she had never met the forms of simple courtesy. She was interested by it as a very novel experience, not very intelligible, but distinctly pleasurable. (p. 79)

This suggests that Lena perhaps misreads 'simple courtesy' as 'friendliness'. It certainly establishes, from the outset, one complicating factor in their relationship: the class difference between them.

In Chapters 4 and 5, Lena's insecurities interact with Heyst's internal conflicts. Heyst's negative expression of his feelings for her ('when one's heart has been broken into' – p. 210) activates Lena's anxieties. She replies: 'But why are you angry with me? Are you sorry you took me away from those beasts? I told you who I was. You could see it' (p. 210). Heyst's 'resentment' (p. 215) at being drawn out of his detachment, out of his false-self system, interacts with Lena's fears and her sense of moral and social inferiority. At the same time, he feels annoyed by Lena's lack of trust in him: she believes that he might have mistreated Morrison or, at least, does not disbelieve the story. Heyst fails to see that Lena cannot disbelieve the story because it echoes her own anxieties. As she says, 'why shouldn't you get tired of that or any other – company?' (p. 214). Lena's substitution of the neutral word 'company' for the more charged word 'friend' (which the echo of Heyst's earlier speech supplies) indicates her attempt to conceal her anxieties about her own position. Lena and Heyst misunderstand each other in these exchanges partly because each is pursuing his/her own thoughts, and each is struggling with his/her own psychological problems. Lena's needs and insecurities and Heyst's doubts, inner conflicts, and self-concealments create a potentially rich field for exploration.

Lena's sense of her unworthiness shapes her interpretation of Heyst's lack of emotional display. He is, for her, someone 'whom she could never hope to understand, and whom she was afraid she could never satisfy': 'as if her passions were of a hopelessly lower quality, unable to appease some exalted and delicate desire of his superior soul' (p. 330). Lena's low self-evaluation also determines the course of action she chooses for herself:

> Such as she was, a fiddle-scraping girl picked up on the very threshold of infamy, she would try to rise above herself, triumphant and humble; and then happiness would burst on her like a torrent, flinging at her feet the man whom she loved.   (p. 353)

Lena aims to prove herself worthy of Heyst's love by sacrificing herself for him. This is, in part, a continuation of the novel's exploration of sexual politics: in this case, the contemporary cultural emphasis on self-sacrifice in the construction of female identity. In part, this springs from another influence on Lena's character: her Christian up-bringing. The intrusion of Jones and Ricardo provides her with the opportunity to cast herself in a drama of redemption. She aims to transcend her low self-evaluation through a voluntary act of self-sacrifice, and, by that means, gain power over Heyst.[80]

Heyst, by contrast, fails to find a way of responding to the new situation on the island. The main emphasis, in the latter part of the novel, is on Heyst as an 'unarmed man' (p. 389), and his failure to act against Ricardo and Jones is used to explore further his failure to respond adequately to Lena. Heyst makes this connection himself: 'I've never killed a man or loved a woman . . . not even in my thoughts, not even in my dreams' (p. 212). Heyst blames his life of thoughtful detachment for his inability to act effectively: 'I have lived too long within myself, watching the mere shadows and shades of life' (p. 318). He does, indeed, seem hampered by a sense of the unreality of the situation and the insubstantiality of his opponents (p. 350). And, at the critical moment, when he has the opportunity to overcome Mr Jones, he does nothing at all:

> In the latter's breast dwelt a deep silence, the complete silence of unused faculties. . . . His very will seemed dead of weariness. He moved automatically, his head low, like a prisoner captured by the evil power of a masquerading skeleton out of a grave.
> (p. 390)

It is not, however, Mr Jones who has captured him and made him prisoner, but rather his false-self system. Where Lena responds to the intrusion of Jones and Ricardo by finding a role for herself that transcends her insecurities, Heyst responds by withdrawing into himself and re-establishing his defences. The final irony is that those defences are, in the end, themselves destructive. Laing suggests that one development, for 'the person who does not act in reality', is the increasing impoverishment of reality and a corresponding impoverishment of the self, until 'the world is in ruins, and the self is (apparently) dead'.[81] This deadness of the self is what Heyst experiences at the critical moment. Indeed, long before this meeting between Heyst and Jones, Heyst 'considered himself a dead man already, yet forced to pretend that he was alive for her sake' (p. 354).

A similar deadness enters into his relationship with Lena. This is epitomised by an incident in Chapter 9, when Heyst asks Lena for her hand. He begins to raise it to his lips, but 'halfway up released his grasp': ' "Neither force nor conviction," Heyst muttered wearily to himself' (p. 350). This derives additional significance by contrast with an earlier incident, when Heyst unexpectedly met Lena in the grounds of Schomberg's hotel:

> White and spectral, she was putting out her arms to him out of the black shadows like an appealing ghost. He took her hands, and

was affected, almost surprised, to find them so warm, so real, so firm, so living in his grasp.   (p. 86)

Heyst moved from the realm of the 'spectral' and shadowy to experience the substantiality and reality of another person: the scene in Chapter 9, by contrast, registers the fact of his emotional withdrawal. The culmination of this process occurs in the penultimate chapter of the novel, when Lena is dying and calls to Heyst: 'Heyst bent low over her, cursing his fastidious soul, which even at that moment kept the true cry of love from his lips in its infernal mistrust of all life' (p. 406). Even at this emotional climax, Heyst remains trapped within his false-self system and (unlike Flora in *Chance*) is unable to express 'the true cry of love'.

The word 'fastidious' provides the key. Heyst is sealed into his false-self system by the doubt of Lena's fidelity that he experienced at the moment when he and Jones saw Lena and Ricardo together. At that moment, Heyst, like Jones, felt betrayed by his partner:

Doubt entered into him – a doubt of a new kind, formless, hideous. It seemed to spread itself all over him, enter his limbs, and lodge in his entrails. He stopped suddenly, with a thought that he who experienced such a feeling had no business to live. (pp. 391–2)

Lena's apparent betrayal of him seems retrospectively to justify his father's advice and to make Heyst's 'apostasy' the more bitter. Heyst had attempted to 'trust in life' and to move outside the defences of his false-self system, but the shock of this apparent betrayal destroys that attempt:

All the objects in there – the books, the gleam of old silver familiar to him from boyhood, the very portrait on the wall – seemed shadowy, unsubstantial, the dumb accomplices of an amazing dream-plot ending in an illusory effect of awakening and the impossibility of ever closing his eyes again.   (p. 403)

Indeed, the shock has not just destroyed Heyst's attempt to emerge from his false-self system and to establish a relationship with Lena, it has also struck at the very basis of that attempt – namely, his contradictory attachment to his father. As Hodges observes, this passage shows how even his father's possessions 'lose their force'.[82]

The immediate effect of this disillusionment is revealed in Heyst's responses to Lena. While Lena is full of a triumphant sense of her victory, Heyst's initial remarks are cold and reproachful: 'You may glory in your resourcefulness and your profound knowledge of yourself; but I may say that the other attitude, suggestive of shame, had its charm' (p. 404). The disillusionment with Lena gives way to a deeper and more general disillusionment in their final exchange: ' "Who else could have done this for you?" she whispered gloriously. "No one in the world," he answered her in a murmur of unconcealed despair' (p. 406). When he realises that she did not betray him, he realises also the full significance of his loss.

IX

Karl, from his comparison of the published text of *Victory* with the manuscript version, argues that Conrad's process of revision has the effect of cutting back the psychologically fuller picture of the manuscript.[83] In particular, he notes how the possibility of Lena's duplicity occurs to Heyst much earlier in the manuscript, and the resulting intensification of Heyst's alienation from Lena, he implies, is more effective.[84] It could be argued, however, that Conrad strengthened the novel by removing from Heyst any early doubts about Lena's fidelity: the early exploration of Heyst's other doubts and conflicts is kept clearer, and the sudden shock of 'betrayal' by her is the more forceful. It might also be argued that, by removing some of the psychological detail in the course of revision, Conrad makes more demands upon the reader's interpretative activity. Conrad's revisions of his manuscript are not so much a reduction of the psychological dimensions of the text as part of a calculated move away from realism and towards an open-ended, multivalent narrative. As part of this process, his exploration of Heyst's relationship with Lena, his presentation of Heyst's struggle against his false-self system and of Lena's response to her sense of lack of worth are overlaid by allegoric and mythic modes.[85]

The novel's allegorical mode has perhaps caused most difficulty. As Heyst and Lena watch Jones, Ricardo and Pedro in the compound, Heyst presents them to her as 'evil intelligence, instinctive savagery, arm in arm' with 'brute force' at the back (p. 329). Later, Mr Jones presents himself to Heyst as 'the world itself, come to pay you a visit' (p. 379). In each of these instances, there is an invitation to allegorical reading, but the allegorisation is the character's interpretation not the narrator's. Conrad develops in *Victory* a device exploited fully in *The Arrow of Gold*: each character interprets what happens in terms of their own view of themselves and the world, and the narrative is then constructed from the intermeshing and alternation of these different world-views.[86] This is seen at its clearest and subtlest in relation to Lena. The terms of Lena's life are those of romantic melodrama, and this romantic perspective explains both her readiness to run off with Heyst and her later decision to sacrifice herself for him. As Secor observes, 'if Heyst has implicated Lena in his dream world, she begins to make it her own according to her vision of her dangers, abilities, and opportunities'.[87] Lena's romantic perspective also enters the prose of the novel:

> The rhetoric of sentimentality and romantic cliche is not Conrad's but Lena's; we are, in other words, given rhetoric not designed to have us take Lena at Conrad's valuation of her but rather intended to reveal Lena's valuation of herself and her world.[88]

Through shifts in narrative-perspective, one idiom is subverted by another, one view of the world is challenged by the next.

Conrad's mythic mode produces a similar result. The narrative superimposes various literary and mythic patterns, and, as with Joyce's 'mythic method', the contradictions between these superimposed patterns build a certain amount of interpretative play into the novel to create a polysemous, indeterminate fiction.[89] This indeterminacy is particularly appropriate to *Victory*, given the novel's scepticism about truth, facts, and reason. The mixed modes, the shifting perspectives, the contradictory mythic and literary patterns work against the production of a coherent and conclusive 'meaning'. As Geddes demonstrates, 'even the most insignificant word or phrase may be seen to assume dimensions that are quite unexpected'.[90] All this accords with Conrad's letter about *Victory*, in which he asserts that 'a work of art is very seldom limited to one exclusive meaning and not necessarily tending to a definite conclusion'.[91] Although Conrad's performance in *Victory* does not stand comparison with what Joyce was to achieve in *Ulysses*, nevertheless, his technical experimentation cannot be seen as evidence of a decline, particularly since that experimentation bore fruit in the two novels which are the subject of the final chapter.

8

Initiation and Invention: *The Rover* and *The Arrow of Gold*

Until comparatively recently, there were only two critical approaches to Conrad's late novels. On the one hand, there was the view established by Hewitt, Moser and Guerard that Conrad's late novels represented a decline after the achievement of the novels of his 'major' period: *Lord Jim, Nostromo* and *The Secret Agent*.[1] On the other hand, there was the view of Bradbrook, Wiley and Wright that there was no decline, and that Conrad's later novels were to be praised as novels of affirmation.[2] More recently, a third approach to the later novels has established itself. This was adumbrated in an essay by Morton Zabel; it was developed further by John Palmer; and it was most fully articulated by Gary Geddes.[3] Geddes argues that Hewitt, Moser and Guerard display 'a misunderstanding of Conrad's fictional aims' and 'a predilection for fictional modes and techniques that were no longer of paramount importance to Conrad'.[4] Their critical approach is biased towards 'fiction that presents the drama of self' and cannot cope with 'the wider, more social manifestations of Conrad's moral imperatives' in his late novels.[5] Conrad, in his later fiction, was interested in 'a certain patterning of events, a certain texturing of the prose', in developing modes and techniques other than those of his earlier work.[6] The late novels are not, as Moser suggests, an exhausted return to old subjects, but a continuing search for the right form for subjects which continue to engage him.[7] The 'achievement and decline' paradigm reveals not so much Conrad's imaginative exhaustion as the exhaustion of its own critical assumptions. Conrad's last two complete novels, *The Arrow of Gold* and *The Rover*, are both works of initiation: the first involves M. George's initiation into passion; the second features Peyrol's initiation into death. And this interest in initiation is combined with renewed technical inventiveness.

251

I

The Arrow of Gold was written during 1917 and 1918, but the idea and
the material were not new. Conrad wrote to Doubleday, on 21 December 1918, that *The Arrow of Gold* was a subject that he had had in
mind 'for some eighteen years'.[8] Conrad was presumably referring
to *The Sisters*, which has obvious points of resemblance. There are
also connections between *The Arrow of Gold* and Conrad's autobiographical writings, *The Mirror of the Sea* and *A Personal Record*: in
both these works, Conrad describes his initiation into the craft of the
sea during his Marseilles years, and, in *The Mirror of the Sea*, he
writes about Dominic Cervoni and the *Tremolino*, which feature
again in *The Arrow of Gold*. In *The Arrow of Gold*, however, Conrad
was concerned with initiation into the life of passion rather than
initiation into the craft of the sea, and he was writing fiction not
autobiography.

Concern with the autobiographical accuracy of *The Arrow of Gold*
has contributed to the critical neglect of the novel, because an approach through Conrad's biography misreads both the mode of the
novel and M. George's narrative function.[9] *The Arrow of Gold*, like
Victory, aims to transcend realism. Wiley, in his sympathetic and
insightful account of the novel, draws attention to Conrad's technique of 'transcribing objectively the illusions of sense', and argues
that 'in no other book does Conrad work quite so steadily as a
painter in prose'.[10] He instances the portrait of Rita, standing in her
pale blue wrapper on the crimson staircase (p. 66); the chiaroscuro
portrait of Therese 'as though she had come out of an old, cracked,
smoky painting' (pp. 138–9); and the monochrome presentation of
Mrs Blunt as a 'picture in silver and grey, with touches of black'
(p. 180). In each case, however, Conrad produces not just a painterly
effect in prose (as Ford had done, for example, in *The Fifth Queen*),
but an effect that is explicitly and self-consciously painterly.[11] It
is not, as Wiley suggests, the objective transcription of sense-
impressions but rather the organisation and evaluation of a description in painterly terms.[12] Consider, for example, the portrait of Rita.
The narrator remarks, at the outset, that 'the visual impression was
more of colour in a picture than of the forms of actual life', and then
notes how the 'white stairs, the deep crimson of the carpet, and the
light blue of the dress made an effective combination of colour'
(p. 66). The reader's attention is drawn, not to an aesthetic object, but
to an aesthetic way of seeing. As in *Victory*, the narrative technique

is based on different perspectives, different ways of seeing, different attempts to interpret what is seen, and the use of self-consciously aesthetic ways of seeing draws attention to this.

M. George is obviously the most important of the various ways of seeing in the novel, since his interpretation provides the narrative. Yet he is not a privileged interpreter: in fact, his actions, responses and perceptions are often (and quite accurately) described as stupid. As he suggests, if he represents anything, 'it was a perfect freshness of sensations and a refreshing ignorance' (p. 31). Nevertheless, the relationship between M. George and Conrad plays a part in the novel, and the text encourages the reader to identify the two. For example, the minimal account of M. George's nautical activities seems to assume the reader's prior knowledge of the *Tremolino* story from *The Mirror of the Sea*, and other passages (pp. 69, 272) resonate against Conrad's earlier writing. At the same time, the use of 'Two Notes' as a framing device for M. George's narrative (and the device of an 'editor') serve to distance Conrad from the narrative.

The 'First Note' introduces a number of thematic concerns. The 'writer' has 'struck out into a pathless desert' (p. 3), and, in doing so, has found an identity which is outside those of his own society. His position resembles Lingard's in *The Rescue*, who had also 'wandered beyond that circle which race, memories, early associations, all the essential conditions of one's origin, trace round every man's life' (*TR*, pp. 121–2). The writer, like Lingard, then has the problem of making this new identity known and understood to his old world. The narrative that follows initially seems to be motivated by the writer's desire to align identity-for-self with identity-for-the-other. Part I introduces the writer's younger self. It begins with him in Marseilles, just after his return from his 'second West Indies voyage':

My eyes were still full of tropical splendour, my memory of my experiences, lawful and lawless, which had their charm and their thrill; for they had startled me a little and had amused me considerably. But they had left me untouched . . . they had not matured me. (p. 8)

Where the young male hero of *The Sisters* was provided with a complicated character, M. George is a much simpler young man, in Jamesian phrase, 'beautifully unthinking – infinitely receptive' (p. 8), and somewhat immature. At the same time, this passage suggests that, if he has been 'untouched' by his recent experiences, his next adventure will not treat him so lightly. This expectation is confirmed almost immediately, when the narrator refers to this evening as 'the last evening of that part of my life in which I did not know that woman' (p. 13). In the course of the narrative, M. George, like the young captain in *The Shadow-Line*, will cross the line that separates youth from maturity, and that journey will take him 'to the point of insanity and past it'.[13]

The narrative starts at the end of Carnival, and the Carnival is used to dramatise M. George's sense of alienation: he is 'neither masked, nor disguised, nor yelling, nor in any other way in harmony with the bedlam element of life' (pp. 7–8). He is joined by two other men, Mr Mills and Captain Blunt, and most of Part I is taken up with a discussion between them, to which M. George listens 'like a yokel at a play' (p. 58). This discussion presents a series of images and impressions of Rita, that provide different perspectives on her. That is, Rita is constructed as the object of male gaze and male discourse. The reification implicit in this is signalled by the role of Allègre in Rita's life. Mills observes that Allègre was 'a collector of fine things' (p. 22), and that Rita was 'without doubt the most admirable find of his amongst all the priceless items he had accumulated' (p. 23). Mills then offers his own disinterested view of her:

> I have known her for, say, six hours altogether. It was enough to feel the seduction of her native intelligence and of her splendid physique. And all that was brought home to me so quickly . . . because she had what some Frenchman has called the 'terrible gift of familiarity'.   (p. 25)

He also registers another characteristic, which is difficult to reconcile with this 'gift of familiarity':

> When saying goodbye she could put in an instant an immense distance between herself and you. A slight stiffening of that perfect figure, a change of the physiognomy. . . . Even if she did offer you her hand – as she did to me – it was as if across a broad river. Trick of manner or a bit of truth peeping out?   (p. 25)

This contradiction in Rita's behaviour announces the enigma which the narrative is designed to solve.

Blunt's perspective on Rita offers an explanation for Rita's combination of familiarity and coldness, but it is an explanation which is inevitably coloured by the difficulties in Blunt's own relationship with her. Blunt describes Rita's Basque peasant background and Allègre's first meeting with her: 'He found her sitting on a broken fragment of stone-work buried in the grass of his wild garden, full of thrushes, starlings, and other innocent creatures of the air' (p. 41). This idyllic, pastoral picture suggests the innocence and naturalness of the young Rita. Allègre's response, however, was to convert Rita into an art object: he not only objectifies her in his paintings; he also makes her into an art object in herself. She appears among Allègre's friends 'manifest and mysterious, like an object of art from some unknown period' (p. 36). As Wiley observes, the supreme achievement of Allègre's 'contemptuous sacrifice of life to art' is his transformation of Rita 'from her childhood state of a wild peasant girl of the hills to her mature position as one of the handsomest and most desirable of the objects in his house in Paris'.[14] In *The Sisters*, Conrad used the same contrast between a Basque peasant childhood and the 'civilisation' of Paris to represent a natural, spontaneous self and the false-self system that replaced it. In *The Arrow of Gold*, there is a further complication: Allègre has not only made Rita into an art object, he has also made her into 'Doña Rita'. He has used his own position of wealth and power to change Rita's social status. This is underlined by his portrait of Rita as the 'Byzantine Empress'. He tells Mrs Blunt, 'The one I had in mind was Theodosia. . . . Originally a slave girl' (p. 28). This expresses precisely Rita's anomalous class position. Allègre uses his position of power to over-ride Rita's moral and social status, and, when he dies, he maintains her anomalous position by making her his hieress. As a result, she has power and status, but not respect: 'They bow with immense deference when the door opens, but the bow conceals a smirk because of those Venetian days' (p. 57). As well as replacing her spontaneous self with a false-self system, Allègre has also placed her in a false position in the world.

Blunt's comment on Rita's social status identifies these two problematic aspects of her identity: 'she's Doña Rita right enough whatever else she is or is not in herself or in the eyes of others' (p. 36). What Rita is 'in the eyes of others' is very clear from Blunt's own response to her, which is infused with 'moral' and social prejudices against her. He compares her to La Vallière, the mistress of

Louis XIV, and he refers bitterly to 'the story of Danae' (p. 37). These comparisons re-affirm her anomalous class position and scandalous moral reputation, while the bitterness (and the obsession with Rita's sexual adventures) derives from Blunt's own crisis of conscience. Blunt also provides various suggestions as to what Rita might be like 'in herself'. He suggests, for example, her response to the transformation that Allègre has effected and to the false position that Allègre has created for her:

> She confessed to myself only the other day that she suffered from a sense of unreality. I told her that at any rate she had her own feelings surely. And she said to me: Yes, there was one of them at least about which she had no doubt.   (p. 55)

Rita's sense of unreality derives from Allègre's reification of her (she was de-personalised by him, as the repeated references to Allègre's artist's dummy imply), but might also be related to the self-experience of the false-self system.

The one emotion about which she has 'no doubt' is revealed to be fear, and the narrative is directed towards disclosing the origins and nature of that fear. Mills speculates that Rita's exposure to the atmosphere of Allègre's circle might explain both her fear and her alleged incapacity to love: 'a young, virgin intelligence, steeped for nearly five years in the talk of Allègre's studio, where every hard truth had been cracked and every belief had been worried into shreds' (p. 56). In this version, Rita appears as a female equivalent of Axel Heyst: she experiences the world as unreal; her ability to love is questioned; and both are explained by reference to exposure to scepticism at an impressionable age. Blunt, however, challenges this reading. He argues that Rita's fear has a deeper origin and has a material rather than a philosophical basis (p. 56). Blunt's challenge prevents interpretative closure and nudges the reader towards the true explanation for Rita's fear, her apparent inability to love, and that 'stiffening' that Mills described earlier.

II

Wiley's interpretation of *The Arrow of Gold* concentrates upon the novel's aesthetic world. He notes how Rita is exploited by Allègre's aestheticism, but he fails to notice that M. George receives similar treatment from the political world of the novel. As Wiley observes, Mills and Blunt through their discussion of Doña Rita create 'a mirage of desire' (p. 268), but that creation is designed to tempt M. George to commit himself to act for the Legitimist cause. In the 'First Note', the 'editor' observes:

> As a matter of fact, on that evening of Carnival, those two, Mills and Blunt, had been actually looking everywhere for our man. They had decided that he should be drawn into the affair if it could be done. . . . Thus lightly was the notorious (and at the same time mysterious) Monsieur George brought into the world; out of the contact of two minds which did not give a single thought to his flesh and blood.   (pp. 5–6)

What seems an accidental meeting is quite deliberate and has an underlying purpose of which M. George is ignorant. The editor's words also echo Nostromo's expression of his sense of betrayal, when he realises how he has been exploited. If Allègre's aestheticism treats Rita as an object, the political schemes of Mills and Blunt take a purely instrumental view of M. George. The novel is not just a satire on the art-world, as Wiley and Geddes suggest, but rather the art-world of the novel acts as a metonym for European bourgeois society: its alienation, its reification of others, its exchange-relations. By the end of Part I, Conrad has established how both Rita and M. George are exploited by their different worlds, and both worlds have been characterised by their tendency to treat people as instruments or things.

Part II begins with M. George's first meeting with Rita. The narrative emphasises M. George's youthfulness and his inability to comprehend the complexities of the world into which he has been introduced. When he goes with Mills to have lunch with Doña Rita, he feels 'as much of a stranger as the most hopeless castaway stumbling in the dark upon a hut of natives' except that he was 'the savage, the simple innocent child of nature':

> Those people were obviously more civilised than I was. They had more rites, more ceremonies, more complexity in their sensations, more knowledge of evil, more varied meanings to the subtle phrases of their language.   (pp. 69–70)

However, once he gets over the intense visual impression that Rita offers, he intuits a 'simple innocent child of nature' beneath the sophisticated social surface: 'that woman was revealed to me young, younger than anybody I had ever seen, as young as myself' (p. 70). As a result, he feels a 'sense of solidarity' with her, and he has the impression of his 'individual life beginning for good there' (p. 70). But his idea that 'there could be nothing more for us to know about each other' soon proves to be an illusion. In the course of Part II, he repeats Mills's puzzling experience of Rita. Her behaviour, during a later visit, combines the 'simple innocent child of nature', to which he had intuitively responded, with the 'terrible gift of familiarity' (p. 25) that Mills reported, but, as he prepares to take his leave, she suddenly reveals that other characteristic that Mills had also reported:

> I took her hand and was raising it naturally, without premedita-
> tion, when I felt suddenly the arm to which it belonged become
> insensible, passive, like a stuffed limb, and the whole woman go
> inanimate all over!   (p. 93)

When M. George was first introduced to her, there was an intimation of this reaction: he noted then that 'she extended her hand with a slight stiffening, as it were a recoil of her person' (p. 67). Most of Part II is taken up with an attempt to explain this puzzling part of Rita's behaviour and personality.

Rita offers the first explanation, and her account of herself, like Blunt's, focuses particularly on her relationship with Allègre. Rita's description of Allègre's 'complete, equable, and impartial contempt for all mankind' (p. 73) seems to confirm Mills's explanation of her 'fear':

> Often when we were alone Henry Allègre used to pour it into my
> ears. If ever anybody saw mankind stripped of its clothes . . . it's
> I! Into my ears! A child's! Too young to die of fright.   (p. 96)

If Rita resembles Heyst, she also, at this point, looks back to that other damaged female, Flora de Barral. As Wiley observes, the 'lady in distress' appears again in Rita, who 'bears under her disguise of a modern Gioconda the same psychic wound of fear as Alice Jacobus or Flora de Barral': 'Her spirit too has been lamed . . . by the scorn poured into her ear as a child.'[15] As with Flora, Rita's subsequent experiences have served to reinforce this early lesson. Until Allègre's death, 'no nun could have had a more protected life' (p. 80), but, when Allègre dies, she is suddenly thrown into a world which she did not understand. In addition, if she was as protected as a nun, she did not have a nun's reputation. She tells Mills that, after Allègre's death, she had 'a sensation of plotting and intriguing' (p. 74) surrounding her all the time, and some of this 'plotting and intriguing' seems to have related to sex. Azzolati, for example, offers her assistance in exchange for sexual favours, and his story is presumably typical. It has obvious similarities to her current relationship with Blunt, as Rita herself suggests:

> I suppose Azzolati imagines himself a noble beast of prey. Just as some others imagine themselves to be most delicate, noble, and refined gentlemen. And as likely as not they would trade on a woman's troubles. (p. 100)

Where Azzolati sought to trade his assistance, Blunt seeks to trade his name for her fortune. And Rita extends her judgement of Azzolati to cover relations with men in general: 'It's like taking the lids off boxes and seeing ugly toads staring at you. In every one. Every one' (p. 100).

Her affair with the Pretender, however, seems to have a different significance: it testifies, in part, to her isolation, and, in part, to an aspect of herself against which she now guards herself:

> My instinct may have told me that my only protection was obscurity. . . . But there were other instincts and . . . How am I to tell you? I don't know how to be on guard against myself, either. (p. 85)

In addition to her disenchantment with men, Rita seems to have acquired a defensive awareness of her own passionate nature. She excuses her recoil from M. George as 'habit – or instinct – or what you like', before she emphasises the idea that she has schooled herself into repressing her natural responsiveness because of her experiences in the social world she has inhabited: 'I have had to practice that in self-defence' (p. 93). Her initial excuses, however, raise the question whether her recoil is merely a habit as she implies or something deeper-rooted.

By the end of Part II, there have been various suggestions as to the nature of the fear which Rita described as the one emotion 'about which she had no doubt' (p. 55). Rita relates her fear to the loss of protection she experienced at Allègre's death (p. 80). Her account of her relationship with Allègre also supports Mills's earlier suggestion that Allègre's scorn had produced Rita's mistrust of life. She offers a third explanation through her account of her relationship with the Pretender: a fear of her own passionate nature. Another explanation is also implicit in the text: Allègre not only protected her, he also transformed her. In transforming her, he suppressed her true nature and replaced it with a false-self system. Rita became the art object that Allègre wanted her to become, and, after Allègre's death, she continued to be treated as an object rather than as a person.[16] The important exception was her relationship with the Pretender: as she says, he 'didn't approach me as if I had been a precious object in a collection' (p. 84). But, in her disillusionment with the Pretender (and after the discoveries she has made about herself through that relationship), she has returned to her false-self system and the object-relations it involves. She tells Mills, 'I soon learned to regret I was not some object, some beautiful, carved object of bone or bronze' (p. 84). After what was (by implication) a painful emotional experience, she has returned to the false-self system as a protection against others and as a defence against her own instincts and feelings.

As Chianese rightly observes, 'she decides to become what others want – an unfeeling beautiful object', but 'she cannot wholly repress her wilful vitality'.[17] The more important question, however, is why she should decide to become what others want, and Laing provides an answer:

> One of the aspects of the compliance of the false self that is most clear is the fear implied by this compliance. The fear in it is evident, for why else would anyone act, not according to his intentions, but according to another person's?[18]

In Part III, Rita goes back to her Basque childhood and reveals the origin of the fear that has motivated her adoption of a false-self system. This fear is related to the 'danger' (to which there are mysterious allusions at the end of Part II), which is associated with her cousin, Ortega. Rita tells George of a childhood incident involving Ortega:

> He got up, he had a switch in his hand, and walked up to me, saying, 'I will soon show you.' I went stiff with fright; but instead

of slashing at me he dropped down by my side and kissed me on the cheek. Then he did it again, and by that time I was gone dead all over and he could have done what he liked with the corpse . . . (p. 112)

This is obviously the prototype for that response of stiffening and becoming passive which both Mills and M. George have reported. In the childhood incident, Rita's response to the threat represented by her cousin was to dissociate herself from her body.[19] This dissociation of herself from her body then becomes one of her standard defences, and the incident with her cousin can be seen as the traumatic experience that determines Rita's subsequent psychological development.[20] What is also striking is the ambiguous nature of her cousin's advance: it is not clear whether he means to attack her or make love to her.[21] This ambiguity characterises his behaviour towards her, as Rita's subsequent narration reveals:

> If I caught sight of him at a distance and tried to dodge out of the way he would start stoning me into a shelter I knew of and then sit outside with a heap of stones at hand so that I daren't show the end of my nose for hours. He would sit there and rave and abuse me till I would burst into a crazy laugh . . . and then I could see him through the leaves rolling on the ground and biting his fists with rage. . . . I am convinced now that if I had started crying he would have rushed in and perhaps strangled me there. Then as the sun was about to set he would make me swear that I would marry him when I was grown up.   (pp. 112–13)

Ortega's actions place Rita in a 'double bind'.[22] On the one hand, he expresses hatred for her and gives the impression of a desire to kill her. On the other hand, he expresses a wish to marry her. Given these conflicting signals, Rita's confusion is understandable. And her sister, Therese, is no help: 'When I showed her my bruises and tried to tell her a little about my trouble she was quite scandalized. She called me a sinful girl, a shameless creature' (p. 113). She disconfirms Rita's true identity and confirms a false identity that involves ideas of wickedness and worthlessness. She interprets Rita's innocence as 'shamelessness', and she accordingly re-writes Rita's narration as Rita trying to lead Ortega astray 'into the wildness of thoughts like her own' until 'the poor dear child drove her off because she outraged his modesty' (p. 158).[23] As Rita puts it, between her cousin and her sister, she was so 'puzzled' that she 'lived in a state of idiocy almost' (p. 113). Since this confusion about her identity was the prelude to her departure for Paris, it now becomes clearer why she allowed herself to be appropriated by Allègre, and why she was so ready to surrender her past for the false identity he gave her.

III

In Part IV, the narrative focus shifts to the Blunts: the mystery of Rita's relationship with Blunt is solved, and Blunt's false position is fully revealed. At the same time, the Blunts serve to characterise the social world against which Rita and M. George are defined. Early in Chapter 2, M. George refers mockingly to the 'perfect finish' of the Blunts. This metaphor links the conventional behaviour of bourgeois society with the products of the art world, while it also points up the gap between the Blunt's self-presentation and their reality. For example, Mrs Blunt tells M. George that her son suffers from 'a profound discord between the necessary reactions to life' and 'the lofty idealism of his feelings' (p. 178). As Part IV proceeds, this statement is gradually decoded: Blunt's 'trouble' is his inability to reconcile his mother's practical solution to his financial problems (the annexation of Rita and her fortune) with his social and sexual prejudices. Where Mrs Blunt refers to 'unexpected resistances and difficulties' (p. 178) in her son, Rita discloses the reality such abstract language seeks to mask:

> His conventions will always stand in the way of his nature. I told him that everything that had been said and done during the last seven or eight months was inexplicable unless on the assumption that he was in love with me – and yet in everything there was an implication that he couldn't forgive me my very existence.
> (p. 210)

Blunt is attracted to her and fascinated by her, but, at the same time, he does not approve of her or respect her. His desire for her is in conflict with his concern for social status, his 'moral' view of her, and his conventional expectations of a wife.[24] Rita's understanding of Blunt's conflicts and her own self-respect ('I have my own Basque peasant soul') combine in her rejection of him: she does not want to think that 'every time he goes away' from her 'he goes away feeling tempted to brush the dust off his moral sleeve' (p. 209).

Part IV also shows the next stage in M. George's relationship with Rita. In Part II, through his 'sense of solidarity' with her, he committed himself to act for the Legitimist Principle, and that commitment has changed his life:

> For good or evil I left that house committed to an enterprise that could not be talked about. . . . It would not only close my lips but it would to a certain extent cut me off from my usual haunts and from the society of my friends. (p. 87)

This recalls Lingard's commitment to Hassim and Immada, and, just as Lingard's commitment represented his discovery of a secret self, M. George's commitment, to begin with, brought him increased self-awareness: 'Never before had I felt so intensely aware of my personality' (p. 89). Subsequently, during the course of Part III, M. George came to realise that he was in love with Rita, but his rhapsodic vision of love (p. 124) was almost immediately undermined by reality: he discovered that the 'great light', the 'emanation' of Rita's charm, cast long shadows, and, in those shadows, lurked 'fear, deception, desire, disillusion' (p. 125). M. George's initiation into passion, like the young captain's initiation into his captaincy in *The Shadow-Line*, is an educative process which is presented in terms of the young man's expectations and the subsequent undermining of those expectations by experience. Accordingly, at the start of Part IV, M. George is going through a 'purgatory of hopeless longing and unanswerable questions' (p. 155). He feels an 'acute consciousness' (p. 154) of Rita's existence; at the same time, he feels angry, because he feels he has been used by her:

> To put her head on my shoulder, to weep these strange tears, was nothing short of an outrageous liberty. It was a mere emotional trick. She would have just as soon leaned her head against the over-mantel of one of those tall, red granite chimney-pieces. (p. 164)

He feels that he has been treated as an object, and he is full of anger, confusion and the sense that 'Nothing could be trusted' (p. 164). Rita takes up precisely this point when M. George goes to see her in Chapter 4. She refers to George and herself as 'simple people' and contrasts them with their world 'which is eaten up with charlatanism of all sorts' so that even simple people 'don't know any longer how to trust each other' (p. 199). She tells him how the falseness of the world has confused her about her own nature. In contrast to the 'mock adulation', the 'mock reserve' and 'mock devotion' (p. 207), she has received in the past, M. George has offered the opportunity for 'the frankness of gestures and speeches and thoughts, sane or insane, that we have been throwing at each other' (p. 217). His naturalness is set against the refinement of the Blunts, his roughness against their 'finish', and, in the end, his direct emotions against the rapaciousness and egotism that their manners are intended to conceal.

However, Rita's idea that there is no 'fear' or 'constraint' lurking in the background in their relationship is as much an illusion as M. George's earlier idea that they had 'nothing more' to know about each other. So far, they have related to each other 'like two passionate infants in a nursery' (p. 163), but once he declares his love for her, she begins to display some of the psycho-sexual disturbance that has already been intimated. When he tells her, 'I just, simply, loved you', her response is to repeat the words 'Just – simply' (p. 217) in a wistful tone. For Rita, love is not simple, and, in the scene that follows, she alternately encourages and frustrates him. The contradiction in her behaviour is most striking as he tries to leave:

> With every word urging me to get away, her clasp tightened, she hugged my head closer to her breast. I submitted, knowing well that I could free myself by one more effort which it was in my power to make. But before I made it, in a sort of desperation, I pressed a long kiss into the hollow of her throat. And lo – there was no need for any effort. With a stifled cry of surprise her arms fell off me as if she had been shot.   (p. 224)

While telling M. George to leave, she simultaneously prevents him from leaving. Rita's behaviour expresses the bind in which she is caught: she fears his love and wants him to go; at the same time, she needs him and wants him to stay. When he responds to her efforts to restrain him, he immediately activates her established defence mechanism of dissociation, and this has the effect of releasing him.

Part V begins with M. George's emotional and psychological state after the apparent termination of his relationship with Rita. As Wiley notes, M. George's development during the course of the novel represents one of Conrad's 'studies in the morbid psychology of passion'.[25] In Chapters 1 and 2, M. George is assailed by a sense of emptiness and meaninglessness: 'I was a mere receptacle for dust and ashes, a living testimony to the vanity of all things' (p. 229). He has lost any sense of himself: 'The observer, more or less alert, whom each of us carries in his own consciousness, failed me altogether' (p. 229). He is 'indifferent to everything', 'profoundly demoralized' (p. 244); he feels as if 'there was no present, no future, nothing but a hollow pain' (p. 244); he experiences a dulled unhappiness as if part of himself were 'lost beyond recall taking with it all the savour of life' (p. 234). At other times, he is conscious of 'a vain passion . . . locked up' (p. 244) within his breast, and he behaves in a way that is explicitly described as mad. For example, his search for some memento of Rita is 'like the mania of those disordered minds who spend their days hunting for a treasure' (pp. 237–8). At another time, after expressing fears for his own sanity, M. George observes: 'I had visited a famous lunatic asylum where they had shown me a poor wretch who was mad, apparently, because he thought he had been abominably fooled by a woman' (p. 238). Like Marlow in 'Heart of Darkness', M. George finds an escape by throwing himself into his work, where he finds 'occupation, protection, consolation, the mental relief of grappling with concrete problems' (p. 242). His work also provides him with a tenuous connection with Rita (since he had received the mission 'from her own hand' – p. 242), and, by continuing to work for the Legitimist Principle, he also demonstrates his 'fidelity and steadfastness' (p. 249) to her.

When Chapter 4 opens, a year has passed since the start of the narrative, and M. George is again sitting in a cafe with the Carnival going on around him. The carnival surroundings now suggest the hell, the 'bedlam', that is George's experience of himself and the world. They also form the context for M. George's meeting with Ortega. Where he had thought of writing a farewell letter to Rita, in which she would 'see her own image . . . as in a mirror' (p. 264), Ortega presents him with a distorted reflection of himself. When M. George realises his companion's identity, he recognises the affinity between them:

> She penetrated me, my head was full of her. . . . And his head, too, I thought suddenly with a side glance at my companion. . . . There was between us a most horrible fellowship; the association of his crazy torture with the sublime suffering of my passion. (p. 274)

Through his perception of this 'horrible fellowship', M. George is able to re-define himself. Where before he felt that he was in Hell, he now feels that Ortega gazes at him in the way that 'the damned gaze out of their cauldrons of boiling pitch at some soul walking scot free in the place of torment' (p. 271). Where before he had felt that the 'moral atmosphere' (p. 238) of his torture would end by making him mad, he now feels 'not the slightest doubt' (p. 274) of his own sanity, when he compares himself with Ortega. This conviction of his own sanity derives also from his response to Ortega's presence – in particular, 'the way I could apply my intelligence to the problem of what was to be done with Señor Ortega'. M. George's main thought is for Rita's safety, and that consideration brings him out of his sense of indifference and futility, but he overestimates the difference between himself and his companion. This is intimated by his changed perception of the Carnival: he hears 'agonizing fear, rage of murder, ferocity of lust' (p. 272) in the yells of festivity, and he sees the Carnival in terms of 'the savage instincts hidden in the breast of mankind' (p. 272). This consciousness reflects his perception of Ortega, but it also reveals something of what is going on within himself. It is no surprise when he suddenly thinks of killing Ortega as the only solution to the problem.

IV

The main focus of Part V, however, is not the morbid psychology of M. George but rather that of Rita, and a recognition of this priority is necessary for a correct understanding of Ortega's character and significance. Wiley, for example, argues that 'Rita's mockery of Ortega has turned him mad enough for passional crime; and George, though he thinks himself sane, has been brought close to the same state through her resistance to his love.'[26] Wiley sees Ortega as 'a symbol of the evil which springs to life when the claims of normal feeling are denied', and he reads his function in Part V as being to 'confront Rita with the human passions disregarded or flouted by the doctrine taught her by Allègre'.[27] Ortega, however, is a singularly inappropriate representative of 'the claims of normal feeling'. Wiley's reading disregards Ortega's role in Rita's psycho-sexual development: it is Ortega who has damaged Rita psychologically rather than the other way round. Ortega's function in Part V is to confront Rita again with the claims of *abnormal* feeling. In the climactic scene in the locked room, Rita re-experiences the trauma that lies at the root of the disturbances in her personality, and, like the young captain in *The Shadow-Line*, she is forced to face up to her fears and responsibilities.

Conrad wrote that 'the inner truth of the scene in the locked room is only hinted at'.[28] As Wiley suggests, this 'scene' in *The Arrow of Gold* is comparable to the scene in the cabin of the *Ferndale* that resolves the impasse in *Chance*; but it also anticipates the locked room on board the tartane in *The Rover*.[29] When M. George reveals that Ortega is in the house, Rita's immediate reaction is unambiguously fearful: with 'the sudden, free, spontaneous agility of a young animal she leaped off the sofa' and 'in one bound reached almost the middle of the room' (p. 306). The 'agility' of this leap is a reminder of Rita's account of herself as a goatherd, being chased across the rocks by Ortega. It is followed at once by Rita's desperate transformation of herself from the spontaneous goat-girl to the reified Rita de Lastaola:

> Suddenly Doña Rita swung round and seizing her loose hair with both hands started twisting it up before one of the sumptuous mirrors. . . . In a brusque movement like a downward stab she transfixed the whole mass of tawny glints and sparks with the arrow of gold.   (p. 307)

As Wiley says, 'her hysterical gesture of transfixing her hair with the golden arrow' is an attempt to defend herself against her fear.[30] She seeks to defend herself against the apprehended threat by transforming herself into 'Rita de Lastaola' – that is, by taking refuge in a false-self system. As in *Chance* and *Victory*, Conrad reveals psychological processes through his character's actions, and he uses melodrama for symbolic, psychologically expressive purposes. Rita's primary defence against Ortega was dissociation. Her second, and subsequent, defence was to take refuge in a false-self system as the sophisticated and apparently invulnerable 'Rita de Lastaola'. This false-self system is not just an 'aesthetic mask', but also a divine mask. Rita de Lastaola is associated, in a way that maintains the ambiguity of her sexuality, with both Artemis and Aphrodite: Artemis, the goddess of chastity, and Aphrodite, the goddess of love and beauty, both warlike, huntress goddesses, armed with bows and arrows. At the same time, on another level, Rita has sought to evade sexuality by remaining a child. Her relationship with George, for example, has been presented consistently in pre-sexual terms. Her desolate appeal to M. George is perceived by him in precisely this way:

> It had all the simplicity and depth of a child's emotion. It tugged at one's heart-strings in the same direct way. But what could one do? How could one soothe her? It was impossible to pat her on the head, take her on the knee, give her a chocolate or show her a picture book.   (p. 307)

In this climactic scene in the locked room, Rita is forced to confront the traumatic experience of her childhood: the events in this part of the novel can be seen as the return of the repressed and as the bringing into full consciousness of the events which have unconsciously directed her.[31]

In Chapter 7, Rita faces again the alliance between Ortega and her sister, the 'family phantasy system', that entrapped her as a child. George imagines Therese 'casting loose the raging fate with a sanctimonious air': she would 'naturally' give the key to the room to 'her dear, virtuous, grateful, disinterested cousin' because 'Righteousness demanded that the erring sister should be taken unawares' (pp. 310–11). The locked room itself recalls the shelter in which she used to hide from Ortega, and provides an appropriate setting for a replay of the earlier drama. Accordingly, she becomes immobile, as she did in her account of her childhood experience, while he repeats his earlier treatment of her. He subjects her to verbal abuse and makes the same contradictory advance:

> You are in all your limbs hateful: your eyes are hateful and your mouth is hateful, and your hair is hateful, and your body is cold and vicious like a snake. . . . You know, Rita, that I cannot live without you.   (p. 318)

As before, Rita responds with 'a crazy laugh' (p. 112), 'an appalling fit of merriment' (p. 319). The obvious difference this time is the presence of M. George. To begin with, his presence creates an additional fear for Rita: she does not want to hear what Ortega will say, but, even more important, she does not want George to hear. Her efforts are directed towards getting him to leave or else covering up his ears. When these efforts fail, M. George's presence acquires another significance which is more briefly and subtly indicated. When George tells her that he spent two hours with Ortega, Rita acquires 'the look of one morally crushed'. Then the following exchange takes place:

> 'What did he say to you?'
> 'He raved.'
> 'Listen to me. It was all true!'
> 'I daresay, but what of that?'   (pp. 314–15)

These last words reveal his willing acceptance of Rita for herself: the truth or untruth of any accusations against her are irrelevant to his feelings for her. The 'searching stare' and 'long breath' (p. 315), with which Rita greets this answer, show that she realises the significance of George's words: he has revealed a trust in her that contrasts sharply with Blunt's mistrust, and this trust holds out the prospect of confirmation of her true identity.

In the final chapter, M. George returns to Rita after taking care of Ortega's wound and observes that she 'seemed to be slowly awakening from a trance' (p. 329). Ortega's verbal abuse forces her to acknowledge what she has tried to deny in order to achieve a position of inviolability, and her initial response is 'a horror' of herself (p. 333). The 'horror' that Rita has to face is her own sexuality. Her earlier account of her traumatic childhood relationship with Ortega began with Ortega telling her that he had been 'thrashed' for wandering in the hills: ' "To be with me?" I asked. And he said: "To be with you! No. My people don't know what I do." I can't tell why, but I was annoyed' (p. 112). Rita's annoyance signals an element that is otherwise screened out of her narration. Ortega's reference to her 'goat tricks' (p. 316), and his anatomising of her limbs, eyes, mouth, hair and body (p. 318), suggest that their relationship had involved some sexual activity. The trauma, and her subsequent hysteric response, were produced by the conflict between the arousal of sexual feelings and her fear of violence from Ortega. Ortega's image of Rita as 'a Parisian woman with innumerable lovers' (p. 269), like Blunt's images of her, foregrounds her sexuality, because he is in the grip of pathological jealousy. But this image also derives from the sexual component of her earlier self which she has attempted to deny and which she prevented from entering her consciousness in her earlier account.[32] When Rita addresses her farewell speech to M. George, she acknowledges this sexual component of her earlier relationship with Ortega, but she is still overwhelmed by the sense of horror at herself: 'I couldn't close my eyes in this place. It's full of corruption and ugliness all round, in me, too, everywhere except in your heart, which has nothing to do where I breathe' (p. 330). Rita recognises that there is a space in his heart which is free from 'corruption and ugliness', and that space offers her the opportunity for re-integration.

Nevertheless, Rita's resistance is not immediately overcome. When she wakes up and finds herself in M. George's arms, her first reaction is the same automatic recoil as before. George's disappointment and grief are expressed in a variation on one of the images associated with their relationship: 'This was no longer the adventure of venturesome children in a nursery-book. A grown man's bitterness, informed, suspicious, resembling hatred, welled out of my heart' (p. 334). The change in the image, however, indicates the advance they have made: the relationship is no longer a regression, an escape into a pre-sexual state. This recoil and retreat mark the end of her resistance. At the door she encounters Therese, and Therese confronts her with the 'family phantasy system' which had confused her in the past:

> Come away from that poor young gentleman who like all the others can have nothing but contempt and disgust for you in his heart. Come and hide your head where no one will reproach you – but I, your sister.   (p. 335)

Given this alternative – the disconfirmation of her true identity, and the bind of a refuge from 'reproach' in her sister's own reproaches – Rita turns back to M. George.

Schwarz offers a summary and criticism of the novel's conclusion:

> Like 'Youth', *The Arrow of Gold* is a voyage of initiation; within the year that comprises the action of the body of the novel, George journeys from innocence to experience. Or, rather, he supposedly matures; in actuality, we do not really see a change in his behaviour; nor do we hear a mature voice or feel the Conradian conflict between a reminiscing speaker and the younger, more impulsive self.[33]

In fact, *The Arrow of Gold* is *not* like 'Youth', and there is no reason why it should reprise that work's interplay between a narrator's older and younger self. Conrad had already returned to the earlier mode in *The Shadow-Line*. In *The Arrow of Gold*, the narrative presents not a journey within the self of the narrator, but rather the establishment of a precarious interdependence between its two central figures, the mature mutuality that Heyst and Lena failed to achieve in *Victory*. Furthermore, the narrator is not a Marlow recounting his past experience within a defined narrative situation; this narrative is a 'selection and arrangement' of M. George's written account made by an anonymous editor. This, in itself, precludes the kind of interaction between the narrator's selves that Schwarz expects: the narrative has the status of an edited text not that of an oral account, and the textuality of the narrative is an important feature of it. More important, although the 'Author's Note' describes the narrative as the story of George's initiation 'into the life of passion' (p. ix), the focus of the narrative is, in fact, on Rita and her psycho-sexual development, and M. George's main function in the novel is to be loyal to her. Like Nostromo, George is a sailor come ashore, but, this time, maritime loyalty is used to expose the 'charlatanism' and self-interest of shore society. In addition, his loyalty to Rita creates a space for the confirmation of her true identity. This reaches its climax in the scene in the locked room, where George's role resembles that of the analyst guiding the analysand through her past experiences.[34]

Conrad's correspondence testifies to the centrality of Rita to his conception of the novel. In a letter to S. A. Everitt, for example, he states that 'the novel may be best described as the Study of a Woman', and all the titles he suggests for the novel refer to Rita and not to George.[35] His description of the novel's subject-matter points to the same conclusion: 'What it deals with is her private life; her sense of her own position, her sentiments and her fears'.[36] As Schwarz notes: 'The major structural principle of the novel . . . is Rita's eccentric and unstable personality. Around her shifting and often unclear identity revolves the entire cast of characters.'[37]

Schwarz, however, fails to notice the skill with which Conrad paces his gradual revelation of the determinants of Rita's character, and the psychological insight or knowledge with which his presentation of her 'case' is imbued. The narrative is organised in terms of the progressive revelation of her psyche: it is directed by (and towards) Rita's own gradual confrontation with her past. In *The Arrow of Gold*, Conrad achieves what he aimed at in *Victory*: the merging of psychological realism with mythic and symbolic modes, and the use of melodrama for the purposes of deeper psychological analysis. Far from representing a 'collapse of form', as Schwarz suggests, *The Arrow of Gold* is a triumph of form, comparable among these late novels to the achievement of *Chance* and *Victory*.

V

Conrad began *The Rover* in December 1919 and finished it in June 1922. Where *The Arrow of Gold* featured 'young Ulysses', *The Rover* represents Odysseus's homecoming. Conrad told Galsworthy that he had 'wanted for a long time to do a seaman's "return" ', and the story of Peyrol 'seemed a possible peg to hang it on'.[38] The narrative begins with Peyrol's return to France after a life-time spent at sea. After this life-time at sea, the affectation 'common to seamen of never being surprised at anything that sea or land can produce had become in Peyrol a second nature': 'Having learned from childhood to suppress every sign of wonder before all extraordinary sights and events . . . he had really become indifferent – or only perhaps inexpressive' (p. 24). The source of his 'indifference' seems to be his mother's death, which is described twice in the opening chapters. The first account presents Peyrol's maritime career as a flight from his mother's death. The second account contrasts his response to his mother's death (and to his first sight of Marseilles) with his subsequent 'indifference':

> The last thing which had touched him with the panic of the supernatural had been the death under a heap of rags of that gaunt, fierce woman, his mother; and the last thing that had nearly overwhelmed him at the age of twelve with another kind of terror was the riot of sound and the multitude of mankind on the quays in Marseilles.   (p. 24)

Like Rita de Lastaola and Flora de Barral, Peyrol has passed through an experience in childhood which has decisively shaped his character. In Peyrol's case, the early traumatic experience has led to emotional self-concealment and an acceptance of 'the new and inexplicable conditions of life'.

Peyrol's apparent emotional detachment is mirrored, in the opening chapters, by his alienation from his native land. The only break in this sense of detachment comes with his first sight of Arlette, when the 'perfect oval of her face, the colour of her smooth cheeks, and the whiteness of her throat' forced 'a slight hiss through his clenched teeth' (p. 21). This 'slight hiss' is not interpreted beyond the statement that 'a feeling that was no longer surprise or curiosity' (p. 21) had lodged in his breast. The nature of this 'soft indefinite emotion' (p. 23) only becomes clear towards the end of the novel. In the mean time, with the entrance of Arlette, the focus of the narrative shifts towards her. In response to Peyrol's words, she smiled 'in a bright flash of teeth, without gaiety or any change in her restless eyes that roamed about the empty room as though Peyrol had come in attended by a mob of Shades' (p. 21). Both her restlessness and that 'mob of Shades' (p. 21) are explained by her history: her eyes 'had been smitten on the very verge of womanhood by such sights of bloodshed and terror, as to leave in her a fear of looking steadily in any direction for long lest she should see coming through the empty air some mutilated vision of the dead' (pp. 48–9). Where Peyrol's 'indifference' has been determined, in part, by his response to his mother's death, Arlette's derangement is the result of her parents' violent death during the French Revolution.

With Chapter 4, the narrative jumps over a time-gap of eight years: Chapters 1–3 are set in the period of republican ascendancy; in Chapter 4, Napoleon has been proclaimed Consul for life. By this time, Peyrol is no longer 'a stranger' (p. 2) but feels 'perfectly at home' (p. 38) at Escampobar. The character for whom this passage of time has brought the greatest change is Scevola. In the opening chapters, he was the master of Escampobar and, apparently, Arlette's husband. (It is only later that the sleeping arrangements of the household are described.) More important, his fierce republicanism had made him seem a formidable figure. He told Peyrol of the struggle against the English:

> The armies of the Republic drove them out, but treachery stalks in the land, it comes up out of the ground, it sits at our hearthstones, lurks in the bosom of the representatives of the people, of our fathers, of our brothers.   (p. 27)

In retrospect, the 'suspicion' that seemed like revolutionary vigilance now looks more like paranoia. By the end of Chapter 4, Scevola has already begun to seem 'a poor creature' (p. 151), as he 'wanders between the buildings like a lost soul in the light of day' (p. 40).

Chapter 4 also introduces Réal. He is 'the son of a ci-devant couple' (p. 70), and, like Arlette, lost his parents to the Revolution. Like Peyrol, he responded to this death by running off to sea, where he found 'another standard of values':

> In the course of some eight years, suppressing his faculties for love and hatred, he arrived at the rank of an officer by sheer merit, and

had accustomed himself to look at men sceptically, without much scorn or much respect.　(p. 70)

As this suggests, he is like Peyrol also in his emotional self-suppression, and it is Peyrol who first breaks through his defensive reserve, 'that schooled reserve which the precariousness of all things had forced on the orphan of the Revolution' (p. 71). This relationship with Peyrol opens the way to others: 'Presently, the peculiarities of all those people at the farm, each individual one of them, had entered through the breach' (p. 71). But the full significance of this statement is not revealed immediately: there are mysteries about Réal's personal motives, and about the nature of his official business at Escampobar. Indeed, the narrative of *The Rover* is constructed as a series of overlapping mysteries: the mystery of Peyrol's motives and purposes; the mystery of Arlette's behaviour; the mysterious mission of the English ship; the mystery of Symons's disappearance as if 'spirited away by some supernatural means' (p. 63); and the mysteries of Réal's personal motives and official mission. Guerard has described *The Rover* as 'a coarse-grained study of feeble-minded and inarticulate people' which somehow makes a recovery 'after two hundred and fifty pages of extreme dullness and ineptitude'.[39] Geddes is more sensitive to Conrad's narrative purposes and achievement. He rightly draws attention to 'the tautness of Conrad's narrative and the intensity and concreteness of his images', and he adds, in reply to Guerard, that the final pages of *The Rover* are not 'a recovery from ineptitude', but 'the culmination of a movement that builds from the earliest descriptions of character and place in the novel'.[40] Conrad himself described *The Rover* as 'a feat of artistic brevity': 'This is perhaps my only work in which brevity was a conscious aim. I don't mean compression. I mean brevity *ab initio*, in the very conception, in the very manner of thinking about the people and the events.'[41]

That brevity is most obvious in Conrad's economic handling of his narrative. The narrative is propelled through the creation of overlapping mysteries, which are resolved as the narrative proceeds. These mysteries are produced by a development of the technique of *Victory*. The main characters are, for various reasons, isolated from each other: Arlette and Scevola are, in different ways, deranged; Réal and Peyrol are both the self-contained possessors of secrets. As a result, the potential for mystery and misinterpretation is very great. The narrative proceeds through the careful control of point of view and the skillful shifting from one perspective to another.

Chapter 7, for example, affords a brief glimpse of a scene that is later revealed to have marked a critical juncture in the relations of the two people involved. The significance of the scene is withheld, because the narrative is focalised through Peyrol:

> Through the open door of the salle he obtained a glimpse of Arlette sitting upright with her hands in her lap gazing at somebody he could not see, but who could be no other than Lieutenant Réal. (p. 82)

Chapter 8 offers an even briefer glimpse of Réal reproaching himself for having 'stumbled against' Arlette, and reminding himself how he 'had endeavoured almost from a boy to destroy all the softer feelings within himself' (p. 117). In Chapter 9, Arlette's memories provide the first details (as well as her interpretation) of what took place between the two of them in the salle; and it is not until Chapter 14 that a fuller account of Réal's view of this incident is given:

> Honour, decency, every principle forbade him to trifle with the feelings of a poor creature with her mind darkened by a very terrifying, atrocious and, as it were, guilty experience. And suddenly he had given way to a base impulse and had betrayed himself by kissing her hand! He recognised with despair that this was no trifling, but that the impulse had come from the very depths of his being. It was an awful discovery for a man who on emerging from boyhood had laid for himself a rigidly straight line of conduct among the unbridled passions and the clamouring falsehoods of revolution which seemed to have destroyed in him all capacity for the softer emotions. (p. 209)

At this point, the incident provides the opportunity for a detailed exploration of Réal's character and feelings. He has constructed an identity for himself according to a strict code of conduct and the suppression of emotions. Now he is torn between his moral principles and his passionate impulses, between the 'rigidly straight line of conduct' on which he has built his identity and the emotions which he has suppressed. In kissing Arlette, he feels he has 'betrayed himself': in fact, it marks his initiation 'into the life of passion' and his entry into a new mode of being.

Chapter 7 also introduces another significant item: the tartane which is purchased by Peyrol. Scevola mentioned a tartane in Chapter 3 in his account of the deaths of Arlette's parents. Peyrol discovers that the tartane he wants to buy, with the 'enormous padlock' on its cabin-door 'as if there had been secrets or treasures inside' (p. 84), is the same boat: 'the tragic craft which had taken Arlette's parents to their death in the vengeful massacre of Toulon and had brought the youthful Arlette and Citizen Scevola back to Escampobar' (p. 85). The secret of the tartane is linked with this bloody memory of the Revolution. The boat acts as a memory symbol for the determinants of Arlette's mental state, and Peyrol's transformation of the ship parallels the effect he has on Arlette and Réal, the two characters damaged psychologically by the Revolution.

Peyrol takes time off from refurbishing the tartane to spend a few days at Escampobar which he passed 'mostly in observing Arlette' (p. 88). Peyrol now hears Catherine's account of Arlette's father's death and of Arlette's return 'pale like a corpse out of a grave, with a blood-soaked blanket over her shoulders and a red cap on her head' (p. 91). Again, there is a delay in decoding this image: it is not until Chapter 10 that Arlette's experiences during the Revolution are recounted from Arlette's viewpoint. There Arlette suddenly announces to her aunt, 'I am awake now!', and begins to reflect on 'the enormous change' which has come over her: every day 'had a tomorrow now', and 'all the people around her had ceased to be mere phantoms for her wandering glances to glide over without concern' (p. 146). Arlette has been 'brought back' (p. 152) to herself by her love for Réal. Now she has a desire to recount her experiences, and, in recounting those experiences, in her confession to the priest, she reveals the full significance of the events which have traumatised her. She reveals details of events after the murder of her parents which are known only to her. In particular, she tells how she was made to accompany the *sans-culottes* in their attacks on the Royalists:

> I had to run with them all day, and all the time I felt as if I were falling down, and down, and down. The houses were nodding at me. The sun would go out at times. And suddenly I heard myself yelling exactly like the others. . . . The very same words!   (p. 154)

Arlette not only witnessed the murder of her parents and others, but also (as these last words signify) colluded in those killings. This is why there has been no abreaction of the experience: her grief at her parents' death was in conflict with her guilty sense of her own collusion. The result of this conflict is described by Arlette. First of all, she was 'raving silently to herself' (p. 154), and then she 'let [herself] go' (p. 155). As a result, when she got back to the farm 'all feeling had left' her: 'I did not feel myself exist' (p. 155). In other words, Arlette escaped from the conflict by de-realizing herself and by depriving the world around her of reality: 'Nothing could matter. Nothing could mean anything. I cared for no-one. I wanted nothing. I wasn't alive at all' (p. 156). She lived among 'mere phantoms for her wandering glances to glide over without concern' (p. 146), until Peyrol's inexplicable arrival at Escampobar gave 'a moral and even a physical jolt to all her being' (p. 219). Peyrol, since he had come, 'had always existed for her' (p. 161), and Réal's arrival built upon this foundation.

Geddes has written appreciatively of Conrad's handling of this part of the novel:

> Appropriately, the bulk of Arlette's experience among the *sans-culottes* in Toulon is related here, as part of her confession, heightening the effect of her deliverance from the spell or possession from which she has suffered for years.[42]

After this confession, 'the narrative looks backward no more, but moves with great speed and force towards its remarkable climax'.[43] In this final section of the novel, the narrative focus shifts back to Peyrol. Hints and suggestions made earlier in the novel now come together in another of the novel's major thematic concerns: 'coming to terms with age and dying'.[44] Schwarz draws attention to the careful orchestration of Peyrol's death:

> Death is a continuous presence. The persistence of death in conversations, interior monologues and the omniscient narrator's descriptions arouses our expectations of death as a structural ingredient of the story.[45]

Through this careful orchestration, 'the reader's mind becomes imbued with suggestions of death', until, 'without his realising quite way, Peyrol's death comes as an inevitable fulfilment of an expected pattern'.[46]

Since Peyrol's running away to sea was a flight from his mother's death, his return to his barely remembered native country is, from the start, associated with death. His retirement from the sea suggests a desire for rest, which might be seen to anticipate a preparation for death. This is certainly the burden of the epigraph:

> Sleep after toyle, port after stormie seas,
> East after warre, death after life, does greatly please.

However, when Peyrol first returns, he has no thought of death: aging and mortality are not yet part of his consciousness. Indeed, when he starts work refurbishing the tartane, this 'congenial task' is described as having 'all the air of preparation for a voyage' (p. 97). Nevertheless, despite the denials of intimations of mortality, there is an obvious irony in that reference to Peyrol's 'preparation for a voyage': particularly since the voyage for which he prepares the tartane actually ends in his death.

To begin with, however, it is Réal rather than Peyrol who seems marked out by death. Catherine's speech about the 'sign from death' (p. 173) is made with reference to Réal, and Catherine's appearance to Réal to wake him for his mission seems to be just such a sign:

> A strange, dim, cold light filled the room . . . and at the foot of his bed stood a figure in dark garments with a dark shawl over its head, with a fleshless predatory face and dark hollows for its eyes, silent, expectant, implacable . . . 'Is it death?' he asked himself, staring at it terrified.   (p. 225)

Catherine's speech about the 'sign from death', however, actually marks the beginning of Peyrol's consciousness of his own mortality. His reaction is significant:

> Melancholy was a sentiment to which he was a stranger; for what has melancholy to do with the life of a sea-rover, a Brother of the Coast, a simple, venturesome, precarious life, full of risks and leaving no time for introspection. . . . Sombre fury, fierce merriment, he had known in passing gusts . . . but never this intimate inward sense of the vanity of all things, that doubt of the power within himself.   (p. 173)

Peyrol's life of unreflecting, unselfconscious action is beginning to give way to reflection and the consciousness of his own declining powers. Ironically, while the conversation has suggested that Réal has been given a 'sign from death', it is Peyrol's emotional response to the conversation that actually constitutes that sign. Peyrol gradually becomes conscious of what was present, but not articulated, within himself earlier. For example, when Réal told him that the Admiralty papers in Toulon recorded him as 'disparu' (p. 106), Peyrol threw the word back at him: 'I am disparu, and that's good enough. There's no need for me to die' (p. 116). But then the word seemed to strike Peyrol from a different angle: 'It seemed to rankle, as Lieutenant Réal observed with some surprise; or else it was something inarticulate that rankled, manifesting itself in that funny way' (p. 117). The most vivid intimation of mortality, however, comes as he shaves himself on the morning of the mission, when the process of aging is unmistakably represented to him by the state of his razors:

> He had always wished to own a set of English blades and there he had got it, fell over it as it were, lying on the floor of a cabin which had been already ransacked. 'For good steel – it was good steel,' he thought looking at the blade fixedly. . . . And here he was holding the case in his hand as though he had just picked it up from the floor. Same case. Same man. And the steel worn out. (p. 233)

Just as Réal's sense of himself is challenged by his unexpected emotional response to Arlette, so Peyrol's sense of himself is challenged by a growing awareness of his own mortality.

Peyrol's death comes about partly in response to these intimations of mortality and partly in response to Arlette and Réal. For much of the narrative, there is a tension between Peyrol and Réal which is only partly explained by the difference between 'a sea-bandit' and 'a sea-officer' (p. 118). Peyrol's insistence on this difference between them is an attempt to conceal a different kind of tension, but it is an attempt which does not succeed: when Peyrol complains of the harm that Réal has done, Réal observes to himself that Peyrol 'can't keep his jealousy in' (p. 109). As Schwarz notes: 'Réal understands even more clearly than Peyrol that their mutual attraction to Arlette is the grounds for the hostility that punctuates the intimacy between the two men.'[47] Peyrol's 'jealousy' is intimately related to his growing awareness of the process of aging. For example, early on he is puzzled by his emotional response to Arlette: 'She produced on him the effect of a child, aroused a kind of intimate emotion which he had not known before to exist by itself in a man' (p. 88). This seems to suggest that the love he feels for her is paternal rather than sexual, and this interpretation is supported by the description of Peyrol, at the end of the novel, as an 'old man on whom age had stolen, unnoticed, till the veil of peace was torn down by the touch of a sentiment unexpected like an intruder' (p. 268). Similarly, when Peyrol describes his relationship with Arlette to Catherine, he observes: 'She did take to me. She learned to talk to – the old man' (p. 169). Peyrol's hesitation suggests a reluctant acknowledgement of Arlette's perception of him, but, however reluctant, it remains an acknowledgement. Accordingly, when Arlette appeals to his love for her (p. 248), he draws on that love to resolve the conflict between the love he feels for her and his awareness of her need for Réal. Peyrol's relationship with Arlette and Réal reproduces the father/daughter/lover triangles of *Almayer's Folly*, *An Outcast of the Islands*, *Lord Jim* and *Chance*, but this time the 'father' sacrifices himself, and his efforts are directed towards the liberation of the younger generation from the burden of the past.[48]

In his death, Peyrol also recovers and re-asserts his former identity. As he walks away from Arlette and Réal, the cool breeze recalled him 'to his old wandering self which had known no softness and no hesitation in the face of any risk offered by life' (p. 250). This recovery is expressed in the skill with which Peyrol manoevres the tartane and tricks the English, a skill which is recognised by himself and by others. As a result, Peyrol's death is also a triumphant assertion of himself.

VI

Schwarz observes that the 'graph' of Conrad's career from *The Nigger of the 'Narcissus'* to his later works 'shows how he had come to appreciate the values of private relationships and attachments based on sentiments'.[49] This is demonstrated in *The Rover* by the emphasis on the happy marriage of Arlette and Réal and by the fact of Peyrol's self-sacrifice to bring that marriage about. Peyrol's role as facilitator of their marriage resembles Marlow's role at the end of *Chance*. Another aspect of Conrad's appreciation of 'the values of private relationships' in *The Rover* is to be seen in its dialectical exploration of 'fraternity': the values of the French Revolution are consciously and systematically opposed to the values of the Brothers of the

Coast. In the opening chapter, Peyrol claims that they 'practised republican principles long before a republic was thought of; for the Brothers of the Coast were all equal and elected their own chiefs' (p. 5). Later, in Chapter 9, when Peyrol is talking with Symons, he recalls his earlier days with the Brotherhood and elaborates this comparison:

> He had known the practice of liberty, equality and fraternity as understood in the haunts open or secret of the Brotherhood of the Coast. . . . Liberty – to hold your own in the world if you could. Equality – yes! But no body of men ever accomplished anything without a chief. . . . He regarded fraternity somewhat differently. . . . In his view the claim of the Brotherhood was a claim for help against the outside world. (p. 132)

This purely personal loyalty lies behind Peyrol's treatment of Symons and his decision to sacrifice himself in Réal's place. Peyrol is thus contrasted with Scevola: Scevola disguises personal impulses in political rhetoric; Peyrol's most significant political intervention derives from 'fidelity to individuals whom he loves and appreciates as individuals' rather than from abstract political ideas.[50] As Réal puts it:

> The sincere lawlessness of the ex-Brother of the Coast was refreshing. . . . When he robbed or killed it was not in the name of the sacred revolutionary principles or for the love of humanity. (p. 209)

At the same time, as this implies, Peyrol is also contrasted with Réal. In Chapter 7, for example, Peyrol thinks: 'There was no trusting those epaulette-wearers. Any one of them was capable of jumping on his best friend on account of some officer-like notion or other' (p. 104).

The portrait of Peyrol, like the presentation of Dominic Cervoni in *The Arrow of Gold*, suggests Conrad's late appreciation of the lawless. More important, it shows how Conrad's political thinking has gone beyond the abstract model of *The Nigger of the 'Narcissus'*: his assertion of 'human solidarity' is not now based on abstractions but on an appreciation of the value of particular human relationships. His exploration of sexual relationships in his late novels has produced a humanising of the earlier political vision.

Notes

Notes to the Introduction

1. Thomas Moser, *Joseph Conrad: Achievement and Decline* (Cambridge, Mass.: Harvard University Press, 1957) p. 10; M. C. Bradbrook, *Joseph Conrad: Poland's English Genius* (Cambridge: Cambridge University Press, 1941); Morton Zabel, *The Portable Conrad* (New York: Viking, 1947); F. R. Leavis, *The Great Tradition* (London: Chatto & Windus, 1948). A. J. Guerard's monograph *Joseph Conrad* (New York: New Directions, 1947) should be added to this list.

2. **(a)** Richard Curle, *Joseph Conrad: A Study* (London: Kegan Paul, Trench, Trübner, 1914); Wilson Follett, *Joseph Conrad: A Short Study.* **(b)** Ford Madox Ford, *Joseph Conrad: A Personal Remembrance* (London: Duckworth, 1924); Richard Curle, *The Last Twelve Years of Joseph Conrad* (London: Sampson Low, Marston, 1928); Jessie Conrad, *Joseph Conrad as I Knew Him* (London: Heinemann, 1926) and *Joseph Conrad and his Circle* (London: Jarrolds, 1935). **(c)** *Five Letters by Joseph Conrad to Edward Noble in 1895* (privately printed, 1925); *Joseph Conrad's Letters to his Wife* (privately printed, 1927); *Conrad to a Friend: 150 Selected Letters from Joseph Conrad to Richard Curle*, ed. R. Curle (London: Sampson Low, Marston, 1928); *Letters from Joseph Conrad, 1895 to 1924*, ed. Edward Garnett (London: Nonesuch Press, 1928); *Joseph Conrad: Life and Letters*, ed. G. Jean-Aubry (London: Heinemann, 1927) – hereafter referred to as *L.L.*

3. Gustav Morf, *The Polish Heritage of Joseph Conrad* (London: Sampson Low, Marston, 1930); R. L. Mégroz, *Joseph Conrad's Mind and Method* (London: Faber & Faber, 1931); Edward Crankshaw, *Joseph Conrad: Some Aspects of the Art of the Novel* (London: The Bodley Head, 1936); J. D. Gordan, *Joseph Conrad: The Making of a Novelist* (Cambridge, Mass.: Harvard University Press, 1940).

4. Douglas Hewitt, *Conrad: A Re-assessment* (Cambridge: Bowes & Bowes, 1952); Thomas Moser, *Joseph Conrad: Achievement and Decline* (Cambridge, Mass.: Harvard University Press, 1957); A. J. Guerard, *Conrad the Novelist* (Cambridge, Mass., Harvard University Press, 1958). Moser was a member of Guerard's 1950 and 1953 Harvard/Radcliffe graduate seminars in the modern novel; he acknowledges a debt to Guerard for 'nearly a decade' of discussions on Conrad (p. vii); and he aligns himself with Guerard and Hewitt (p. 3). In particular, the account of Conrad's 'anticlimax' in Guerard's earlier work, *Joseph Conrad* (pp. 27–30) is credited as influencing Moser's view of Conrad's 'decline' after *The Shadow Line* (p. 2).

5. For recent work that pays some attention to the early fiction, see William W. Bonney, *Thorns & Arabesques* (Baltimore: The Johns Hopkins University Press, 1980); Cedric Watts, *The Deceptive Text* (Sussex: The Harvester Press, 1984); Stephen K. Land, *Conrad and the Paradox of Plot* (London: Macmillan, 1984). More representative, however, are Aaron

6. Fogel, *Coercion to Speak* (Cambridge, Mass.: Harvard University Press, 1985); Suresh Raval, *The Art of Failure* (London: Allen & Unwin, 1986); Jakob Lothe, *Conrad's Narrative Method* (Oxford: Clarendon Press, 1989) – all of which concentrate on the canon of texts established by the 'achievement and decline' paradigm.

6. John A. Palmer, *Joseph Conrad's Fiction: A Study in Literary Growth* (Ithaca, N.Y.: Cornell University Press, 1968) p. 10. Palmer's account of the development of the paradigm ('Achievement and Decline: A Bibliographical Note', pp. 260–86) can be read as complementary to my own. Thomas Kuhn's concept, the 'paradigm', has an obvious applicability to changes and developments in literary critical traditions. For Kuhn, paradigms are 'universally recognised scientific achievements that for the time provide model problems and solutions to a community of practitioners' (*The Structure of Scientific Revolutions* [Chicago: University of Chicago Press, 1962] p. x).

7. Palmer, p. ix. For more recent criticism of the late novels, see Chapter 8.

8. After describing the 'rediscovery' of Conrad as 'a profound psychologist', 'a political prophet' and an 'audacious craftsman', Moser asserts that 'over these three' and 'including them all, stands Conrad the moralist' (pp. 10–11). For a similar privileging of 'Conrad the moralist', see Paul L. Wiley, *Conrad's Measure of Man* (Madison: University of Wisconsin Press, 1954); C. Cooper, *Conrad and the Human Dilemma* (London: Chatto & Windus, 1970); J. E. Saveson, *Conrad: The Later Moralist* (Amsterdam: Rodopi, 1972); R. A. Gekoski, *Conrad: The Moral World of the Novelist* (London: Paul Elek, 1978).

9. Guerard, p. 146. Compare: 'Fictional characters are representations of life and, as such, can only be understood if we assume they are real. And this assumption allows us to find unconscious motivation by the same procedure that the traditional critic uses to assign conscious ones' (M. A. Kaplan and R. Kloss, *The Unspoken Motive* [New York, 1973] p. 4).

10. Guerard, p. 12. Leo Gurko's criticism of Morf can be transferred to this part of Guerard's work: 'To read *Lord Jim* as a compendium of clues to Conrad's personal feelings is to shrink its range of discourse and turn literature generally into a treasure hunt for disguised personal references' (*Joseph Conrad: Giant in Exile*, p. 18). Guerard suggests, for example, that by the time Conrad came to write his late novels, he was bereft 'of certain unconscious drives' (p. 255). Guerard is at his worst with *The Arrow of Gold*. His particular psychological approach leads him to focus on Conrad's 'evasion' of the biographical truth about the 'duel'. This concentration on an event described briefly in the second 'Note' is of a piece with Guerard's belief that 'the interest of the novel . . . is extra-literary' (p. 284).

11. Bernard C. Meyer, *Joseph Conrad: A Psychoanalytic Biography* (Princeton, N.J.: Princeton University Press, 1967).

12. Notice that Freud himself observed, in his *Introductory Lectures on Psychoanalysis* (The Pelican Freud Library, I): 'Interpretation based on a knowledge of symbols is not a technique which can replace or

compete with the associative one. It forms a supplement to the latter and yields results which are only of use when introduced into it' (p. 184). The principle, he noted earlier, was that 'psychoanalysis follows the technique of getting the people under examination so far as possible themselves to produce the solution of their riddles' (p. 130), and this is obviously not possible when the subject is a dead author.

13. See, for example, Freud's *Studies in Hysteria* (The Pelican Freud Library, III) pp. 389–92, or *Introductory Lectures on Psychoanalysis* (The Pelican Freud Library, I) pp. 482–500 (e.g.: 'what turns the scale in his struggle is not his intellectual insight . . . but simply and solely his relation to the doctor' [p. 497]). See also Jacques Lacan's 'Intervention on Transference' (1951): 'What happens in an analysis is that the subject is, strictly speaking, constituted through a discourse . . . psychoanalysis is a dialectical experience' (*In Dora's Case*, ed. Charles Bernheimer and Claire Kahane [London: Virago Press, 1985] p. 93).

14. See, for example, Freud's *Studies in Hysteria*, pp. 380–1.

15. Gilles Deleuze and Felix Guattari, *Anti-Oedipus*, trans. Robert Huxley, Mark Seem and Helen R. Lane (New York: Viking, 1977); Fredric Jameson, *The Political Unconscious* (London: Methuen, 1981) p. 99. See also Freud, *Introductory Lectures on Psychoanalysis*: 'there is no justification for carrying this shift of interest so far that, in looking at the matter theoretically, one replaces the dream entirely by the latent dream-thoughts' (p. 217).

16. Richard Brown, 'James Joyce: The Sexual Pretext', Ph.D. thesis, University of London (1981); revised version published as *James Joyce and Sexuality* (Cambridge: Cambridge University Press, 1985).

17. Frank J. Sulloway, *Freud: Biologist of the Mind* (London: Fontana, 1980).

18. Wiley, p. 14. See also Ralph Tymms, *Doubles in Literary Psychology* (Cambridge: Bowes and Bowes, 1949) pp. 93–4.

19. J. Galsworthy, 'Reminiscences of Conrad', *Castles in Spain* (London: Heinemann, 1927) p. 91. (In a 1908 letter to Galsworthy, Conrad commented on the character of Hilary Dallison in Galsworthy's *Fraternity*: 'Morbid psychology, be it always understood, is a perfectly legitimate subject for an artist's genius' [*L.L.*, II, p. 78].) S. Freud, *Selected Papers on Hysteria & other Psychoneuroses* (Nervous & Mental Disease Monograph Series No. 4; New York, 1912). C. G. Jung, *Psychology of the Unconscious*, trans. Beatrice M. Hinkle (New York: Moffat, Yard, 1916). Hinkle prefaces her translation with an introductory essay on psychoanalysis. (Conrad's copy was included in Hodgson's catalogue for their 1925 sale of books from his library.)

20. Jeffrey Berman, *Joseph Conrad: Writing as Rescue* (New York: Astra Books, 1977) pp. 149–50. Berman, however, does not make much of this observation: after suggesting that 'genuine loneliness, feelings of abandonment, and submerged hostility towards her imprisoned father . . . prompt Flora to repudiate her life', he goes on to say only that Flora 'still does not have the intellectual or psychological complexity that Conrad's solitary males possess' (p. 154).

21. Richard Brown, p. 26. J. D. Patterson has attempted to do this for the earlier novels in 'The Representation of Love in the Novels of Joseph Conrad: 1895–1915', D.Phil. thesis, Oxford University (1984).

22. Paul Kirschner, *Conrad: The Psychologist as Artist* (Edinburgh: Oliver & Boyd, 1968); Zdzisław Najder, *Conrad's Polish Background* (London: Oxford University Press, 1964); Avrom Fleishman, *Conrad's Politics* (Baltimore: The Johns Hopkins University Press, 1967); Eloise Knapp Hay, *The Political Novels of Joseph Conrad* (Chicago: University of Chicago Press, 1963). Two other works were also influential in the early stages of my research: Edward Said, *Joseph Conrad and the Fiction of Autobiography* (Cambridge, Mass.: Harvard University Press, 1965) and Robert R. Hodges, *The Dual Heritage of Joseph Conrad* (The Hague: Mouton, 1967). More recently, I have been indebted to Cedric Watts, *Conrad's 'Heart of Darkness': A Critical and Contextual Discussion* (Milan: Mursia International, 1977) and Ian Watt, *Conrad in the Nineteenth Century* (London: Chatto & Windus, 1980).

23. Kirschner, p. vii.

24. Ibid. Contrast this with Meyer, who interprets characters as 'multiple self-portraits of the author' (p. 122). The inadequacy of this approach is evident in the example Meyer offers: 'Viewed in this light the picture of James Wait as a child-like helpless creature, whose physical weakness appears to be admixed with malingering . . . may be regarded as an incisive and scornful confession' (p. 122).

25. Kirschner, pp. viii–ix. Although I have accepted Kirschner's terms for Conrad's three phases, my disagreement with the details of his reading of Conrad will be clear.

26. 'Against the distant background of British, Dutch and Arab struggle for domination of the islands, the local Arabs and Malays compete for trade and political power' (*Conrad the Novelist*, p. 71). Eloise Knapp Hay used the word 'psychopolitical' in her account of *Nostromo* (*The Political Novels of Joseph Conrad*, p. 189). More recently, Cedric Watts has argued, in *The Deceptive Text: An Introduction to Covert Plots* (Sussex: Harvester Press, 1984), that the political struggle is not just an over-elaborated background, but constitutes a covert plot that prompts and contains the overt plot.

27. Eloise Knapp Hay, p. 10. This idea is taken further by Robert Hodges in *The Dual Heritage of Joseph Conrad* and by Zdzisław Najder in *Conrad's Polish Background* and in *Joseph Conrad: A Chronicle* (Cambridge: Cambridge University Press, 1983).

28. Jameson, *The Political Unconscious*, p. 20.

29. *The Metaphysics of Darkness* (Baltimore: The Johns Hopkins Press, 1971) p. viii.

30. Bruce Johnson, *Conrad's Models of Mind* (Minneapolis: University of Minnesota Press, 1971) p. 15. Johnson's approach is philosophical and ethical rather than psychological.

31. Ibid., p. 26. G. B. Ursell, in 'Conrad's Early Writing with Particular Reference to "The Rescue" ("The Rescuer")', Ph.D. thesis, University of London (1973), argued the importance of a consideration of 'The

Rescuer' for an understanding of Conrad's early work. Roussel also argued for the need to discuss *The Rescue* as 'a product of Conrad's early years' (p. 55): he sees it as 'an investigation of the most obvious alternative to Willem's last vision' (p. 56).

32. By 'existential psychology', I refer to the early work of R. D. Laing and the associated work of David Cooper and Aaron Esterson. For a critical account of Laing's early development, see Juliet Mitchell, *Psychoanalysis and Feminism* (Harmondsworth: Pelican Books, 1975) pp. 227–92. See also Robert Boyers and Robert Orrill (eds), *Laing and Anti-Psychiatry* (Harmondsworth: Pelican Books, 1972).

33. R. D. Laing, *The Divided Self* (Harmondsworth: Penguin Books, 1965) p. 33 (hereafter referred to as *D.S.*).

34. *D.S.*, p. 32.

35. Ibid., p. 26. Laing is referring specifically to Ludwig Binswanger's term 'being-in-the-world'. See Ludwig Binswanger, *Being in the World*, trans. Jacob Needleman (London: Souvenir Press, 1975).

36. Aaron Esterson, *The Leaves of Spring* (Harmondsworth: Penguin Books, 1972) pp. 38–9. Juliet Mitchell suggests a serious limitation to Laing's approach: 'Laing's account makes the mistake of supposing an already-constituted discrete subject. . . . Freud's child does not have the separate, pre-existent essential self . . . his discrete self is set up in the moment of this recognition of absence which is the recognition of difference' (p. 384). On the child's compulsive-repetition game in front of the mirror (to which Mitchell refers), see Freud, 'Beyond the Pleasure Principle' (1920), and Jacques Lacan, 'The Mirror-phase as Formative of the Function of the I', *New Left Review*, 51 (Sept./Oct. 1968) pp. 72–3.

Notes to Chapter 1: Two Prototypes of Betrayal

1. Guerard, *Conrad the Novelist*, p. 3.

2. *A Personal Record*, p. 5. All references to Conrad's works are to the Uniform Edition (London: J. M. Dent, 1923–8).

3. In *Joseph Conrad: A Personal Remembrance*, Ford refers to 'the copy of *Madame Bovary* upon the end papers and margins of which *Almayer's Folly* was begun' (p. 94). Even if this is not factually true, it has the truth of impression that Ford sought. Notice that, on 6 April 1892, Conrad wrote to Marguerite Poradowska that he had 'just reread' *Madame Bovary* (*Collected Letters*, I, p. 111; hereafter *C.L.*). For a discussion of Conrad's debts to Flaubert, and a comparison of *Almayer's Folly* and *Madame Bovary*, see Watt, *Conrad in the Nineteenth Century*, pp. 50–5; Guerard, *Conrad the Novelist*, pp. 70–89; see also Johnson, *Conrad's Models of Mind*: 'Almayer and Willems are a variation on Flaubert's description of the character destroyed by illusions, Villiers's and Huysman's peculiar isolattoes, and the familiar late-nineteenth-century pattern of the disintegrating colonial' (p. 12).

4. G. Flaubert, *Madame Bovary*, trans. Mildred Marmur (New American Library, New York and Toronto, 1964) p. 217 (all subsequent refer-

ences are to this edition). P. J. Glassman, *Language and Being* (New York and London: Columbia University Press, 1976), writes: 'Almayer does not remark that the supposed partners of his visionary purpose have developed equally forceful needs of their own' (p. 101).

5. Significantly, Almayer admits this truth to himself only in Chapter 11 ('There used to be a half-caste woman in my house'), where it is part of the dynamics of his rejection of Nina.

6. For an analysis of narrative technique in *Almayer's Folly*, based on Gérard Genette's *Narrative Discourse*, see Allan H. Simmons, 'Ambiguity as Meaning: The Subversion of Suspense in *Almayer's Folly*', *The Conradian*, 14:1/2 (1989) pp. 1–18.

7. See Cedric Watts, *The Deceptive Text*: 'As in the later *Outcast of the Islands* and *Heart of Darkness*, at the centre of the hidden machinations is a scheme by a trader to eliminate a rival and secure for himself the control of a commercial territory' (p. 47). In this case, 'the fulcrum of the plot is provided by the Arab traders' betrayal of Dain' (pp. 50–1).

8. See Laing's account of schizogenesis in *Self and Others* (Harmondsworth: Penguin Books, 1971) pp. 100–2. For schizogenic family situations, see R. D. Laing and A. Esterson *Sanity, Madness and the Family* (Harmondsworth: Penguin Books, 1970).

9. Reshid anticipates Dain both as prospective husband for Nina and as the object of attention from the Dutch authorities. In the same way, Nina is mirrored by Taminah and Almayer by Jim-Eng.

10. The significant detail, though, is that Nina stands 'irresolute' (p. 150) and doesn't immediately give way under this ultimatum.

11. See Moser, pp. 41–52. Moser reads this misogyny as personal to Conrad. I will argue below that it is culturally produced.

12. Cf. John H. Hicks, 'Conrad's *Almayer's Folly*: Structure, Theme and Critics', *Nineteenth Century Fiction*, xix.1 (June 1964) pp. 17–31. Hicks argues that Nina's commitment to Dain enables her to find her self and a 'socially valid identity' (p. 24).

13. Moser, p. 52.

14. Watt, *Conrad in the Nineteenth Century*, p. 45.

15. Ibid., p. 46.

16. *C.L.*, I, p. 247.

17. See Watts, *The Deceptive Text*, pp. 47–53.

18. The ambiguities of power in sexual politics find a curious echo in the colonial politics of Sambir: when Lakamba flies the Dutch flag, 'this emblem of Lakamba's power . . . was also the mark of his servitude' (p. 108). More interestingly, the generally disregarded slave-girl, Taminah, briefly finds herself in possession of the information (about Dain's whereabouts) upon which the whole political plot depends.

19. See Chapter 2.

20. A. Schopenhauer, *Essays and Aphorisms*, trans. R. J. Hollingdale (Harmondsworth: Penguin Books, 1970) p. 86. Galsworthy observed, in *Castles in Spain*, that Conrad had 'read a good deal' of philosophy and that 'Schopenhauer used to give him satisfaction' (p. 121). Conrad could have come across this passage in the essay 'On Woman' in A. Schopenhauer, *Studies in Pessimism*, selected and trans. by T. Bailey

Saunders (London: Swan Sonnenschein, 1891) p. 113. In *The Bourgeois Experience: Victoria to Freud*, vol. II (Oxford: Oxford University Press, 1986), Peter Gay observes: 'Once Schopenhauer became fashionable in the 1850s, his ideas on love came to command a sizable and enthusiastic following. They seemed to fit into that widespread fear of women that literature and the arts were exemplifying and spreading' (pp. 82–3).

21. Thomas Mann, *Schopenhauer*. See also Schopenhauer, *Studies in Pessimism*, p. 35.
22. *Studies in Pessimism*, p. 112.
23. A. Schopenhauer, *The World as Will and Representation*, trans. E. F. J. Payne (New York: Dover Publications, 1969) vol. I, p. 328.
24. J. S. Mill, 'On the Subjection of Women', p. 168.
25. J. D. Patterson, 'The Representation of Love'.
26. Steven Marcus, *The Other Victorians* (London: Weidenfeld, 1966); William Acton, *The Functions and Disorders of the Reproductive System* (1857). For a dissenting view, see Brian Harrison, 'Underneath the Victorians', *Victorian Studies*, x (1967). Harrison casts doubt on Acton's representativeness. However, as Patterson points out, *Functions and Disorders* was popular enough to go through six editions between 1857 and 1875.
27. Quoted Marcus, p. 31. As Marcus points out, Acton's category 'women' does not include working-class women or prostitutes.
28. Otto Rank, *The Trauma of Birth* (London: Kegan Paul, Trench, Trübner, 1929) p. 93.
29. Marcus, pp. 13, 28.
30. For example, Acton comments on instances from the insect world, where the male of the species dies after copulation: 'Do the males die from excess? Is the act of copulation a suicidal one? Is the orgasm too strong for the tender organization of the insect?' (p. 34).
31. Kirschner, *Conrad: The Psychologist as Artist*, p. 34.
32. Roussel notes that Almayer has the chance to sacrifice his egoism and follow Nina, but that he turns the chance down: 'Almayer's "folly" refers not only to the house into which he sank his last hopes and assets, but also his resolve "in the undying folly of his heart" . . . to forget Nina' (p. 42).

Notes to Chapter 2: The Unshared Ideal of Self

1. *'Twixt Land and Sea Tales*, p. 94; *An Outcast of the Islands*, p. 3.
2. This image is clearly proleptic of the destructive effect of Aissa on Willems later.
3. Jocelyn Baines, *Joseph Conrad: A Critical Biography* (Harmondsworth: Pelican Books, 1971): 'The subject of *An Outcast of the Islands* is the enslavement and eventual destruction of a white man, whose self-respect has already been undermined by a piece of dishonesty, by his passion for a Malay woman' (p. 199). Baines's terminology of 'self-respect' is inappropriate to Willems. As Conrad himself put it:

'First, the theme is the unrestrained, fierce vanity of an ignorant man who has had some success but neither principles nor any other line of conduct than the satisfaction of his vanity. In addition, he is not even faithful to himself. Whence a fall, a sudden descent to physical enslavement by an absolutely untamed woman' (*C.L.*, i, p. 185).

4. Dostoevsky, *Crime and Punishment* (Harmondsworth: Penguin Books, 1951) p. 133.
5. Kirschner, p. 35.
6. Willems, significantly, seems to experience his emotional response to Aissa as depravity: 'Willems never remembered how and when he parted from Aissa. He caught himself drinking the muddy water out of the hollow of his hand, while his canoe was drifting in mid-stream. . . . He drank again, and shuddered with a depraved sense of pleasure at the after-taste of slime in the water' (pp. 72–3).
7. *An Outcast of the Islands* can be read as a sequel to *Almayer's Folly*. The question left at the end of *Almayer's Folly*, what happened to Nina after the discovery of her 'new principle', is answered here: following the new self of passion is shown as leading only to possession. As in *Heart of Darkness*, we are given a 'choice of nightmares' (p. 138): the unrealiseable ideal of self or the horrors of the instinctual self. Glassman, in *Language and Being*, argues that a pessimistic prognosis for the relationship was implicit in *Almayer's Folly*: 'We cannot feel confident . . . about the final yield of Nina and Dain's temporarily self-justifying vision. Like every other fantasy construction examined in *Almayer's Folly* its authority is likely to be impermanent because it does not take into account the irreconcilable divergence of individual purposes and needs' (pp. 114–15). Roussel is more optimistic (pp. 40–2).
8. The narrative is built upon a series of father/lover/child triangles: Hudig/Willems/Joanna; Lingard/Almayer/Mrs Almayer; Omar/Willems/Aissa; and, above all, Lingard/Willems/Aissa.
9. Guerard has noted the ambiguity of the erotic feelings of the novel: desire was strong enough to lead to betrayals, but turned rapidly to disgust (*Conrad the Novelist*, p. 80). An explanation for this is to be found in the suicidal rather than the sensual basis of his 'obsession', and in its relation to the negative pole of his dual self-evaluation (which is the obvious significance of his relationship with a woman whom he considers 'racially' inferior).
10. This instance parallels Almayer's jibes about 'those new relations of yours' (p. 88).
11. Willems is clearly subconsciously troubled by the crime he consciously denies: he has Jim's hypersensitivity to remarks and gives himself away by unnecessary denials.
12. As with Nina in *Almayer's Folly*, the father acts as a block to the daughter's emotional and sexual fulfillment.
13. See Hampson, 'Chance, Pattern and Plan in Dostoievsky's "The Gambler" ', *Footnote*, ii. 1 (October 1973) pp. 8–16, and Freud, 'On the Universal Tendency to Debasement in the Sphere of Love', *On Sexuality* (The Pelican Freud Library, vol. vii) pp. 243–60.

14. Ironically, this wish is fulfilled later as Lingard's punishment. As in *The Secret Agent*, plans misfire and bring about results the opposite of those intended.

15. Just as, later, his refusal to fight back stops Lingard from killing him (p. 260).

16. For example, Morf, p. 158. Gekoski sees Lingard's confrontation with Willems as 'a confrontation with an obscure and deadly aspect of his own behaviour' (p. 41).

17. Compare Kirschner's suggestion that Lingard's sympathy for Willems short-circuits his will: he is unable to punish because that sympathy is tantamount to assuming responsibility for his own betrayal (p. 38).

18. Notice Nina's statement, during this episode: 'I am a white child. . . . Father says so' (p. 194).

19. *'Twixt Land and Sea Tales*, pp. 147–238.

20. In this false estimation of his success, Lingard is also like Babalatchi.

21. Note, however, how Conrad is quietly critical of Lingard: he includes the information that Lingard's assistance (or interference) at sea was, in fact, not 'the right way' but was 'in defiance of nautical etiquette' (p. 199).

22. Compare George Orwell, 'Shooting an Elephant', *Inside the Whale* (Harmondsworth: Penguin Books, 1962). In each case, the personality-structure is exemplified in a colonial context, where the issue for the white man is precisely that of identifying with an alterated identity.

23. Compare Charles Gould in *Nostromo* and his attitude towards his mine: he would blow it up rather than give it up.

24. This viewpoint comes as a surprise, although there has been, in fact, some preparation for it: for example, in the conversation between Lingard and Almayer about their policy of economic indebtedness 'backed by loaded rifles' (p. 171).

25. Kirschner, pp. 37–8.

26. Lingard needs to be able to believe in a meaningful universe of simple values, and it is this which Willems threatens: 'the picture of Willems ranging over the islands and disturbing the harmony of the universe by robbery, treachery, and violence, held him silent, entranced – painfully spellbound' (p. 209).

27. When Willems had claimed 'The evil was not in me', Lingard interrupted him: 'And where else – confound you! Where else?' (p. 273).

28. See pp. 36–9 above.

29. Kirschner, p. 38.

30. Consider his comment on his embezzling from Hudig: 'It was an error of judgement. I've paid for it' (p. 266), and his words to Almayer after the attack on the trading post: 'You will keep the bitter taste of this humiliation to the last day of your life, and so your kindness to me shall be repaid' (p. 185).

31. See p. 39 above, for an analysis of his first self-justificatory conversation about Joanna with Lingard. It ended with Lingard placing the blame firmly back on Willems.

32. Notice his punishment of Almayer – leaving him tied up 'like a bale of goods' (i.e. humiliating him by depersonalising him and turning him

into an object). Willems does to Almayer what he most fears for himself.

33. Compare St Paul: 'What I would do, that I do not; but what I hate, that I do. . . . Now then it is no more I that do it, but sin that dwelleth in me' (Romans, 7:14–22).

34. Consider: 'He shuddered at the thought of what might happen in the impenetrable darkness of that house if they were to find themselves alone' (p. 336). See Patterson, for a discussion of erotophobia as an aspect of Victorian patriarchal culture.

35. Consider 'like a nightmare' (p. 270) and 'a devil' (p. 273); and 'a ferocious creature' (p. 269), 'a wild animal' (p. 269), 'an animal as full of harm as a wildcat' (p. 270), 'a damned mongrel' (p. 271).

36. Almayer's attitude to his environment is described as follows: 'He hated all this. . . . And yet all this was very precious to him. It was the present sign of a splendid future' (p. 292). For a detailed discussion of this aspect of the novel, see Hampson 'The Mystic Worshipper and the Temple of Self: Egotism and Idealism in *An Outcast of the Islands*', *The Journal of the Joseph Conrad Society (U.K.)*, ii.4 (September 1976) pp. 9–12.

37. The third figure on the island at the end, the old woman, represents, in contrast to Almayer and Willems, the resigned acceptance of facts without striving for the 'escape', the 'refuge', the 'consolation', of hopes, dreams, idealisations: 'The third, the decrepit witness of their struggle and their torture, accepted her own dull conception of facts' (p. 328).

38. Guerard, *Conrad the Novelist*, pp. 80–1.

39. The echoes relate particularly to the parricidal incident between Omar and Aissa. As Aissa returned from depositing Omar back at the hut: ' "Nothing but misfortune," she whispered, absently, to herself. "Nothing but misfortune to us who are not white" ' (p. 151). Later, when she misinterpreted Willems's fears as the fading of his love: 'her eyes looked fixedly, sombre and steady, at that man born in the land of violence and of evil wherefrom nothing but misfortune comes to those who are not white' (p. 153). The whisper, 'Kill! Kill!', also retrospectively clarifies (or verifies) a detail in this episode: when Aissa carried Omar back into the hut, after his attempt to stab Willems, Willems 'heard her voice speaking inside, harshly, with an agitated abruptness of tone; and in answer there were groans and broken murmurs of exhaustion. She spoke louder. He heard her saying violently – "No! No! Never! . . . I would sooner strike it into my own heart" ' (p. 151).

40. *D.S.*, p. 17.

41. 'The ontologically insecure person is preoccupied with preserving rather than gratifying himself: the ordinary circumstances of living threaten his low threshold of security' (*D.S.*, p. 42).

42. Ibid., p. 44; compare *An Outcast of the Islands*, pp. 80–1: 'He struggled with the sense of certain defeat – lost his footing – fell back into the darkness. With a faint cry and an upward throw of his arms he gave up as a tired swimmer gives up: because the night is dark and the shore is far – because death is better than strife.'

43.   It is arguably this psychological condition of ontological insecurity that lies behind Said's polarisation of will/surrender and Kirschner's opposition of master/slave.

44.   For example, Aissa tells Lingard: 'I live with him all the days. All the nights. I look at him; I see his every breath, every glance of his eye, every movement of his lips' (p. 249); and again: 'I waited, watching his face, his eyes, his lips; listening to his words. – To the words I could not understand. . . . Day after day, night after night, I lived watching him – seeing nothing' (p. 252).

45.   'The risk consists in this: if one experiences the other as a free agent, one is open to the possibility of experiencing oneself as an *object* of his experience and thereby of feeling one's own subjectivity drained away. One is threatened with the possibility of becoming no more than a thing in the world of the other, without any life for oneself, without any being for oneself' (*D.S.*, p. 47).

46.   W. R. D. Fairbairn, *Psychoanalytic Studies of the Personality* (London, 1952) pp. 42 and 145.

47.   Roussel, p. 30.

48.   Laing comments on the case of Mrs R: 'Her longing was always to be important and significant to someone else. There always had to be someone else. Preferably she wanted to be loved and admired, but, if not, then to be hated was much to be preferred to being unnoticed' (*D.S.*, p. 54).

49.   'Moreover, this shut-up self, being isolated, is unable to be enriched by outer experience, and so the whole inner world comes to be more and more impoverished' (*D.S.*, p. 75).

50.   'The individual who may at one time have felt predominantly "outside" the life going on *there*, which he affects to despise as petty and commonplace compared to the richness he has *here*, inside himself, now longs to get *inside* life again, and get life *inside* himself, so dreadful is his inner deadness' (*D.S.*, p. 75).

51.   Esterson, *The Leaves of Spring*, pp. 120–1.

Notes to Chapter 3: The Real Existence of Passions

1.   In *The Time Machine* (London: Heinemann, 1895), Wells had already developed various technical devices (including the use of a frame-narrative) which seem to have had an influence on the writing of 'Heart of Darkness'. For some discussion of connections between *The Time Machine* and 'Heart of Darkness' see Watts, *Conrad's 'Heart of Darkness': A Critical and Contextual Discussion*, pp. 22–7, and Hampson, 'The Genie out of the Bottle', in Peter L. Caracciolo (ed.), *'The Arabian Nights' in English Literature* (London: Macmillan, 1988) pp. 218–43. For a discussion of the use of narrators and frame-narrative by Wells and Conrad, see Sandra Penney, 'The Role of the Narrator in Selected First-person Novels', unpublished Ph.D. thesis, University of London (1984).

2. Guerard, in *Conrad the Novelist*, suggests that Jim arises from a fusion of Lingard and Willems. He notices how Lingard prefigures Jim's romantic egotism and self-deception; how, like Jim, he takes pride in the 'benevolent despotism' of his colonial rule. He also points out a number of situational prefigurations of *Lord Jim* in *An Outcast*: as Lingard gives Willems a second chance in Sambir, so Marlow and Stein give Jim his second chance in Patusan; as Aissa questions Lingard on Willems's status in the outside, 'white' world, so Jewel questions Marlow; as Lingard shakes his head when asked if Willems is great in the white world, so Marlow has to admit to Jewel that Jim was 'not good enough' (*Lord Jim*, p. 318).

3. Roussel, p. 56.

4. It is the difference between a seaman's commitment to a code of conduct and the sense of 'duty' ('je me dois à moi-même') of a Julien Sorel (Stendhal, *Le Rouge et le Noir* [Paris: Garnier-Flammarion, 1964] p. 103). In Roussel's words: 'Lingard comes from the sea not the shore, and his commitment is not to himself but to the values of his world. Consequently his egoism takes on an entirely different quality' (p. 56).

5. *The Sisters* (New York: Crosby Gaige, 1928) pp. 6–8. Ford refers to canonical rather than biological incest. Ford himself, of course, had been in a similar situation with the Martindale sisters.

6. Baines writes: 'There is no evidence to support Hueffer's assertion that the story was to be about incest, and as Hueffer had not even noticed the similarities between *The Sisters* and *The Arrow of Gold* his comments are not worth much' (p. 208). Both Stephen and 'M. George' have connections with a French bohemian/artistic world; Rita and Rita de Lastaola share a Basque peasant childhood and early adolescence as part of a Paris orange-merchant's family; the 'moral avenger' is still called Ortega, but in *The Arrow of Gold* he is a distant cousin rather than a priest, and the priest-uncle is a separate character.

7. *The Sisters*, p. 6.

8. Conrad has already revealed to the reader that Stephen is not long for this world: 'Only a small band of the good and the smart hated him. . . . Doubtless they would not have been so bitter . . . had they known then how short his life, how faint his trace on earth, was fated to be' (p. 23). Stephen looks back to Willems, whose flight had a similar suicidal motivation, and interestingly anticipates 'Lord Jim'.

9. Meyer, p. 49.

10. He wrote to Garnett on 23 March 1896 saying that he had decided to abandon *The Sisters* in response to Garnett's criticism and that he planned to begin 'The Rescuer' 'on the lines indicated to you' (*C.L.*, I, pp. 267–8).

11. The note on the manuscript to this effect is corroborated by a letter to Garnett (10 June 1896): 'I send to you today a registered envelope containing all that there is of the *Rescuer*. It is the whole of the first part' (*C.L.*, I, p. 286).

12. 'The Rescuer', B. M. Ashley 4787 – all references in this chapter are to this manuscript unless *The Rescue* is specifically indicated. See 'Intro-

duction' for reasons for attending to 'The Rescuer'. For a discussion of
the dating of the manuscript, see Gordan, *Joseph Conrad: The Making of
a Novelist*; Thomas Moser, ' "The Rescuer" Manuscript: A Key to
Conrad's Development and Decline', *Harvard Library Bulletin*, x (1956)
pp. 329–30; and G. B. Ursell, 'Conrad's Early Writing', unpublished
PhD thesis, University of London (1973). Gordan suggested that much
of Part IV of the manuscript dates from 1916, and Moser agreed with
this suggestion. Ursell argues that the entire manuscript was the work
of the period 1896–9: Conrad broke off at the start of Part IV in
December 1898 to take up 'Heart of Darkness', but then returned to
Part IV after completing 'Heart of Darkness' and worked on it from
February to June 1899. (I have followed Ursell's dating.)

13. Although this polarity, at times in 'The Rescuer', finds expression in a
     rather childish contrast of sailors and landsmen, of bachelors and
     married men, it initiates a set of contrasts of sea and land that are also
     of central importance in subsequent works.

14. As Benita Parry convincingly argues, the initial praise of the 'true
     adventurer' (pp. 3–4) 'has the status of a thesis whose axioms are to be
     spectaculary invalidated by the fiction's action': 'the mystique of the
     chivalrous and disinterested adventurer is stripped away, leaving the
     more ambiguous figure of a maverick and dreamer motivated by
     altruism and self-interest, compassion and egoism, a man cut off from
     his ethnic roots and without roots in his place of exile' (Parry, *Conrad
     and Imperialism* [London: Macmillan, 1983] pp. 44–5).

15. This contrasts with Fleishman's ideas about Conrad's view of the
     colonist in *Conrad's Politics*, Chapter 4.

16. Thus Roussel comments on Lingard: 'The independence and wilful-
     ness of his character appear as the fundamental qualities which allow
     man to dedicate himself to an idea and carry this idea through to
     realization. . . . Since the will is the agency by which the mind shapes
     the world to its own ideals, its strength along with its integrity be-
     comes the central issue of his life' (pp. 56–7).

17. In *The Fellowship of the Craft* (Port Washington: Kennikat Press, 1976),
     C. F. Burgess writes: 'Lingard's uncomplicated view of the great world
     beyond the confines of the brig *Lightning* is harmless enough. What is
     not so innocuous, however, what is, in fact, critical and ultimately
     fatal is Lingard's innocent belief in his own infallibility and invulner-
     ability' (p. 146). Lingard's belief in his own infallibility is, of course,
     supported by various imperialist myths, in particular by what Benita
     Parry calls 'that sado-masochistic political nexus celebrated in colo-
     nial legend as a natural bond between a master-race and peoples born
     to servitude' (p. 29).

18. Parry, however, again convincingly argues that Jörgenson can be read
     as 'the fiction's unacknowledged hero' (p. 50). From the Malay per-
     spective, he is 'one white man who remained to the end, who was
     faithful with his strength, with his courage, and with his wisdom'
     (p. 111). Parry less convincingly argues that 'The Rescuer' 'inverts the
     assumptions informing the "conquest/surrender" dichotomy' of or-
     thodox imperialist discourse: 'Because Jörgenson, who had "gone

native" retains an unwavering fidelity to his commitments, while Lingard who dominates his environment and asserts his authority as a white man is unfaithful to a trust, what is demonstrated is that "surrender" can imply and reinforce integrity' (p. 49).

19. We might also relate it to the world of 'The Return' in *Tales of Unrest*. Lingard, by contrast, is imaginatively responsive to people and events; and he, literally and metaphorically, inhabits a region that is off the beaten track.

20. At this point, two of Conrad's early concerns merge: the problems of the man of imagination, and a feeling of alienation from European society.

21. Compare Shaw's angry reaction to Carter: 'What do you think? Think I am a dummy here? I ain't mate of this brig for nothing' (p. 354). Shaw feels his position is undermined by his ignorance, and, as he unintentionally reveals, he fears that he will be exposed as 'a dummy'.

22. Travers's comments on the Malays, which Parry describes as the 'implacable cliches of colonialist propaganda' (p. 43), also have an obvious psychological implication: 'And if the inferior race must perish it is a gain, a step towards the perfecting of humanity which is the aim of progress. Our duty to these regions lies in the ruthless, merciless repression of natural instincts' (pp. 282–3).

23. The comparison of her gaze to the 'shallow sea' recalls the earlier association of Lingard's eyes with the 'narrow seas' (p. 45). The earlier passage, however, included the idea of 'glimmers of fire' and 'masterful depths'. The echo serves to ironise the concluding words ('stilled forever') and to re-inforce the expectation of a relationship between Lingard and Mrs Travers in which their suppressed passions will emerge.

24. Edward Said, *Orientalism* (New York: Vintage Books, 1979) p. 3.

25. For an account of 'The Rescuer' in terms of social class and the idea of the 'gentleman', see Jeremy Hawthorn, *Joseph Conrad: Narrative Technique and Ideological Commitment* (London: Edward Arnold, 1990) pp. 79–100.

26. Parry, p. 46. The 'modulated, gentle' sound of her voice is perhaps to be read as a sign of class.

27. In the same way, in Chapter 3, it is Mrs Travers's interpretation of one of his comments – 'they are to be saved' – that he takes as the guide as to what he should do about Travers and Linares.

28. Parry, p. 56.

29. Ibid., p. 57. There will not be space to consider *The Rescue* later in the context of Conrad's late fiction. Juliet McLauchlan, in 'A Reconsideration of *The Rescue*,' *The Ugo Mursia Memorial Lectures* (Milan: Mursia International, 1988) pp. 201–26, animadverts to the changes Conrad made to 'The Rescuer' and notes particularly the 'introduction of imagery associated with acting and the stage' (p. 216), which contributes to the literary self-consciousness of *The Rescue*.

30. Roussel asserts: 'The contradictory demands made on him flow from the same source in his character' (p. 70). Roussel then defines this source as 'his unconscious acceptance of responsibility for the lives of

those around him' (p. 69), and interprets Lingard's failure as 'the inadequacy of the world of the sea to accommodate any world more complex than the deck of a merchant ship' (p. 70). In this chapter I have suggested that 'The Rescuer' is not primarily concerned with the code of the sea, but uses Lingard's character to explore quite different issues.

31. Lingard understands the significance of this decision: 'If he woke her, nothing would remain of all these other gifts that had gone to the building of his life' (p. 527). Compare Roussel's assertion that: 'Lingard does not choose another course of action. His fall consists precisely in the fact that, robbed of his belief in the validity of things, he is unable to choose at all' (p. 62). Roussel interprets this journey as the experience of 'infinite and eternal darkness' (p. 61): 'The experience of the irrational, Lingard's passion for Mrs Travers . . . undercuts the ability of consciousness to will effectively by violently wrenching the will from the control of consciousness. . . . Mrs Travers's perception that all existence is "less palpable than a cloud" . . . attacks the will in precisely the opposite way. Instead of directing the will uncontrollably toward one object, it destroys the whole orientation of mind toward willing by undermining any sense of a reality toward which the mind can move' (p. 60).

32. *C.L.*, II, pp. 121–2. Compare the 'Author's Note' to *The Rescue*, where Conrad notes how he laid aside 'The Rescuer' 'at the end of the summer of 1898': 'Several reasons contributed to this abandonment and, no doubt, the first of them was the growing sense of general difficulty in the handling of the subject . . . I saw the action plainly enough. What I had lost for the moment was the sense of the proper formula of expression' (vii–viii).

Notes to Chapter 4: The Brotherhood of the Sea

1. Ford Madox Ford, *Joseph Conrad*, 67.
2. Frederick Marryat, *Peter Simple* (London: Saunders and Otley, 1834) 3 vols.
3. Vernon Young, 'Trial by Water', *Accent* (Spring 1952) pp. 80–1, suggests that 'Wait' also contains a symbolically significant play on 'weight'.
4. See the Preface, pp. viii and x.
5. Conrad to Henry S. Canby, 7 April 1924 (*L.L.*, II, p. 342). Compare this with Conrad's letter of 9 December 1897 to an unidentified reviewer: 'I also wanted to connect the small world of the ship with that larger world carrying perplexities, fears, affections, rebellions, in a loneliness greater than that of the ship at sea' (*C.L.*, I, pp. 420–1).
6. *The Nigger of the 'Narcissus'*, p. 25.
7. 'To my readers in America', *The Children of the Sea* (Garden City, N.Y.: Doubleday, Page, 1914).
8. For a detailed account of contradictions in *The Nigger of the 'Narcissus'*, see Jeremy Hawthorn, *Joseph Conrad: Narrative Technique and Ideological Commitment*, pp. 101–32.

9. Contrast Guerard's interpretation: 'In their hidden laziness the members of the crew sympathize with Wait's malingering' (*Conrad the Novelist*, p. 108).

10. Notice, however, that when one of the crew complains that the captain prefers to risk the lives of all his crew rather than cut the ship's masts, the chief mate replies: 'Why should [the captain] care for you? Are you a lot of women passengers to be taken care of? We are here to take care of the ship' (p. 79). Not only is the individual less important than the group, but all the members of the group can be sacrificed to a transcendant ideal (the ship or the nation). And this 'brotherhood of the sea' is not a democratic body, but a feudal, authoritarian, hierarchical society. The captain is 'the ruler of that minute world' (p. 31): he is both 'father' and 'God'. The duties of the crew are to obey: to serve and to sacrifice themselves, if necessary. (Notice also the gender roles implied by the chief mate's rebuke and how they are reproduced by Marlow in 'Heart of Darkness'.)

11. Guerard comments on the pattern of Wait's 'presences and absences': 'He is virtually forgotten (after the first dramatic appearance) while the men get to know each other and the voyage begins; he is something they are too busy to be concerned with. We return to him only when they have little work to do. . . . And he is literally forgotten (by crew as well as reader) during the worst of the storm. After he is rescued, he is again neglected for some thirty pages, and returns only with the sinister calm of a hot night and beshrouded ocean' (p. 111). Guerard suggests that this pattern contains 'the clue to any larger meanings', and notes, in particular, that the 'menace of Wait is greatest when men have time to meditate' (p. 111).

12. 'Heart of Darkness' is included in *Youth: A Narrative and Two Other Stories*. Conrad's 'Congo Diary' is included in *Last Essays* (London: J. M. Dent, 1926) pp. 231–53.

13. 'Geography and Some Explorers', *Last Essays*, p. 25.

14. Notice also that this passage describes the two main groups of Marlow's story: where the 'pilgrims' are *mutatis mutandis* 'hunters for gold', Kurtz is revealed to be a pursuer of fame.

15. See Hampson, 'Conrad and the Idea of Empire', *L'Epoque Conradienne* (Limoges, 1990) pp. 9–22, for a more detailed discussion of this issue.

16. It could also be argued that Marlow is driven by guilt relating to the lie he told the 'Intended' – indeed, that he is compelled to tell the true story of Kurtz, a narrative that breaks out of the conventions of imperialist adventure-romance, because he surrendered to that conventional pressure in the story he told the 'Intended'. See Peter Brook, *Reading for the Plot* (Oxford: Clarendon Press, 1984).

17. For a detailed account of 'Heart of Darkness' and its relation to the literary tradition of *katabasis*, see Cedric Watts, *Conrad's 'Heart of Darkness': A Critical and Contextual Discussion*, pp. 55–9; Lilian Feder discusses parallels with *Aeneid* VI in 'Marlow's Descent into Hell', *Nineteenth-Century Fiction*, IX (March 1955) pp. 290–2; Robert O. Evans discusses the parallels with Dante's *Inferno* in 'Conrad's Underworld', *Modern Fiction Studies*, II (May 1956) pp. 56–62; Peter Carraciolo includes a comprehensive listing of articles on Buddhist elements in

'Heart of Darkness' in 'Buddhist Teaching Stories and their Influence on Conrad, Wells and Kipling', *The Conradian*, XI.1 (May 1986) pp. 24–34. The 'long staves' (p. 76) of the European traders at the Central Station provides a visual parallel with the pilgrims of *The Pilgrim's Progress*: Hopeful and Christian are described as 'leaning upon their staves (as is common with weary pilgrims, when they stand to talk with any by the way)' (*The Pilgrim's Progress* [Harmondsworth: Penguin Books, 1965] p. 157).

18. Karl Marx, 'Future Results of British Rule in India', in Karl Marx and Frederick Engels, *Selected Works* (London: Laurence & Wishart, 1950) I, p. 323.

19. For a brief summary of the range of possible meanings see Watts, *Conrad's 'Heart of Darkness'*, p. 117.

20. Compare Conrad's statement in an 1894 letter to Marguerite Poradowska: 'One must drag the ball and chain of one's self-hood to the end. It is the [price] one pays for the devilish and divine privilege of thought; so that in this life it is only the elect who are convicts – a glorious band which comprehends and groans but which treads the earth amidst a multitude of phantoms with maniacal gestures, with idiotic grimaces. Which would you be: idiot or convict?' (*C.L.*, I, pp. 162–3).

21. Thus Guerard, for example, describes Marlow's pilgrimage as 'a journey towards and through certain facets or potentialities of self' (*Conrad the Novelist*, p. 38). Frances B. Singh, however, usefully draws attention to the contradiction between the political and psychological levels of the narrative: 'Historically Marlow would have us feel that the Africans are the innocent victims of the white man's heart of darkness; psychologically and metaphysically . . . Marlow equates the primitive with the evil and the physical blackness of Africans with a spiritual darkness' ('The Colonialistic Bias of "Heart of Darkness"', *Conradiana*, x [1978] pp. 41–54). See also Patrick Brantlinger, *Rule of Darkness: British Literature and Imperialism, 1830–1914* (Ithaca: Cornell University Press, 1988): 'Conrad portrays the moral bankruptcy of imperialism by showing European notions and actions as no better than African fetishism and savagery. . . . His version of evil – the form taken by Kurtz's Satanic behaviour – is going native. Evil in short *is* African' (p. 262).

22. Of all the groups in the novella, it is only the cannibal crew men who can meet 'the truth' of the jungle with their own 'true stuff', who exhibit real restraint even under the extreme pressure of hunger, and the basis of their restraint remains inexplicable: 'Was it superstition, disgust, patience, fear – or some kind of primitive honour? No fear can stand up to hunger, no patience can wear it out, disgust simply does not exist where hunger is; and as to superstition, beliefs, and what you may call principles, they are less than chaff in a breeze' (p. 105).

23. For further discussion of attitudes to work and language implicit in Marlow's response to this document, see Jeremy Hawthorn, *Joseph Conrad: Language and Fictional Self-Consciousness* (London: Edward

Arnold, 1979) pp. 9–10. *An Inquiry into Some Points of Seamanship* is set against Kurtz's 'report' (with its 'postscriptum').

24. He is also, of course, the Fool to Kurtz's Lear. See P. J. Glassman, *Language and Being*, p. 223; Adam Gillon, *Conrad and Shakespeare* (New York: Astra Books, 1976) p. 135.

25. Edgar Allan Poe, 'A Descent into the Maelstrom', *The Complete Tales and Poems of Edgar Allan Poe* (Harmondsworth: Penguin Books, 1982) pp. 127–40.

26. Marlow's attitude can be seen as conventional in this genre. It is comparable to Gulliver's response to humanity after his fourth voyage. It might also be compared with Edward Prendick's mood at the end of Wells's *The Island of Dr Moreau* (London: W. Heinemann, 1896): 'Though I do not expect that the terror of that island will ever altogether leave me, at most times it lies far in the back of my mind, a mere distant cloud, a memory and a faint distrust; but there are times when the little cloud spreads until it obscures the whole sky. Then I look about me at my fellow-men. And I go in fear. . . . I feel as though the animal was surging up through them. . . . When I lived in London the horror was wellnigh insupportable . . . I would go out into the streets to fight with my delusion, and prowling women would mew after me, furtive craving men glance jealously at me' (pp. 216–17). Wells's exploration of the human/animal boundary is also connected to an interest in food, eating and being eaten. See Peter Kemp, *H. G. Wells and the Culminating Ape* (London: Macmillan, 1982) pp. 7–72. Conrad's collocation of policemen and butchers re-appears in *The Secret Agent*.

27. 'It's queer how out of touch with the truth women are. They live in a world of their own, and there has never been anything like it, and never can be. . . . Some confounded fact we men have been living contentedly with ever since the day of creation would start up and knock the whole thing over' (p. 59).

28. The original idea for 'Heart of Darkness' was, in fact, written on the manuscript of 'Tuan Jim', the short story from which *Lord Jim* grew.

29. Letter to David S. Meldrum, 19 May 1900 (*C.L.*, II, p. 271).

30. Burgess, *The Fellowship of the Craft*, p. 96. This is a distinction that Roussel, for example, misses, when he writes of 'Jim's effort to validate the ideal of the brotherhood of the sea' (p. 21).

31. Wiley, *Conrad's Measure of Man*, p. 52.

32. Ibid., p. 51.

33. Some critics have picked up the similarities of the names *Patna* and Patusan, and have suggested that Patusan represents a second chance that is given to Jim, the chance that he had felt he had missed on board the *Patna*. See, for example, Guerard, *Conrad the Novelist*, p. 128.

34. Robert Secor, *The Rhetoric of Shifting Perspectives in Conrad's 'Victory'* (University Park, Pa.: Pennsylvania State University Press, 1971) p. 7.

35. For this view of the Brownlow–Maylie world, see Arnold Kettle, *Introduction to the English Novel* (London: Hutchinson, 1951) I, pp. 115–29.

36. See R. Hampson, '*Chance*: The Affair of the Purloined Brother', *The Conradian*, 6.2 (June 1981) pp. 5–15.

37. Chapter 3 indicates that it was during Jim's watch that the accident

occurred (p. 17), and that Jim was certainly inattentive if not actually dozing at the time of the accident: 'The line dividing his meditation from a surreptitious doze on his feet was thinner than a thread in a spider's web' (p. 25).

38. Jim's failure to live up to the code of conduct of the sea is emphasised by comparison with the Muslims on the *Patna*, who are described as 'pilgrims of an exacting belief'.

39. Watt, *Conrad in the Nineteenth Century*, p. 343. Watt draws attention to Marlow's observation that Jim 'made so much of his disgrace while it is the guilt alone that matters' (p. 177). Watt comments: 'it is usually agreed that shame is much more directly connected than guilt with the individual's failure to live up to his own ideal conception of himself. . . . Guilt anxiety accompanies transgression; shame, failure'; 'what really matters to Jim is his personal failure to live up to his ego-ideal' (p. 343).

40. Watt writes: 'There is something ominous about the words "only" and "name" here. . . . Brierly sees solidarity as something based not on any internal ethical foundation, but entirely as a response to the need to maintain public esteem for the group to which he belongs. His own self-esteem is grounded on equally external and insecure foundations' (*Conrad in the Nineteenth Century*, p. 278).

41. Martin Green, in *Dreams of Adventure: Deeds of Empire* (London: Routledge & Kegan Paul, 1980), discusses Conrad in the context of adventure-romance. For an adventure-romance hero of the type Jim physically resembles, consider, for example, Jack Martin in R. M. Ballantyne's *The Coral Island*: 'Jack Martin was a tall, strapping, broad-shouldered youth of eighteen, with a handsome, good-humoured, firm face. He had had a good education, was clever and hearty and lion-like in his actions, but mild and quiet in disposition' (p. 7). *The Coral Island* was first published by T. Nelson & Sons, London, 1858. All references are to the Everyman's Library edition (London: J. M. Dent & Co., 1907). J. S. Bratton, in *The Impact of Victorian Children's Fiction* (London: Croom Helm, 1981), refers to the mid-Victorian transformation of Arnold's attitude to boys as exemplified by Kingsley's *Westward Ho!* She writes: 'The new ideal is to be a lad like Amyas, who is tongue-tied and thoughtless but strong, brave, and simple in his faith in God, England and himself, and in his right to rule not only his social inferiors at home, but all the world abroad' (pp. 133–4). The passage she quotes from *Westward Ho!* provides an appropriate context for the romance world of Patusan: 'As he stands there with beating heart and kindling eye, the cool breeze whistling through his long fair curls, he is a symbol, though he knows it not, of brave young England longing to wing its way out of its island prison, to discover and to traffic, to colonise and civilise.' *Westward Ho!* was dedicated to Rajah Brooke. Gordan suggested Brooke was a source for Lord Jim, in *Joseph Conrad: The Making of a Novelist*, pp. 64–73. In *Conrad's Eastern World* (Cambridge: Cambridge University Press, 1966), Norman Sherry gave qualified support to this suggestion (p. 135).

42. Old Robinson's alleged piracy and cannibalism express, in extreme form, the implications of the amoral selfishness that Chester represents.

43. For example, Marlow's friend, Denver, takes the attitude: 'I guess there is something – some awful little scrape – which you know all about – but if I am sure that it is terribly heinous, I fancy one could manage to forgive it. . . . Perhaps you ought to have told me; but it is such a long time since we both turned saints that you may have forgotten that we, too, had sinned in our time?' (p. 188).

44. In *Joseph Conrad: The Major Phase*, Jacques Berthoud writes: 'I have argued that the first part of the novel has been concerned with establishing the truth revealed by conduct. This being so, the second part is concerned with exploring, under the sponsorship of the German merchant Stein, the truth inherent in vision' (p. 80). In *Conrad in the Nineteenth Century*, Watt observes 'how deeply representative Stein is of German romantic idealism': 'There is the twin enthusiasm for geographical exploration and scientific discovery . . . there is the fact that Stein . . . is also an exile from the 1848 revolution, and thus a representative of German political liberalism; and there are his poetic quotations, which make him the spokesman of German romantic literature' (p. 323). See also Leo Lensing, 'Goethe's *Torquato Tasso* in *Lord Jim*: A Note on Conrad's Use of Literary Quotation', *English Literature in Transition*, 19(1976) pp. 101–4.

45. Tony Tanner comments on this: 'Marlow speaks for the world of hard daylight, of solid matter: but Patusan is lit by the moon which rises above the harsh division of the material world and produces an insubstantial realm of shadows and dreams. And note this: the moon is to the sun what the confusing echo is to the sound. "Patusan" is, literally, the confusing echo of "Patna". Jim has moved out of the world of firm substance, bright light and clear sound . . . and into an unreal world where appearances are subservient to the dreaming imagination' (*Conrad: Lord Jim* [London: Edward Arnold, 1963] p. 45).

46. When Jim arrives in Patusan, he is imprisoned in the stockade but escapes by leaping over the stakes. As Tanner notes, Jim had felt 'imprisoned within an enclosure of high stakes' (p. 31) at his trial: 'The image has become real – and in this magic world Jim does manage to make a successful leap out of the stockade of facts' (p. 47). With this second 'jump', Jim apparently cancels the first. Notice, however, how Brown establishes a bond with Jim partly through the chance of hitting on this word: 'There are my men in the same boat – and, by God, I am not the sort to jump out of trouble and leave them in a d——d lurch' (pp. 382–3).

47. Berman notes that 'Jim has used the same word to characterize himself to Marlow' (p. 81): 'Of course I wouldn't have talked to you about all this if you had not been a gentleman . . . I am – I am – a gentleman, too' (*Lord Jim*, p. 131).

48. As Tanner has suggested, Brown can be seen as playing Iago to Jim's Othello (p. 53).

49. As Dorothy van Ghent has pointed out, this act of self-sacrifice cannot truly be seen as an atonement for Jim's crime on board the *Patna*: Jim has never consciously acknowledged his guilt for that crime, and you cannot expiate a crime for which you deny your responsibility ('On *Lord Jim*', *Twentieth-Century Interpretations* [Englewood Cliffs: Prentice-Hall, Inc., 1969] p. 70).

Notes to Chapter 5: The Betrayal of Land-entanglements

1. In effect, Conrad had explored the ideal code psychologically and exposed some of its limitations. Compare Roussel: 'Just as Kurtz symbolized to Marlow his own commitment to the ideal . . . Jim is most obviously a test case for Marlow's allegiance to the group' (p. 80).
2. See 'Introduction', p. 6. As Raval points out, *Nostromo* is the first of Conrad's political novels 'overtly to dramatize the unavoidably political nature of human life' (*The Art of Failure*, p. 73).
3. Conrad to Henry S. Canby, 7 April 1924 (*L.L.*, II, p. 342).
4. *Nostromo*, pp. 84, 116, etc.; also 'Autocracy and War', *Notes on Life and Letters*, pp. 107, 113. As Frederic Jameson observes: 'the sea is both a strategy of containment and a place of real business' (*The Political Unconscious*, p. 210).
5. *Lord Jim*, p. 4.
6. For a brief account of some of these contrasts and affinities in relation to the major characters, see F. R. Leavis, *The Great Tradition* (Harmondsworth: Penguin Books, 1962) pp. 210–21.
7. Arnold Kettle, *An Introduction to the English Novel* (London: Hutchinson, 1951) II, p. 66.
8. Conrad to Ernst Bendz, 7 March 1923 (*L.L.*, II, p. 296).
9. Irving Howe, *Politics and the Novel* (New York: Horizon Press, 1957) p. 108.
10. Compare Conrad's description of his intention in *The Nigger of the 'Narcissus'*: 'I tried to get through the veil of details at the essence of life' (Conrad to Helen Watson, 27 January 1897 [*C.L.*, I, p. 334]). For semic and symbolic codes, see Roland Barthes, *S/Z* (Paris: Seuil, 1970).
11. *Nostromo* uses parallels and contrasts to produce effects similar to those produced by irony in *The Secret Agent*. In particular, through these parallels and contrasts, all positions are questioned, undermined, undercut. For example, as Irving Howe has pointed out, Gould shows the flaw of idealism while Decoud shows the shortcomings of cynicism (see *Politics and the Novel*, p. 112). The multiperspectival narrative of *Nostromo* looks forward, in different ways, to *Chance*, *Victory* and *The Arrow of Gold*.
12. 'Nostromo' is the Italian for 'bosun' (which was Gian-Battista's position when he arrived in Sulaco). As Cedric Watts suggests, in *A Preface to Conrad* (London: Longman, 1982), Captain Mitchell's mispronunciation presumably relates to the phrase rather than to the noun (p. 178).

13. Conrad's presentation of economic and political processes bears comparison with Lenin's *Imperialism: The Highest Stage of Capitalism* (Petrograd, 1917; Moscow: Foreign Languages Publishing House, 1947). The immediate context was America's 1898 war against Spain, as a result of which America acquired Guam, Cuba and the Philippines. The war was closely followed by Conrad: see his letters to Cunninghame-Graham of 1 May and 30 July 1898. America's role in the 1903 secession of Panama from Colombia provoked Conrad's critical comments about 'Yankee Conquistadores': see his letter to Cunninghame-Graham, 26 December 1903, and Cedric Watts, 'A Note on the Background to "Nostromo"', *Joseph Conrad's Letters to Cunninghame-Graham* (Cambridge: Cambridge University Press, 1969) pp. 37–42.

14. As Howe remarks, Captain Mitchell, 'the epitome of endurance and faithfulness', appears ridiculous in the complex world of Costaguana in a way that Captain MacWhirr, for example, never does in the crises of sea-life (*Politics and the Novel*, p. 110).

15. Ibid., p. 111.

16. According to the 'Author's Note', Nostromo was derived from Dominic Cervoni: 'Dominic, the *padrone* of the *Tremolino*, might under given circumstances have been a Nostromo' (p. xx). Conrad writes about Dominic Cervoni and the 'Tremolino' in *The Mirror of the Sea* and *The Arrow of Gold*. In *Nostromo*, the 'brotherhood of the sea' appears in the diminished and parodic form of the 'swaggering fraternity of Cargadores' (p. 127): 'The Cargadores of the port formed, indeed, an unruly brotherhood of all sorts of scum' (p. 95).

17. Similarly, he tells Decoud: 'I am going to make it the most famous and desperate affair of my life. . . . It shall be talked about when the little children are grown up and the grown men are old' (p. 265).

18. Howe, p. 108.

19. Both, however, can be seen as rationalisations growing out of his sense of betrayal.

20. Jameson observes: 'these two great lines of the book's character-groupings, that which descends from the mine owner Charles Gould and that which descends from the Italian immigrant and Garabaldino Viola, sort themselves out into an immediately identifiable opposition: they correspond to the two great forces of nineteenth-century history – industrial capitalism, expanding into its imperialist stage, and "popular" (that is, in the strictest sense, neither peasant nor proletarian) revolution of the classic 1848 type' (*The Political Unconscious*, p. 273). Jameson, however, oversimplifies the picture, since Mrs Gould's aunt was married to a follower of Garibaldi (p. 60), and that example of 'a sacrifice offered to a noble ideal' (p. 75) influences Mrs Gould's own idealism.

21. *The Art of Failure*, pp. 74–9. Gould attempts to ignore an aspect of reality that is represented in *Nostromo* but suppressed in *Lord Jim*. (See *The Political Unconscious*, pp. 206–80.)

22. Conrad's presentation of Gould clearly depicts the socialisation of

production. Compare Lenin, *Imperialism*: 'In spite of themselves the capitalists are dragged, as it were, into a new social order, a transitional social order from complete free competition to a complete socialisation' (p. 32).

23. See Berthoud, pp. 105–6; Hawthorn, *Joseph Conrad: Narrative Technique and Ideological Commitment*, pp. 205–12.

24. For ideal/idol, see Patrick Brantlinger, *Rule of Darkness: British Literature and Imperialism, 1830–1914*, p. 262 ('Conrad universalises "darkness" in part by universalising fetishism'); for Gould's alignment of capitalism and morality, see Raval, pp. 92–4.

25. Ernst Fischer, *Marx in his own Words*, trans. Anna Bostock (Harmondsworth: Pelican Books, 1973) pp. 50–1.

26. See Marx, *Capital* (London: Lawrence & Wishart, 1977) I, pp. 88–9: 'It is plain that commodities cannot go to market and make exchanges of their own account. We must, therefore, have recourse to their guardians, who are also their owners. . . . In order that these objects may enter into relation with each other as commodities, their guardians must place themselves in relation to one another, as persons whose will resides in those objects. . . . The persons exist for one another merely as representatives of, and, therefore, as owners of commodities . . . the characters who appear on the economic stage are but the personifications of the economic relations that exist between them'.

27. Howe, p. 109.

28. Compare Conrad's statement, in 'Autocracy and War': 'A swift disenchantment overtook the incredible infatuation which could put its trust in the peaceful nature of industrial and commercial competition. . . . The true peace of the world . . . will be built on less perishable foundations than those of material interests' (*Notes on Life and Letters*, pp. 106–7).

29. Berthoud, p. 100.

30. J. Hillis Miller, *Poets of Reality: Six Twentieth-Century Writers* (London: Oxford University Press, 1966) p. 39. Guerard called *The Secret Agent* 'the very darkest of Conrad's books' (p. 219).

31. Hillis Miller, p. 46; Jameson, pp. 240–2.

32. See, for example, Hillis Miller, pp. 39–41.

33. Hillis Miller, p. 45. Ossipon, for example, expresses 'virtuous indignation' at the explosion: 'for the even tenor of his revolutionary life was menaced by no fault of his' (p. 78). Inspector Heat's response to the explosion is similar to Ossipon's: 'The complexion of that case had somehow forced upon him the general idea of the absurdity of things human' (p. 91).

34. Guerard, *Conrad the Novelist*, p. 230. For detailed discussion of Conrad's use of irony, narrative perspective, analepsis and prolepsis in this scene, see F. R. Leavis, *The Great Tradition*, pp. 236–7, and, more particularly, Jakob Lothe, *Conrad's Narrative Method*, pp. 244–8.

35. Hillis Miller, p. 46.

36. Ossipon presents himself as a disciple of Lombroso (pp. 46–7). See Hampson, ' "If you read Lombroso": Conrad and Criminal Anthropology', *The Ugo Mursia Memorial Lectures*, pp. 317–35. See also Robert

G. Jacobs, 'Comrade Ossipon's Favorite Saint: Lombroso and Conrad', *Nineteenth-Century Fiction*, 23 (June 1968) pp. 74–84; J. E. Saveson, 'Conrad, *Blackwoods*' and Lombroso', *Conradiana*, 6 (1974) pp. 57–62; Norman Sherry, *Conrad's Western World* (Cambridge: Cambridge University Press, 1971) pp. 275–6; Allan Hunter, *Joseph Conrad and the Ethics of Darwinism* (London: Croom Helm, 1983) pp. 153–219.

37.   Hunter, p. 188.

38.   C. Lombroso, 'Criminal Anthropology', in *Twentieth-Century Practice: An International Encyclopaedia of Modern Medical Science* (London, 1897) XII, p. 402.

39.   For further discussion of this passage and of Conrad's views of 'idleness', see Hawthorn, *Joseph Conrad: Narrative Technique and Ideological Commitment*, pp. 71–9. Hawthorn notes: 'There is a clear identification of the embassy spy and the idle rich, a relationship which is structural, ideological and temperamental' (p. 75). See also Michel Foucault, *Madness and Civilisation* (1961; Random House, 1977), which introduces an account of idleness and labour with Voltaire's question: 'Have you not yet discovered the secret of forcing all the rich to make all the poor work? Are you still ignorant of the first principles of the police?' (p. 46).

40.   Hillis Miller, pp. 39–41.

41.   Hawthorn, *Joseph Conrad: Language and Fictional Self-Consciousness*, p. 82. Compare Lombroso's views as expressed in his essay 'L'Anarchie et ses héros', *Revue des Revues* (15 February 1894). After stating that 'toutes les institutions sociales et gouvernementales sont, d'après la conception puissante de Max Nordau, un énorme mensonge, un mensonge conventionnel', Lombroso asserts 'Ceci ne justifie point l'anarchie, mais on comprend comment elle a pu naître de la protestation d'une âme sincère contre le mensonge ambiant, contre l'injustice régnant en souveraine et faulant aux pieds le mérite.'

42.   Sherry, *Conrad's Western World*, pp. 228–47, 379–94.

43.   Leavis, *The Great Tradition*, p. 231.

44.   Richard Curle, *Joseph Conrad: A Study* (London: Kegan Paul, Trench, Trübner, 1914) p. 96.

45.   F. Engels, *The Condition of the Working Class in England* [1845] (Moscow: Progress Publishers, 1973) p. 64. Compare Carlyle's picture of London as 'a huge aggregate of little systems, each of which is again a small anarchy, the members of which do not *work* together, but *scramble* against each other' (journal of 1831; quoted in Raymond Williams, *The Country and the City* [London: The Hogarth Press, 1985] p. 215).

Notes to Chapter 6: Independence and Community

1.   See 'Autocracy and War', *N.L.L.*, pp. 93–101, and compare Lombroso's view of anarchists (Chapter 5, footnote 37).

2.   Berthoud, p. 172.

3.   *N.L.L.*, p. 85.

4. Guerard, *Conrad the Novelist*, p. 231; Raval, p. 73.

5. Michael Holquist, *Dostoevsky and the Novel* (Princeton, N.J.: Princeton University Press, 1977) pp. 96, 75.

6. Holquist, p. 88.

7. Holquist, p. 88. As the 'detective of his old self's motive', he 'isolates three different motives, each of which becomes the iconic attribute of a self who is presented as a suspect, only to be cleared, in favor of one of the other motive-defined selves' (p. 89).

8. Fleishman discusses *Under Western Eyes* as a confrontation between Russian organicist theories and Conrad's own organicist ideology: 'At the root of all forms of Russian thought, as exemplified in these speeches – the czarist general's autocracy, the mystical student's populism, the revolutionary's nihilism – lies a conception of society as an organism, a real unity of its members, which has not only a histori-cal tradition but a divinely shaped destiny, a spiritual law determin-ing its course. . . . It is the religious absolutism that lies behind much Russian nationalism (Dostoevsky's, for example) that Conrad con-demns as obscurantist' (*Conrad's Politics*, p. 224). Conrad, however, had lost faith in organicism before he wrote *Under Western Eyes*, and this novel arrives at a more complex view of the collective and com-munal nature of human life. For other considerations of Conrad's ideological confrontation with Dostoevsky, see Carola Kaplan, 'Conrad's Attempted Occupation of Russia in *Under Western Eyes*'; Daphna Erdinast-Vulcan, 'Dostoevsky, Bakhtin and Conrad'; Keith Carabine, 'Conrad, Korzeniowski, Dostoievski', *The Joseph Conrad So-ciety Sixteenth Annual International Conference*, University of Kent, Can-terbury, 1990.

9. Guerard, *Conrad the Novelist*, p. 233.

10. As Berthoud points out, Razumov is under no 'external pressure to betray him to the authorities': the decision 'is wholly his own' (p. 177). Haldin is quite ready to remove himself as soon as he senses Razumov's disapproval of his act; and General T—— makes it clear that, if Razumov had not betrayed him, Haldin 'would have disappeared like a stone in the water'.

11. See Robert B. Heilman, 'Charlotte Brontë's "New" Gothic', in Robert C. Rathburn and Martin Steinmann, Jr. (eds), *From Jane Austen to Joseph Conrad* (Minneapolis: University of Minnesota Press, 1958) pp. 118–32.

12. Jeremy Hawthorn, 'Introduction', *Under Western Eyes* (Oxford: Oxford University Press, 1983) p. vii.

13. Guerard, p. 234.

14. Ibid., p. 235.

15. Ibid., p. 236.

16. Ibid., p. 235.

17. The parallel with Raskolnikov is obvious: Sonia's 'feminine compas-sion' plays an important part both in bringing him to confess and in guiding him towards his new conception of himself. Peter Ivanovitch's account of himself, weeping with joy 'in the manner of a converted sinner' (p. 124) also echoes the final stage of Raskolnikov's develop-

ment. Just as *The Secret Agent* satirised anarchists while incorporating certain of its anarchists' ideas, *Under Western Eyes* satirises Peter Ivanovitch's feminist idealism while inscribing a similar view of women.

18. Sophia Antonovna plays the role that Porfiry plays in relation to Raskolnikov: she is even described, at one point, as frowning 'in the manner of an investigator' (p. 246). In addition, where Razumov had earlier been described as 'Mephistophelian' (p. 60) or 'satanic' (p. 228) in relation to Haldin and Peter Ivanovitch – the adjective acknowledging his superior position – it is now Sophia Antonovna who is experienced as 'Mephistophelian' (p. 247) by Razumov.

19. See Chapter 2 for a fuller discussion of this inner experience. Razumov has tried to escape from 'the toils of a false position' (p. 307) by taking on an identity which he knows to be false, but this strategy has not solved the problem. He cannot shake off the sense of unreality which the false-self system casts over all his experiences: 'The futility of all this overcame him like a curse' (p. 316).

20. As Hawthorn points out, there is a further irony in this setting: 'the ironical juxtaposition of Razumov, writing his secret report to Mikulin, and the statue of Rousseau, author of *The Social Contract*', which expresses the 'tension between self-interest and collectivity' ('Introduction', pp. ix–x).

21. Raskolnikov, too, falls into a fever after his murder of Alyona and Lizaveta: 'He was not completely unconscious, however, all the time he was ill; he was in a feverish state, sometimes delirious, sometimes half-conscious' (Fyodor Dostoevsky, *Crime and Punishment*, trans. Constance Garnett [London: William Heinemann, 1914] p. 109).

22. In *Self and Others*, Laing notes that in 'typical paranoid ideas of reference', the person 'feels that the murmurings and mutterings he hears as he walks past a street crowd are about him' (p. 136). In *The Divided Self*, Laing discusses the case of 'Peter', and describes one of the strategies 'Peter' used to try to escape from 'ideas of reference': 'The phantasy he put into action of being anonymous, or incognito, or a stranger in a strange land, is a common one in people with ideas of reference. . . . They are often found to move from job to job, or from place to place. This defence works for a short while, but can last only as long as they are anonymous; it is very difficult not to be 'discovered': and they are liable to become as suspicious and cautious as any spy in enemy territory that others are trying to "catch them out" into "giving themselves away" ' (p. 128). This suggests a curious link between *Lord Jim* and *Under Western Eyes* in terms of 'ideas of reference'.

23. See Hawthorn's chapter, '*Under Western Eyes* and the Expressive Body', *Joseph Conrad: Narrative Technique and Ideological Commitment*, pp. 236–59. Hawthorn observes how Razumov's 'inner conflict' is signalled by his bodily movements; how his confession to Nathalie Haldin involves a silent pointing to his own body; and how, subsequently, he achieves the control of his bodily movements that had eluded him 'during the period of his duplicity' (p. 254).

24. Guerard, p. 231.
25. Hawthorn, 'Introduction', p. xii.
26. Guerard, p. 243.
27. Gekoski, p. 159.
28. According to the date on the typescript, *Under Western Eyes* was completed on 22 January 1910. 'The Secret Sharer' is based on an incident which took place in 1880 on board the *Cutty Sark* (see Basil Lubbock, *The Log of the 'Cutty Sark'* [Glasgow: J. Brown and Son, 1924]). Conrad combined this with memories of his own experiences on board his first command, the *Otago*.
29. *'Twixt Land and Sea Tales*, p. 93.
30. Guerard, p. 22. Hewitt, similarly, notes that Leggatt is 'only able to come on board because of the state of mind of the captain' (p. 71).
31. At the same time, as Hewitt notes, the narrator also tells us that Leggatt 'was not a bit like me really' (p. 105). The doubt that this statement creates produces the kind of hesitation that is characteristic of the narrative-technique of Gothic fiction. 'The Secret Sharer' might usefully be compared, in this respect, with James Hogg's *The Confessions of a Justified Sinner*. Todorov has suggested that it is precisely this hesitation that characterises the fantastic as a genre. See Tzvetan Todorov, *Introduction à la littérature fantastique* (Paris: Editions du Seuil, 1970).
32. Hewitt, p. 73.
33. Guerard, p. 23.
34. Ibid., p. 24.
35. For a discussion of self-consciousness in relation to the ontologically insecure person, see *The Divided Self*, pp. 106–19. In 'Closing, Enclosure and Passage in "The Secret Sharer"', James Hansford offers a reading of the captain's duality, which traces a passage from the captain's '*conscious* alertness' which earlier separated him from his ship, his command and from himself' to 'the internalisation of division' expressed in the oxymoronic phrase 'unconscious alertness' (*The Conradian*, 15.1 [June 1990] p. 38).
36. Guerard, p. 22.
37. Ibid., p. 25. Josiane Paccaud's Lacanian reading of the story does not encounter this problem: 'The fundamental split has to be achieved within the captain, which requires that the fantasies evoked by Leggatt's presence be repressed into the unconscious' ('Under The Other's Eyes: Conrad's "The Secret Sharer" ', *The Conradian*, 12.1 [May 1987] p. 59).
38. Guerard, p. 23.
39. For 'obscure tenacity', consider 'Heart of Darkness'; for 'immaculate command', consider *Lord Jim*; for 'pitiless obligation', consider *The Nigger of the 'Narcissus'*.
40. Guerard, p. 24.
41. It is, perhaps, significant that the captain of the *Cutty Sark* (on whom the narrator was partly based) committed suicide, four days after letting Leggatt's prototype go free, by stepping over the side of his ship.

42. Hewitt, p. 77. Hewitt regards 'The Secret Sharer' as the pivotal work in his argument for Conrad's late-novel 'decline'. He argues that the narrator splits off a part of himself in order to perform his role as captain, and that, in the same way, Conrad suppresses a part of himself, the questioning and doubting part of himself, in his later novels. Despite her very different approach, Paccaud makes the same assumption about Conrad's identification with his narrator and about his subsequent decline as a novelist: 'But the cost to be paid for the mastery of the imaginary fantasies aroused by Leggatt . . . is dear in terms of artistry since it led to a generally acknowledged impoverishment of the imaginative vein upon which Conrad drew' (p. 67).

Notes to Chapter 7: The Wisdom of the Heart

1. In Wiley's words, 'neglected though it is, [love] stands forth as the single value transcending the egotism of a materialistic world' (p. 99).
2. *C.L.*, III, p. 194. See R. W. Smith, 'Dates of Composition of Conrad's Works', *Conradiana*, XI: 1 (1979) p. 77, for a detailed account of the chronology of composition.
3. Quoted by Smith, p. 77.
4. *L.L.*, II, pp. 145–6.
5. Powell's reminiscences, in both matter and manner, recall Conrad's own memoirs, *The Mirror of the Sea* and *A Personal Record*, whose writing was contemporaneous with the writing of *Chance*. According to Smith, Conrad started *The Mirror of the Sea* in February 1904, and he started *A Personal Record* in September 1908 (p. 210). See also Thomas Moser, 'Conrad, Ford and the Sources of *Chance*', *Conradiana*, VII:3 (1975) pp. 207–25.
6. Mégroz, *Joseph Conrad's Mind and Method*, pp. 220–1. Conrad makes clear, in his 'Author's Note', the centrality of Flora: 'it is Flora de Barral who is really responsible for this novel which relates, in fact, the story of her life' (p. vii).
7. See, in particular, the fine article by Frances Wentworth Cutler, 'Why Marlow?', *The Sewanee Review*, 26 (1918) pp. 28–38; and C. E. Montague, *The Manchester Guardian* (15 January 1914), reprinted in Norman Sherry (ed.), *Conrad: The Critical Heritage* (London: Routledge & Kegan Paul, 1973) pp. 273–6.
8. Henry James, 'The New Novel', *The Times Literary Supplement*, 635 (10 March 1914) pp. 133–4; 637 (2 April 1914) pp. 157–8. These articles were revised and expanded for reprinting in *Notes on Novelists* (London: J. M. Dent & Sons, 1914) pp. 249–87.
9. See Hampson, '*Chance*: The Affair of the Purloined Brother', *The Conradian*, 6:2 (June 1981) pp. 5–15. (For a discussion of the use of the 'police-tale', see also the 'Epilogue' to R. L. Stevenson's *The Wrecker*.)
10. Guerard, p. 270.
11. Graham Hough, '*Chance* and Joseph Conrad', *Image and Experience: Studies in a Literary Revolution* (London: Duckworth, 1960) p. 212.

12. Moser, p. 164.
13. As Todorov suggests, the detective-story has an inbuilt tendency to-
     wards literary self-consciousness: 'This novel contains not one but
     two stories: the story of the crime and the story of the investigation.
     . . . The first story, that of the crime, ends before the second begins.
     . . . The characters of this second story, the story of the investigation,
     do not act, they learn. . . . This second story, the story of the investiga-
     tion, thereby enjoys a particular status. It is no accident that it is often
     told by a friend of the detective, who explicitly acknowledges that he
     is writing a book; the second story consists, in fact, in explaining how
     this very book came to be written' (T. Todorov, 'The Typology of
     Detective Fiction', *The Poetics of Prose*, trans. Richard Howard [Oxford:
     Basil Blackwell, 1977] pp. 44–5).
14. Moser, p. 39.
15. Hough, p. 217.
16. Palmer, p. xv.
17. See, for example, Hewitt, pp. 98–102; Moser, p. 165; D. R. Schwarz,
     Conrad: The Later Fiction (London: Macmillan, 1982) pp. 42–3; Meyer,
     Joseph Conrad: A Psychoanalytic Biography, pp. 235–6.
18. The change in Marlow's character raises the question: are we right to
     talk of 'Marlow' as if there were a single, consistent character, or
     should we rather think of four separate Marlows?
19. Berman observes: 'In the interval between *Heart of Darkness* and *Chance*
     Marlow has aged; and for reasons which Conrad refuses to divulge,
     apparently acquired an invulnerability that eluded him in his youth'
     (p. 150).
20. William York Tindall, 'Apology for Marlow', in *From Jane Austen to
     Joseph Conrad*, p. 278.
21. Moser, for example, sees Conrad's 'almost irrepressible misogyny' as
     contributing to the artistic failure of 'crucial scenes' (p. 159). Meyer
     gives this assumption of misogyny the authority of science: 'with few
     exceptions the earlier Conrad kept his misogyny within the bounds of
     artistic taste, exercising sufficient control over his dormant prejudices
     to prevent their dominating his material. Following his breakdown he
     appears to have lost that control, and what had been a random or
     minor nuisance became a virtual rallying banner' (p. 239n).
22. See pp. 63, 80, 94, 117, 212, 281, 327.
23. Gary Geddes, *Conrad's Later Novels* (Montreal: McGill, Queen's Uni-
     versity Press, 1980) p. 22.
24. Consider, for example, Hewitt's criticism of Marlow in *Lord Jim*: 'The
     effect of muddlement which is so commonly found in *Lord Jim* comes,
     in short, from this – that Marlow is himself muddled. We look to him
     for a definite comment . . . on Jim's conduct' (p. 37).
25. Moser, p. 49.
26. Cutler, p. 38.
27. For a brilliant account of the novel's construction of layers of percep-
     tiveness/imperceptiveness and its implication of the male reader in
     its dialectic of male understanding/ignorance of women, see Andrew
     Roberts, 'Secret Agents and Secret Objects', *The Joseph Conrad Society
     (U.K.) Sixteenth Annual International Conference*, Canterbury, 1990.

28. Moser, p. 107.
29. As Moser says: 'Her reaction to the governess's cruelty is as determining to her career as Jim's jump is to his' (p. 136).
30. Geddes, p. 14.
31. Marlow chides Fyne later with the words: 'The liability to get penal servitude is so far like genius that it isn't hereditary' (p. 188). Later still he suspects that Mrs Fyne has made such a fuss about the elopement in order to alienate the couple and thus remove 'this embarrassing connexion' (p. 194) from her life.
32. Kirschner, p. 146. Moser also suggests that the 'first half of *Chance* is, in some ways, a feminine version of *Lord Jim*' (p. 136).
33. Geddes, p. 15.
34. For a discussion of the double bind, see Laing, *Self and Others*, pp. 144–8. For an analysis of the letter Raskolnikov receives from his mother, see *Self and Others*, pp. 165–73.
35. Kirschner, p. 146.
36. Ibid., pp. 149–50.
37. Henry James, *The Spoils of Poynton* (London: W. Heinemann, 1897). Conrad had received a copy of this novel from James in return for the copy of *An Outcast of the Islands* which Conrad had sent him. See Conrad's letters to Edward Garnett of 27 October 1896 and 13 February 1897 (*C.L.*, I, pp. 311–12 and 339–40).
38. Guerard, *Joseph Conrad*, p. 24; Moser, p. 108.
39. Kirschner, p. 153.
40. Hough, p. 220.
41. Schwarz, *Conrad: The Later Fiction*, p. 47. Cf. Geddes: 'When de Barral is released from prison, he remains the prisoner of his own blindness and obsession' (p. 18). If Flora and her father resembled the Dombeys earlier, they now resemble the Dorrits.
42. Schwarz, pp. 46, 48.
43. Kirschner, p. 154.
44. Geddes, p. 31.
45. Hewitt, p. 89.
46. Kirschner, p. 151.
47. Ibid., p. 150. It is worth noting that Anthony's response to his initial disappointment in this relationship is the same as Flora's: 'I ought to have known that you could not care for a man like me' (p. 337). As Wiley observes, 'Anthony's passion for Flora grows out of complicated roots in morbidity, violence, and profound sympathy' (p. 146).
48. Cf. Marlow's comment on Flora, after his first meeting with her: 'She looked unhappy. And – I don't know how to say it – well – it suited her. The clouded brow, the pained mouth, the vague fixed glance. A victim. And this characteristic aspect made her attractive' (pp. 45–6).
49. Leavis, p. 244.
50. See E. E. Duncan-Jones, 'Some Sources of *Chance*', *Review of English Studies* 20, (1969) pp. 468–71; and Thomas Moser, 'Conrad, Ford and the Sources of *Chance*', *Conradiana*, VII:3 (1975) pp. 207–25.
51. Kirschner, p. 144.
52. Ibid., p. 144.
53. Ibid., pp. 147–8.

54.   Henry James, *The Bostonians*, 3 vols (London: Macmillan, 1885); Kirschner, p. 144

55.   Kirschner, p. 145

56.   See K. West, *Chapter of Governesses: A Study of the Governess in English Fiction, 1800–1949* (London: Cohen & West, 1949).

57.   *The Bostonians*, I, p. 215.

58.   In *Socialism and the New Life* (London: Pluto Press, 1977), Sheila Rowbotham and Jeffrey Weeks argue that 'The feminism of the 1900s was much wider than the vote and brought up again all kinds of questions about the relations between the sexes' (p. 19). D. H. Lawrence provides evidence in support of this statement. He wrote to Edward Garnett (18 April 1913): 'After all, it is *the* problem today, the establishment of a new relation, or the readjustment of the old one, between men and women' (Harry T. Moore [ed.], *Collected Letters of D. H. Lawrence*, 2 vols [London: Heinemann, 1962] I, p. 200).

59.   See F. R. Karl, '*Victory*: Its Origin and Development', *Conradiana*, xv:1 (1983) p. 23; and R. G. Hampson, 'Introduction' and 'Note on the Text', *Victory* (Harmondsworth: Penguin Books, 1989) pp. 9–32, 37–42.

60.   Geddes, p. 42.

61.   'It is clear that, at the very least, Conrad wishes the reader, as the recipient of all these strange perceptions and impressions which have accumulated in the mind of the narrator, to hesitate before trying to pin down the central character of his novel' (Henry J. Laskowsky, '*Esse est percipi*: Epistemology and Narrative Method in *Victory*', *Conradiana*, IX:3 (1977) p. 276. See also Secor, *The Rhetoric of Shifting Perspectives: Conrad's 'Victory'*.

62.   Laskowsky, pp. 276–7. 'Lena', 'Alma', Magdalen' might similarly be seen as allotropic forms of the same element.

63.   D. B. J. Randall (ed.), *Joseph Conrad and Warrington Dawson* (Durham, N.C.: Duke University Press, 1968) p. 159.

64.   Leavis, pp. 224–5.

65.   Gurko, *Giant in Exile*, p. 214.

66.   Dike offers a different reading of Heyst's relationship with Lena: 'Lena does not understand Heyst's attentions: that he is drawn not to her but to her plight. Though unexpectedly he is stirred by her physical presence, his conscious motive is to redress a social wrong' (Donald Dike, 'The Tempest of Axel Heyst', *Nineteenth-Century Fiction*, 17 [September 1962] p. 109). Dike has not attended closely enough to the conflict between Heyst's conscious view of himself and his unconscious processes, that is foregrounded in Part Two, and he accordingly fails to register the significance of Heyst's response to Lena as a stage in that conflict.

67.   Schwarz, p. 70.

68.   Schomberg's behaviour to his wife recalls that of Willems in *An Outcast of the Islands*. The picture of Mrs Schomberg shows Conrad's deepened awareness of the position of women. It is not just the terrible sense of her silent suffering, that passes unnoticed, as she sits at her post in the hotel 'concealing her tortures of abject humiliation and terror under her stupid, set, everlasting grin' (p. 95), but it is also the

equally terrible implication of her interventions in the novel's plot. Mrs Schomberg acts to protect her husband and to maintain this life of suffering, because the alternative is even worse: 'his swollen, angry features awakened in the miserable woman over whom he had been tryannizing for years a fear for his precious carcass, since the poor creature had nothing else but that to hold on to in the world' (p. 106). Mrs Schomberg is trapped by her position as a woman as surely as Flora was.

69. For example, Schomberg's 'manly exterior' (p. 104), his 'manly, care- less attitudes' (p. 106), and the 'deep manliness' (p. 108) of his voice. Note also Karl's remarks on changes from the manuscript to the book: 'In the revision, Conrad altered Heyst's phantom-like quality and stressed to a greater degree his muscular embodiment' (*'Victory*: Its Origin and Development', *Conradiana*, xv:1 [1983] p. 38).

70. See Jeffrey Meyers, *Homosexuality and Literature, 1890–1930*, for discus- sion of 'the homosexual element in Heyst' (p. 87).

71. Cf. his reaction to the news of how others see him: 'So that's how the business looked from outside! . . . Strange that it should hurt me . . . yet it does' (p. 208).

72. Hodges, *The Dual Heritage of Joseph Conrad*, pp. 53–8.

73. Ibid., p. 55.

74. Ibid., p. 57.

75. Leavis, p. 227.

76. *D.S.*, pp. 65–73, 78–93. Laing notes that this detachment of the self means that 'the self is never revealed directly in the individual's expressions and actions' (p. 80).

77. *D.S.*, p. 80.

78. *D.S.*, p. 84.

79. *D.S.*, p. 82.

80. The oxymoronic phrase 'triumphant and humble' registers precisely the transfiguration she desires and the low self-evaluation from which the project springs.

81. *D.S.*, p. 85.

82. Hodges, pp. 58–9.

83. Karl, p. 33.

84. Ibid., p. 35.

85. For a more detailed account of Conrad's use of 'allegoric and mythic modes' in *Victory*, see my 'Introduction' to the Penguin edition, pp. 14–19.

86. Bonney has commented on 'the solipsistic epistemology operant throughout *Victory*' (p. 185), and Secor shows how this 'solipsistic epistemology' operates through the novel's foregrounding of percep- tion and cognition by its shifts in narrative perspective.

87. Secor, p. 37.

88. Ibid., p. 45.

89. See Hampson, 'Joyce's Bed-trick: A Note on Indeterminacy in *Ulysses*', *James Joyce Quarterly*, Summer 1980, pp. 445–8.

90. Geddes, p. 69.

91. Written 4 May 1918 to Barrett H. Clark (*L.L.*, II, pp. 204–5).

Notes to Chapter 8: Initiation and Invention

1. The continuing influence of this view is evidenced in a number of more recent works. In *Conrad: The Moral World of the Novelist* (1978), for example, Gekoski deals with *Chance*, *Victory* and *The Shadow Line* in one brief concluding chapter. The chapter begins: '*Chance* (1913) and *Victory* (1915) are generally agreed to be transitional works, sharing many of the characteristics and virtues of Conrad's earlier novels, yet beginning also to reveal those defects that mar the later work' (p. 172). These 'later works' (which are not even named) get no further mention. Berthoud's *Joseph Conrad: The Major Phase* (1978) ends with *Under Western Eyes*. He refers to 'the often undervalued later novels, especially *Chance*, *Victory* and *The Rover*' (p. 187), but he does not discuss them, and the title and organisation of his book serve to maintain that undervaluation.
2. Bradbrook, *Joseph Conrad: England's Polish Genius*; Wiley, *Conrad's Measure of Man*; Walter F. Wright, *Romance and Tragedy in Joseph Conrad*.
3. Morton Zabel, 'Joseph Conrad: Chance and Recognition', *Sewanee Review*, LIII (Winter 1945) pp. 1–22; Palmer, *Joseph Conrad's Fiction*; Geddes, *Conrad's Later Novels*.
4. Geddes, p. 1.
5. Ibid., p. 5.
6. Ibid., p. 6.
7. Moser, p. 180.
8. See Smith, p. 81.
9. For an examination of the autobiographical aspects of the novel, see Baines, pp. 51–80; Karl, *Joseph Conrad: The Three Lives*, pp. 156–78; E. H. Visiak, *The Mirror of Conrad*, pp. 99–103; Hans van Marle, 'Young Ulysses Ashore', *L'Epoque Conradienne*, 2 (1976) pp. 22–35; Watts (ed.), *Joseph Conrad's Letters to R. B. Cunninghame Graham*, p. 77.
10. Wiley, pp. 158, 163.
11. For an account of Ford's reproduction of painterly effects in prose, see Arthur Mizener, *The Saddest Story* (The World Publishing Co., 1971) p. 469.
12. Geddes offers a valuable supplement to Wiley's discussion of *The Arrow of Gold*. He argues that images of paintings 'turn out to be structurally important, determining not only the method of presenting character, but also the kind of narrative frame that is used' (p. 9). He notes that the approach to characterisation 'is far more visually oriented than is usual for Conrad; and the seeing eye is obviously that of the painter or art-critic' (p. 121). See also Bickley and Hampson, ' "Lips That Have Been Kissed": Boccaccio, Verdi, Rossetti and *The Arrow of Gold*', *L'Epoque Conradienne* (December 1988) pp. 77–91.
13. Harold E. Toliver, 'Conrad's *Arrow of Gold* and Pastoral Tradition', *Modern Fiction Studies*, 8 (Summer 1962) p. 149.
14. Wiley, p. 164.
15. Ibid., p. 163. The governess, however, attacks Flora's sense of her own worth, whereas the effect of Allègre's scorn more closely resembles the education of Heyst. Rita, like Heyst, acquires a false-self system as

a consequence of 'scorn' that is primarily directed at others. Rita's 'mystic wound' has a very different source.

16. See *D.S.*: 'In conformity . . . with what one perceives or fancies to be the thing one is in the other person's eyes, the false self becomes that thing' (p. 99).

17. Robert Chianese, 'Existence and Essence in Conrad's *Arrow of Gold*', *Conradiana*, IX.2 (1977) p. 152.

18. *D.S.*, p. 99.

19. In *Selected Papers on Hysteria* (New York: Nervous and Mental Disease Monograph Series, 1912), Freud noted his conviction that the splitting of consciousness 'exists rudimentarily in every hysteria' (p. 8), and that a severe trauma 'or a painful suppression (perhaps of a sexual affect)' (p. 9) may bring about a splitting of consciousness. Laing similarly suggests that a 'normal' individual in a threatening situation that offers no apparent escape 'develops a schizoid state in trying to get outside it, if not physically, at least mentally: he becomes a mental observer who looks on . . . at what his body is doing or what is being done to his body' (*D.S.*, p. 79).

20. In *Selected Papers on Hysteria*, Freud observes that 'every expression which produces the painful affect of fear, anxiety, shame or of psychic pain may act as a psychic trauma' (p. 3). He also notes: 'Very often they are experiences of childhood which have established more or less intensive morbid phenomena for all succeeding years' (p. 2).

21. Ford's statement that Conrad wanted to deal with incest in *The Sisters* was, perhaps, not so wide of the mark.

22. See *Self and Others*, pp. 144–5. Laing derives this idea from G. Bateson, D. D. Jackson, J. Haley and J. Weakland, 'Towards a Theory of Schizophrenia', *Behavioural Science*, I (1956) p. 251.

23. Therese's account of Rita's 'shamelessness' is a model example of the operation of a family phantasy system. She tells M. George that Rita 'was always ready to run half-naked about the hills' (p. 158). When M. George points out that Rita's 'half-naked' state was because of Therese's neglect, Therese asserts that she did not mend Rita's frocks because of the unpredictability of Rita's temper: 'I could never tell when she would fling over her pretended sweetness and put her tongue out at me' (p. 158). The evidence she then produces to demonstrate this unpredictability of temper is Rita's angry response to Therese's neglect of her clothes (p. 159). (For 'family phantasy systems', see *Self and Others*, p. 40; see also Laing and Esterson, *Sanity, Madness and the Family*, passim.)

24. Rita criticises Blunt's desire for 'innocence' (p. 211); by contrast, there is the attitude, expressed by Dominic Cervoni, that 'lips that have been kissed do not lose their freshness' (p. 127).

25. Wiley, p. 168.

26. Ibid., p. 171.

27. Ibid., p. 171.

28. Letter to Mrs Thorne on 2 November 1919 (*L.L.*, II, p. 232).

29. Wiley, pp. 169–70.

30. Ibid., p. 166.

31. In his *Selected Papers on Hysteria*, Freud recorded that 'the individual hysterical symptoms immediately disappeared without returning if we succeeded in thoroughly awakening the memories of the causal process with its accompanying affect, and if the patient circumstantially discussed the process giving free play to the affect' (p. 4).

32. In *Selected Papers on Hysteria*, Freud observes that 'where hysteria is to be newly acquired one psychic determinant is indispensable; namely, that some presentation must intentionally be repressed from consciousness' (p. 23).

33. Schwarz, p. 128.

34. Compare George's role in this scene with Freud's description of the basis for the cathartic treatment of a patient: 'The interest shown in her, the understanding which we foreshadow, the hope of recovery extended to her' (*Selected Papers on Hysteria*, p. 34).

35. Conrad to S. A. Everitt, 18 February 1918 (*L.L.*, II, p. 201).

36. Ibid.

37. Schwarz, p. 132.

38. Conrad to Galsworthy, 22 February 1924 (*L.L.*, II, p. 339).

39. Guerard, p. 284.

40. Geddes, pp. 179 and 174–5.

41. Conrad to Garnett, 4 December 1923 (*L.L.*, II, p. 327; 326). Schwarz observes that 'Conrad's artistic economy is appropriate for the barely verbal and unself-conscious characters of *The Rover*' (p. 139). As Geddes says, '*The Rover* is the work of a writer very much at one with his art' (p. 186).

42. Geddes, p. 182.

43. Ibid., p. 182.

44. Schwarz, p. 145.

45. Ibid., p. 146.

46. Ibid.

47. Ibid., p. 149.

48. For an anthropological reading of this triangle, see Hampson, 'Frazer, Conrad and the "truth of primitive passion",' in Robert Fraser (ed.), *Sir James Frazer and the Literary Imagination* (Macmillan, 1990) pp. 172–91.

49. Schwarz, p. 145.

50. Ibid., p. 152.

Index